Also by Will Wight

The Last Horizon
The Captain
The Engineer
The Knight

The Traveler's Gate Trilogy
House of Blades
The Crimson Vault
City of Light

The Traveler's Gate Chronicles

The Elder Empire

Of Sea & Shadow	*Of Shadow & Sea*
Of Dawn & Darkness	*Of Darkness & Dawn*
Of Kings & Killers	*Of Killers & Kings*

For the most up-to-date bibliography, please visit **WillWight.com**

CRADLE

I
UNSOULED

II
SOULSMITH

III
BLACKFLAME

IV
SKYSWORN

V
GHOSTWATER

VI
UNDERLORD

VII
UNCROWNED

VIII
WINTERSTEEL

IX
BLOODLINE

X
REAPER

XI
DREADGOD

XII
WAYBOUND

THRESHOLD

STORIES FROM CRADLE

WILL WIGHT

THRESHOLD

Copyright © 2024 Hidden Gnome Publishing

Book and cover design by Patrick Foster
Cover illustration by Seth Rutledge
Icon Illustration by Teigan Mudle

All rights reserved. No part of this book may be reproduced in any form by any electronic or mechanical means including photocopying, recording, or information storage and retrieval without permission in writing from the author.

This is a work of fiction. Names, characters, places, and incidents either are the product of the author's imagination or are used fictitiously, and any resemblance to actual persons, living or dead, businesses, companies, events, or locales is entirely coincidental.

www.WillWight.com

1 2 3 4 5 6 7

Trade Paperback: 978-1-959001-64-5

PUBLISHED BY

THE STORIES

The First Uncrowned King	1
A Light Chat in a Dark Place	39
Anagi's Regret	45
Testing Northstrider	79
A Bloody End	103
The Wolf and the Reaper	125
Threshold	163
Daughter of Dread	205
The Return of the Prince	233
A Day in the Life of Akura Pride	247
Harness	267
The Gang Creates a World	313
Homecoming	341
How Cradle Should Have Ended	359

The First Uncrowned King

Information requested: the original Uncrowned King tournament
Report location: Long before the events of the Cradle series.
Context: The reader should have read at least through the eighth Cradle volume, *Wintersteel*.
Authorization confirmed.
Beginning report...

Reigan Shen's eyes bled as he watched the Monarchs do battle with the Wandering Titan.

Under a yellow sky, light and thunder crashed against the Titan's sword, churning the horizon into a wall of dust and debris that stretched from north to south. He could see little more than that; just holding his eyelids open took all his effort.

Certain spots stood out among the carnage. Highlights shining through the clouds, which he could pick out with ease.

Where one Monarch shifted through a portal, and where leaves disappeared and reappeared to shift aside the Titan's technique. Spatial manipulation.

Shen's Remnant never spoke to him anymore—Truegolds digested their Remnants completely—but its instincts had never merged as fully as he wished. A consequence of swallowing a Sage's spirit during his advancement to Gold.

Though it didn't speak, it directed his attention. He could learn those techniques. Space was his territory, his inheritance. He was special like they were.

Reigan had never wanted anything so much. He'd never imagined such glory.

One movement of the Titan's hand upended the heavens and earth, blinded the spiritual sense, and strained the fabric of space. Monarchs contended with that force, matching it blow for blow.

They commanded the world.

One day, Reigan Shen would too.

A few short years later, Underlord Shen led his pride into the heart of the Rosegold continent. The center of human power.

The old lions, still in their original forms, crept behind him like whipped cats. They had asked him not to go, to stay back, to hunt the plains as their ancestors had done for generations.

The plains were gone. Countless leagues of the grasslands had been chewed up in the Dread War, and yet his elders wanted to cling to tradition formed before their world had been destroyed.

Embrace tradition *and* feed their people. They begged him to keep their pride prosperous, but also not to change too much.

Reigan Shen had neither time nor patience for them. They faced a choice between innovation and starvation, and that was no choice at all.

In a mostly human form, Reigan strode boldly into a newly constructed...city, he supposed he should call it. He wasn't sure of the settlement's name, and it had been clearly made from buildings taken whole from elsewhere and transplanted here. He saw massive granite edifices with their cracks cemented together standing next to stores of painted wood that had been scooped up from their original location grass and all.

This was a collection of survivors and whatever shelter they could salvage, with one clear exception.

House Arelius stood at the top of a hill, golden and pristine, a palace untouched. Its spires of white marble, gold accents, and sapphires shone in the sunlight, unharmed by the Dreadgods. Blue banners showed crescent moons backed by lightning.

Those unscarred walls were magnets for Reigan's eyes.

According to rumors, House Arelius had a stockpile of treasures unmatched in all the worlds. The Silent King itself had challenged the wards and slunk home, defeated.

That was the power of their legacy, the might of the House's ancestors handed down generation by generation. It was said that their armories were endless, filled with weapons that allowed their Sages and Heralds to challenge Monarchs.

House Arelius had no Monarch and hadn't in living memory. It was a point of honor for them, that they stood as one of the greatest families in the world with only Sages and Heralds.

They were the true kings of Rosegold, and Reigan would surpass them. One day.

His visit to their territory was the first step.

Reigan led his pride—or, as they were known to the wider world, the Shen tribe—to the grandest of the patchwork buildings. It was a spidery castle, built with sturdy walls of iron and stone, but everything was thin and so stretched it looked weak.

A few days before, this castle had been on the other end of the continent. Reigan could still feel the invisible cracks from the technique that had brought it here, the scars in space.

Banners flew throughout the castle, and indeed from many of the mismatched structures. Plain gray banners bearing a black X.

The simple mark of House Gray.

Servants in gray ushered the Shen tribe to their housing, but Reigan wasn't put with them. He was brought beneath a massive, shadowy dome, its walls reinforced by scripts and constructs until they felt unbreakable.

And he was far from the only one. Dozens of Underlords surrounded him, all youthful, and few from the same faction. Most stood apart, as Reigan Shen did, and they looked so wary and suspicious that he immediately adopted a relaxed posture.

All the better to stand out, to pretend to be unworried, so he could catch them off guard.

On a balcony over the Underlords, a thick gray mist gathered until a hooded figure stepped out of it. Shen's Remnant pricked his attention; that had been a spatial technique.

"Young Underlords, lost and alone, I share your pain," a woman said from within the hood. "Our Houses and families have been destroyed. We've buried loved ones with our own hands. And with them, we must bury the old ways."

The ears on top of Reigan Shen's head perked up. She was speaking exactly as he'd hoped she would.

"I am Valketh, the Mist Sage, formerly of House Wylan. But House Wylan is no more, and neither are your Houses. So let me welcome you to House Gray."

They had been welcomed already. That was what had brought them here; the creation of a House that contained the fragments of destroyed factions and the families that had never been part of a great House.

All were accepted in House Gray, and the protection of a Sage was enough of an advantage to draw people from all over Rosegold.

Most of the Underlords gathered here weren't leaders, as Reigan was. Some groups had Overlords or even Archlords in charge, while others were led by older Underlords. Those leaders had already been ushered in and agreed to pledge their loyalty to the newborn House Gray.

Each family had been requested to send their strongest Underlords of the younger generation. Therefore, this greeting wasn't for their families. It was to them as individuals, as warriors.

The Mist Sage's hood passed over them all equally. "You are the future of our continent, of our world, and the Monarchs see that.

Now, we will ask you to prove yourself in a series of tests and duels. The best of you will represent House Gray and do battle before the Monarchs themselves."

Excitement ran through the Underlords in lightning-charged whispers. Reigan Shen was no exception, though he had no one to whisper to.

His memory of the Monarchs was branded into his mind. Now was his chance to catch their attention. To show his greatness.

"The better you perform in this tournament, the more support the honored Monarchs will provide us...Not to mention the treasures you yourself will receive. They're not merely looking for the best fighters but for those among you with the potential to become future leaders. The Uncrowned Kings and Queens of our world."

The Sage's words danced in Reigan's ears. He could swear he sensed her gaze on him specifically.

And if she hadn't noticed him, she would soon.

The blood didn't have a chance to dry on Reigan's fur before he was ushered into a private audience with the Mist Sage.

He'd earned it.

When he was finally allowed through a delicately carved black door, he was surprised to see that the Sage didn't live in the opulence he associated with people of her advancement level.

It was a simple sitting room, with the Sage herself in a wooden chair behind a desk. She tinkered with dream tablets and shimmering constructs as he entered, though she pushed them aside and gave him her full attention a moment later.

"Reigan Shen. That's a very unique Path you have. What do you call it?"

She was younger than Reigan had expected, or at least she appeared so. A small human woman with a round face, mud-brown hair, and skin that reminded him of desert sands.

No wonder she wore a hood. Without it, she didn't look intimidating at all.

"The Path of the King's Key," Reigan announced proudly.

Valketh shifted in her chair, which squeaked. "Who's the king?"

"Lions are often referred to as kings of the natural world."

"Really? I've never heard that. Is that a lion saying?" The chair squeaked again, and she frowned at it.

Reigan Shen thought it was a shame that all the powerful Sages had been killed in the Dread War. At least, he assumed so, though this was his first time meeting one. She clearly hadn't outlasted the others on the basis of strength; she didn't have the dignity of one truly strong.

"A human one, I believe," Reigan said, restraining his contempt. "I was fortunate enough to encounter a Sage's Remnant when I was little more than a cub. It agreed to bond with me as a reward for my bravery."

He expected her to acknowledge him at that—after all, he was something of a peer to her—but instead she only grunted. Most of her attention was taken up by the squeaky chair as she shifted from side to side, trying to find the source of the noise.

Irritated, Reigan opened a gold-edged portal and reached inside.

He seized a varnished chair—careful not to scratch its finish with his claws—and plopped it down beside her.

"A seat worthy of your station," he announced. "Polished whiteblood wood, made by artisans from the late House Druilic. Irreplaceable, now."

He ached at the loss, but any gift to a Sage was an investment.

Valketh rose from her cheap, original chair somewhat reluctantly. She gazed at it even as she moved it to one side. "No matter how many times I restore it, it wears down faster and faster. Even so, it seems like a waste to throw it away." She sank down into the pale, contoured wood of Reigan's chair and sighed. "That *is* a comfort, thank you."

As he watched the human woman slump down in a work of art, almost sliding off the cushion, it was even more of a struggle to keep disdain from his face.

"May I know what is expected of me as the victor?" he asked, in a blatant attempt to get the conversation on track.

"You'll be part of our team for this Uncrowned King tournament, of course, and I'd *like* you to serve as team leader. It's obvious that you have the most potential of all the candidates."

Well, a Sage was still a Sage. Whatever her deficiencies in grandeur, she obviously had keen insight.

Reigan tucked hands behind his back and lifted his chin. "I would be honored to lead House Gray to victory in this event."

"To victory? You think you have what it takes?" Valketh's voice didn't get any louder, but it suddenly seemed to fill the room, billowing from all around him.

"You face the scions of Monarchs, the apprentices of Heralds.

Those with bloodlines that can be traced back to the birth of this world. You, an Underlord of the wild Rosegold plains, think you can face them with your Remnant of a nameless Sage? You've found one gold coin in the grass and you imagine yourself the richest of all kings."

Her words crept inside him, and he shivered in the crawling cold. Something had changed as she spoke, something *real,* but he couldn't identify what it was.

The Mist Sage leaned forward, her voice soft but inescapable. "In most, arrogance is only a danger to the arrogant. They overestimate themselves, but reality will humble them. In those like *you,* arrogance becomes a danger to all."

Reigan struggled to speak and eventually managed to force out a response. "I am a danger only to my enemies."

"Your pride is blind," the Sage continued. "It is founded on insecurity and ignorance. Tragically, you're *right.*"

Reigan Shen stood stiffly and turned over her words until he understood them. When he did, another jolt of electric excitement passed through him. "That is no tragedy."

"Sometimes, treasure is found by those with no map." The Sage leaned back in the chair and sighed, and the subtle pressure in the room released. "Between your madra, your talent, and the natural gifts of your species, you have a real chance at victory. I never expected to find one like you, and that frightens me."

Reigan's tail curled in eagerness, though humans couldn't read that reaction. Striking fear into this improper Sage told him that he had been right; right in his evaluation of her, of himself, of his future.

The Mist Sage rubbed the side of her head. "Your triumph is by no means guaranteed, but I'll give you what you need to fight for it. But I will state my misgivings plainly. Envy and ambition are a poor foundation on which to build your empire."

"No amount of ambition is too great for these times," Reigan said. He stroked his whiskers, proud of his own wisdom.

Valketh let out a long breath. "Come on. You've been moving space intuitively; the least I can do is tell you what you can't see."

In the year of training before the Uncrowned King tournament, Reigan Shen transformed entirely.

Even his form was smoother than it had been at the beginning— less fur, more dexterous fingers, shorter claws. He couldn't fully transform into a human, as he would be able to eventually, but he could borrow their combat arts.

He'd especially grown to love their weapons.

There were no young Underlords in House Gray that could serve as his opponents, so he had to train against the older Underlords. Even those couldn't *beat* him, merely help him practice.

Recognizing his own power and potential felt like unfolding into his true self. Like he'd been locked away in a box but finally got the chance to stretch his limbs.

The trip to Everwood took two months, and that may have been his greatest education. The Mist Sage brought them through space, and he detected her burden in carrying so much of House Gray along. Sometimes, while she spent days recovering, a sandstorm transported them instead of a cloud of fog.

That sandstorm's authority over space was significantly stronger than the Sage's, but strangely, Reigan sensed that it wasn't quite so refined. That surprised him, as he suspected it was a technique of the Dragon Monarch. Perhaps the Mist Sage was more skilled than he'd realized.

Nonetheless, they were both operating outside their specialty. One day, he would make them look like novices.

At the end of their journey, they emerged on the site of the Uncrowned King tournament: a deep woodland of towering trees, each with branches large enough to hold towns. Many of them *did*, carrying entire networks of living wood and Forged madra that supported a whole civilization.

This was the territory of Emriss Silentborn, the Forest Monarch.

Reigan could feel her presence everywhere, comforting and protective, as though her spiritual perception cradled them like a blanket.

For the first time, he began to doubt his chances to win.

Surely, the omniscient Queen of Everwood wouldn't allow someone to overturn her own champions. If he were in charge, he would ensure that his Underlords won. Anything less would be a stain on *his* honor.

How could he defeat Emriss' fighters without provoking her wrath?

All the competing factions gathered at the top of a tree that contained a massive arena and the city-sized infrastructure needed to support it. His spiritual senses suggested that the tree had been grown recently, leading him to conclude that the entire facility and the trunk on which it rested were created specifically to host this tournament.

That was the wealth of a Monarch.

Only two of the eight organizations remaining after the Dread War still had Monarchs to lead them. The gold and green dragons banded together under Seshethkunaaz, King of East Ashwind; though the Monarch didn't show himself, Reigan felt his presence as well, like an earthquake holding itself back.

The people of Everwood were the most numerous, of course, but Emriss had put forward no more fighters than anyone else. Her people, primarily humans with skins of various dark shades, used strange sacred arts. Each was accompanied by a spirit, and some by Remnants.

As he'd expected, those two groups gave off intimidating pressure that stood his fur on end. He eyed them warily.

But there was a third faction, almost as strong as the first two: Reigan's neighbor from Rosegold.

The Arelius clan, blond and smug, stood behind Herald Cenilia Arelius. She wasn't the only Herald, either. They had half a dozen remaining at her level, meaning that they were stronger than anyone except the Monarch factions.

Given their untold treasures, they might actually *match* the gold dragons in total strength, and Reigan seethed at the thought.

What had they done to earn such riches? They were rewarded simply for being born.

The others of his House Gray seemed no more happy with the Arelius clan, though House Arelius had provided them with protection and supplies. How could they feel anything but resentment?

Arelius had survived where almost every other House had been obliterated. House Gray hadn't risen from the ashes of the Dread War, merely crouched in them.

But the mutual grudge of Houses Gray and Arelius was nothing compared to the tension he sensed between the followers of Seshethkunaaz and the Blackflame Empire.

The Mist Sage had tutored them all on the different factions they'd face in the tournament, so Reigan had learned something of the history of other continents. The Blackflame Monarch was long dead, their Empire in a steady decline after untold devastation by the Dreadgods.

Once, the Blackflames had controlled half the Ashwind continent, with the gold dragons holding the other half.

Over the years, the east had prospered and the west had splintered. One of the few remaining Blackflame Heralds led the team here, but he was scarred and sullen, glaring angrily at the healthy dragons on the other side.

Reigan *was* pleased at the relative scarcity of humans in the tournament. The Utarian Collective, Iceflower representatives, were a united force binding together many tribes of sacred beasts. Their leader, the Sky Sage, was a sacred eagle, and their champions a variety of species.

The Tidewalkers had a human or two on the team, but were mostly sea creatures of various descriptions gathered behind a shark Herald. From what Reigan had heard, they were devastated by the Weeping Dragon, but they put forward a strong front.

Finally, the Ninecloud Court made the third human-dominated faction, but they were a threadbare group. Despite their bright rainbow colors and ostentatious decorations, anyone could see they were barely holding together.

They had the smallest entourage, some of their fighters had been Underlords for mere days, and most of the rest came from the same Sha family.

They didn't even have a Sage or Herald with them. Their 'Luminous Queen' had made known that she was isolating herself after the death of her mother, a true Monarch. But this princess was merely an Archlord.

Reigan didn't see why they'd been invited at all. House Sha, or whatever they called themselves, wouldn't last another generation.

Once the factions settled into the arena, entering with appropriate fanfare, the leaves far overhead began to fall. They drifted down, green with a hint of purple light passing through, and Reigan got the odd impression that each floating leaf was watching him.

A motherly voice spoke into their minds, and Reigan needed no introduction to recognize Emriss Silentborn.

"Welcome, children. We bring you here in the hopes that you will learn from one another, to spread the sacred arts across the world..."

A cloud of sand rose in the distance, and Reigan sensed irritation.

"...and that the strongest among you would prevail," Emriss added, though Reigan was certain that the last part was an afterthought. *"Fight not only for glory, but for the advancement of us all."*

After a few more words of greeting, the Monarch reached the point in the introduction that Reigan cared about. *"For your first test, I will bring you into a dream realm where you will display your abilities for a panel of judges to evaluate."*

He felt an instant of doubt. Why weren't the Monarchs judging the competition themselves? There could be no one more qualified.

"Would you trust our decisions if we did so, Reigan Shen of House Gray?"

Reigan's tail went stiff and he shivered.

"I'll explain the rules to you in a moment, but I expect you'd rather hear about the prizes."

A vision expanded in his mind; tools, weapons, and treasures of every description, each carefully preserved and labeled in cases of metal and glass. They filled a hall so long he couldn't see the end.

"The Underlord instruments that survived the war," Emriss said. *"If you pass the evaluation of the first round, you may pick one prize of your choice."*

Reigan embarrassed himself by reacting aloud. "One!?"

He heard her smile. *"Ah, but that's only the first round."*

No matter what their tests were, he resolved to tear them apart.

Reigan Shen came in seventh in the first round.

His entire body tensed with shock. He had been certain he was first. They tested him thoroughly, bringing him into a world where he couldn't separate dream from reality.

He'd fought squads of enemies, individual duelists, and unspeakable monsters. He'd climbed burning mountains, identified clues with his spiritual senses, solved riddles, and wielded strange weapons.

Each time, he gave his best effort, even on the tasks that were beneath him. He could have coasted lazily and still passed, but he pushed forward with diligence to gain the respect of the Monarchs.

Yet *six* people of his generation had still surpassed him.

He glared at the list, committing their names to memory. His rivals were four beasts and two humans.

From the Utarian Collective, Del'rek of the Shann came in sixth. A sacred elephant, he'd made a shameful display by leaping up and down at his ranking, trumpeting his trunk and then wilting when he realized how loud he'd been.

He was young, though, for an elephant. He could certainly compete in the next tournament, if he didn't win this one. Reigan wouldn't need such insurance.

In fifth came Shadeseeker, the sacred shark who was clearly more talented in shapeshifting than the rest. Her human form was almost entirely complete except for a fin sticking out from her shoulders and her serrated teeth. She grinned broadly at her father, the leader of the Tidewalker sect, whose answering smile was even more sinister.

In fourth and third place were the gold dragon twins, Laranatoth and Zaraxius. Their tails lashed and they studied the list of names with as much obvious anger as Reigan himself felt. He knew why.

Both the top places were held by humans.

In second was the man who represented everything Reigan hated. His short blond hair was styled, his clothes a layered mix of white, gold, and azure silk. His eyes crackled with blue electricity, and he regarded the list with casual amusement, cracking a joke to the young woman at his side and laughing at her response.

Tiberian Arelius did not deserve to be there. Reigan *knew* that, though he'd never interacted with the man. He knew what House Arelius was like. They were only so strong because they'd hid from the Dread War like cowards.

Nonetheless, there was Tiberian's name. The second-best Underlord of his age. Reigan would have to use the rest of the tournament to prove that judgment wrong.

At least House Arelius wasn't first.

A girl from Emriss Silentborn's team sat cross-legged on the arena floor as the scores were announced, and she seemed indifferent rather than excited. She played with her spirits instead; a pair that resembled goldfish, one pure white and the other black.

Their madra was light and shadow, two opposites that should never coexist in the same body, but her spirit held both in harmony. The spirits swirled around her, and the three of them were lost in their own conversation.

Dellei Twinfire. Reigan marked her too. Though it was only the first round, her spirit felt strange, and he didn't understand her Path. That was enough to make him unwary, not to mention that she was the favored champion of a Monarch.

By winning, he would prove himself better than those humans.

The eight Uncrowned were no surprise to anyone, least of all Reigan Shen. The only addition of any note was Sha Jeska, niece of the absentee Luminous Queen, who managed to scrape her way into the top eight.

For the rest, they had traded the top spots back and forth since the first round. In each confrontation, Reigan's respect for his competitors grew.

As did his estimation of his own abilities.

Dellei Twinfire was the apprentice of a Monarch, and the gold dragons descended from one, but Reigan was keeping up with them. He learned as he watched them, as he clashed with them, as he outwitted their teammates and as he fell into their traps.

The other Uncrowned were those he considered his equals. At least in potential.

Of course, he had more to be proud of than they did. His only inheritance was the Sage's Remnant. He had no ancestors giving him advice, no resources he hadn't fought for, and no armory full of treasures.

Though he was quickly working on that last one.

Each round, he selected a new prize from the Monarchs. Emriss and Seshethkunaaz had pooled the supplies left behind after the Dread War, repurposing the weapons of the fallen into motivation for the next generation.

They allowed more valuable selections as the rounds progressed, so Reigan's treasure hoard grew. With that start, he would rival the old Rosegold Houses soon.

But still not House Arelius.

Each prize that Reigan Shen won was another tool for him to use in the future competition, but not Tiberian. The Arelius champion hadn't changed his fighting style through the entire tournament, having been provided plenty of weapons and training materials by his rich family.

He was a spearman whose weapon crackled with multicolored lightning that reminded Reigan of the Weeping Dragon. As needed, Tiberian's madra shifted between a fluid river, a powerful gust, and a devastating thunderbolt.

Reigan watched his every match live, then reviewed dream tablets of the fights afterward. He gnashed his teeth over Tiberian night and day.

The Arelius man had a clear advantage: familiarity with his Path.

Original and potent Reigan's techniques may have been, but Tiberian's fighting style was flawlessly polished. He could adapt to any situation without ruffling a strand of his perfect hair.

Reigan's biggest opponent in the rounds thus far, by contrast, was his own Path.

The Mist Sage had taught him what to expect from the manipulation of space, but he was still fumbling in the dark. He wouldn't be able to directly perceive what he was doing until reaching Sage.

Valketh had tested his aptitude and suggested he would advance into a Sage eventually, but she recommended he not pursue that before Archlord. It would be a distraction from conventional advancement, and the power of his body and spirit were his biggest advantage.

Overlord would be a far more reliable source of power, but unfortunately, sacred beasts could not advance in a burst of insight as humans did.

Normally, Reigan would say that sacred beast advancement was more natural and convenient. But the longer he lingered at the peak of Underlord, the more jealous he grew of humans. They could simply meditate until they surged through and reached the next stage.

He had to mold his body into its superior form. And while he felt as though he could reach a higher level at any point, his great power was becoming a disadvantage.

If he forced it, he would destabilize his spirit and cost himself time in the long run. So he settled for patience.

At least his first fight as one of the eight Uncrowned should be winnable at his current level.

Shadeseeker, the Uncrowned of the Tidewalkers, was the shark-girl who was so close to human.

He'd studied her, as he had all his opponents, and she was a worthy fighter. She hadn't merely ridden here on the grace of her Herald father, as he'd first suspected.

She grinned, baring teeth to intimidate him, as she twirled a pair of jagged daggers. "I love cats. They're delicious."

He gave her a look of disdain and fiddled with a ring in a show of boredom. "Did you think you were going to scare me?"

"Oh, you're already scared. I can smell it."

Reigan stifled a yawn, but it didn't seem to bother her.

"Not of me," Shadeseeker went on. "You're scared everywhere you go, every fight you watch. I think you're scared you're not going to make it. Scared they're going to see you aren't good enough to be here, and they'll toss you back in the grass where you were born and forget you ever left."

Hackles raised on the back of his neck and he missed his chance to feign composure. She grinned wider.

Reigan had known the others were aware of him. Of course they were; he was one of the Uncrowned. But Shadeseeker had been *watching* him.

He hadn't noticed.

"*Begin,*" one of the judges called.

Shadeseeker's daggers were swallowed in madra, which mixed aspects of swords, water, and a touch of blood. They formed jagged fangs of what appeared to be black water; it had taken several matches and close observation, as well as consultation of some texts from the Everwood library, before Reigan had figured out their composition.

Reigan opened his King's Key and activated a sacred instrument.

The Tempest Jar was, in fact, a large ceramic jar painted to resemble a furious ocean storm. It contained madra very similar to Tiberian's, and it had been a potential solution to him as well as Shadeseeker.

A green lightning bolt, thick as a tree, shot out to impact the shark's Forged blades of black water. She pulled her daggers back, severing her contact with her own technique, and began molding aura.

Which was the point where she lost. Reigan's lip curled as his tail swished from side to side.

Another portal had already opened behind her, releasing a school of tiny Remnants. Razor-toothed fish, each the size of a human hand, that glistened like jewels. Together, they were worth an Underlord.

They sought out blood madra, which was the smallest component of her madra. It was enough. They devoured her power, stealing her attention, and they were highly resistant to her techniques.

Meanwhile, the Tempest Jar recovered for another shot.

Reigan made a show of pulling a bottle of wine and a golden goblet out of his vault, pouring himself a drink, and taking a sip.

The crowd *loved* it. They laughed and cheered wildly, more than he'd heard from any fight before the winner was declared. He tried not to preen too obviously under their praise as he watched his plans finish off Shadeseeker.

She fought through the Remnants, though she was heavily

burned by the lightning, and struggled toward him with limbs covered by an Enforcer technique. He waved a hand idly and knocked her back with a pulse of golden force.

The whistle sounded. The fight was over.

That had been closer than it seemed. If she'd made arrangements of her own, or discovered his, she could have adapted and kept him on the back foot. In a straight fight, without preparation, she would no doubt defeat him.

But he *was* prepared. He'd won before stepping into the arena.

Shadeseeker was healed a second later, sitting up and glaring at him. He stood over her, swirling his wine.

"I was glad to hear your positive opinion of cats," Reigan said. "Myself, I love fish."

She snapped at him, but was pulled away by aura. In the next match, he defeated her again and was declared the victor.

In celebration, he treated himself to some roasted fish.

"Brace yourself," the Mist Sage said. "You're fighting Tiberian."

Reigan let his portals vanish and hopped down from the raised dais on which he'd stood while training. His fur was matted with sweat, so he began toweling off.

"About time. I've been waiting far too long."

"You're not ready."

"Of course I am. He's only human." Reigan gave her a bold smile, but the Mist Sage was unfazed.

Valketh looked off into the distance, her eyes filling with dark mist. "Everywhere I look, he defeats you."

"If your predictions were so precise, why fight at all? Why would the Monarchs not award the prizes and save us all the time?" He spoke lightly, but inwardly he burned with frustration.

He knew he was no match for Tiberian. He simply didn't accept it.

"I didn't say your victory was impossible. I'm sure it's out there, somewhere in the mist. But it is far from likely."

"Advance me to Overlord, then."

She tossed one of her wide sleeves. "You don't need me to give you a truth about your soul, and we have plenty of natural treasures. Advance yourself."

"If I could do it as easily as humans do, I'd be an Overlord already."

"And yet none of your human opponents are Overlords. If we'd held this tournament ten years ago, I'd expect half of you to have advanced."

That was a stroke of luck born from the Dread War. All the Underlords close to advancing had forcibly done so during the war, even if they burned out their future potential.

The young Underlords left with talent and bright futures had all been far from advancing. At least, they had been before the competition. Now they were all peak Underlords only a hair from becoming Overlords.

Except, perhaps, Dellei Twinfire. Her strange spirit-bonding Path made her hard to read. She didn't seem any closer to advancement than she'd been at the beginning, though she'd inexplicably demonstrated greater strength every round.

"Despite what you may believe," the Mist Sage said, "humans

have it harder to advance than sacred beasts. They just tend to do it faster. With your talent, you're guaranteed to reach Overlord eventually, but Tiberian has no such assurances."

Reigan glared into her hood. "And yet, with the right words whispered into the air, he could be Overlord in a moment."

There was no precedent in his pride for advancing to Overlord, but there was plenty for advancement in general. When Reigan had advanced to Underlord, he'd been surrounded by the elders of his kind as they awaited the return of a hunt.

Each species of beast tended to advance a little differently, though they all had common traits. The feel of the spirits around him, the advice of his peers, and the power of their shared bloodline had all helped Reigan Shen define his Underlord form.

Once that vision was clear enough, the soulfire had run through him and given birth to his Lord body.

In his case, he'd become more human-like than most, but such was to be expected. The Sage who'd left his Remnant to Reigan had been a human, and his madra was easier to use in a humanoid shape.

The Mist Sage spread her hands out, swirling dark clouds of madra in the air and watching something in them. After swirling her fingers through the conjured mist and examining the shapes, she sighed.

"Top four is a great honor," she said.

When Reigan Shen finally faced Tiberian Arelius across the arena, his fury stoked hotter and hotter.

Tiberian was hardly paying attention. He posed in the best lighting he could find and propped his spear up on his shoulder, waving to the crowd. Blond hair gleamed, and his robes were fine silk in half a dozen shades of blue to green.

The judges usually allowed the candidates a moment to address the people, to get them excited for the upcoming match and to appeal to them. Tiberian even showed off his techniques, making it rain lightning around himself and catching the liquid bolts on his spear.

Even those not from House Arelius cheered for him.

Reigan hadn't brought any of his family along. For the journey here, it had been important to reduce the burden on the Mist Sage as much as possible, and they were too weak to make a difference.

As for those in House Gray...they supported him, but only because he was on their team and they respected his ability. It wasn't as though he had any friends there.

House Arelius had friends everywhere, of course. They had everything.

"Are you a sacred artist or a street performer?" Reigan asked, after Tiberian sent tiny bolts bursting into the sky over spectator's heads.

"Most of the best street performers are skilled sacred artists," Tiberian responded, without turning from his show.

Reigan ground his teeth. "Your disrespect desecrates this sacred tournament."

"Isn't that up to the Monarchs?" Tiberian made himself glow and levitate, surrounded by crackling clouds, accompanied by the roar of the audience.

"You're lucky they haven't smited you already."

Tiberian hopped down and gave Reigan a small, casual smile. "A Monarch who let themselves be bothered by a little Underlord wouldn't be a very good Monarch, would they?"

A signal pulsed from the judges, indicating that the fighters should take their positions, and Reigan snapped into place. Tiberian strolled over, spinning his spear in the air and catching it as he walked.

Reigan knew he wasn't favored to win the match, but Tiberian had underestimated him. This was his opportunity to steal victory from an unwary opponent.

And even if he didn't win, he would savor the chance to punch a smile off that smug face.

"*Begin!*" the judge shouted.

Reigan moved his hands to open a pair of portals, and *Tiberian was already there.*

Yellow, blue, and green sparks crackled over the Arelius Underlord, his hair lifted and shone with three-colored lightning, and power gathered in his spear. He had closed the gap with Reigan *instantly,* and his weapon was mid-strike.

Reigan managed to turn the madra for a portal into a shield, blocking the spearhead with a dark, golden pulse of energy.

With the opponent knocked off-guard, Reigan struck with his claws to tear the skin from the human's face.

Tiberian casually bent to the side, released his spear with one hand, and sent a burst of tiny fingers of lightning leaping for Reigan's face like vipers striking from a bush.

Reigan defended once again with King's Key madra, still trying to bring together a technique of his own, but the Arelius didn't let up.

Reigan Shen had the more powerful body. Even his soul was

stronger, at least in terms of their potency of madra. In a head-to-head contest, Reigan was certain he would win, and that was without considering the uniqueness of his Path or his weapons.

But Tiberian's techniques were an extension of himself. He flowed like water, with spear strikes blowing craters into the living wood of the arena floor like devastating thunderbolts. The wind carried him gracefully, and Reigan could no more escape him than he could escape a storm.

Worst of all, Tiberian moved like he had seen the fight play out in advance.

Sliding to avoid punches, slipping aside to dodge traps, deflecting weapons launched from what should have been a blind spot. Once, he stabbed into the air an instant *before* Reigan opened a portal in that location, and Tiberian destroyed a launcher construct as it activated.

His bloodline ability. The ultimate inheritance from his all-too-generous ancestors.

Reigan slipped further behind with every exchange. He desperately sought a way out right up to the moment when he fell *too* far behind, and his left side exploded.

One well-Enforced thrust of a spear that he was too slow to dodge, and furious lightning detonated his shoulder, taking with it his entire arm and a chunk of his ribs.

Reigan looked down at himself with shock.

The next thing he knew, he was in his waiting room with the Mist Sage looking down on him. In pity.

He shot up, flexing the left arm he had just missed. Reigan didn't need to ask the outcome of the fight.

"That went as expected," Valketh observed.

Reigan roared and struck out blindly, but the Sage caught his blow with a frail human hand. Well, she had the base strength of an Archlord, after all.

The pity in her gaze intensified. "One more round, Reigan. You've done us proud."

"No." He pushed his way up from the bench on which he lay, tearing open one of his vaults. The one that contained natural treasures.

He began tossing them out, arranging them around himself as though to weave soulfire. "I advance to Overlord here, now."

"Your body and spirit are strong enough," the Sage said. "But your mind? Your will? They are in conflict. These are not problems that resolve themselves quickly."

"Perhaps not for you." Reigan assumed his place at the center of the treasures. "Assist me or leave me."

The Sage gazed into her mist again and seemed surprised at what she saw. "This may not be as hopeless as I supposed. Even so, your best course of action is to give up on the tournament and advance to Overlord once we have safely returned home. I'm no substitute for the guidance of your people."

It was Reigan Shen who cared for his people, not the other way around.

"They cannot tell me what it means to be a lion. I will show *them*."

With that, Reigan reached out to the buzzing vital aura. The Mist Sage had already surrounded him with her perception, her spiritual energy filling the room as a subtle but powerful presence.

Forcibly, he drew in aura and ignited his soulfire. The transformation began.

Reigan Shen held in his heart the image of true power, of the king of lions that he would one day become. He would be untouchable, inviolable, above, apart. A king had servants to act for him, but when *he* acted, the heavens and earth trembled.

No one had left him anything, but his own descendants would lack for nothing.

His fur shrank away little by little. Reigan seized onto it, imagining a powerful lion, though one that stood on two legs. He needed something of a human form to wield his Path; besides, everyone knew that madra was more flexible for humans.

It was harder to reconcile that vision than he'd expected. The intuition remaining in his madra, his own techniques, and the Mist Sage's spiritual influence all seemed to push him into a more-human form.

His madra channels, which were naturally sturdier even than others of his own kind, began to strain. If he kept holding on to his fur and his tail, he was going to lose the transformation.

Well, so what?

Those were mere aesthetic changes, discarded as easily as clothes. A king did not let such things define him. What did the appearance of his body matter?

He focused on his future dignity, as he ruled from a palace of white and gold. Grander than the palace of House Arelius, larger and greater. As he himself would be.

With that image to guide him, he continued to transform.

Reigan Shen stepped out as an Overlord, looking smugly down on the human woman who hadn't believed in him. "My will is stronger than you realize," he said.

A smile slowly crept onto Valketh's mouth and she laughed. "I suppose it is. Cenilia Arelius is going to think I'm a genius."

Reigan had established his own talent, and the Sage had indeed helped him on his advancement. He could be gracious. "Aren't you? You saw the potential in me, when no one else did. I do not easily forget a debt."

She flipped up her hood and raised a mask over the lower half of her face, but a smile glittered in her eyes. "Go win for us, and all of House Gray will be in *your* debt."

"Then gather my reward." If Reigan's tail hadn't vanished in his advancement, it would have been lashing. "House Arelius stands unrivaled no longer."

When he emerged as an Overlord, the crowd cheered in his honor. With no undignified shows, he had recaptured their attention.

Tiberian himself only lifted his eyebrows. "Congratulations to House Gray! If you listen close, you can hear a thousand people rushing to change their bets."

"They should have bet on me from the beginning," Reigan said. He stroked his mane calmly, giving off a regal bearing.

Tiberian laughed and readied his spear. "Show me why."

Reigan kept irritation from his face, because a king shouldn't be annoyed by such taunts, but the Arelius hadn't given him the satisfaction he wanted.

Only one of them was an Overlord. The match was a foregone conclusion.

The judge called for them to begin, and Reigan spread a barrier of King's Key madra. Let Tiberian rush headlong into it and dash himself to pieces.

Tiberian didn't open the fight as he had before. Instead of hurtling in, he'd risen into the air and launched a Striker technique. Madra blasted from his spear, a beam of braided green, blue, yellow, and white.

As far as the tempo of battle went, Tiberian had gained the upper hand. But he was still only an Underlord.

Reigan's madra moved more easily, filled his body more naturally, and responded to his will more quickly. Even at the same advancement level, he'd held the advantage in raw attributes, and that edge was only magnified.

He countered the Striker technique with ease, opening a rift onto a half-formed vault. The space itself hadn't stabilized yet, so Reigan had nothing of value within, but it was enough to absorb the attack as a shield.

Meanwhile, he crafted another portal to strike back.

But Tiberian didn't roll over and give up. He'd begun a Ruler technique, controlling the aura in the arena to his benefit. As a storm gathered overhead, Tiberian Arelius attacked.

Reigan Shen unleashed his arsenal. He hadn't been able to fill his vaults with Overlord weapons, but his portals were still superior in every way. They opened faster, he could make more of them, and he could project them farther from his body.

Even so, Tiberian kept up.

He was a frustrating opponent, a biting fly powered by lightning, flitting here and there. Reigan brought forth more and more weapons, more traps, but launchers fired and puppet-constructs were torn apart by a shining figure they couldn't catch.

Once again, the first to strike a blow was Tiberian.

Reigan turned aside another thunderbolt, redirecting and returning it, when the aura-storm overhead struck down with lightning and caught him on the back.

He roared in pain as burning heat hammered down on him, singeing his hair and clothes. His flesh burned, and if he hadn't advanced, that would have been the end of the battle.

Tiberian took the opening, rushing into Reigan as a bolt of living lightning, but Reigan's hand snapped up to grab him. The Arelius reacted just as quickly, avoiding the hand, but King's Key madra of burnished gold tightened around him.

Finally.

Reigan squeezed, Tiberian's bones crunched, and the fight ended.

Despite the call of victory, Reigan returned to his waiting room in worse spirits than before. He seized a bench and threw it into the wall.

"Tell me his secret!" Reigan demanded.

The Mist Sage scratched inside her hood. "He's extremely gifted and well-trained. Are you talking about his bloodline?"

"I should have crushed him! I'm an Overlord!"

"The gap between Overlord and Underlord isn't so large a gap. It's a major advantage, certainly, but it isn't so rare for experienced Underlords to defeat less-talented, off-guard, or recently advanced Overlords."

"Could he have advanced as well? Maybe he veiled his spirit."

The Mist Sage waved a hand in front of his face. "Reigan. Why are you acting like you lost?"

Reigan cradled the burning shame in his heart.

"The Monarchs are watching. The *world* is watching. Anything less than overwhelming victory may as well be defeat."

"Good luck, then." The Mist Sage began to walk out of the room. "He won't make it easy for you."

In the final round of the Uncrowned King tournament semifinals, Reigan Shen unleashed all his fury.

As he had before, Tiberian backed off and set up a Striker technique. This time, Reigan anticipated him.

A half-dozen portals tore open, straining Reigan's spirit to the limit. He pulled javelins of blood madra and hurled them bodily, activated constructs, released imprisoned Remnants, and summoned flying swords to control.

He overwhelmed Tiberian in a tidal wave of accumulated wealth. It wasn't a reliable tactic, nor one he could repeat often, but Tiberian couldn't predict it. Reigan lit up the arena with his fury, emptying all his vaults to push the Arelius onto the back foot.

Tiberian emerged from the chaos of the arena, spear ready.

He didn't make it unharmed. Torn and bleeding, one eye closed, with half of his hair burned away. The other half lifted, filled with the three-colored lightning of his Enforcer technique.

Reigan caught a lightning bolt on several crossed flying swords, but Tiberian had already begun Ruling the vital aura. Storm madra seized Reigan, sending jolts of lightning madra pouring through him.

His body charred, his spirit followed, and Tiberian's spear lanced into his ribs.

Where it stuck.

Reigan grabbed the weapon with a half-formed grip of King's Key madra, locking it in place. He held it there, imprisoning his enemy for a crucial instant.

Tiberian's eyes, crackling with electricity, widened as he sensed what Reigan was about to do. But he was too late.

Reigan Shen leaned forward and tore out Tiberian's throat with his teeth.

The audience roared, and their approval mixed with the taste of blood and the judge's declaration of victory.

Though it hadn't been an overwhelming win, Reigan threw his head back and laughed. The tournament wasn't over, but he felt like it was.

Even the prince of House Arelius was nothing but another human.

As he was walking out of the arena, chin lifted, waving to the crowd, Emriss Silentborn's power quietly cleansed him of all his injuries. He felt better than he ever had. Stronger. More like a lion.

Before he reached the door, he sensed a surprising presence: Tiberian.

The Arelius hurried out of his waiting room, though the rules said not to reenter the arena after defeat. He was also unscathed, and Reigan looked forward to seeing the rage and frustration on his face.

"Well fought!" Tiberian said. He smiled and extended his right hand. "Let's duel again, Reigan Shen of House Gray. Once I've caught up to you, of course."

Reigan suppressed his initial distaste that the human would pretend they were friends. He was saving face for his family in front of the crowd, and Reigan didn't mind being a gracious winner.

"I hope you can," Reigan said, as he clasped the human's hand.

Tiberian Arelius laughed heartily. "As do I! You'll have to share your wisdom with me when we get back home."

"If you can pay the price."

Tiberian laughed again, clapped Reigan on the back, and left.

That wasn't the final round of the first Uncrowned King tournament, but it held that spot in Reigan Shen's heart.

Dellei Twinfire was his last opponent, and—though she hadn't advanced to Overlord—her twin spirits emanated pressure that made Reigan wary. The two fish, each the size of a human head, echoed her techniques and coordinated so well that he felt he was facing half a dozen sacred artists rather than only one.

The pure white goldfish controlled madra of light to blind him, to craft visual illusions, and to camouflage or distract. The black one manipulated shadows to grasp, to hide, and to disguise.

Dellei herself could somehow switch between a Path of darkness and a Path of light, and the largest threats came from her pair of swords. Every time Reigan thought he could tear through with sheer force, he found himself tearing apart only an immaterial curtain of shadow.

He'd prepared countermeasures for her, but had burned them all against Tiberian. Even so, he regretted nothing.

And eventually, in the third match, he managed to run her out of madra by virtue of his superior endurance as an Overlord and a sacred lion.

When he defeated her, the world celebrated. He was even ushered in to meet the two remaining Monarchs themselves.

Before them, he dropped to his knees willingly.

"You may stand," Seshethkunaaz said. The King of Dragons radiated obvious approval, his gold reptilian eyes warm. "You've done us proud and brought honor to this competition. In you, I see the spirit all sacred artists should strive for. State your wish, and let it be granted."

Reigan stood, though he kept his head lowered. "You are merciful to this humble lion. I come from no great family, and I do not have the resources of my peers. I wish for nothing more than the wealth to support my clan and to fund my own advancement."

"A wise request," the dragon Monarch said. "Greed is a trap for the weak, but a virtue for the talented. You will have one of my own treasuries."

Reigan let his excitement show. He was afraid to kneel again, since a Monarch had told him to stand, but he bowed as deeply as he could.

Seshethkunaaz turned to his counterpart. "Surely you would do no less, Emriss?"

The Queen of Everwood leaned on a staff of living wood topped with a softly glowing crystal. Her skin was dark, and appeared human except for a few patterns where Reigan detected the texture of tree bark. Her eyes shone purple and green, and she inspected Reigan with a gaze that reminded him of the Mist Sage.

But her attention was far deeper, far older, and far wiser than that of any human.

"Reigan of House Shen," she said, "if I am to reward you appropriately, I need to know you. Where will your ambition take you?"

Reigan hesitated. He liked the sound of *'House Shen,'* but he wasn't sure he would be allowed to speak the full breadth of the dream lest the Monarchs take it as disrespect. Or, worse, laugh at him.

"You may be honest," Emriss said gently.

Reigan would take the Monarch at her word. "I witnessed the Dread War with my own eyes, and I keep my memories of your battles deep within my soul. One day, if the heavens are kind, I wish to stand with the two of you as a Monarch in my own right."

Rather than mockery, the Dragon of the Wasteland radiated approval. His intent was so clear that it felt like a fatherly hand on the shoulder.

Even victory hadn't ignited Reigan's heart like that encouragement. He would advance to Monarch if only to prove the gold dragon's faith justified.

"If you truly seek to join us as a Monarch," Emriss said, "I believe you will succeed."

His heart glowed again, though her tone puzzled him.

She welcomed him, not with pride, but with deep, deep sorrow.

A Light Chat in a Dark Place

Information requested: the missing conversation between Eithan and Ozmanthus Arelius.
Report Location: Chapter 21 of *Reaper*.
Context: Lindon and Eithan are together in the labyrinth, and they have just stumbled on a Forged echo of Ozmanthus Arelius.
Authorization confirmed.
Beginning report...

In the depths of the labyrinth, Eithan stood next to Lindon and watched his own ghost take shape.

Even the ancient scripts and devices operating in the labyrinth strained to replicate him, capturing only a fragment of his will, an approximation of his personality and memories. It drew more power than the hunger echoes they'd faced thus far, though Ozmanthus Arelius looked relatively unassuming.

He bore the classical good looks of the Arelius family, of the sort Eithan admired every day in the mirror, but his current body was altered enough that they looked like brothers rather than clones. Ozmanthus wore a gentle smile, pale hair cascading down his back, as he propped a broom up on his shoulder.

Lindon set his jaw and braced his spirit, leaning forward to face the new opponent. "Leave him to me."

He looked so young. He *was* so young, to bear the power Eithan had helped him gather.

Eithan adopted an expression of surprise, looking to Lindon. "You want me to face Reigan Shen on my own?"

"Apologies, Eithan, but I saw you fight earlier. He's weakened, and you could break through to Sage at any time. Go face your family's killer."

It was times like these where Eithan regretted having to balance so many lies.

He sighed and gestured for Ozmanthus to wait. The echo nodded and waited, as Eithan had known he would.

Now was the time for a little truth.

"Everyone misunderstands me," Eithan said. "Reigan Shen isn't the one I'm trying to surpass. *He* is."

Ozmanthus waved.

Confusion flickered through Lindon's entire body before showing itself on his face, and the Arelius bloodline senses made each detail crystal clear.

He saw every physical micro-change as Lindon brushed aside his puzzlement and steeled himself once again. "Then let's face him together."

Eithan had no intention of doing that. This was an irreplaceable opportunity, both for himself and for Lindon. He couldn't say so, but his ghost would help him out.

"Yes, of course! If you think he'll allow that."

On cue, Ozmanthus put a black-and-white hand on a panel in the labyrinth wall and exerted his authority.

A tiny sliver of the influence Ozmanthus Arelius once wielded over this place, but more than enough to create some privacy. Lindon vanished immediately.

"My thanks," Eithan said, with a polite dip of the head. "Now..." He brandished his scissors. "Shall we?"

For a moment, Eithan and his past self faced each other across a gulf that spanned millennia, one bearing fabric scissors of dark metal and another a broom of pale madra.

Then they both sheathed their weapons and sat side-by-side on a nearby stair.

"It went that badly in the heavens, did it?" Ozmanthus asked.

"It did," Eithan responded. "It *really* did."

Ozmanthus steepled his fingers and frowned. "That's concerning. I may not have access to a complete record of our memories, but I remember being quite confident in our preparations."

"The plan worked. The Abidan organization hadn't seen a talent like us since the first generation."

Pride leaked into Ozmanthus' smile. As well it might. This echo was taken from an era when Ozmanthus Arelius had spent years studying the first Abidan, gathering the relics and knowledge they left behind to infer everything possible about the world beyond.

Eithan's ghost was still drunk on his own hubris.

"The enemies of the Abidan must be formidable, then, if they drove us back here," Ozmanthus mused. "Or did you retire, as Judges are said to do when their job is finished?"

"The problem was not quite so...external."

Ozmanthus' sense of superiority melted into a faint sadness. "Ah. Unrivaled even in the heavens."

"It defies all probability."

"I suppose the novelty of it would wear off after the first few centuries. Still, that problem alone would be well within our capacity to solve. You don't seem averse to taking disciples."

They both glanced toward the wall, far beyond which Lindon was traveling to Subject One.

"It was the job," Eithan said. He hadn't left all his memories in this form—most of them were a burden rather than an asset—but he felt the crushing weight of even the fraction he had remaining.

Ozmanthus scanned him with a quick flick of their bloodline power, then sighed. "They had us making weapons."

"Using them. When an Iteration could not be saved, it met the Reaper of Worlds."

Rage rippled out of the echo, sending sparks flying from nearby scripts and evoking an ear-piercing screech from the network of projector bindings. Ozmanthus surged with power, his broom appearing almost real.

"I can only assume you left them in ruins," he said, colorless eyes blazing.

"If I had," Eithan said, "then I would have learned nothing at all."

Ozmanthus mastered himself and the bindings settled down. He smoothed out his Forged clothes and rearranged his hair.

Once he had composed himself, he arched an eyebrow. "So we learned our lesson. Was that what convinced us to give up?"

"It convinced us to try one last time."

They sat together, quietly, as they both watched the battles taking place above and below them. As much as they had shared in their speech, they shared more in their silence, communicating as two versions of the same man.

The anger and sadness and pride that Ozmanthus carried were still in Eithan. Older, certainly. Maybe deeper. But he had a better understanding of them.

And they brought him here, to look for something else. Something different.

Simultaneously, they both exchanged beaming smiles and stood.

"Perhaps I should be ashamed of you," Ozmanthus said, "but I find myself hoping for your success."

"I unfortunately cannot reciprocate," Eithan responded, "because I *am* ashamed of you."

"I see manners did not survive into our old age."

"At least we kept our hair."

Ozmanthus' attention was pulled by strands of his awareness, back to Lindon. "Shall I redirect him? Confronting Subject One and a foreign Monarch one after the other, he's likely to break."

"I believe in him. Don't you?"

Ozmanthus chuckled dismissively. "I don't even believe in *you*."

Eithan patted his ghost on the shoulder. "That much, we have in common."

Anagi's Regret

Information requested: the fate of Yan Shoumei, and the identity of her long-time antagonist, Anagi.
Multiple reports detected. The following file contains a total of *four* reports. Proceeding with Report #1.

Report #1 Location: Chapter 20 of *Wintersteel*.
Context: This first report takes place just before Yerin's tournament fight against Yan Shoumei.
Authorization confirmed.
Beginning Report #1...

Yan Shoumei returned to the Uncrowned King tournament through a portal, and she immediately sensed a difference.

Reigan Shen's faction was almost empty. She sensed only a handful of people in their tower, and no one powerful.

"Where did everyone go?" she asked the Blood Sage.

"They are awaiting the rise of a Dreadgod. Somehow, they believe that it will have more import than what happens here." The Sage shook his head at their foolishness. "Do not make that mistake. The development of your Blood Shadow and Yerin's will have vast ramifications for all sacred artists in the future. As such, you should be well-rested and psychologically at your peak, so use these to focus yourself."

He casually tossed her a bundle, which she only recognized when she caught them.

They were letters from home.

She couldn't get back to her room fast enough.

She spent hours reading, though there weren't so many of them. It was only that she went over them again and again, squeezing out every detail.

As a baby, Yan Shoumei had been abandoned on a dock. She'd been picked up by a group of six fishermen coming in from the night's catch, and while they looked for her birth mother, they had passed her around from family to family.

They'd never found her parents. In fact, if her mother showed up now, she would probably be driven out of town.

One and all, the six fishermen had treated her like a daughter. She'd grown into the lynchpin uniting their families into one, and she considered them all like fathers.

As she was the only one among them all with any talent for the sacred arts, she had become their defender. And eventually, somehow, for the entire town.

In that position, she'd learned there were more threats to a town than she'd ever realized. She was able to do her work as a Truegold for years, until an Overlord named Anagi had set his sights on their town.

She'd managed to fend him off thus far with her connections in Redmoon Hall, but only a year ago, he'd advanced to Archlord.

Since she couldn't advance so quickly, only influence could help her. And there were few people more influential than the winner of an Uncrowned King tournament.

The letters told the whole story. A gang of fish-men had stopped raiding the docks when they found out it was the hometown of an Uncrowned. Nearby sacred arts schools had sent presents to her family, or invitations for their children to come and train. A large city had increased its trade with them, hinting that they wanted Yan Shoumei to visit.

Her Blood Shadow stirred inside her, ready for violence, and Yan Shoumei soothed it.

The more she won, the more her family would prosper.

So tomorrow, they would win once again.

Report #1 complete.

Report #2 Location: Chapter 21 of *Wintersteel*.
Context: Yan Shoumei has lost one round to Yerin, but the match has not yet ended. There's still a chance for

Yan Shoumei to bring home victory.
Beginning Report #2...

Yan Shoumei hoped no one back home saw that fight.

It wasn't that she minded them seeing her lose—no one could ensure victory every time—but it was humiliating to have lost without the chance to show her full capabilities.

When Yerin's Blood Shadow had begun Forging the claw, she had poured soulfire into her Red Crystal technique, sure that she didn't need anything stronger to protect her. She had her Iron body and her Ancient Scale, after all.

She could have defended herself further, but had opted to try and disrupt the Shadow with a Striker technique to the chest instead.

Only when the Forger technique had completed did she notice the sensation of danger from her spirit, and then it was too late.

Foolish. She'd made a split-second judgment, and it had been the wrong one. She was too reckless. She was meant to fight carefully and let Crusher take all the risks.

The Blood Sage silently chewed on his finger as she berated herself. When she could take his silence no longer, she finally said "You don't have to say anything. I won't hold back anymore."

She'd wanted to keep one secret left to beat Sophara, but if she didn't reveal her weapon now, she wouldn't make it so far.

His eyes widened. "No, you've done perfectly. This is ideal. You have pushed her to cooperate with her Blood Shadow, and even the Shadow itself is acting with a degree of independence. Do you have any concept of how difficult it is to manifest a Blood Shadow so sturdy that it can withstand the activation of such a weapon?

The Akura clan spared no expense in her training. Though that can cause problems of its own..."

He continued chewing on his finger, leaving Yan Shoumei to stew in irritation. He was focused on Yerin's progress. Of course he was.

Without moving his eyes to her, he pulled a letter from his pocket. "Ah, but of course I need *you* to win. A loss will push her to develop her Blood Shadow further, we will still reap all the benefits of victory, and we have a chance to test the limits of the bestial Shadow. With that in mind, I have some further motivation for you."

He tossed her the letter.

As she scanned the page, her heart seized up.

This wasn't a message from her family, though it was from her home. A Redmoon acolyte sent to the area reported that the Archlord Anagi was positioning his students for invasion. The scout speculated that he was waiting only to see the results of the tournament.

She looked up to the Sage, trying to keep from tearing the paper to shreds. "Top four is good enough. He will restrain himself. Even top eight...why would an Archlord with no greater backing knowingly attack the family of an Uncrowned?"

"We lack the information to speculate. Maybe he does have greater backing. Maybe he just hates you that much. Maybe he won't act at all. Life is rarely certain."

He was still chewing and watching the door as though waiting for it to open.

Yan Shoumei's imagination was going wild with panicked speculation, but she calmed herself. Her situation hadn't changed, not really.

The only thing she could do was win.

REPORT #2 COMPLETE.

REPORT #3 LOCATION: CHAPTER 27 OF *WINTERSTEEL*.
CONTEXT: LINDON HAS DEFEATED YAN SHOUMEI AND LEFT HER FOR DEAD. HE IS CURRENTLY BATTLING SOPHARA NEARBY, BUT THAT LEAVES YAN SHOUMEI A CHANCE TO SNEAK AWAY.
BEGINNING REPORT #3...

EITHAN EASED HIS BROKEN, BRUISED, AND BLOOD-CAKED BODY down to sit on a chunk of rubble. His tender wounds and spinning head aside, he was feeling rather good.

Not far away, Lindon was draining a Remnant dry, and his newfound authority would be the fastest way out of this crumbling tower. Sophara's body was still warm outside—he knew from experience that it took dragon corpses entirely too long to cool—and the Blood Sage had scuttled off.

But that didn't mean the tower was clear of enemies.

Debris shifted next to him, and Yan Shoumei crawled out from beneath a pile of timbers, coughing dust. Eithan instinctively slid to the side, only for his ribs to scream protest. Gritty gray clouds landed on his robes.

Trying to stay clean was like sweeping sand at this point. The only thing that kept his robes decent was his blood sticking them together.

The girl leaned on Eithan's chunk of masonry for support, still hacking her lungs up, black hair powdered gray-brown from her time in the tower's wreckage.

Even weak as she was, she could have burst forth in a show of power. She could have used her sacred arts to protect herself and made her life a lot easier.

Instead, she had wrapped herself in layer after layer of veils. She was thoroughly cocooned, having wisely deduced that using blood madra here would draw attention far more than filling the halls with hacking coughs.

She was wise. Lindon had been fighting until a moment ago, but currently he was preoccupied with the fruits of his victory. He had overlooked her, so it was the perfect time for her to sneak off.

"I'm impressed," Eithan said to Yan Shoumei, and the Redmoon artist stumbled away from him in shock.

Her spiritual sense was completely deafened by her veils, and her eyes were still gummed shut with blood and grime. He had assumed she would have at least noticed his presence, but from the way she rapidly blinked and swiped at her eyes, she'd had no idea anyone was there until he spoke.

He smiled brightly at her. Surprises were always fun, as long as you were the one doing the surprising.

She froze, and he could practically see the thoughts crawling across her mud-caked face. Should she run? No, he'd catch her. Should she fight while he was injured and weak? No, he was too advanced. Should she scan him to see if he was too injured to fight? Maybe unleash her Blood Shadow? What if that drew Lindon down on her?

As she was paralyzed between fight and flight, he gave her a gentle wave. "I mean it, I'm impressed. I know how hard it is to keep yourself restricted when you're in danger. It was the right call."

Yan Shoumei's voice scraped out, even more dry and ghostly than usual. "Don't toy with me."

"Why not? Isn't that better than killing you? I hope you realize that you were part of an assassination attempt against a Monarch's children. The survival rate for such a failed operation is...not high."

"Then kill me."

That time, her voice shook. There was something of a quiver to it, so her defiance came out more like a plea.

He read danger in that tone. Not danger to him, but danger nonetheless. If he left this situation alone, she would draw a blade and lunge at him, trying to force him to kill her.

She knew better than to be caught by Malice.

Maybe light banter hadn't been the best approach.

Eithan frantically shook his head. "No, no, I'm sorry, this is a bad time for jokes. I do apologize."

She stared at him as though she couldn't believe he'd just used the word 'joke.'

"Yes, I see that I have failed to uphold the gravity of this situation. Let me cut to the bone: you should run away. I will cover for you with the Monarch."

She crept warily a few steps closer to the entrance. "Why?"

"Because if I chased down everyone who was bullied or bought into doing Reigan Shen's bidding, I would be a grim, black-clad specter of vengeance rather than the bright, fresh-faced soul you see before you."

He spoke more gently now that he didn't have to worry about a suicide rush. "You had no choice. I know that's the coward's favorite defense, but in this case it is literally true. You had to choose between killing and dying, which is no choice at all. Go home."

With an underhand toss, he threw her a void key.

Not his, of course. He'd scavenged this one from a Redmoon Overlord, and there was nothing interesting inside.

"I don't know what's in your key, but that one has several weeks' worth of rations, scales, and other supplies. Keep your veil on, your head down, and your Blood Shadow quiet until you're out of Akura territory. You can make it."

She stared at the void key in her hand as a tiny whisper of her spiritual perception leaked out of her veil, so she could sense the storage and verify his words.

He had responses prepared for her distrust, for her gratitude, and—most likely of all—for another expression of stunned disbelief.

So he was caught with his mouth open and no idea how to respond when she said, "Come with me."

There was an awkward moment of silence before she filled the silence herself. "You're not the son of a Monarch. You can walk away."

"I really, really can't." He gave her his best smile. "But I am flattered by the offer. Alas, it is the curse of the truly gorgeous; I can never escape attention from anyone who sees me shirtless."

He expected rolled eyes.

But she nodded sadly, wearily, as though he had told her he planned to work himself to death in an iron mine. He suspected she might be reading too much into his words, but all she said was, "Thank you."

In a sudden flurry of motion, she dashed off, leaving Eithan alone with his thoughts.

For a moment.

Lindon landed nearby, having jumped down from the roof, so Eithan immediately flopped down again and pretended to be dying.

One of his jokes had already failed, but that meant he had to try another.

REPORT #3 COMPLETE.

REPORT #4 LOCATION: CHAPTER 33 OF *WAYBOUND,* THE FINAL BOOK OF THE CRADLE SERIES.
CONTEXT: THE FOLLOWING TAKES PLACE AFTER YERIN'S ASCENSION BUT BEFORE LINDON'S. ON THE OTHER SIDE OF THE WORLD, YAN SHOUMEI RETURNS TO HER LIFE AND CONTINUES HER ADVANCEMENT.
BEGINNING REPORT #4...

THIRTEEN SACRED FISH, THEIR BODIES RESEMBLING MEN WITH GILLS AND webbed hands, crept up from between the docks of Sailfin Port. Scales gleamed in the moonlight as they snuck ashore, and they spoke to one another only in hisses and the occasional spurt. Not a language, but a code.

Cracking the code wasn't necessary. It was clear why they were here. The same reason they had come once or twice a month for the last year: to raid the local Soulsmith foundries.

Security around the foundry warehouses by the docks had been significantly increased, with constructs patrolling the street and skies, new scripts freshly painted, and hired Highgold guards standing in doorways.

The fish-men had brought their own countermeasures. A twisted shell sprouted Truegold-level claws and latched onto a nearby alarm script, disabling it while not setting it off. Thirteen webbed feet moved from sand to slapping wet planks without making a single sound; veiled by a sound-dampening construct.

Weapons glistened in their hands, still wet from the sea, each made from the pieces of an aquatic beast or Remnant, most with aspects of water. Fish-men positioned rapidly to attack, sighting guards or constructs to eliminate.

Well-armed, well-prepared, and well-informed.

But not well-informed *enough*.

Yan Shoumei spoke one word in her harsh, whispering voice. "Go."

Crusher rose into the night from where he'd been concealed on the rooftop next to her. His muscled bulk looked like it belonged on a short-haired bear, or perhaps a gorilla, and he snarled with a wolf's snout. His ears, which stuck up from his skull like a rabbit's, twitched as they attuned themselves to prey.

Her Blood Shadow leaped, landing among the fish-men and crushing one in a red spray.

The invaders shouted to one another, but it was all inaudible to Yan Shoumei. Their stealth construct was still active.

Crusher tore them to pieces, unstoppable. The strongest of their number was Truegold, so they may as well have dropped to their knees and waited for death.

'In silence, the fish died. The quickest Remnant began to rise only ten seconds later, but Yan Shoumei didn't wait for the others.

She hopped off the roof next to a guard, who jumped and straightened his spine when she landed.

"Remnants around the corner," she said. "Free dead matter for your employer."

The guard put his fists together. "Thank you, Overlady!"

He rounded the corner as she recalled Crusher, and she heard his shout of surprise as he saw the gore and the rising spirits. If she hadn't been there, he would have been killed.

Yan Shoumei had been on stakeout nearby for the last two weeks, waiting for her prey. Finally, it was over. She'd never had the patience for fishing.

And now she could go after the next task on her list.

She withdrew Crusher back into her soul, which became harder and harder to do as Crusher grew in strength. When she'd first advanced to Overlord, she'd had an easier time for a while, but her Blood Shadow continued to represent the majority of her power. If it weren't for special preparations—thanks to the Sage of Red Faith and Reigan Shen—she wouldn't have been able to hold Crusher at all.

With the Blood Shadow withdrawn, she hopped onto a flying boat—the people of Sailfin Port preferred them to Thousand-Mile Clouds. It was a small rowboat that lifted when she activated the script, shooting through the air.

Flying boats had the advantage of sailing on water aura, which was abundant here, so they rarely had to be maintained and never needed their cloudbase replaced as cloudships did.

Of course, they had their share of disadvantages; for one thing, they weren't a smooth ride. Due to some quirk of water aura, the boats flew as though over the surface of a choppy sea.

Yan Shoumei was growing used to hers, but she still missed the flat, comfortable flight of a cloudship as she sped past row after row of wood-and-plaster houses that made up Sailfin Port.

She had to follow the halfheartedly cobbled streets up to the hills, where a small wall indicated the home of the Broken Waves sect. Not a large sect, nor a powerful one, but one that had been local to Sailfin Port as long as she could remember.

A Thousand-Mile Cloud could have flown up and over the walls, descending onto a blue-tiled roof of her choice. In other words, it would have allowed her to approach without being seen.

Instead, she sailed up the road, past the bows of those who spotted her. The sect was a village in its own right, and more people than usual were out tonight. Sacred artists dropped bags or put aside tools as they recognized her.

Yan Shoumei shrunk further and further into herself with every salute. She was too late, she could tell. She should have run around the back of the sect and leaped over the wall; she was tired, but at least that would have spared her from their examination.

Finally, she pulled up to the Gold training hall of the Broken Waves sect, a grand building by the standards of a remote port town. Its doors, each carved with cresting waves, were thrown wide open.

The sect leader, a grandfatherly Truegold man, waved away the healers that tended to him. Bandages wrapped half his face, covering his eye, and her heart lurched.

Sect Leader Yan Loumai had more of a gut than most active sacred artists, and a gray beard that fanned over his chest, but he still had the burly arms and healthy tan of a career fisherman. The corner of his one visible eye wrinkled as he smiled at her and spread his arms for a hug.

"Shoumei, you made it! Come over here, I'm a little slow this evening."

His head wasn't the only place on his body bandaged; his left knee was wrapped as well. Crusher boiled inside her, in tune with her own heart.

"Your eye?" Yan Shoumei rasped.

He touched the bandage in obvious surprise and then laughed. "No, not as bad as it looks! I still have it."

Her spirit eased, but not much. He *could* have lost the eye, and she wouldn't have been around to help.

"You're still not going to give your father a hug?" he asked.

Yan Shoumei's hair fell around her face and her cloak hid her body. She struggled with herself—her instincts told her to rush out and get revenge immediately.

But she did walk up and embrace her first adoptive father. The only one without another family of his own; the one who had named her after his own grandmother.

"How did it go at the docks?" he asked.

That was a transparent attempt to stop her from asking questions, and she didn't fall for it.

"How long ago did the Flashing Knives leave?" Yan Shoumei asked in return.

He looked away from her. His beard fluttered in a heavy breath. "*We* accepted their challenge, Shoumei. I can't have my daughter taking vengeance."

Yan Shoumei turned to one of the healers, a member of her own generation whose water and life Path was one of the more prominent supplementary Paths in the sect. "How long ago was it?" she asked.

The healer spoke without moving her eyes from the carpet. "Less than an hour, Overlady!"

Yan Shoumei knew this girl. They weren't close friends, but they had trained together. Long ago, before her father had taken over the Broken Waves sect.

Time had changed much, and power changed more. But Shoumei still couldn't change enough.

"Shoumei, please," her father said. "What will it say about our sect if my daughter avenges every offense?"

Yan Shoumei shifted within her cloak, uncomfortable. The only reason Yan Loumai was the Truegold sect leader instead of a barely-Highgold fisherman was his daughter. She'd brought him resources to supplement his advancement, making up for his lacking talent.

She was the protective spirit of the sect, the guardian that kept Broken Waves intact. Or she was supposed to be.

"They should have been too frightened to injure you," she responded.

He stroked his beard as he chose his words. "You work in the weather you have, not the weather you want."

Factions with one Underlord didn't challenge territory under the protection of an Overlady. Not only would her intervention spell certain death for anyone who crossed her, but her displeasure could mean the end of all the Flashing Knives.

"I won't forget this," she promised. "Anagi can only have his way until I reach Archlord."

Loumai waved a hand. "This is only a minor disagreement. The most important thing at stake was my own pride."

"They took no prize from you?" Yan Shoumei asked.

"Nothing irreplaceable."

She took a moment to cycle and focus on her spirit. If she didn't calm her shame and anger, she might accidentally release Crusher. He wouldn't hurt her friends, but he would give them a good scare.

Her father sensed the turmoil in her spirit...or perhaps he simply saw it on her face. He moved closer to her again, resting a hand on her shoulder.

"It's already over, Shoumei. We have hot food and a bed ready for you."

When *had* she last slept? Overlord bodies could be pushed far past their limits, especially hers; blood madra was good for strengthening muscles.

But she did still have limits. Even if she ignored the sensations from her body, her aura told the story. She needed rest.

"Overlords don't need sleep," she said, and leaped back into her flying boat.

If she let the Flashing Knives go, they would continue to make trouble. She could fight them off, but she wasn't allowed to kill them, and she certainly couldn't destroy their headquarters.

So they thought, but only because they had an Archlord backing them. Their safety extended only so far as Anagi's support.

She'd endured this disrespect, this constant testing of her own boundaries, for too long. Her reputation as an Uncrowned had served her well for a time...until the Dreadgods had been killed and the Monarchs vanished.

Just like that, the illusion protecting her family had disappeared.

Anagi still wouldn't move on her hometown. Officially, she was the Overlady of Sailfin Port, with the surrounding lands under her jurisdiction.

He didn't violate her territory. He just protected the ones who did. And there was nothing she could do, because he was an Archlord.

Yan Shoumei sped along the roads in her flying boat for almost two hours. She knew where the Flashing Knives' headquarters was, and sure enough, she caught a group in her spiritual perception before they reached safety.

Sword and blood artists one and all, they didn't follow the Path of the Flashing Knives. As far as she knew, they didn't have any Paths in common, even if they shared some techniques.

They were slaughter artists, growing powerful from the aura of live battlefields. Yan Shoumei resented them, though she shouldn't.

Compared to run-of-the-mill slaughter artists, Redmoon Hall was far worse.

She couldn't make moral judgments, but she could beat them at their own game. As soon as she sensed them, she tucked away her flying boat—they weren't using vehicles and didn't seem to be in much of a hurry.

The Flashing Knives had circled up behind their leader, a tall and gangly Underlord with a pair of Goldsigns like crimson slashes across his eyes. His dark hair was tangled and dirty, and he carried twin knives that shone with silver aura.

Truegolds and Highgolds backed him up, standing in a circle

beyond him and activating tiles attached to their belts. They created a formation circle, one that funneled aura of force and wind into armor around the Underlord.

Crusher crashed into him.

Outside the stealth construct the fish-men had used, Crusher was deafening. The ground cracked as he made impact with the Underlord, the wind howled away from them in a hurricane, and many of the Golds had to brace themselves. Without the protection of their formation circle, they would have been seriously injured and possibly killed, but they managed to hold their positions.

To Yan Shoumei's bitter surprise, the Underlord stayed in place as well.

He'd been too old to enter the last Uncrowned King tournament, but even if he had been allowed, he wasn't Uncrowned material. Anyone in the top sixteen could have defeated him in two techniques.

Yan Shoumei looked past the daggers, past the formation, and noted the man's armor. His robes had been torn, revealing silver threads of glistening chain. They burned with activated script.

An Archlord-level sacred instrument. Combined with the protective formation and the Underlord's own techniques, it was enough to protect him from Crusher.

"You're outside your territory, Overlady!" called the leader of the Flashing Knives. He didn't sound as casual as he no doubt intended. Crusher, furious at being unable to kill his prey, had begun to hammer at the Underlord's crossed arms.

The armor would break eventually, but Yan Shoumei didn't have so long. She didn't need two guesses to figure out who'd given this no-name bandit chief a protective treasure.

Anagi would be on his way, so she had to send her message before he arrived.

Yan Shoumei rushed for the circle of Golds.

They shouted and strengthened the formation, pushing it to hold against her attack. She would need a technique or two to pierce it, given that her madra better at damaging flesh than inanimate shields.

So she bypassed the barrier entirely. Her Ruler technique latched onto all of them, the aura in their blood boiling.

Though reaching through the powered script weakened her aura control, she didn't require full power. The enemies began to choke, faces turning red, as their own blood rebelled against them.

All were blood artists, so they resisted, but Yan Shoumei had gotten what she wanted. Their concentration on the script-circle lapsed.

She punched through the script, the armor over her skin cracking, as she tore away the scripted plate on the nearest man's belt. She crushed it, and the formation faded.

Three seconds after her arrival, Yan Shoumei conjured blood madra into a Striker technique to slash through all the Golds.

A spirit of water dove down toward her, driving her away. She canceled her technique and leaped backwards.

The spirit was a winged dolphin seemingly forged entirely from blue, sun-dappled water. It was a natural spirit, or at least a Remnant that looked like one, and Yan Shoumei's chest seized with fear and deep hatred when she saw it.

Anagi's voice echoed out through the night, slippery and warm like a squirming eel. "Slaughtering my Golds in the night? Such a shame to see an Overlady conducting herself like this."

Crusher let off his assault on the Underlord so he and Yan Shoumei could glare at Anagi together.

The Archlord stood on a flying boat, proud and noble, pretending to be the perfect hero. Three soulfire baptisms had perfected his body, so his build was young and athletic, his hair long and dark, and his face handsome.

He disgusted her. If his appearance matched his spirit, he would be a bloated wretch.

Anagi tucked his hands behind his back and turned on her with a stern look of disapproval. The Flashing Knives rushed over to gather beneath him.

Yan Shoumei had to hold Crusher back from leaping at Anagi immediately. The Blood Shadow snarled, saliva dripping from the edges of his fangs as clawed fingers opened and closed with impatience.

Of course, she didn't want to restrain him, but she had little choice.

"Lawless and reckless," Anagi said sadly. "I knew you'd turn on us. Dreadgod cultists can't keep themselves from feeding on real sacred artists."

Yan Shoumei shivered inside her cloak with the effort of restraining herself and her Shadow. "Leave my town."

His winged dolphin chittered as it swam around her. The sound echoed like laughter.

Anagi swept a hand to indicate the countryside. "Does this look like Sailfin Port? I've honored *your* territory."

Yan Shoumei wasn't particularly suited for trading arguments, but she wasn't an idiot. She didn't bother to speak.

Who was here to witness their argument? An Underlord and his gang of Golds?

Without turning her back, she called her flying boat. There was nothing else to gain here.

"The duel was mutual, wasn't it?" Anagi asked his Underlord.

The wiry leader of the Flashing Knives gripped his weapons and nodded, keeping a wary eye on Crusher.

"So it was. Then I expect an apology, Overlady. You've attacked my men and disturbed my own esteemed self."

She sneered at him. "My apologies." The flying boat arrived and she stepped aboard.

"A *material* apology, you idiot."

Crusher took one running step toward Anagi before Yan Shoumei wrested control back.

Anagi didn't betray a single sign of disturbance, but his dolphin-spirit swooped down to hover between him and Crusher. "My time has been wasted. Show me your sincerity in scales, or I'll tell all the local Lords about our exchange here. I'm quite happy to swear that you attacked a group of weak sacred artists after a legitimate duel, then refused to pay recompense when asked."

Yan Shoumei was having trouble breathing.

As early as she could remember, Anagi was the evil spirit haunting her family. Compared to the Monarch families, he was nothing; a petty provincial ruler that enjoyed exercising his authority over those beneath him.

To her, he was a nightmare that didn't vanish upon waking. No matter how much power she gained, no matter how high she climbed, he was always one step ahead of her. No matter what advantages she kept, he still had more.

For a while after she'd returned home, she'd had peace. Then the Monarchs were gone, their factions splintered. Sages and Heralds were the greatest powers left, but most places in the world had no one so advanced.

She could look thousands of miles in any direction and find no one above Overlord. No one but Anagi.

Yan Shoumei was the second-most powerful, but the others could join hands and crush her easily. She had few allies. Who could trust a Dreadgod cultist?

For months, the noose around her neck had grown tighter and tighter.

But Yan Shoumei had one final problem. She was weaker than Anagi, certainly. But not *too* much weaker. If she was only an Underlord, or even an ordinary Overlord, she would have folded under his pressure immediately.

Sailfin Port might have had a harder time, subject to Anagi's whims, but Yan Shoumei would have led an easier life.

Unfortunately for her, she *could* fight. That option remained always in the back of her mind.

Until Anagi put that last bit of pressure on her. Then it moved to the front.

A needle of blood streaked toward Anagi, a scarlet spear that tore through the air. He raised a hand coated in blue madra to slap away the Striker technique.

It gouged through his technique and split his hand in half.

Crusher struck the winged dolphin, which was reduced to a

spray of water. Thunder rolled, and several of the Golds screamed and clapped hands to bleeding ears.

No one but Anagi and Yan Shoumei would recognize it, but Crusher was made with more than just madra. He carried stolen willpower and the weight of a dozen unique sacred beasts. Even a sliver of the Strength Icon.

Yan Shoumei leaped away and summoned Midnight Rain.

The bow was oversized for her, its limbs smooth and dark but glistening red. It had been made from petrified wood, she was told, with the blood of a Herald sword artist worked through it. Its binding came from an Archlord-level sacred beast, a lizard whose cries once caused the blood of its prey to erupt.

Yan Shoumei put her entire spirit into the weapon, all her soulfire and madra, and pulled the string back. The arrow that appeared was a shivering, crackling mass of strange light, capped with an energy shaped into a spiky crimson star.

Back in the Uncrowned King tournament, when the Sage had helped her select this weapon, he had warned her that she wouldn't draw forth its full power for years. At that time, she hadn't even been able to fully Forge the weapon, just to use it as a half-formed Ruler technique.

The arrow streaked toward Anagi, dragging a Ruler technique behind it.

Golds exploded, their blood turning to needles within them. The Underlord's own skin was pierced, and he screamed, but he survived.

Anagi took the arrow on his arm. Script on his sleeve lit before the fabric unraveled, revealing armor beneath that was identical to what he'd lent his Underlord. The arrow struck the armor and sent him hurtling back. He coughed up blood as he flew.

Crusher gathered himself to pursue, but the dolphin-spirit reformed. It crashed over her Blood Shadow in a wave, shoving him back.

Yan Shoumei had spent a year rebuilding Crusher after his near-destruction at the hand of Lindon Arelius. Her own advancement had made it easier, but Crusher still wasn't what he would have been if he had been allowed to advance freely.

Even so, he was greater than any other Overlord-level Blood Shadow. That he could clash with an Archlord spirit at all was to his credit.

He would struggle with the winged dolphin, though, and Yan Shoumei couldn't help him. Her own Path wasn't useful against those with no blood.

Anagi had landed on his own feet, but she was drawing back another arrow. She released it and drew another. Midnight Rain exhausted her, straining her madra channels to their limits. She might even injure herself permanently by using it so freely.

But it could kill him.

The Archlord had been caught off guard, and he staggered as he took the second arrow. Her rage burned happily; one or two more shots and he was dead.

Something slammed into Yan Shoumei from the side.

She felt no pain; the combination of her Silverscale Iron body and the Ancient Scale she'd received from Seshethkunaaz meant she was always wearing armor comparable to Anagi's.

But it dispersed her shot. Midnight Rain was hard to handle even when she was at her best.

Of *course*, it was the Underlord of the Flashing Knives who had attacked her. The man had tried to stab her in the side with his daggers filled with soulfire and madra, but they only cracked her outer defenses.

Yan Shoumei seized his entire face in one hand, and his eyes barely had the chance to widen before she stopped his heart.

As his body dropped, she regained her grip on the bow, but it was too late.

Anagi drew an Archlord weapon of his own. He whirled a long, fluid metal chain with a sickle-blade on the far end. It shone blue, and its binding carried the fury of an ocean storm.

As she tried to activate Midnight Rain again, Anagi's blade cut across her. She blocked with the bow, but his weapon had a Ruler technique as well.

Waves suddenly struck her out of nowhere, condensed from water aura, tossing her aside. She righted herself quickly, but she couldn't find enough concentration to use her bow properly.

Anagi was just getting started. The sickle-and-chain whipped faster as it gained momentum, the blade striking as though it had a mind of its own—which it very well might. Each time, the wave that shoved at Yan Shoumei grew stronger.

If that were all she had to deal with, she would adjust. But his spirit still engaged Crusher. And he was an Archlord in his own right.

A Striker technique slashed at her; water madra condensed enough to fell trees.

Yan Shoumei was drowning.

She couldn't get her bearings, could barely strike back, and couldn't catch a breath to think. Blood streaked down Anagi's face; he had even wept crimson tears as Midnight Rain's binding struck him.

He was hardly unscathed, but she wouldn't last another minute.

Anagi had more soulfire, could use his weapon more freely, and had a stronger body and soul. Only her iron-clad defense kept her afloat, and that was cracking.

With what she was sure would be her final thought, Yan Shoumei turned her hatred for Anagi to herself.

She could have let the Flashing Knives go. She could have chosen not to attack Anagi. Once she was dead, he would go straight for her family. He would not be a gracious winner, or merciful.

Her own stupidity would cost them everything.

A clawed, red hand bigger than her entire skull shot out in front of her, and Anagi's sickle-blade embedded itself into crimson flesh.

Yan Shoumei felt no pain from her Blood Shadow, only anger and a grim resolve. Crusher hauled himself away from the dolphin-spirit, though it stripped pieces from him. He left a leg behind as he crawled between the enemy and Yan Shoumei.

Striker and Ruler techniques crashed into him, mangling his body.

For the first time, his bestial thoughts condensed into something Yan Shoumei heard as an actual word: *Flee.*

Desperate, she obeyed.

Yan Shoumei tossed herself into the flying boat, fueling it with everything she had left. It sailed down the road as Crusher kept the enemy occupied behind her.

The night was blurry through her panic and her tears, but she steered the boat as straight as she could. This would buy her only a few hours, if that. She was fleeing from an Archlord water artist on a boat; he had likely *let* her run so he could guarantee the destruction of her Blood Shadow. He knew where she was going.

By dawn, she and everyone she loved would be dead.

Yan Shoumei scrambled to open her void key. She fumbled around in the space with one hand, looking for her last resort. The route she'd convinced herself she'd never take.

Finally, she found it: a sealed bottle of glass, filled with blood. An emergency option left by the Sage of Red Faith.

She crushed it, and the madra and authority of a Sage spread through the night in a red cloud.

"Please!" she begged Redmoon Hall. "I need help!"

Her hoarse words were choked with tears, and she repeated herself over and over.

When a woman's voice answered her, it felt like the heavens themselves had opened and lowered a lifeline.

"Yan Shoumei," the cold voice said. "You're bolder than I thought, to come to us for help."

The red cloud formed into the face of a woman, and Yan Shoumei's recognition was accompanied by total despair.

Archlady Kahn Mala's hair was streaked with gray and pulled back almost as tight as her skin, which looked as though it had been attached directly to her skeleton. Her Blood Shadow wrapped around her neck in the form of a cobra, which lifted its head and flared its hood as it saw Yan Shoumei.

"I, please, he's going to kill me!" Yan Shoumei sobbed.

Kahn Mala was clearly unmoved. "And why would Redmoon Hall offend Anagi for you? You abandoned us."

"I'm sorry, I'm sorry! I'll do anything!"

"What can you do for us? The last anyone heard from you, it was after a battle with the Void Sage, and Redmoon Hall is now under *his* protection. You are the enemy."

"Lindon Arelius?" Yan Shoumei asked blankly. Hadn't he been eaten by the Dreadgod, or become one of them?

If he was alive, and in a position to protect Redmoon Hall, she would throw herself on his mercy. "I'll serve him! Tell him I'm sorry!"

Kahn Mala looked down on her in scorn. "I'm not disturbing the most powerful sacred artist in the world for *you*. Now, control yourself. You were an Uncrowned and a member of Redmoon Hall. At least die with some dignity."

The red cloud dispersed. The connection vanished.

Yan Shoumei's heart crumbled.

Something in her spirit snapped as she felt Crusher's destruction. It was a piercing spiritual pain, but she was beyond screaming. She stared dully into the grass without recognizing anything.

Some time passed before she realized she wasn't even fueling her flying boat anymore. The spiritual trauma of losing Crusher had disturbed her use of her own madra, and she hadn't bothered reactivating the script. She'd even gone off-track, and now she was lost in the moonlit woods.

Her madra channels ached, her core was all but empty, her soulfire down to a single gray wisp. Her muscles throbbed all over; her Iron body had taken the brunt of her attacks, but the force still transferred through.

She gazed up at the moon, tracing the new scar that the Weeping

Dragon had left across its face. Dreadgods had such power. She'd been given the chance to reach those heights.

And she'd wasted it.

A powerful presence washed over her as Anagi approached, but she only knelt on the ground and watched the sky. When she felt him near, she spoke without looking.

"Leave my family alive," she said tonelessly. "I'll do whatever you want."

She heard him spit. "I *would* have taken you as a servant, but now I'm tempted simply to kill you. Are you even any good to me without your spirit?"

"I don't know."

Was she any good even *with* Crusher?

"Swear on your soul to follow my orders. We'll start there. If you can serve me well, I might—"

A perception swept across them both. A spiritual sense so powerful that Yan Shoumei had thought she'd never feel it again.

That was the gaze of a Monarch.

Anagi extended his own senses warily as he waited for a change, but the perception seemed not to pay them any special attention. Whichever Sage or Herald had developed such a powerful spiritual sense would rule this region soon, if not the entire continent.

The sensation jostled Yan Shoumei out of her trance. She looked to Anagi, swallowing her revulsion. She'd rather die than serve him, but if that would keep her alive, maybe she could appeal to this new ruler for her freedom someday.

As she was about to speak, a blue line slashed down in front of her. It didn't feel anything like water madra, and a moment later the air tore like a curtain.

She found herself staring into black-and-white eyes.

"Yan Shoumei of Redmoon Hall," the man said, "why have you called my name?"

Only then did she realize, to her absolute shock, that the man was Lindon Arelius.

He had the same build as before—that was to say, *huge*—but his bearing had changed completely since she'd seen him last. He carried the air of a Monarch.

Even though, as far as she could tell, he was in the middle of an ordinary dinner. He sat at a wooden table with a half-empty plate, his sleeves rolled up so they didn't dangle into the food.

Yan Shoumei prostrated herself before the portal. "Void Sage, please! I beg you to save my life!"

A blue spirit, resembling a young woman, peeked into the edge of the portal and gave a bright chirp. Somehow, Yan Shoumei took the sound as encouraging.

It took a few seconds to remember that Lindon had carried such a spirit back at the Uncrowned King tournament. It had simply been much smaller.

Lindon leaned back in his chair. "Tell me the situation."

"My enemy, an Archlord named Anagi, has kept his heel on my family for years."

She intended to continue, but Anagi cut in, stepping up and bowing to the portal.

"Excuse me, Sage Arelius, but this is nothing more than a private grudge between the two of us. It is nothing that deserves your attention."

Yan Shoumei fought against the panic that tried to set in again. "I beg you for just a minute of your time. My life and the life of my family is at stake. Anything within my power is yours."

Another spirit appeared over Lindon's shoulder, this one purple and one-eyed. It licked its lips and sprouted a halo, one that reminded her of the Silent King.

[Where's Crusher?] the spirit asked in her mind. [My old friend, Crusher. I don't sense him in you, and that's a shame, because I expected he would be nice and ripe. Plump.]

Yan Shoumei didn't like the spirit's interest in Crusher, but the truth would serve her well. "Anagi destroyed him only moments ago."

A purple eye narrowed. [And *you're* Anagi.]

The Archlord bowed smoothly. "I'm more than willing to compensate you, if you wanted her Shadow for yourself."

[I like you. Let's take his side, Lindon.]

"Wait!" Yan Shoumei blurted. "I have more to offer, I can—"

Lindon cut her off with a wave. She would say he looked exasperated. "I don't want anything from you. Just answer my questions, all right? Tell me the truth: How did Anagi wrong you?"

Yan Shoumei's words spilled forth with more honesty than she intended. "He *choked* my family. Strangled my town with demands, with taxes, protection fees, he kept all the sacred artists under his thumb, he hired slaughter artists to kill anyone he disagreed with. He's a petty tyrant, and I did everything I could to get away from him. Everything I..."

She swallowed, trying to continue, but Anagi inserted himself into the silence.

"I'm sorry for wasting your time, Sage. This should never have been brought to your attention."

"I don't recall giving you permission to speak."

That was not like the Lindon Arelius she recalled. She'd studied his matches for the tournament, and she remembered him as polite to a fault.

Anagi drew himself up and gave a tight smile. "My apologies once again, but I don't *require* your permission. If you were here, I would of course defer to your authority, but you are not. Though I have not achieved the distinguished title of Sage, I am an Archlord as well."

Only at Anagi's words did Yan Shoumei recognize that the window in front of her was not a door. She couldn't sense Lindon's presence; it was only an image, an advanced version of the construct she'd used to contact Kahn Mala.

The one-eyed spirit winced. [Why did you have to do that, Anagi? I liked you.]

"Apologies for the disrespect, Archlord Anagi," Lindon said. "Yan Shoumei. How did you escape Sky's Edge?"

Now that she knew Lindon couldn't save her, Yan Shoumei's hope was fading by the second, but she clung to the last thread. "Eithan Arelius. He let me go."

"Mmm. Then I should forgive you as well. **Restore.**"

Something twisted around Yan Shoumei, and—so suddenly that it shocked her—she was whole. Better than whole. Her madra channels were fresh, her core full, and her Blood Shadow was nestled in her soulspace.

Tears rose in her eyes and she bowed wordlessly.

"You are merciful, Sage," Anagi said. "Let me take it from here."

Lindon laced his hands together, one whiter than the other. "What will you do, Archlord?"

"I will take Yan Shoumei into my service. I think you'll agree that we cannot allow a Dreadgod cultist to run free."

The purple spirit gave a look of pure astonishment. [You don't keep up with the news, do you, Anagi?]

"The cult of the Bleeding Phoenix is protected by Yerin Arelius, and I carry her burdens now. Therefore, Yan Shoumei is under my authority. You will not harm her."

Anagi drew himself up and looked down his chin at the Sage. "If you wish to claim this girl, come do so in person. I'll be waiting."

Yan Shoumei couldn't see the blue spirit anymore, but she heard a tinkling chime from elsewhere in the room. It sounded like laughter.

"You have been warned," Lindon said. A moment later, the vision cut off.

Yan Shoumei rose to her feet immediately, summoning Midnight Rain once more. Anagi was still wounded, his madra depleted. Now that she was at full power, she had a much better chance.

Anagi already had his chain-and-sickle in hand, the winged dolphin hovering over his shoulder. "Sages are not as powerful as you imagine them to be," he said. "The next time you see the Void Sage, he will beg *my* forgiveness."

He slashed out with the blade, a probing strike. The blade missed her, but the follow-up Ruler technique battered her with waves.

At that point, Anagi burst into black flames.

He didn't get a chance to scream. Yan Shoumei barely recognized what was happening. In a blink, he went from a powerful Archlord to a pile of scorched bones with beautiful silver armor lying on top.

While Yan Shoumei stared at the ashes, a voice echoed in her mind.

[And he even offered to pay us. Ah, well. Hey there, Crusher! Remember us?]

In the depths of Yan Shoumei's soul, Crusher shuddered.

Testing Northstrider

Information requested: the ascension of the Monarch Northstrider.
Report Location: *Waybound,* between Northstrider's ascension and Lindon's.
Context: No further context required.
Authorization confirmed.
Beginning report...

Northstrider stood in a *line* and waited to be tested.

So far, the heavens had not lived up to his expectations.

He'd avoided ascending for so many years only because he'd wanted to have a real voice in the worlds above. He had studied enough history to know that the Abidan were just another human organization—

if the most far-reaching one—but they had the resources of many worlds and a legion of people all able to manipulate the Way directly.

From what he'd seen since ascending, their advanced technology and techniques had done them little good.

The golden, planet-spanning city of Sanctum was impressive enough, with even the most meager citizen living like the child of a Monarch. They didn't even need to worry about offending a more powerful sacred artist, a level of social stability that had almost gotten him arrested twice.

But there was still a pall of dread over the citizens, and the Abidan acted like their worlds were all ending. There was little dignity in them, and they did not conduct themselves with the bearing worthy of Monarchs.

Northstrider intended to teach them what that meant, but first he had to join their organization. They had him standing in a line of hundreds of other people, all clean and well-dressed, all meager in power.

Even so, they didn't skip him to the head of the line. They didn't acknowledge him in any way.

Not only was his pride offended, but his sense of pragmatism was violated. He was worth more in a fight than any given legion of those around him, but the Abidan—in a state of emergency—had no method of sorting him from the masses.

A smiling blue ghost of a woman, clearly a construct, beckoned him forward. [Northstrider of Cradle, yes? We've had quite a few new recruits from your world in the Wolf Division.]

Northstrider folded his arms and said nothing. She hadn't asked him a question.

[I expect you'll do well there,] she continued. [And who's that? Have you made yourself a friend?]

She is scanning me, his oracle codex reported.

Northstrider had nothing to hide. He let the smooth, black orb rise out of his spirit. "My creation," he said.

The blue ghost inspected his codex and nodded. [Very good! You'll have a head start in learning to use a Presence, if and when you pass the tests. And I believe it's your turn now!]

A golden door slid open and Northstrider marched in, finding himself in a garden of white stone. A ball floated in the center of the room, one woven from blue light that was infinitely more substantial than the translucent body of the ghostly woman outside.

Her voice echoed throughout the room. [This is simply a method to understand your initial aptitudes. Take a seat however is comfortable for you and begin to focus on the nexus of Waypower. As you're from Cradle, you're familiar with meditation, aren't you?]

Northstrider didn't sit. He reached out a black-scaled hand to the ball of blue light, exerting his will as he would if he meant to toss someone across the world.

The ball expanded into a hollow ring with a tunnel visible inside, though it looked only wide enough to admit his arm.

[You have quite the aptitude for Fox techniques!] the woman's voice reported. [That's the third most common result for ascendants of Cradle, after Wolf and Titan. Why don't we try those next? Attempt to convince the Way to strengthen yourself.]

With disdain, Northstrider Enforced himself. Madra of blood and hunger wrapped his body and, drawn by his iron will, so did a slender vein of blue light. It drew into his technique and lent it an absolute aspect that his oracle codex spun to analyze.

He couldn't call up the Way so directly with his normal Enforcer techniques, but with the energy from the Way materialized in front of him, he had no issue.

[As expected, Wolf compatibility! Now—]

Northstrider knew what was required of him, so he conjured a barrier. He extended his awareness through the Way, touched Fate, and cracked a nearby stone before restoring it to perfect condition.

On his own initiative, he passed three more tests.

The room's Presence, if that was the nature of the ghostly woman, began to sound excited. [Six for six! Remember that this is only an initial compatibility test, and it does not determine your ultimate potential, but fewer than five percent of our applicants demonstrate aptitude for six of seven Abidan disciplines. The seventh, however, is often considered the most difficult.]

Before she could elaborate further, Northstrider focused on one of the nearby stones. He had done his research on the Abidan, and he'd reasoned out the seventh property of the Way.

"**Rise**," Northstrider commanded the stone.

The blue orb in the center of the room let out a formless blue haze, followed by a ripple of sapphire light, as Northstrider reinforced his command with the Way.

The stone, of course, rose as ordered. It floated in the air. Not suspended in vital aura or gripped directly by his will, but freed from gravity.

[Wonderful!] the room's Presence called. She manifested a moment later, smiling broadly. [You've done what few in your position have ever managed to do, Northstrider. Fewer than one percent of our applicants demonstrate compatibility with all seven properties of the Way. Even among the current generation of Judges, only one had such talent.]

Northstrider's proud mood soured. "Ozriel." It was hardly a guess. He had heard plenty about Eithan Arelius' title since coming here, and half the stories were about his divine skill. Of course, *all* the stories were about how he had selfishly abandoned existence to its own demise.

The ghostly blue woman waggled a finger. [Actually, no. While this is not commonly known, Ozriel was compatible with only six of the seven disciplines. The Judge skilled with all seven was the late Makiel, the Hound, leader of the First Division. May the Way guide his soul.]

Northstrider's mood improved immensely. He was thousands of years behind, but it seemed his ultimate potential was superior even to Eithan's.

Initial compatibility, his oracle codex reminded him. *Not ultimate potential.*

Northstrider ignored that.

[Recruits such as you are extremely rare and prized, especially in times like these. You will spend time in each of the seven divisions before you find the one where you may do the most good, but you'll start with the one where you show the most promise.]

"Where is Akura Fury?" Northstrider asked.

[He is on the verge of promotion to two-star in the Wolf Division. One of the best of our current batch of recruits. If you end up joining the Wolves with him, the future of that division will be secure.]

Northstrider silently waited for transport. He knew what his test results were, and he knew where his talents lay. Once he arrived at the Wolf Division, he would have to test himself against Akura Fury. To see where he fell by their standards.

The blue woman waved a hand, which trailed information so dense that Northstrider couldn't catch it all. [Customarily, we would arrange for a tour of the various divisions first, but many recruitment procedures are abbreviated in the current circumstances. Would you like to visit the Ghost Division tomorrow morning, or shall I send you right now?]

Ghost Division? Northstrider thought.

He let nothing show on his face.

His oracle codex began organizing what they knew about the Abidan divisions, but only a blink or two had passed before a skeletally thin man in a gray cloak *burst* from the white stones on the ground.

Northstrider reacted as a Monarch with many centuries of experience. Madra filled his hand, a sliver of the Way reinforced his Enforcer technique, and he slammed a punch into the newcomer.

In another world, an attack with such force would have broken space, not to mention detonating the air. Sanctum was far more stable, with a greater weight to its natural laws and defenses in place even Northstrider didn't understand. It was as though the world itself had a will working against his.

Nonetheless, it didn't actually *weaken* him, just reduced the collateral damage from his techniques. He struck the gray-cloaked man with a technique that should have liquefied flesh.

Instead, his punch passed right through the stranger, and not merely as though the gray-cloaked man had turned to air. It was like Northstrider had punched into a hole shaped like an intruder in a gray cloak.

Hands grabbed Northstrider's shirt, but the stranger was completely focused on the room's Presence. "I'm taking him! Right now! Okay?"

[We acknowledge your request, as long as the recruit agrees—]

"Thanks!"

Northstrider didn't follow up with a second attack yet. He'd recognized the newcomer, at least through logical processes. This was a member of the Ghost Division.

He looked young.

The gray-cloaked Ghost seemed like he was no older than twenty-five, with a scraggly excuse for a beard, wild hair, and wide, anxious eyes. Though Northstrider knew it was foolishness to judge the people of the heavens by their outward appearance, the Ghost looked like he had missed more than a few meals and never done a day of hard training in his life.

Nonetheless, it was with respectable strength that the young man hauled Northstrider through...

Not the Way itself. Some kind of barrier, or border. It was as though he'd pulled Northstrider through a curtain, and on the other side was the headquarters of the Ghost Division.

Or so Northstrider assumed.

All the Abidan divisions were headquartered within great golden pyramids, each large enough to contain a major city. He presumed that was where the gray-cloaked Ghost had brought him, but it was impossible to tell from the inside.

In fact, the place was disorienting even to Northstrider.

He found himself in a vast room, which twisted in on itself like a three-dimensional maze. One that had been repurposed for office space. Desks were planted on a diagonal ceiling, where people stood upside-down and drank from cups that didn't spill. They walked down a staircase that turned sideways and inside out, only to come out right-side-up from Northstrider's perspective.

The same thing, and stranger still, was happening all around him. He saw a man draw a sketch of a vehicle, bring it to life as a structure resembling a Remnant, then shrink it down to fit in a palm. A woman opened a door for one of her colleagues, then a moment later, someone just walked straight through the same door. A single pen—at least, a writing device Northstrider took to be a pen—sat on a desk, and no fewer than three people took it away. Though it was simultaneously taken in three different directions, the pen remained sitting on the desk.

Such scenes wrapped around him, as normal parts of daily life. He could see at least a thousand people.

Of course, he had his codex take detailed records.

He was the latest in a batch of recruits, and the only one who was taking appropriate stock of his surroundings. Then again, from the feel of them through the Strength Icon, he was the only one *capable* of true vigilance. His awareness contained everything in his immediate vicinity, even without specifically expanding his spiritual perception.

There were fifty-one trainees other than him, and he surmised that they had all been taken just as suddenly by other Ghosts. The one who'd brought him was the only one who remained, the others having dissolved in strange ways.

Not that the remaining Ghost seemed happy with the situation. He'd started to fade into a gray shadow himself before something snapped him out of that state and he staggered back to full physicality in front of the group.

"Oh. What? I'm...Okay, yes, I'm your...I'm the one who's going to take you for the day. Welcome to the Ghost Division."

A woman to Northstrider's left lifted her hair to puke on the floor. Their host reached out a bucket, which he'd pulled from nowhere, and put it beneath her without looking.

"That's going to happen," the Ghost said. "Most of you are here because you scored well on the aptitude test for the Ghosts, so anyway, now it's time."

They stared at him.

"Time for what?" one asked.

"I didn't take an aptitude test," another protested.

Northstrider was, once again, unimpressed with the hiring procedures of this otherworldly bureaucracy. Despite what power this young man might actually possess, *he* was weak.

"Tell us your name," Northstrider commanded.

The Ghost straightened. "Hallister Halloway, one-star Ghost! Most people call me Hall."

Northstrider wasn't going to call him that. "Organize yourself, Ghost."

"Right, yes. Thank you. Ahem." Hall plucked at his gray cloak. "I'm going to take you to a world where we're needed. Just do the best you can."

Hall gave the group an encouraging smile and pushed open a nearby door, which led into the buffeting blue of the Way. The

Ghost stood to one side and beckoned people through; some entered without hesitation while others looked as though he was tossing them into a bottomless hole.

Northstrider loomed over the Abidan. "That was not organized."

"I know you're scared, but we *really* need you. It's bad out there."

It was far from the first time that Northstrider considered killing an Abidan, but it might have been the first time Northstrider decided the act was beneath him. Perhaps he'd done better than he thought in attempting to make himself a powerhouse even by Abidan standards.

We have observed an enormous gap between the lowest of the Abidan ranks, which struggle to maintain their connection to the Way or to direct it at scale, and the higher ranks. It was a timely reminder from his oracle codex, though Northstrider had hardly forgotten.

The Judges were as far above him as he was above a meager Lowgold, so surely there were some Abidan among the middle ranks who commanded true authority.

Hall, however, was clearly not one of them.

"When we arrive," Northstrider said, "instruct the trainees. Tell them the nature of Ghost techniques and our purpose at our destination. Then you may begin your work."

Hall looked up in pure astonishment. "Everybody knows. And we have work to do!"

"Lead. Or I will."

Northstrider intended it as a threat, and Hall seemed to take it as one. He busied himself in beckoning people through the portal, as though that had suddenly become vitally important.

When the rest of the recruits had marched through the doorway,

Northstrider followed. He was used to steering through the fabric of space, even diving into the shallowest currents of the Way itself, so he found it uncomfortable to be held to a defined course.

This stretch of the Way had been shaped and bound to a specific destination, and no deviation was possible. Clearly, someone had built infrastructure for this mission.

The Fox Division, his oracle codex reported. *Foxes bind the Way to destinations, allowing travel between and within Iterations.*

Northstrider appreciated the handiwork of the Foxes even as their tunnel through reality made him feel restricted. He didn't relish the idea of working as a glorified courier, but he had always been comfortable manipulating space.

In fact, he had expected to test better as a Fox than as a Ghost. Finding himself in the Third Division had surprised both him and his codex, though he'd taken it in stride.

They arrived in a world that looked...fine.

From Hall's attitude, Northstrider had anticipated arriving in an apocalypse, like a Dreadgod attack or the obvious collapse of local reality. Instead, fifty-two new recruits stood in a sunlit forest one might find anywhere. If it weren't for the absence of spiritual power, he would have believed that they might be back on Cradle. Birds chirped and clouds drifted lazily overhead.

The Abidan was the last out of the portal, and he stared up at the clouds when he arrived. After he examined them for a second, he drew a glass lens out of nowhere and watched the sky through it.

Then he paled. "Bad bad bad! Okay, I'm going to go straight for the temporal structure. Everybody else, look for anomalies and fix them!"

He started to vanish, but Northstrider was prepared for him. He focused willpower onto his grip and sensed the echo of the Strength Icon, then reached out and grabbed the back of Hall's cloak.

The man came up short with a *'grk'* like an over-eager dog reaching the end of its leash.

"Explain," Northstrider ordered.

"*Really?* We have...Fine! Everyone, you're honorary members of the *Ghost* Division, which builds and maintains the laws of reality. They're falling apart here, as you can *see*, so just pick something and fix it!"

He threw out his hands and turned to Northstrider as though asking to be dismissed.

Northstrider fixed Hall with a stare. "They don't understand."

Of course they didn't. Even with his oracle codex, his prior research, his connection to multiple Icons, and his observation of Hall's initial reaction, Northstrider was only just beginning to see what the Ghost was talking about.

Though it looked peaceful on the surface, this world must be unraveling at the seams. Ghosts dealt with worlds on the brink of death, or those in the process of being born.

Hall took a breath and gathered himself. "Listen, I know you ascended from the lower worlds, but this is common sense. If you don't get it, just watch someone, you'll pick it up. Right, everybody?"

The others stared blankly or shifted in place.

One woman raised a hand. "I know what you're talking about, but I don't know how to feel it. Or fix it."

A nearby man, disturbed by spatial travel, bent over to vomit. This time, Northstrider caused it to vanish before it hit the ground.

One may infer that Abidan recruits are usually more qualified, the oracle codex suggested. *Also, Hall himself is not suited for this position.*

Northstrider wondered if something he'd done had made his oracle codex state the obvious or if that was Dross' influence.

A stunned Hall pressed the heels of his hands to his forehead for a moment before he said. "All right! One of the fundamental properties of the Way is that it sustains coherent existence. Those who can manipulate those properties have the potential for joining us. As the Ghost Division, we're guarding…"

He struggled to find the words. "…You know, time. Space. Existential weight. Substance. How *real* and *rational* something is."

"So we fix broken time?" someone in the crowd asked.

"Yeah, sometimes. Fixing is a Phoenix job, but Phoenixes can only restore things to how they were before. When we need to write *new* rules, or break ones that are wrong, that's when you call us."

Urgently, Hall stabbed his finger at the sky. "Look at that cloud! That one. That cloud is *not moving left.*"

The cloud was indeed drifting left.

"It's traveling to the right, it's just doing that *backwards in time.* That means something is very broken. Work on repairs—None of you have a Phoenix rating, do you? Never mind—Fix whatever you can so things hold together while I do the real Ghost work."

He vanished, and Northstrider let him. That left a crowd of recruits in a clearing with nothing to do other than trying to fix the timeline.

"Heed me," Northstrider called. "When I was tested by the Abidan, I rewrote the properties of a stone so it was no longer affected by gravity. You all should have done something similar."

A few started telling what they would do or held up their hands, but Northstrider let a little spiritual pressure leak out to silence them. "Whatever you did then, do it now. We restore the natural order. If you see areas where it is broken, repair it. If you do not, reach out to the Way and seek order. If you can do neither of those, observe me."

With that, Northstrider levitated into midair and cast his senses into the substance of the world around him.

As he'd suspected before, this world was held together by little more than rusty nails and twine. He found towns where time ran backwards, palaces isolated from space, and sleeping people whose nightmares slithered out of their minds to stalk the night.

His first instinct was to patch the holes, but his experience in restorative authority told him the likely outcome. This wasn't a healthy world that had been attacked and wounded. It succumbed to a wasting disease it had held all along.

A Phoenix could prolong this world's life by restoring it to a state of order, but that would only delay the inevitable. It would slowly slide into this condition once again.

They needed to put things right.

To attempt this is to tinker with the fundamental principles of reality, his codex warned. *Collateral damage and unintended effects are impossible to predict.*

Repairing this world would require great power, but power alone would not do it.

It would need knowledge and insight, but not only those.

It required a firm hand, a strong mind, a bold heart, and an artist's touch. Even then, there was no one to guarantee it would work.

Only such a challenge was worthy of Northstrider.

He focused on the severed space around the palace, which was the most straightforward problem to fix. "**Mend.**" The work of a Phoenix.

Under his authority, the spatial cracks surrounding the vast building were slowly squeezed away.

He maintained his will on them, keeping his full attention, until they were gone. Then he moved on to the next problem.

"**Be not,**" he commanded the nightmare. Already thin, it should have puffed out of existence, but the creature snarled and fought back.

Several other, lesser wills joined his. Some of his fellow recruits had sensed what he was doing and followed his lead. He approved.

Under their combined focus, the nightmare creature vanished.

Such problems were far from the central issue, and fixing them was like patching leaks in a boat that had already exploded. But every minor source of chaos that they repaired was a small amount of pressure taken away from the Ghost's work.

Once the simplest issues were solved, Northstrider opened his eyes and surveyed the recruits around him. Many were breathing heavily or blinking rapidly, showing their mental exhaustion.

He favored them with a compliment. "Good. Now, I will attempt to restructure time. This is the true test, and even I may not succeed. Support me."

Northstrider returned his attention to the fabric of the world. Any assistance they gave him would be welcome, but he did not count on it.

He had to sink deeper into the Iteration to address this problem, which altered his perception. At first, he was sensing his surroundings as he had on Cradle; he touched the powers of the recruits, the interlocking patterns of intention and significance that reflected on his Icons, and the strange energy of this world.

That felt similar to the spiritual elements of Cradle, but still distinct, in a way that he was growing used to since leaving his home behind.

All of those sensations were familiar enough, and created a map of a planet—smaller than Cradle, but still vibrant and full of life. He had to go deeper.

As he did, the picture changed. Rather than a map of the planet, he began to see it as a tangled set of threads, stretching out from the past to the future. Even those threads were just the smallest piece of a machine whose complexity he was only beginning to understand.

But that was as far as he could see. Pushing himself so much was a feat to be proud of, given that he had already evolved his perception from that of a Monarch since ascending.

The threads running through the Iteration were brightly colored and stretched infinitely far, but they had been tied into knots. They weren't *supposed* to be tangled at all, and Northstrider could sense why the Ghosts were concerned.

He could revert this logic to a previous state, but it would only end up tangled again. He needed to not only untangle them, but leave some structure to prevent the problem from recurring.

Northstrider was operating beyond his experience, and by any measure, beyond his power. He didn't let that stop him.

He'd always had a gift for working with time.

Dragons felt that they owned the world, as though reality itself should bend to their arrogance and the essential weight of their existence. Northstrider tapped into that confidence from the many dragons he'd made part of himself, hearing the song of the Dragon Icon grow louder and louder.

In his vision, which had grown so strange and esoteric, he saw the ghosts of dragons looming up behind him. Thousands, overlapping one another.

Northstrider used thir authority, and he commanded the most fundamental principles of this world to obey him.

Outside, in the physical world, a cloud stopped drifting left.

The strings shivered and obeyed only reluctantly, slithering around each other as they re-ordered themselves to his direction. But this was a command greater than any Northstrider had issued before, and it was a world to which he had no connection.

Even his willpower was strained to its limits, his authority lacking. He was making a change, but not enough of one.

A handful of other, weaker wills had joined his own, shoving against the strings to push them closer to order.

He let them shoulder a higher proportion of the burden—which might harm their real bodies, but he couldn't concern himself with that—to reach deeper.

Northstrider called the Way to support him.

It was far harder than it had been in his test, as no one had conjured the Way for him. During his normal workings, he could *reach* the Way Between Worlds, but commanding it? That had been beyond him, once.

Perhaps it still was.

As the other recruits collapsed beneath the task he'd left for them, Northstrider found that the Way wasn't responding. He needed more.

Though it made little sense, he acted on instinct. He cycled madra, Enforced his limbs, and reached out. Physically.

If the Way existed outside the world, wasn't any direction as good as another?

Northstrider *grabbed* a fistful of the Way and *seized* it for his service. The Strength Icon resonated with the Dragon Icon, bound to the same purpose.

And a faint wisp of blue light reinforced his working.

Suddenly, the shining threads at the heart of existence snapped into place. They looked like strings on an instrument, side by side and taut. Blue mist wove between them, ensuring that when one moved, the others were plucked in harmony.

Northstrider returned to the real world to find himself surrounded by death.

Many of the recruits who aided him had simply dropped to the ground, dead. Others convulsed or clawed blindly at the air.

Northstrider's body was perfect and unassailable, but even his own concentration was reaching its limits. His will had been pushed far beyond its usual constraints, and like a torn muscle, it needed rest.

Nonetheless, these people had harmed themselves while following his lead.

"**Return**," he commanded.

The dead returned to life, the wounded were healed, and Northstrider determined that he would *not* pass out before the working was finished. It was beneath his dignity.

The operation has succeeded beyond expected parameters, his oracle codex reported. *Intervention of the Way is likely.*

Once the working was completed, Northstrider placed his arms behind his back and pretended to be unaffected, instead of passing out. With his stance steady, he contemplated the significance of what had just occurred.

The Way had supported his healing. Only a fraction of its aid, a small percentage of what a true conjuring of the Way should be capable of.

But he hadn't called upon it. The Way had aided his actions. Or, as the Abidan seemed to put it, it had flowed through him.

A shadow peeled away from a nearby tree and paled to gray as Hall materialized, panting. "Who did all that? Where are they? Did you see them?"

Northstrider glared at him. "Use your eyes."

"Yes! I sense their power in you!" Hall grabbed Northstrider's collar. "Call them back! Why did they leave before we were done?"

Northstrider couldn't use even the slightest working any longer, but he was still physically healthy and full of madra. He could likely slap the young Ghost's head into the woods.

"That was me," he said instead.

Hall snorted. "You don't need to *lie.*"

Northstrider seized him by the hair. "Tell me what you know of the situation. And do not question my honor again."

Hall tried to shake him, but of course failed. "We're going to lose this Iteration! We have temporal stability, sure, but our void membrane is *completely* gone, and our existential infrastructure is..." Hall lost his words, so he mimed an explosion. "Do *you* want to be stuck on a fragmenting Iteration with no causality anchor?"

Northstrider's oracle codex was busy looking up those references, but he could make an educated guess. He understood enough to take command of this situation; he was clearly more suited to lead through an emergency than the panicking Ghost.

And his curiosity was not merely piqued. It resonated with hunger madra. Even if Hall knew little, he was part of an organization where they studied the machinery of existence. What greater knowledge could there be?

After this mission, whether Northstrider joined them or not, he would certainly conduct more research with the Ghosts.

"Where is our exit?" Northstrider asked.

"That doesn't fix it! If we don't do something *now*, we're—"

"Answer me."

"I have it." Northstrider released his hair so Hall could pull out a silver handheld device. "But we can't use it yet! This is *my* assignment, and if we leave, we won't be able to come back. It will dissolve, and how am I going to explain that?"

Northstrider snatched the device and activated it. The process was simple, merely a press of a button that called to preexisting workings in the Way.

Hall stared at him with slack-jawed horror as another Fox-made portal opened before them. Northstrider turned to the other recruits.

"Leave."

Several rushed in. Others said petty things, beneath Northstrider's notice, like *'I'm almost finished here!'* or *'My friend isn't back yet!'*

Northstrider tossed those in with wind aura. He found the stragglers with his spiritual perception and hauled them back, hurling them into the Way without explanation.

Hall stood back as though afraid to be associated with him, pointing a trembling finger at Northstrider. "I won't take the blame for this! This was you!"

"We had minutes before this world collapsed," Northstrider said. "Is that not so?"

Hall shuffled, ran his hands through his messy hair, and inspected the grass. "If we could have patched something together for the void membrane..."

"You kept disciples in danger that you could not handle. You have failed as a leader. Your choices were to accept that failure or to remain in danger and rely on rescue, which is a foolish risk."

Northstrider stepped closer to the Ghost, and when Hall tried to flinch back, Northstrider didn't let him.

"I am not a fool. And I will not follow one. Get into the portal."

Red-faced, Hall breathed heavily. "I'm going to report you! I'll tell them what you did!"

Northstrider reached the end of his patience. He backhanded the young Abidan.

The strike never connected.

It was as though each fraction of an inch was further away than the last, and Northstrider watched as his hand grew slower and slower, never fully stopping. His entire body felt the same; as though he were locked in a prison of time.

If Hall could perform workings like that, why was he so incompetent otherwise?

His oracle codex blared a warning. One that reminded him of another, far more ominous warning in the past. *The Ghost has come.*

It wasn't talking about Hall.

A woman in white armor stepped out from behind Hall as though she'd been hidden there all along. Her skin was so pale it looked unnatural, her dark hair falling around her face, and she carried a tall staff.

Everything else was stopped. Hall's eyes moved in his sockets, but the rest of the world was completely still.

The newcomer looked from Northstrider and then beyond him. "Beautiful," she said, and a spark of passion kindled in her eyes. "It has the rough signs of an amateur's touch, but I see creativity. Vision. And with nothing but your native energy system and your own authority...*This* is craftsmanship! Tell me your name."

So delicately that he hadn't noticed, he'd been released.

"I am Northstrider, of Cradle."

She gave a quick, fluid sketch of a curtsy. Instead of armor, she wore a dress of gray smoke spun into fabric. "Once, I was known as Eiras Luriana of Obelisk. Now, most call me Durandiel." She lifted her staff—*The* Staff of *the* Ghost—and tapped it onto the ground. "You'll appreciate this."

In that instant, Northstrider found himself in the world he'd envisioned when he looked beneath the substance of the Iteration. It had only existed in his mind, but now he floated within it, and without strain.

He and Durandiel hovered over the ordered strings that represented the world's time. Not Hall. Just the two of them.

"This is what you saw," she said. "Your idea would have worked, if you were able to command but a bit more of the Way." Sapphire mist flowed out of the darkness and wove itself among the strings, coating them and playing beneath them.

Northstrider could see how each time one of the strings was plucked and began to vibrate out of place, the mist would carry over to the next string. Each would reinforce the others, compensating for any disorder.

It was the evolution of his theory, executed perfectly.

She rolled her Staff between both palms as she warmed up, visibly excited. "That shows creativity and foresight, and it's very clever. But watch *this*."

Durandiel glanced at him to make sure he was paying attention, then reached out with a single finger. She tapped as though touching one of the strings.

Far away, it quivered. A tiny echo passed through the mist, and the other strings vibrated at the same frequency.

They carried that sound into the distance, where it shivered into deeper mechanisms. Without Northstrider's intervention, his vision adjusted to see so far.

A song wrapped the planet, shaking a protective membrane into place.

Mechanical pieces he could scarcely understand clunked and rattled as they tumbled, seemingly random...but then clicked with one another, settling in order.

It was as though the Ghost had plucked a flower in Moongrave that she knew would lead inevitably to the fall of House Arelius two continents away. Northstrider's mind was overwhelmed by an awe even greater than what he'd felt when he saw Eithan Arelius do battle with the man who blotted out the stars.

As the Ghost's restructuring of reality completed and that strange deeper world faded away, Northstrider remained staring blankly, trying to hold on to his comprehension of what he'd just witnessed.

Durandiel's eyes sparkled. "You have the talent to join whichever division you like, but they won't teach you *that* in the Wolves. Leave word at our headquarters when you decide to join. You're the first recruit we've had in years that's worth my personal attention."

She turned and walked past Hall, who fell to his knees in front of the Ghost.

"Thank you, Judge!" he shouted. "Please, I don't know what to tell the supervisors. Would you put in a word for me?"

Durandiel looked down on Hall, and in stark contrast to a moment before, she looked distant and cold. For a long ten seconds, she let Hall sweat.

"No," she said at last.

Then she vanished.

Contradiction, the oracle codex said. *The Judge implied she did not know your name, but she was aware of your compatibility scores.*

Northstrider paid no attention to its voice. He was occupied with remembering the Judge's lesson, but he found that his memory lingered on different details. The elegance of her motion as she reached out her hand. Her artistic passion. The contours of her face, which used imperfections to transcend mere perfection.

The codex buzzed in his head again. *Your objectivity is compromised. Recommend investigating the other divisions before making your decision.*

Northstrider fully intended to visit the other divisions. He would learn what he could of their ways and techniques.

Before he joined the Ghosts.

A Bloody End

INFORMATION REQUESTED: ERROR. REQUEST NOT FOUND.
REPORT LOCATION: LOCATION UNKNOWN.
CONTEXT: CONTEXT UNKNOWN.
AUTHORIZATION CANNOT BE CONFIRMED.
BEGINNING REPORT...

THE WAR WAS ALREADY LOST, BUT THEY COULD STILL SAVE the world.

Zeth Baker was convinced of it. He had to be. He had no doubts, no reservations, no fears.

He lied to himself, because that was the first step in changing the truth. Then he passionately lied to others, praying his words would turn to facts.

Zeth stood in a small room, a cramped storage closet that had been hastily cleared out for the purpose of exchanging messages. Inches away, his friend Brani stared into the distance as she looked through the eyes of her other self.

"The royal palace wants to hear about the evidence," Brani reported.

As a Twin Messenger, Brani could temporarily exist in two places at once. As she stood before him, she also stood in a Message Stall back in the Delarian royal capital, serving as their only link to the nobles.

Zeth knew she could give the report herself, but it was important the story came from him. Somehow, the people had given them their trust. He had to carry that trust carefully.

"High Consort Seredash believes he can summon his goddess," Zeth reported. "He's convinced of it. There's no doubt that it's true, or at least the Empire believes it is. I've never seen the Tanakite priests so excited. They're rounding up prisoners, driving them into the Tomb of Scrolls."

It had taken Zeth and his team months to unearth that much. Most of it had been spent behind enemy lines, living on the edge of death every day.

Brani's face darkened as she listened to the response, and Zeth's heart quivered. A moment later, she delivered the words of the royal palace, "If what you say is true, they have to proceed carefully. He'll ask for permission to withdraw us and send a force after the Tomb."

Zeth held himself together so he didn't collapse completely. "How long does he need to receive permission?"

"The consuls won't convene until the end of the week, and

the Outer General is in the field. Messengers will be sent to them immediately."

He had no doubts. No fears. He was nothing but certainty and determination. Zeth lied to himself again, trying to make the lie true.

"The danger is *imminent*," Zeth insisted. "They move prisoners into the Tomb as we speak. The Tanakites have locked themselves inside and brought no food; they intend to finish this before dinner. We need immediate intervention."

Brani was born in a forest and still dressed the part. Her muddy brown hair was tied back with twine, she was dressed all in furs, and she carried almost as many knives as Zeth himself did.

As she listened to the palace's return messages, something feral crept into her expression, and she returned the newest message with a snarl. "They say to keep *watch*."

Zeth was glad he hadn't constructed the Twin Pattern, as Brani had. She was usually a good Twin Messenger, but if he was face-to-face with the royal palace's representative, he would have a hard time not punching the man in the face. She was holding back better than he would.

"No," Zeth said, still feigning certainty. "We require immediate intervention. Unsheathe the Sundown Sword, give us a contingent of Sky Knights, or at least put the Tomb under Imperial Sanction. *Something.*"

"The Tanakites have conquered more territory than they can hold," Brani said, clearly repeating what she was told. "They'll have to withdraw before winter, even with no intervention."

Zeth wished he could stab the other party through his own Messenger. "This winter? We won't live to see dawn! They're going to summon Mul'Tanak!"

Brani's face went through several contortions as she had an argument on the other side, an argument he heard nothing of.

Hope had drained from her face by the time she responded. "The Pattern Construction process for summoning a goddess is too intense for even the Tanakite Empire to sustain. Our scholars all agree. We've calculated the risk and found it minimal in the short-term, but we will still pass the issue up the chain of command. We assure you, this report will not be forgotten."

Zeth lost his breath. He tried to argue back, but he couldn't even form words. Only a moment later, Brani sagged in place as she let her Twin drop. She looked up at him hopelessly.

"They dismissed me," she said. "What are we going to tell the others?"

Zeth didn't know what to say. He couldn't come up with a comforting lie, not even to himself.

Powerlessly, he shoved open the door onto a recently blasted landscape. Dust blew over a sharp cliff that was only a week old.

Far beneath them, filling a desolate valley, was the army of the Tanakite Empire.

They were a swarm of ants from this height, carrying banners with the image of their goddess. There was a fat, black spider on those banners, each of its razor-edged legs and mandibles glistening with freshly drawn blood.

Mul'Tanak, Spider Goddess of Blood and War. It was in her name that this entire war was fought.

The Tanakites had begun as a small splinter faction; before Zeth had been born, they were relatively unpopular. Who wanted to serve a spider goddess?

But her priests had suddenly grown in power when Zeth was but a child, led by the man who called himself High Consort Seredash. The High Consort had made some kind of breakthrough in his Pattern Construction, tapping into what he called the "world beyond all worlds" and—according to him—glimpsing Mul'Tanak directly.

Whatever the case was, his Worldweavers had suddenly become more powerful than all others. They had become an invincible force on the battlefield, so various kings and nobles had suddenly become devout Tanakites.

Their tenets were simple. The Spider Queen would trade power for blood and pain, and neither the blood nor the pain needed to be your own. *That* message had plenty of adherents.

The Empire was less than ten years old, and it had moved like a furious blaze, chewing up all the small countries in the region. Every time the Empire was predicted to stop, to consolidate their power, they moved feverishly onward.

All had brought them here, to an ancient historical site: the Tomb of Scrolls. Tanakite forces crawled all over the temple, which was made from huge blocks of sandstone and stained glass.

The Tomb itself wasn't special, except in an academic sense. It had originally been a library where a series of kings had kept all their knowledge of Worldweaving, but future generations had stopped adding to the knowledge and begun worshiping what was there instead.

Zeth didn't know what was special about the Tomb that would allow the High Consort to break through to his goddess. Maybe there was a scroll inside that taught him how, or maybe it was some property of the Tomb itself.

But he could see with his own eyes the lines of people being driven at spearpoint into side entrances of the sandstone building. Crimson-robed priests scurried past those lines, visibly excited even from this distance.

Whatever plans the Tanakites had, they were imminent. It was going to happen soon, so soon that Zeth wasn't even sure his team would have time to make it down there.

Even if they did, it would be a one-way trip.

The supply closet in which he and Brani had held their conference had once been attached to a wooden house. Only a day before, a giant claw had torn the house down the middle, leaving a stretch of sand and dry air between the closet and the rest of the building.

His team had tied a tarp across one torn-open wall, blocking off the wind. The other two huddled inside, looking up when Zeth and Brani entered.

When they saw Brani's expression, their hope melted away. Zeth could feel it.

"When will they take action?" Yarech asked softly. He had been a noble himself, once, and he sounded like it.

"They're sending messages," Zeth reported. "They're confident the Pattern Construction can't be completed quickly."

Most of Yarech's body was stitched up or taped together, leaving him looking like a patchwork golem of flesh. He would heal eventually, but the last few months hadn't given him much time.

His Pattern was that of suspended death; he could postpone destruction and injury indefinitely, but he was reaching the end of what his Worldweaving techniques could sustain.

Yarech rubbed at the stitch crossing his forehead. "How do

we know they're not correct? The Tanakites could have rushed to conclusions."

The three of them looked to the fourth and final member of their group, who floated with her face close to the ceiling.

Wuraia drifted on her back as though floating on the surface of a pond the rest of them couldn't sense. Dark hair hung down, but the rest of her body acted as though she were drifting in water.

That was the effect of her own Pattern in action. For any purpose that benefited her, she acted as though she were suspended in water. If it didn't benefit her, she counted as being in normal air; for the purposes of breathing, for instance.

She was also their resident expert in Worldweaving theory, and she spoke with toneless despair. "This is the greatest expenditure the Tanakites have made in a decade. They fought a war just to get here. I would not bet against them."

Yarech crouched in a corner, picking at the edges of his most recent stitches and scowling. Brani had melted onto the floor and looked entirely powerless. Wuraia drifted quietly over all their heads.

None of them had to be here. They'd volunteered.

All of them skilled Worldweavers with unique Patterns, all willing to risk their lives to sneak behind enemy lines.

Zeth couldn't ask them to give any more. But he, himself, still had a little more to give.

That was the last lie he could tell himself.

He moved over to his pack and picked it up, slinging it onto his shoulder. "Leave at dark. Yarech, take command. It should only take a week to get across the border."

Wuraia peeked down. "Put that down, Zeth."

"I can get in. I might be able to stop it."

Yarech groaned and placed his palms against his eyes. "This isn't heroic. You're abandoning us."

"I'm not—"

Brani pushed herself to her feet. "We all leave together."

"I can't—"

"And how do you plan to stop their Pattern Construction?" Wuraia asked. Her voice was filled with a hint of scorn. "You don't even know what they need. Tell us your plan, Zeth."

"What am I supposed to do?" Zeth shouted. He hurled his own pack against what remained of a wall, and the metal within the pack clanged loudly.

Unsatisfied, he kicked through a nearby chair. "I...don't...know...what...to do!" As he shouted, he kicked the chair to splinters.

He stood, panting, with tears in his eyes as he looked at them. "How can I walk away?"

All three of his friends were quiet for a long time.

"You won't make it out," Yarech said. "In the best-case scenario, you still die. And if you do succeed, there will be no proof you were ever right. The people will believe you died for nothing."

Zeth looked out through a gap in the tarp they were using for a wall. The Tanakites hoisted up an idol of their goddess, a black-bladed spider covered in fresh blood.

"They're going to summon *that*," Zeth said.

Yarech looked at the floor beneath the tarp, where wood had been torn apart by a giant blade. The Tanakites claimed that their sudden power—the same power that had destroyed the house and conquered most of the continent—was a gift from Mul'Tanak.

What was the real Queen capable of?

Brani grabbed fistfuls of her own hair. Her eyes flitted here and there and her breaths came faster and faster. Finally, she forced words out. "We have to run. We have to run, we have to run. We have to."

Yarech was silent. So was Zeth.

It wasn't in a brave, heroic moment of triumph that they decided to go. The air was choked with terror, despair, and anger. They came to an agreement in almost total silence.

But in the end, they all left the house and walked to their deaths together.

From overhead, Wuraia's tears fell on them like rain.

Descending the cliff was easy for their team. It was a process they had repeated many times during their months together.

Wuraia could levitate herself, while Yarech could simply leap to the bottom and crash into the ground with only minimal damage to himself. Together, the two of them could rig ropes for Brani and Zeth to follow.

Approaching the Tanakite camp was the part Zeth had dreaded. No matter how they discussed it, they couldn't think of a way to approach before dark, so they crouched nearby as the scorching desert sun sank.

As they waited, Zeth blindly hoped that the enemy wouldn't begin the Pattern Construction ritual before sundown. If the Tanakites succeeded in their summoning before Zeth and his party arrived, he would have put four lives at risk for nothing.

Darkness finally fell, but Zeth felt no relief. In a way, the Pattern Construction's success would have been more relieving.

Now that they had the cover of night and the ritual hadn't been conducted yet, he had to move on. He had to lead his friends on a one-way trip.

None of them had Patterns useful for stealth, but they needed it less than he expected. The entire Tanakite camp stirred in celebration, buzzing with excitement and gossip, and there was no enemy force camped nearby. The guards were hardly alert.

Wuraia swam up and over the makeshift fortifications of hastily constructed wood, opening a gate for them as soldiers passed. The other three of them came in after.

Once in the camp, the task became much harder. Not that anyone would recognize them on sight; Tanakites came from all over the continent, and Zeth Baker was hardly a famous face.

But the attention of everyone was fixed on the Tomb of Scrolls. Even those who drank, sang, and celebrated still turned to the sandstone building every few seconds. Some raised toasts to the building, others glanced up in fear or nerves or reverent prayer.

To make your lies into truth, you had to lie to yourself first.

Zeth told himself he belonged. He made himself believe it, and he walked out as though he had nothing to hide. And with boldness, he strode through the Tanakite camp.

Wuraia walked like a normal person, as the effects of her unique

Pattern would at least give her away as a Worldweaver. Then they just...walked.

Zeth casually stole a patch of cloth off a saddle. It was scarlet and worked with the symbol of Mul'Tanak, her razor-edged legs and mandibles dripping. He wore it over his shoulders as a sort of scarf and marched with greater confidence.

Each step felt like it took a minute. His ears strained at every second, sorting through the noise of the camp for a cry of alarm or a challenging question.

But the confidence of the Tanakites was to his advantage. There were no enemies nearby, and no one had any reason to think that would change.

At least, that was the attitude until they reached the steps of the Tomb of Scrolls itself.

There, soldiers in red-and-black leaned on their spears and stopped them. There were four of them in sight, a pair on either side to the steps, and Zeth could hear a few more nearby. One out of armor, running errands, and at least two out of sight behind a stall.

"Not here," one soldier snapped. "Turn around."

Zeth knew what to say. He had talked his way through Tanakite patrols before; the soldiers were used to dealing with civilians and unknown members of their own order. They didn't tend to suspect strangers.

But he didn't say anything.

Worldweaving was the art of lying to reality. You had to create your own lie, Construct your own Pattern, and convince the world to believe it. Most Worldweavers were illusionists, but the best could change reality in limited ways. The more limited, and the more plausible, the easier.

Zeth Baker had always been known as a talented Worldweaver, even in his hometown. Only he knew the truth: he wasn't talented. He was just very, very specialized.

He drew a dagger in each hand.

Daggers filled his pockets and his pack. They were tucked into his belt, and hung on chains from his neck. He had daggers in his boots and daggers hidden in his hair.

He hid daggers anywhere he could. And he *might* have hidden daggers anywhere. Everywhere.

In fact, who was to say he hadn't already hidden daggers in this very camp? Even slipped them into the armor of his enemies?

At the sight of his weapons, the soldiers readied themselves, only to scream and gurgle and spit blood as their own motions impaled themselves on the razor-edged daggers that had suddenly appeared in the crevices of their armor. Or daggers that, just maybe, had always been there.

Seven bodies fell, spurting blood. The four soldiers on the stairs, the one delivering messages, and two out of sight.

Zeth sprinted up the steps, and he didn't need to look to know his team was behind him. They would be seconds away from a raised alarm.

His gaze was fixed on the top of the stairs and his goal—the ritual inside. But he allowed himself a moment of vicious satisfaction.

If Mul'Tanak liked blood and blades so much, he was about to be her favorite.

Luck favored them more than Zeth expected, because they made it inside the Tomb of Scrolls before the shouts caught up to them and the soldiers went on high alert. They dashed down a hallway, one set with candles that had all been recently lit. A preparation for the ritual, he suspected.

"Which way?" he demanded.

Brani, their scout, concentrated as she conjured her own Pattern. She looked through her Twin-self for a moment, which she would have positioned at a junction ahead, and reported.

"They're in the main library. Straight ahead, take a left. But there are a lot of—" she cut off with a choked scream as blood appeared on her thigh.

An arrow had hit her Twin-self. The copy would disappear, but the original kept the wound.

Zeth's stomach dropped as he held her. She couldn't run with that wound, and they couldn't simply stop to administer first aid.

Brani pulled out her bow and, with Yarech's help, strung it. "Get to the corner. I'll give cover."

This was as far as she could go.

Zeth didn't even have the chance to say goodbye, because a Tanakite priest jogged around the corner at that moment. Brani released an arrow, but all full priests were Worldweavers.

He batted the arrow aside with his arm, which temporarily transformed into a spider's leg that was as flat and sharp as a sword.

When the priest's arm transformed back, Yarech was in front of him, swinging his war-hammer.

The head was a fist-sized chunk of diamond, suspended in place by Yarech's Pattern. It crunched into the priest's skull, and then three of them rounded the corner.

Soldiers faced them. Four holding shields and spears covering for archers behind. A volley was loosed.

The arrows wobbled in midair, caught by unseen currents as Wuraia extended her own Pattern. Brani brought up the rear, blood streaming from her leg as she took aim and loosed an arrow.

That arrow slid through the tiny gap between shields and found an eye. All of her arrows did.

It was incredibly rare to construct a second Pattern, but Brani had done so. They were two of the more common Patterns—Twin Messenger and Marksmanship—but even so, that was quite the achievement.

She could be in two places at once *and* her shots never missed.

Twin archers stood behind them, Wuraia covered them, and Zeth and Yarech advanced.

He found himself breathless and burning a while later, surrounded by the dead. Yarech was fine, though exhausted, and Wuraia had stopped floating. She leaned against the wall, wincing and nursing a new wound as she tried not to look at the bodies of those who had drowned in a dry hallway.

Zeth nodded to them, turning back to look at Brani.

She lay on the ground, alone.

All four of them were legends in their own right, but the people told more tales of Brani than of the rest of them combined. Not of her marksmanship or her skill as a scout.

Everywhere she went, Brani fed the hungry. The poor knew when Brani was in town by the packages of food that mysteriously showed up on their doorsteps. They called her Brani the Kind.

She would be remembered, Zeth promised. She would be honored.

He had to lie to himself first, to make it the truth.

Still unable to speak, he forced himself to march on.

The doors to the main library were propped open. Guards forced two parallel lines of chained prisoners into the doors, and the halls were filled with weeping and pleas. The prisoners cried out when they saw Zeth and his team, and the guards raised the alarms again.

This time, arrows caught Wuraia in midair. First one found its mark, then—as her Worldweaving weakened—three more.

She fell to the ground, but Zeth and Yarech didn't slow.

Yarech took more arrows than anyone, but they were bloodless as they punctured his flesh.

And once they were close enough, Zeth's Pattern took over. *Maybe* he had managed to sneak up and plant a dagger in the nearest soldier's back.

The prisoners in the hallway fled in all directions, screaming. The soldiers were all dead, the Spider Goddess' believers felled by daggers.

Zeth couldn't get a full breath. His left eye was matted down by blood, and he tried to force it open, only to feel searing pain. Maybe he'd lost the eye.

That was fine, he told himself. He could keep moving.

The main library of the Tomb of Scrolls was a tall, vaulted cathedral to knowledge, its shelves covered in ancient texts that had been reverently preserved. It was a huge and open room, its bookshelves arranged like walls, but they all led up to a stone altar. It was beneath a stained-glass window depicting a regal figure reading an unfurled scroll.

Zeth could imagine that, once upon a time, scholars had lectured or performed readings from that place.

The Tanakites had put it to a very different purpose.

Prisoners—dead, alive, and everywhere in between—had spilled their blood over the stone until it was soaked. Tanakites held ritual knives high, tormenting their captives.

At least a dozen of them. A dozen powerful Worldweavers.

Over them, the High Consort stood with a ritual knife in each hand, his back to Zeth. He looked up at the stained-glass window, which was filled with the bloody light of sunset.

It occurred to Zeth, after a painfully stretched-out moment, that the sun had set long ago.

The High Consort only noticed their arrival after hearing angry shouts among the priests, and he spun around at the sound.

He was hideous. A tall but twisted man, wearing red robes decorated with designs of spider's legs. He had painted symbols on his face: six extra eyes and a pair of mandibles at the edges of his lips to mirror the face of a spider.

Without a word, he snarled at Zeth, swiping the ritual dagger in his right hand.

Following that motion, a bladed arachnid leg fell from the sky. It cleaved down, splitting a nearby bookshelf in two; it was large enough to break houses.

Yarech caught the blade on the haft of his hammer. He prevented his own weapon from breaking, exercising his Pattern to suspend death.

The spider-leg unraveled, and Yarech fell to his knees. Blood was leaking from the seams in his stitches and bandages.

"I...can't..." he began to say.

A second spider's leg came out of nowhere and crushed him.

Zeth stared at the spot, numb. Suddenly, it was so absurd that he had come here at all. He had only wanted to do...something. Anything other than sitting back and waiting for the end of the world.

But what would have been so bad about waiting?

If Mul'Tanak led her people to conquer the world, at least he would have lived a little longer. The idea of doing something leaned on the idea that he *could* do something.

And how could he? The High Consort had constructed a Pattern so strong that he could manifest the limbs of impossible beasts. That wasn't plausible. It wasn't even *possible*.

Zeth was challenging the impossible.

He hurled a dagger, which a red-clad priest batted aside with a sleeve. Thrown daggers weren't good weapons.

But *maybe* he had thrown *two* daggers.

The second cut the priest's cheek, disrupting his concentration, and Zeth closed the gap. He stabbed the man in the gut, then ten more wounds erupted where Zeth *could* have stabbed him.

Not that it would make a difference.

Although...

Who said it wouldn't make a difference? It might. In fact, it definitely would.

The fewer the priests, the less likely the ritual would succeed. Zeth convinced himself of the truth of that as he forced his body to move, as he overlaid his Pattern over reality. If he killed all the priests, their Pattern Construction would end.

From priest to priest he moved.

That lasted a few seconds before a spider's limb caught him and kicked him into a bookshelf.

The shelf was old and sturdy. He sent scrolls spilling everywhere, but the shelf stayed in place.

Something inside him broke, but he didn't feel it. Zeth lifted his head to see the High Consort peering down at him with two real eyes and six painted ones.

The man smiled, revealing yellowed and crooked teeth. "You have constructed a beautiful Pattern," High Consort Seredash said. "The Queen will be pleased to see it."

The surviving priests, in their red robes, were no longer paying attention to Zeth. They had collapsed to their knees, murmuring rituals and prayers as they bowed toward the stained-glass window.

It was painfully bright red. The High Consort rushed back to join them, bowing to the light as well. The light took on a life of its own as their chants filled the Tomb of Scrolls, drowning out the screams of dying prisoners and even Zeth's own pain.

"Mul'Tanak! Mul'Tanak! Mul'Tanak!"

Fuzzy darkness closed in on his vision, and that name was all Zeth could focus on. He had too many memories associated with that name, and not all of them were bad.

He had sat across a fire from Wuraia, and she'd tucked hair behind her ear as she taught him with infectious enthusiasm. 'Mul'Tanak,' she said, wasn't some name they'd conjured from beyond the world. It had its own roots in mundane language.

'Mul' was a prefix used for female deities, and 'Tanak'—roughly translated—meant 'swords unending.'

The crimson light split apart, and for a moment, Zeth thought he saw a flash of blue light. Perhaps it was just a trick of his dying brain.

Then sharpened blades peeled back the wall of the world and Mul'Tanak arrived.

Zeth had no doubt it was her. She carried with her a divine aura, one that made him feel every dagger he carried. His death seemed more *real* suddenly, as though an actual specter hung over his form, breathing down his neck.

Despair choked him as much as blood, and he forced his one remaining eye open to witness Mul'Tanak as he died.

The goddess had descended in human form. Her black carapace covered her from the neck down like armor, her legs sprouted from her back and were formed from scarlet-stained steel, and her dark hair had a single streak of bloody red.

"Bleed and bury me," the goddess said. "Who's been screaming my name?"

High Consort Seredash pressed his forehead into the bloody altar, and Zeth could hear tears in the man's voice. "Divine Mother! O Mother, deliver us!"

The other priests, who likewise had pressed their faces against the bloodstained ground, echoed him. "O Mother, deliver us!"

The goddess was quiet for a long moment. Something about her silence struck Zeth as...wrong. She was pinching the bridge of her nose and sighing.

"Before I get to delivering, answer me a question, and answer true. Whose blood is this?"

"The blood of the weak!" Seredash cried. "The blood of those who opposed us, who denied your entry! And now, should it be your will...it is *your* blood. The blood of Mul'Tanak!"

"Yeah, let's give that back. **Return.**"

A great force passed through the world upon that spoken command, and Zeth felt a shiver that he hadn't sensed outside of his own Pattern Construction. That was the feeling of the world as it accepted a lie and turned it to truth.

A moment later, the blood was gone. And the prisoners were standing up.

Every one of them, even the dead, now found themselves alive and whole. They patted their bodies where wounds once were.

Yarech was one of them. He gasped and inspected his stitches; old wounds were still there, but there was no trace of where he had been torn apart by the Tanakite Worldweavers.

Relief warred with disbelief inside Zeth, but only then did he realize that his own body was no exception. All his recent wounds were gone; he was simply sitting against a bookshelf, whole and healthy.

He didn't dare stand up.

The priests muttered in confusion, but the High Consort prostrated himself before Mul'Tanak again. "Tell us what blood you will accept, Mother, and we will drain it for you!"

If anything, he sounded more excited than before.

Tanakites, one and all, had been drawn in by the promise of power. That one command from her had demonstrated truly divine ability. It was for that power that Seredash had committed this entire campaign.

Zeth understood the enemy well enough to read the man's thoughts. In his mind, this would be proof that all his atrocities were worthwhile.

"Bet every drop of my *own* blood that Ziel doesn't have to deal with murder-cults," the goddess muttered. "Wonder if it's too late to change my Path."

"Who is Zeal, Mother?" Seredash asked eagerly. "We've never heard the name of such a god."

One of the crimson, bladed legs reached out from Mul'Tanak's back. It tucked under the High Consort's chin. "One last question for you. How many people have you bled dry in my name?"

"Many and more," Seredash whispered reverently. "Legions."

The goddess leaned down, and her crimson eyes blazed bright. "One was too many."

Mul'Tanak stretched out the six bladed arms on her back, and a single, pure note filled the Tomb of Scrolls. Like the chime of a great bell.

Zeth felt a power just as great as her previous command. It passed over him, resonating with his daggers...but leaving him untouched.

The ritual knives, however—the ones carried by every Tanakite priest—exploded.

Invisible blades erupted from the knives, instantly killing every priest in the chamber. Zeth was certain that the effect had not ended at the walls. He suspected that every Tanakite who had spilled blood with such a blade had already suffered the same fate.

Except one. The High Consort bled from a thousand cuts, but he was still alive, looking up at his goddess in shock for a few more seconds.

Only then did he, too, collapse in his own blood.

The goddess brushed black-armored hands clean and hopped away from the altar. "Guess I can't skip the cleanup. Oi, you."

Red eyes met Zeth's, and his heart stopped.

"Y-yes! How may I...serve?"

Mul'Tanak waved that aside. "Cut that right now. What legends do they tell about me?'

Zeth looked down to the Tanakite cloth that remained over his shoulders. Hurriedly, he tore it off; she was obviously killing her own priests. What if she thought he was with them?

"I'm not one of them!" he insisted. Then he froze. What if this goddess felt like he was denying her to her face?

"Have eyes, don't I? And hold a second. Why all the spiders?"

Zeth held the cloth and pointed to it in confusion. "That's...you. Mul'Tanak."

The goddess stared at the symbol for a moment. Then she gave a single, clear shudder.

"We're going to put a stop to that right now."

The Wolf and the Reaper

Information requested: the fate of Akura Fury, a new recruit of the Wolf Division, and his half-sister Mercy.
Report Location: *Waybound*, between Mercy's ascension and Lindon's.
Authorization confirmed.
Beginning report...

Despite the name, Mercy liked being a Reaper.

For one thing, she didn't have to do much actual reaping. At least, she hadn't yet. Most of the time, she was given enough information to enter a world and help fix it. She left the worlds better off than they had been before she arrived.

That had been Eithan's goal the entire time, she'd learned, but he regularly warned her not to grow complacent. Eventually, one of their solutions wouldn't take.

Or, worse, the people of a world would reject their help and steer into their own destruction.

Mercy would have to face those fates eventually, but the Joy Icon helped her maintain perspective.

In the future, it might not be enough. But for the time being, she was doing good.

She let that thought fill her as she burst into the monitoring room at the heart of The Grave, ready for her next assignment.

The Grave was a mass of steel and stone hanging in orbit above the central world of Sanctum, and it was built with an aesthetic that she could charitably call "industrial." If she were more honest with herself, the entire station felt like it had been cobbled together from destroyed buildings, wrecked spaceships, and fragmented asteroids.

[Don't you love *asteroids*,] her Dross asked, savoring the last word. [And to think, we didn't have those in Cradle.]

Sure we did! We just never saw them.

[No, I mean, we didn't *have* them. As in I didn't own nearly as many as I do now.]

Mercy laughed as she saluted her Judge, Ozriel.

"Insolence!" Eithan cried. "Fifty demerits for laughing at your superior. And an improper salute!"

Each Division of the Abidan had their own structure and culture; some were big enough to have multiple distinct factions. Their Eighth Division, currently made up of only three official members and a Judge, didn't have such strict rules.

"I accept my punishment! What does that bring my demerit total up to?"

"Four thousand and twelve," Eithan said immediately. He had never mentioned demerits before. "You may redeem yourself with your next mission."

He swept out one black-gauntleted hand to the console behind him. Most of the room was taken up by a wide, sweeping screen where they often displayed the details of assignments.

At his gesture, the screen transformed into a vast field of grain as it was processed by a host of building-sized threshing machines. The field stretched out to the horizon, with at least a hundred identical vehicles visible.

"Pioneer world six hundred and two," Eithan introduced. "Miraculously untouched by the Collapse, it remains a source of food and materials that we can't harvest from any world with a stable connection to the Way."

Dross gasped in delight, manifesting and leaning forward. [Ooooh, and why not?]

"They retain unique qualities we can't replicate within the rules of stable reality," Eithan responded easily. "The fields you see before you produce a grain whose quantity is uncertain. Were there five bales in that crate? Perhaps twenty? A hundred? We can exploit such qualities, making a highly efficient source of support for nearby worlds."

Mercy sighed. "Lindon would fight me for this one, wouldn't he?"

"I have quite the list of locations with anomalous properties for him once he finishes his business in Cradle." Eithan rubbed hands together in apparent glee. "In fact, every day he's gone, I come up with enough schemes to occupy him for a year. But that's not the issue you should focus on!"

Mercy peered into the scenery, looking for the problem he spoke of. "How big is this operation?"

"Pioneer Six-oh-two has a stable population of only ten thousand, but they get along perfectly well. Or well enough for our purposes, at least. If this were one of your usual assignments, it wouldn't count as much of a punishment, would it?"

Mercy looked up in surprise. In the last few months, Mercy had mostly been sent into worlds whose problems had diplomatic solutions. Ziel was chosen to solve crises with long-term solutions, which made him grumble every time he returned. When the problem could be killed, they sent Yerin.

This assignment looked to be different in more than one way. For one thing, it was taking place in a Pioneer world, where the Abidan could typically operate freely. That was outside the remit of the Reaper Division, who focused on intervening where others couldn't.

It was also last-minute. Usually Mercy spent longer studying a world and their potential solution than she spent implementing it.

Above all, this didn't sound like a problem that required a diplomatic solution.

Eithan swept white hair behind him and regarded the planet, and his eyes gained a bit more of the cold depth that Mercy associated with Ozriel. "Considering the value of each remaining world, it won't be long before this world receives an official Iteration designation and we transplant a much larger population there. At that point, its physics-defying characteristics will condense into a stable energy system, which is highly valuable to those whose power does not derive directly from the Way."

"So you want me to..." Mercy vaguely punched the air. "Fight...robbers?"

"Very possibly!" The screen shifted, showing several violet-edged visions of the future. In one, the farm equipment exploded, leaving the crops to burn. In another, silver-crowned invaders floated down from orbit, levitated vast containers of the farm's produce into the sky, and vanished. In another, the grain itself multiplied visibly as workers scurried away, trying to escape a tidal wave of vegetation.

Dross narrowed his eye. [I see, I see. Too much variance.]

"As expected of a Presence, you've cut to the heart of it. The Hound Division is stretched very thin these days, so they can only give us a rudimentary breakdown, but they don't understand their own report. *Something* is going to happen to this Pioneer world, but in each projection, Fate shows us something different. Once upon a time, I would have looked into this myself."

Eithan sighed, but Mercy was sure he wasn't as disappointed as he pretended to be. She comforted him anyway.

"That's why you have us!" she said brightly. "But how do we know this is in our jurisdiction?"

"We know it might be! And who could object to us helping defend Abidan territory? Spend a week or two with the workers of this world, get a sense for the most likely disasters, and have Dross run some projections."

Mercy pressed her fists together. "I'll leave right now!"

No one was around the Grave anyway, with Yerin on assignment and Ziel down on the planet for his time off. He spent it fishing.

"Of course, the Court has already assigned a low-ranking Abidan to this world," Eithan went on. "Another promising recruit, such as yourself. I feel that the two of you could learn much from one another."

Mercy's brow furrowed as she wondered why Eithan had broached the subject so indirectly. "Sure! I don't mind making a new friend."

"I wouldn't call him *new*."

The first face Mercy saw in Pioneer 602 was her half-brother's.

Fury wore the seamless white armor of the Abidan, but otherwise, he hadn't changed. His shadow-like hair drifted up as though underwater, and his crimson eyes blazed with joy the moment he saw her.

Mercy had only manifested in the world for a few seconds before Fury was upon her, grasping her arms and laughing.

"Mercy, I can't believe it! Finally! This is better than I could have ever hoped!"

"Glad to see you again too, Uncle Fury!" And it was, though Mercy felt a little trepidation. She knew her "uncle" too well.

"I've been getting so *bored*. Follow me; there's a desert a few hundred miles that way."

[Do you think he wants to find a desert because he really loves sand?] Dross asked.

That's not why, Mercy thought back. She knew what Fury wanted, and so did Dross.

[That's a shame. Sand is great.]

Before Mercy could suggest an alternative, Fury flew off into the distance, his armor blurring into a streak of white.

Mercy sighed and looked around at all the witnesses. The people of this Pioneer world had been taken from Abidan-settled Iterations, especially Sanctum. They were used to Abidan, but that only meant they didn't panic at the otherworldly figures.

Instead, they bowed or waved or stared or huddled together and whispered in awe. Some gasped or blushed as Mercy's gaze passed over them.

They were hardy folk, by and large. Weathered and muscular from exercise, with durable clothes stained with dirt and grease. The nearby buildings were made with machines that reminded Mercy of the most complicated works of Soulsmiths, though they had been built from metal instead of Remnant pieces.

Despite their advanced technology, they resembled workers you might find anywhere. The tools changed, but the people were just here to do a job.

Once, those groups had looked up to her as an heir so powerful and distant she might as well have been the daughter of a goddess.

Now, their looks were much the same. Mercy had hoped she'd left this sort of regard behind on Cradle.

Nonetheless, she gave a beaming smile and waved to the crowed. **"Be well!"** she commanded, and the Joy Icon flared overhead in the form of a bright violet flower.

It was a minor working, spread as it was over a large area and expansive population, but the blessing spread over all of them. It would improve their mood and health—only a little on an individual level, but enough to make a subtle difference.

Then she flew out to fight.

When she arrived at the desert, Uncle Fury was already bouncing from foot to foot impatiently, shaking his shoulders as he loosened up. "I've been waiting for you, Mercy! The other recruits are doing their best, but they just can't keep up."

"I'm sure they're grateful for your help," Mercy said.

She was confident they *would* be grateful eventually, though most of the rumors she'd heard about Fury's adventures in the Wolf Division suggested that his fellow newcomers found him terrifying.

Fury laced his fingers together and stretched them out. "Haven't seen much talent in the family, sorry to say. Naria's keeping an eye on some kids who might have potential, but it'll be decades before any of them can stand up to a real battle."

Mercy hadn't seen Fury much since ascending—in keeping with his normal behavior, he was usually out fighting someone—but she had plenty of relatives in Sanctum. She'd been pleasantly surprised by how much time she'd been able to spend with people she knew, though the Grave itself still felt too empty for her taste.

"I could help train them," Mercy suggested. She'd been waiting for the opportunity to suggest that; busy as she was, she still had responsibilities to her family.

"No! You'll take it easy on them."

She would. Hard to deny that.

"They don't *need* to get much stronger," she persisted. "Sanctum is safe, and most of the population has no combat ability at all." An Underlord would be stronger than most any of the citizens. Only the Abidan or their candidates were a real threat, and those were a vast minority of Sanctum's population.

Fury groaned. "Are you really okay with *our* clan being full of normal, average citizens? They'll never get into the Abidan with that attitude!"

"I did," Mercy said.

"But did you earn it?" Despite the words, Fury didn't sound judgmental. He grinned like a boy looking forward to opening a present, and he made a show of folding his fingers into fists.

His smile was infectious. There was only one way to talk to Uncle Fury; she had to speak his language.

Fury moved himself directly over her, launching a downward punch with his white gauntlet.

She caught it on her own black armor.

Red eyes blazed with joy, and she could feel power flowing through her own eyes, which must have been shining as bright as his.

With joy that Mercy could feel radiating from his heart, Fury let loose.

A fist of shadow crashed into her, Forged into the size of a mountain and reinforced by blue light. A Wolf technique, bending the Way to empower his attacks with the weight of the world's laws.

For that, Mercy unleashed her bloodline armor. A purple crystalline fist, the same size as his attack, followed her straight punch and met his technique.

Both shattered, but Mercy had blinked out of existence and into the air, gaining distance. Or attempting to do so.

Fury followed her, merciless, raining attacks from every angle. Though he lacked the bloodline armor that his descendants had developed, he wore Abidan armor and could reinforce himself with the techniques of the Wolf Division. She had a more varied toolset, but he had honed his own abilities to perfection over centuries.

Seventh page, Mercy thought, and she summoned the projection of the Netherworld Empress.

She'd consumed most of the resources in her Book of Eternal Night to fuel her rapid growth, but its structure was still helpful for her to unleash her techniques. This one had begun as a technique molded around Akura Malice's will, theoretically the ultimate expression of a Path Mercy's mother had designed.

An image loomed behind Mercy, reinforcing her willpower and her authority, an Empress carrying a spear and clothed in black, white, and violet. The face of the Empress had once resembled Malice's, but now it looked more like a statue modeled after Mercy.

The projection struck out at Fury, who met the blow, but it kept him occupied enough.

Mercy had a surprise for him.

She reached into her storage device, an upgraded version of a standard void key.

And she summoned her new bow.

Shattersight wasn't black, as her old bow had been. It looked as though it had been made from purple mist and rainbows, like a dream or a hologram Forged into reality.

[That's not too far from the truth,] Dross commented. [I'm pretty sure Eithan made it from nothing.]

When the bow manifested, the entire Iteration changed imperceptibly, like a boat rocking at the introduction of an unexpected weight. Purple-tinted clouds appeared overhead, trailing for miles behind her like a train of silk. The desert sands suddenly swirled and shimmered as though they contained mysterious power.

Fury skidded to a halt in midair. "What is *that?*" he asked in obvious delight.

"Shattersight! It's supposed to hold me over until Lindon joins us. Eithan thinks he'll give me the Silent King's bow."

"And where did he get this one?"

Mercy smiled without responding. The answer was obvious anyway.

Her bow was crafted by Ozriel himself.

Eithan had complained about his lack of materials and how much better he could have done with the Dreadgod pieces Lindon had to work with. All the while, he spun this bow into existence from what might actually have been daydreams.

Mercy imagined nocking an arrow and one was on the string, sharp and shining, a shaft of purple metal.

Nocking, drawing, and taking aim took no time, and not just because of her own speed. It was one of Shattersight's features; imagining the process took less time than doing it.

She loosed the arrow and time moved again, but it split through the space containing Fury. He crashed to the ground, his armor and own protective techniques defending against attacks from strange vectors, but he hadn't been given a chance to dodge.

Mercy knew better than to let him up. She listened to an echo of the Bow Icon, releasing an arrow that split into the possibility of all the arrows she might have loosed. A volley split out of her bow, raining down on Uncle Fury's landing point.

Then it was Dross' turn. He sped his calculation until he was catching a glimpse of Fate, spinning out Fury's possible moves.

Mercy shot at each of those branching possibilities, her arrows dragging shadows behind them. They were layered with various techniques, each of which would require different defenses.

As always, Akura Fury was quick to adapt.

While the first arrow from Shattersight had left him with no chance to resist, he almost slipped past a second one and fully defended against a third.

Blue light flared, and for a moment Mercy saw it as more than merely *blue,* but rather the color of existence itself. She glimpsed the foundation of reality, as endless as the sky and implacable as truth.

That weight reinforced his movement technique and he arrived in front of her.

He shrugged off her shadows as though walking through cobwebs, striking out when he reached her. Crystal armor took the blow, but she found it harder and harder to shake him off.

Finally, a kick cracked her defenses and sent her blasting into the desert, defended only by the black armor of the Reapers.

She spat sand from her face and dismissed Shattersight. "You got me, Uncle Fury!" she called into the sky.

He descended eagerly, wiping blood from a scalp wound that had already healed. His white armor was cracked here and there, though it sealed itself at visible speed.

"Only round one!" he said happily. "I know you have more to show me. And I can't wait to see what other tricks are in that bow!"

Dross sent a message into both of their minds. [Not that I

wouldn't mind helping Mercy beat you up, but don't you think we should at least *pretend* to do some work?]

Jek'nan, the Flourishing Disease, had been embedded in the heart of this Pioneer world since the Abidan Collapse began.

He had wormed through this reality, spreading his roots in their minds and hearts, sowing discord to one day reap the rewards of the energy that would be released when the world collapsed.

That was how he fed. He was one-of-a-kind, a mighty tree left to drift in the Void until it became something greater. He would latch onto fragments of destroyed worlds, corrupting and feeding on them, growing mightier century by century.

This was merely his latest meal, but the most substantial one so far. It had the greatest risk, targeting a world under Abidan protection. He wouldn't have tried if he weren't confident in his subtlety.

Fate was all but blind to Jek'nan's actions, as long as he remained careful. He spread his influence far and wide, inciting a rebellion here, a spreading virus there, the occasional would-be tyrant. Abidan Hounds saw his actions as a cluster of equally unlikely probabilities, but nothing that would lead them to suspect a Fiend.

Unlucky, to have them dispatch an agent here just before he was ready for his harvest. At least he was fortunate enough that they had only sent a Wolf.

Their organization would call him a Class Three Fiend, or a threat that required a small squad to deal with. In times like these, with their resources spread so thin, they didn't have a squad to spare.

He could kill a Wolf, if it came to that, though he saw no reason to expend such energy. The Flourishing Disease could ruin a world gradually, and certainly escape from a single warrior. Even overpower him, under the right circumstances.

Jek'nan had no reason to fear the Wolf Division. Hounds, Spiders, and Ghosts would be more troublesome to deal with. The first two would have means of detecting him from within Pioneer 602, while the latter could target him more effectively than any of Razael's fighters.

The second Abidan, however, caused him to pause and reconsider his thoughts.

Black armor. There was something about her outfit which scratched at his memories, or rather his instincts.

Jek'nan had no direct experience with the Abidan. The only 'memories' he had came from the pieces of worlds he devoured, and from exchanges with other Fiends. Those weren't conversations, as humans thought of them, but rather something of a brushing of minds.

The clearest memories of the Abidan that he had were formed from faded impressions and secondhand emotions. Even so, the black armor filled him with a distant dread.

He couldn't figure out why. He didn't even sense much of a connection to the Way in the newcomer. Was she even an Abidan? She felt more like a Silverlord, and those were...if not exactly *allies,* at least not inclined to hunt Fiends on sight.

The network of roots that Jek'nan had spread throughout the

Pioneer world lurked beneath reality, easily avoiding anything but a deep scan, and his thoughts spread all throughout that network. After hours of conversation with himself, he came to a final conclusion.

No need to change his plans. No need to change anything.

By the time the Abidan found him, the world would already be collapsing. Their greatest advantage—the reinforcement from the Way—would be far out of reach.

The Flourishing Disease would feed, and replicate himself, and grow. Forever.

Mercy felt Uncle Fury's attention focus on her only a second before he kicked open the door to the tavern, striding in without a glance to anyone else.

"I'm bored," he said. "Let's fight!"

"The tavern" was just what the locals called the place where they relaxed. It was a large, open building that had been printed from plastic, concrete, and metal, then—over time—filled with the tools of recreation.

There were tables for games, food, or both. A pair of bartenders worked a bar where they summoned bottles out of storage devices. A robot drone flew around, taking orders. A screen on one wall played a movie no one was watching, and at least three different songs were playing in different corners.

When Uncle Fury entered, Mercy was standing with one foot

braced on a chair, reaching up and moving her shadow madra to form shapes. Dross enhanced her images with special effects as she recounted the story of her battle against the Dreadgods.

Of course, Fury's entrance both interrupted and ruined the story. Everyone who had been listening stood up hastily as Fury arrived. Drinks were spilled, conversations cut off, and two of the three songs stopped instantly.

A moment later, a gunshot rang out, and the machine playing the third song exploded.

Thanks to the Joy Icon, Mercy was sensitive to the emotional state of the people around her, and she felt their intentions as a mix of fear, awe, and wary respect. Most of the workers on Pioneer 602 had grown up seeing the Abidan as divine beings, and those that hadn't had quickly learned the stories.

Mercy understood what it was like to go from a mortal to a citizen of the heavens, but she had never truly been powerless. To these people, a divine warrior had just walked in.

She'd spent the past week getting to know them, eroding their wariness one forced conversation at a time. Just when she'd been making progress, here came Uncle Fury to remind them that she was one of the outsiders too.

She had to set the example.

"Uncle Fury!" she called happily, breaking the silence. "I was just telling them about fighting Dreadgods!"

Red eyes brightened. "Were you? Well, I have plenty of stories myself."

She reached out to a chair that someone had vacated in panic on sight of Fury. "Why don't you pull up a seat and tell us about it?"

"Eh, maybe later. I'm really itching for a fight right now."

Mercy made a disappointed sound, though at least three men around her released breaths of relief that Fury wouldn't be joining them. "If you insist. I'll be back later, though, okay everybody?"

"Yes, Abidan," half the crowd said in unison.

Mercy reminded herself that she was making progress.

As they exited, Mercy spoke in a low voice to Fury. "They wouldn't be so scared of you if you spent more time with them."

Fury returned an odd look. "If they knew me, they'd only be more afraid."

"That's not true! I'm not afraid of you, and neither is Aunt Naria."

"Yeah, but you're strong. They're weak." He shrugged. "It's okay, we're just not going to be friends."

"Don't you want to know the people we're fighting for?"

"Why?" Fury spread his hands. "I'm going to fight for them whether they like me or not."

Mercy still felt that it would be better for everyone if Uncle Fury made himself a little more human in the eyes of the Pioneer workers. Not only would it be better for the Abidan's reputation, but Fury's popularity would solve problems he'd never considered.

Then again, Fury had more experience than anyone in Cradle short of some Monarchs. He was more insightful than most gave him credit for, and she'd known him to take interest in people far weaker than he was. Provided he saw potential in them.

He'd befriended her own father, and more recently Lindon. Perhaps she would take a longer view in a few hundred years as well.

Without warning, Fury moved to the door. "Well, I'll think about it. For now, we have work to do!"

"We do?" Mercy asked. But she followed him anyway.

They were already almost out of "town"—the main collection of structures at the heart of the grain fields—before Mercy realized that Fury hadn't taken off flying.

Instead, he tilted his head and looked into the sky, his shadowy hair drifting in unseen currents.

Only then did Mercy understand that something was wrong.

[I noticed immediately. He was putting on a show. Then again, if I weren't more perceptive than you, I'd be out of a job.]

Before Mercy could ask what Fury had noticed, he spoke again.

"You've been getting to know everyone," Fury said conversationally. "How do you think they feel about being here?"

Mercy took his cue and continued as though nothing was wrong. "Better now than last week. I've been smoothing out their worries, but I don't think there was ever much to be worried *about*. Just some rumors that got out of control."

"That's right, that's right. And what were those rumors?"

"Nothing too crazy. That we were being targeted by the Vroshir, that the Abidan had abandoned them, that they were going to run out of food or not get paid. You put a stop to most of it just by showing up."

As she spoke, a shape appeared over Fury's shoulder. It was like an orange diamond made from fire and light.

A standard-issue Presence of the Wolves, one without enough individuality to have developed a personality. It beamed something to Dross, which he received and transmitted to Mercy.

Information streamed into her and Dross wove that data into a graph.

The chances of this world's population dropping due to a violent rebellion or bloody civil war had dropped sharply, approaching zero. Their chances of revoking the Abidan, calling in a Vroshir, contracting a plague, or attacking Fury had also virtually vanished.

But the Fate of the world hadn't changed.

Pioneer 602 still had weeks left before most of its people died.

Other possibilities had manifested to replace those that Mercy and Fury had headed off by their arrival. An incursion from low-level Fiends, failure of the wards that kept the influence of the Void out from the unstable Pioneer world, and a sudden spike in the multiplicative properties of the grain causing a destructive wave; these were all much more likely than they had been before Mercy's arrival.

It was as though someone had determined that this world would be destroyed within a month, but they hadn't decided how.

"If there's one thing I hate," Fury said, "it's when there's just no enemy to fight."

Mercy wanted to continue following his lead, but she wasn't sure what he meant. There clearly *was* an enemy somewhere, and one capable of actively manipulating Fate. "You think we should look somewhere else?"

"I think we should give up," Fury said, and he sounded like he was putting on an unconvincing performance for an unseen audience.

"What about the people here?" Mercy asked. She had an easier time matching Fury's acting when she was expressing genuine concern.

"Yes, we'll probably just pack up and leave," Fury shouted without answering her question. "We might even take everything with us!"

Dross cut into their thoughts. [I'm not sure who that...enthusiastic...performance was for, but maybe I can make this easier. You think there's an enemy here watching us, right?]

Another Presence's voice responded, dry and crackling like a fire. [Yes. My host expresses frustration. We must bait out the enemy to strike him.]

Mercy sent her own opinion, but Dross had begun speaking for her already. [From the way I understand fishing, we have to know what the fish wants before we can dangle it on the hook.]

[My host would rather reach into the water and grab the fish with his bare hands.]

[Oooh, that's how Lindon does it too!]

Dross, Mercy thought, *ask them how an enemy might hide from us.*

She'd sensed nothing spiritually, and since ascending to the Abidan, she'd learned that the spiritual sense of Cradle was very useful for detecting the energy systems of other worlds.

As a member of the Reaper Division, she'd been encouraged to develop her skills that didn't rely on the Way. That was an advantage when she was going into dying worlds, but not so much here, when the techniques of a Spider or Hound would give her access to several more senses.

Dross and the other Presence interacted briefly, then sent her and Fury their analysis. There were too many *potential* hiding methods to count, but they boiled down to a few likely categories.

The enemy was either a Fiend—what the Abidan called any creature warped by the Void—or a person using the energy system of another world. That was the signature method of the Vroshir.

No matter which it was, they were either hiding in this world or operating remotely.

[But let's all agree that there *is* an enemy involved, even if we don't know what they want,] Dross suggested.

That's the only thing that makes sense.

[My host says that of course there's an enemy. He expresses irritation that the opponent is such a coward.]

Let's call for help, Mercy proposed.

If she couldn't sense the source of the problem and neither could Fury, they only had one choice: call in someone who could.

Eithan could resolve this problem in seconds, but he was both in hot demand among all the worlds and bound by a web of strict rules. Mercy was technically bending her jurisdiction as a Reaper by intervening in an Abidan-supervised world, but she would never be punished for it as long as she didn't break anything. The Abidan were too shorthanded to complain about a little extra help.

They were of a very different opinion about Ozriel. The Reaper of Worlds could not intervene lightly, and all his actions would be under intense scrutiny by the Court of Seven.

[My host mentions that he has a few contacts among the Spiders. They often work closely with the Wolves.]

Dross sent an image into their minds of himself raising a hand. [Before we go looking for outside help, let's make sure to consult the genius already present. I have an idea that Mercy, at least, never considered: we could break this world.]

Fury nodded rapidly before his Presence had a chance even to say anything.

How would that help? Mercy asked skeptically.

[Vroshir want the contents of this world, we want the people, and the Fiends want the world itself. All right, then let's take the people away and start to break it so nobody gets what they want, but not so bad we can't bring in a Phoenix to fix it. The evil villain comes out of hiding and we smack him down, then we put everything back the way it was. Everybody wins!]

Fury started gathering madra as though he meant to punch through the planet.

Mercy waved her hands in front of his face to get his attention. "Hey, whoa! Hold on a second. We've got to evacuate the people before we blow everything up, right?"

"I know how to hold back," Fury said defensively.

Dross manifested next to Mercy, arms on his nonexistent hips. [After all the effort we went through to converse in silence, you had to go and ruin it!]

"We're going to break the whole Iteration. Why do we care if the enemy knows that or not?"

[Oh, I guess...I guess we don't.]

In fact, it would help them if the enemy believed that was what they would do. Dross spun out some hypothetical scenarios and confirmed that the threat was likely to work, though he was forced to rely on Abidan compiled estimates due to a lack of firsthand information.

Evacuation, they knew, would only take a few days. Especially if they planned to put everything back the way it was afterwards. Evacuation protocols were well-practiced on most Pioneer worlds.

That didn't mean it would be popular, though. Simply announcing the need to leave would spread fear throughout the worker population, so Mercy left that to Uncle Fury.

He was used to delivering bad news.

If Jek'nan had the biology to do so, he would have begun sweating.

Theoretically, the Abidan destroying this world was a lucky break for him. It wasn't possible to erase an Iteration without leaving fragments—not even a small, unstable pseudo-Iteration like this one.

Those fragments were what Jek'nan meant to digest. The Abidan intended to do his work for him.

And in the process of dismantling this reality, they would discover him.

That was what sent Jek'nan's network of minds to whispering among themselves. There was no way these Abidan would miss him once the world began to fade; even the population leaving would remove most of his camouflage.

If Pioneer 602 died due to "natural" causes, that would be a different case entirely. He could arrange things so that he remained concealed as the fabric of reality crumbled.

But to destroy this world, the Abidan would effectively be stabbing swords blindly into the box in which he was hidden. He would either be driven out of hiding or run through.

His mental network came to an agreement quickly. It was clear that his first plan had already run its course.

Now, he needed to rely on his second advantage: raw power.

Jek'nan was stronger than the Wolf, certainly. He was an even match for a squad of four average Wolves. The black-armored one was something of a mystery, and he couldn't investigate her more thoroughly without breaking his cover.

Even so, if she was a combat-oriented Abidan, she would have been a member of the Wolf Division. And if she were a Judge in disguise, she would have seen through Jek'nan instantly.

The Fiend had earned his identity as the Flourishing Disease by spreading through many fragmented worlds, and he had a good estimation of his own ability. He should have no trouble breaking cover, pushing away the Abidan, and tearing off a significant chunk of the world.

If he was lucky, he'd even have an Abidan to feed on. Such a meal might be enough to propel his existence to new heights.

But if he wanted the prize, he'd have to act. The moment the Way weakened, he would strike.

He would start the battle on his own terms.

The first ship, a great wedge of steel, had already been loaded with thousands of workers. They took off into nothingness, a swirling blue portal swallowing them in an instant. They would stop at the nearest Iteration, holding in deep space while they waited for further ships to arrive.

At the very moment they disappeared, something in the Iteration changed. Weakened. Mercy didn't have a good sense for it, not being tied to the Way as closely as a traditional Abidan would have been, but she knew what it was.

A world's human population tied them to the Way. Only a quarter of the workers were evacuated so far, but the rules of reality had already slackened.

No corruption would set in for a while, but they planned to demolish the reality, so existential decay was something of a moot point.

Sector Control had approved their plan, though the Phoenix Division was perhaps the most overworked of all the Abidan. They had also made it clear that, should the plan fail, both Mercy and Fury would be investigated.

Which, as Dross reminded Mercy every few seconds, would likely carry penalties for the entire Reaper Division. They were hanging by a thin thread as it was.

Mercy was far more concerned about what would happen to the people in the transports. She didn't feel much relief at seeing the first one vanish. Her attention moved immediately to the second one.

And at that moment, when she fixed her senses on a second transport vessel, the enemy struck.

A fragment of the horizon peeled away like a strip of paint curling off a wall. Mercy reacted before she even had time to wonder what was happening, pulling Shattersight and taking aim.

Fury was faster even than she was, clad in shadow and laughing, charging the distant anomaly with madra and Way-power gathering around his fist.

Time seemed to freeze, and Mercy heard two mental voices speak in unison.

[Information Requested: Identity of the unknown Fiend.]

The information request echoed through reality as the Presences reached into the Way for answers. Only a moment later, Dross had a response.

Not that it was encouraging.

[That was a vast database of nothing,] he said. [This must be a Void scavenger, because it's never done its work around the Way before. They're usually Class Four.]

Mercy hadn't interacted much with Fiends yet, but she still knew the broad classifications. Class Four Fiends were threats to cities or low-power civilizations, but could be resisted by powerful mortals. Combat-capable Abidan were usually overkill.

Is this one a Class Four?

[Hm. Eh. Well...We haven't seen it *do* anything, and usually the Class rating is based on its scope of impact, so it's hard to say *no*...]

You think it's Class Three, don't you?

[There are cities back home bigger than all of Pioneer 602. This hasn't even formed a proper planet. A Four could affect the whole thing, but doing that while hiding from you and Fury?]

Fury's Presence was much more succinct. [Estimated Class: Three-point-six-five.]

Class Three Fiends weren't threats to a full, stable Iteration, in much the same way that Gold-level sacred birds weren't a threat to a well-defended cloudship. But Pioneer 602 was more like a Thousand-Mile Cloud on its last wisps of energy.

Squads of Abidan were dispatched to deal with Class Threes.

Strips of the horizon continued peeling away as time resumed, resembling tendrils or knotted roots. Spots of darkness buzzed around each one, like flies gathered to rotten meat.

Layered with every technique Mercy could use, an arrow streaked out from Shattersight. It arrived at what seemed to be the central nexus of the roots, a twisted knot deep inside the wheat field.

The heart of this world's corruption reminded Mercy of a golden whirlpool of twisted space, as though something were beneath the soil, sucking everything into it.

Mercy's arrow hit its target just ahead of Fury, piercing through.

And it seemed as though the entire world screamed in pain.

Dross manifested on Mercy's shoulder, shading his eye with one tentacle. [You know, I think he underestimated us.]

Monarchs were known to be capable of tearing open spatial rifts. In Cradle, which Mercy now understood to be a huge world with a population in the hundreds of billions. It had a connection to the Way more stable than Mercy could fully understand.

Class Three Fiends were opponents for entire groups of Abidan. Of the two guardians in Pioneer 602, only one was truly an Abidan. But both were full Monarchs of Cradle.

Mercy had prepared that arrow to break the world.

One more target in the way wouldn't slow it down.

Jek'nan screamed harder, deeper, and in more tones than a human could comprehend. He screamed in frequencies their technology could not perceive.

He had never felt, not even imagined, such pain.

From his observation of the Abidan and his limited understanding of their capabilities, he had been confident that he understood what these two could do. He'd seen the black-armored one's bow, and he'd felt their blows shake the desert as they fought.

It had never occurred to him that they might have been holding back so much.

That one arrow carried with it a dense energy of shadow so complex it made the wards defending the world look simple. The arrow was infused with a venomous intention, a cleansing warmth concealed within the shadow, a will intended to drive out hostile invaders. The vaccine to his disease.

Paired with the properties of the bow, it seemed to ignore everything—his defenses, the stability of the world, logic itself—to pierce him straight to the core.

With that strike, Jek'nan realized for the first time that his life was in danger.

Then the second Abidan arrived.

The Wolf loomed overhead, looking darker than his partner in spite of his pure white armor. Eyes blazed scarlet, hair drifted in a banner of night, and his wide grin belonged more to the madness of the Void than the order of the Way.

He harnessed the power of shadow too, but in a very different way than the woman. His fist was simpler but deeper, and it carried a measure of infinite power. Of Strength itself. Jek'nan realized, for the first time, that this low-ranking Wolf could have always shattered Pioneer 602 with a single punch.

Before that strike landed, the Flourishing Disease reversed his plan. He no longer wanted even a fragment of this world. He needed to get back into the Void, where the Abidan could not follow.

To do that, he had to strip away the final anchors holding this world down.

And quickly, before that fist and those arrows reduced him to splinters.

The Presences both erupted into alerts when the Fiend changed its tactics.

Mercy sensed it anyway. The tendrils of the enemy had split, taking their focus away from the Abidan to the workers surrounding them.

Clearly, the Fiend didn't like its chances in a straight battle. It was trying to reduce the world's connection to the Way and thus escape. Dross confirmed her read of the situation.

Mercy didn't need to think about what she would do. Strings of Shadow erupted from her in a city-sized web, covering the people and their departing ships. Her madra and intentions slammed into the branches of the enemy, and while her techniques were somewhat weaker, they still formed a defense for the people.

Fury, meanwhile, had acted according to his nature as well. He'd redoubled his attack.

Shadows blotted out the sky and reality itself shook with each blow. Shook too much.

Fury's voice echoed in Mercy's mind, transmitted through his Presence. *One more arrow, Mercy! Now, before he gets away!*

Together, they were more than a match for this entity. Separately, maybe one of them could win, but it would require a battle that would devastate Pioneer 602. And certainly they couldn't stop the Fiend from escaping back into the Void.

Let him go, Mercy sent back, through Dross. *We can't hold him here and keep them safe.*

The impression she received from Fury's Presence was like a long, heavy sigh. *I know it's hard, Mercy. I do. But this* is *the way to save the most people.*

Instead of a further verbal explanation, Fury sent his own memories.

He turned from a battle with a young gold dragon, letting her leave so he could cover a village from the assault of her armies. Years later, he hovered over the wreckage of that same village, leveled by the dragon he'd allowed to escape. Xorrus had grown in power and wreaked her revenge a thousand times over.

Fury had dozens, maybe hundreds, of such memories.

Mercy could cover the people in her web and support Fury at the same time, but that would require splitting her attention. What he required was the weight of her full willpower.

When she took her will away from the web, it would collapse and the people would die. But in that moment, they could strike a fatal blow to the Fiend.

Fury sent her pity but unshakeable resolve. He had made up his mind years before.

Unfortunately for him, so had Mercy.

Look out, Uncle Fury, she warned him.

Then she turned her attention fully to the people. Otherworldly branches flogged their temporary city, branches that resembled flexible windows onto other places and times. The black fly-like spots that swarmed around the Fiend's flesh ate into Mercy's shadows, corroding them from existence.

Behind her, the Netherworld Empress stepped forward and swept out her bow, which transformed into a spear.

The strike swept the city clean. If not for the dome of Strings of Shadow over the people, even the aftermath would have killed the workers.

At the same time, Pioneer 602 trembled and flickered, becoming less real, and not because of Mercy's technique. The whirlpool effect at the center of the grain fields intensified, twisting into a knot in space and time.

Fury roared, gathering up madra in his hands for a Striker technique.

Then the Fiend vanished, tearing itself out of reality and into the vast ocean beyond existence.

Spatial cracks spidered across reality, showing a depth of darkness filled with sparks of eye-twisting color. The enemy undulated into the distance like a squid, rapidly moving further away.

Fury whirled on Mercy, though his expression was sad rather than angry. "I know you're young," he said, "but you *have* to learn these lessons, Mercy. There's too much at stake."

Mercy was focused on controlling the dissolution of her madra as the massive dome of shadow faded into essence. If she banished it all at once, people or structures leaning on her Strings of Shadow might collapse.

"Yerin would have helped you to kill the Fiend as fast as possible," she said. "Ziel would have done what you wanted while protecting as many people as he could. Lindon would have looked for a way to do both."

She beamed at him. "I'm going to try something else."

Mercy didn't believe Fury was wrong. But she knew her Archlord revelation, she'd seen her own Remnant, and she could hear the song of her Icon.

It might be the right choice to sacrifice the few to save the many, but that didn't feel very *joyful*.

[This is naïve,] Fury's Presence observed.

"Not as much as you think!" Mercy responded brightly.

Then, before the spatial cracks had time to heal, Mercy tossed herself into the Void.

Dross had been complaining in the back of her mind ever since she'd thought of this idea, and his complaints got louder as she found herself drifting in the hostile emptiness outside of the cosmos.

[And there it is,] he said, resigned. [You know how much good I'll be to you out here? None! Just a glorified memory construct!]

Dross' connection to the Way had thinned, greatly reducing his predictive ability, though he still had his own memories and intelligence. Mercy herself felt the lack of connection to existence, and not just in a spiritual sense.

She felt disconnected from her own flesh, like she floated in a dream. If she lost concentration, she thought she'd fall apart. And that wasn't even considering the darkness around her, which seemed to gnaw at her from the outside in.

To her, the Void didn't feel empty so much as it felt filled with emptiness. Those two concepts seemed distinct, at the moment. It was hostile, trying to break her down. Even the Joy Icon drifted distantly, its warm song a bare whisper.

She lifted Shattersight, pulling an arrow to its transparent string.

The Reapers had one advantage over the other Abidan: her powers were not dependent on the presence of the Way.

Even her black armor was more suited to being here; she felt a strange resonance, as though it had been crafted from metallic slices of the Void itself. Most Abidan were helpless here, except to preserve their own existence. She was almost unaffected.

The Fiend, on the other hand, was much stronger.

It was far away by the time she entered, just a relatively large spot of swirling color, but it stopped when it sensed her enter. The enemy unfolded into the form of a tree that almost seemed made of liquid glass, its roots and branches surrounded by swarms like flies.

Its senses reached out to her, brushing her and confirming her presence.

Then the tree shot back toward her, a hungry predator pouncing on its prey.

[You don't need a Presence to predict *that*.]

Weight, power, significance, and continent-shattering madra gathered in Mercy's arrowhead. The Fiend would reach her in seconds, but *in* those seconds, she would have created an attack too powerful for a Pioneer world to survive.

The tree gathered its branches into a shield as it rushed forward, clearly intending to weather the attack.

Mercy released her shot, and layers of darkness streaked across the Void.

Empowered by Shattersight's ability to break apart existence, her arrow speared through the outer layer of the Fiend. She hit the enemy like a lightning bolt hitting a dry oak, leaving it split and broken.

But still advancing.

A psychic scream shook the Void, even attracting some of the nearest "stars." Those were other Fiends and fragments of destroyed worlds, floating in emptiness, and some of them drew closer at the sounds of battle.

Mercy gathered amethyst armor around herself and retreated, diving toward Pioneer 602, which looked like a steadily closing pinprick beneath her.

A twisting root seized the armor around her ankle, and she felt her mind and spirit seized as well. It was a more than physical grip, like the Void itself refusing to let her retreat.

She clawed at the exit, but that was where her lack of authority over the Way proved a liability. A full Abidan would have been able to expand the pinprick into a full gateway immediately, but Mercy's connection was too distant.

Fortunately, she had an ally.

A white-armored hand punched out from the Pioneer world. It grabbed onto her wrist and hauled her back, where she came to a tumbling stop in the middle of a field of grain.

Mercy, panting, raised a thumb to her half-brother. "I knew I could count on you, Uncle Fury!"

His expression was a picture of befuddled confusion. "What was *that?*"

"I hurt it!" She hopped to her feet. "I know it's not dead, but I couldn't let it get away for free."

Fury stared at her for another long moment before he burst out laughing. "Well, all right! Next time you plan to do something crazy, let me know so I can help."

Jek'nan drifted in the Void, unleashing his true form. His remaining branches spread freely, no longer requiring concealment. To a passing human's eye, he would resemble a tree-shaped mass of twisted ribbons, though the color would be difficult to describe. Each of his branches could blend into the fabric of a world, and with no context, they resembled a twisting nest of every color at once and none in particular.

He nursed his wounds and reached out for what little nourishment he could grab—passing Fiends, tiny debris too small to even be called fragments, and some of the loose energy left behind by the black-armored Abidan's arrow.

Far from enough to restore him, but he would heal eventually. The next time, he would have to conceal himself more carefully. Operate more quietly.

And avoid the Abidan in the black armor.

Sight was not Jek'nan's sharpest sense, especially not in the Void, but he spotted something floating toward him. Something with a tantalizing scent of deadly stability; it smelled like one of the Abidan had lost a weapon down here. An appetizing meal.

Jek'nan willed himself closer, drifting through the Void toward the tiny speck of black-and-white. Oddly, no matter how close he came, he still couldn't see the thing clearly. Perhaps that was one of its properties, though such things rarely functioned in the Void.

He reached out with his branches, wrapping around the object. Just as he did, the thing spoke.

Jek'nan had a decent understanding of humans. He had observed them for centuries, and had devoured thousands. So he was surprised at how calm the thing's voice sounded. Usually, anything left in the Void that could talk was terrified.

"I think we're far enough away from prying eyes, don't you?" the speck said. His tone was—the Fiend spent a moment thinking of the right word—*conspiratorial.*

The Flourishing Disease responded by sending its infection into the speck. The black spots swirling around his form flowed down, infecting his target. By destroying it, he would make it part of him.

His infection found no purchase. It was stopped completely.

By what he now recognized as a suit of black armor.

Suddenly, whatever power had been concealing the speck's identity fell away, revealing a black-armored human with long, white hair.

Something deep in Jek'nan's instincts shuddered, and his recent memory fervently agreed. He had no desire to make enemies of the black-armored Abidan again. In fear, he struck out, trying to drive the human away.

The Abidan stroked his chin, ignoring the barrage of attacks that rained down on him. Even in the depths of the Void, his power seemed undiminished.

"You met my apprentice," the Abidan said. "She's new. Eventually, she'll learn to clean up after herself."

Jek'nan tried to squirm away, but one black gauntlet held his branch tightly. He tried to suppress his rising panic. An Abidan couldn't kill him, not in the Void; even a small piece of him would regrow someday.

A shard of razor-edged darkness appeared in the human's hand, and Jek'nan saw hope die.

A bright smile bloomed in the Void, even sharper than the weapon. "You were a wonderful teaching assistant! My thanks, and goodbye!"

One swipe of the Scythe, and Jek'nan the Flourishing Disease was no more.

Threshold

INFORMATION REQUESTED: LINDON'S FIRST MISSION AS A REAPER.
REPORT LOCATION: JUST AFTER THE EVENTS OF *WAYBOUND*.
AUTHORIZATION CONFIRMED.
BEGINNING REPORT...

Lindon had barely been in the Grave for two days before Eithan put him to work.

"I'm very sorry to disturb you," Eithan said, "and that's only *slightly* because Yerin threatened to kill me."

Lindon dipped his head. "No apology necessary. I'm here to work."

[Yerin couldn't kill him anyway,] Dross noted.

Neither of them were used to Eithan's new look. His hair was still long and flowing, but it was pure white instead of blond. In place of flashy clothes, he wore sleek, black armor that covered him from the neck down.

His face was still the same—familiar and smiling—but he was Ozriel now, not just Eithan.

Then again, it was easy to recognize him when he staggered back, with a hand held to his chest as though he'd been struck a blow. "Dross! For shame! The Court of Seven has restricted my abilities, to be released only in the most dire of emergencies. I am now just as vulnerable as any mortal man. Or at least as vulnerable as Lindon is."

You didn't send that to Eithan, did you? Lindon asked.

Dross materialized over Lindon's shoulder, one-eyed gaze pointing at Eithan. [No, I didn't. This *is* for you, Eithan, and I want you to remember it: I've missed you. It's so nice to have an equal around.]

Lindon almost choked on the word "equal," but Eithan beamed.

"Likewise, Dross! It has been many long years since I've seen my own Presence, but he's not nearly as charming as you are."

The entire ascended world was new to Lindon, so he was eager to hear more about it, but alarms were flashing everywhere he looked.

They stood in the briefing-room of the Grave, a broad chamber that reminded him of a cloudship's bridge. The wide, sweeping arc of a 'window' didn't look out on Sanctum, though Lindon knew they floated above that world.

Instead of the view outside, the window showed scenes from dozens of different worlds, most of which were outlined in violet. From what he'd understood so far, the violet border meant they were scenes from a likely future.

Warnings flashed here and there, between the scenes, in bright red. Every few seconds, there were more.

Dross whistled and spun closer to Eithan. [Ever since you left, I've wondered what your Presence is like.]

"Why don't you guess how my Presence manifests?" Eithan suggested.

Behind him, the words "URGENT REQUEST" flashed rapidly in dire, shining red.

"Apologies," Lindon said, "but didn't we need to get to work?"

[I guess...A pair of scissors! No, a weasel! It's not a mirror, is it?]

"I'm not sure if I should be offended by the weasel, but otherwise, you're getting closer! Lindon, would you like to have a guess?"

"Do we have time for this?"

"We wouldn't have time to handle *everything* even if there were a thousand times more of us and we all worked around the clock. Rest assured that I have prioritized carefully."

"Then I do have a guess. Your Presence is a clone of you."

Eithan's shoulders sagged. "Lindon! How little you think of me." He held out a hand and a figure manifested on his palm, six inches high. A figure with long, blond hair, colorful outer robes, and a beaming smile.

[Not *merely* a clone,] Eithan's clone said. [A mental copy brought to glorious life and granted independence. His ideal self, you might say.]

Eithan looked down fondly on the Presence in his hand. "I asked myself, 'Whose advice would I most like living in my head and controlling a portion of my powers?'"

[Of course, the answer was clear! There is only one being in all existence who could handle such a burden.]

Dross' gaze flickered from one face to another. [Wow, this is amazing! In a horrifying way, of course.]

The flashing alarms still bothered Lindon, but if Eithan didn't think they were as urgent as they seemed, he supposed there was no need to worry. "I suppose I can see why you were so lonely up here. All you had to talk to was a copy of yourself."

Both Eithans frowned at him.

[Is that really what you want to talk about right now?] the Presence asked.

Eithan picked up without interruption. "Don't you see the alerts behind you?"

[Do you realize how urgent those are?]

"Shameful," Eithan said with a sigh. "Lindon, if you don't mind focusing for once, we can finally get down to business."

Lindon knew what Eithan was after. He wanted to provoke a reaction.

But they hadn't seen each other in about two years. Just interacting with Eithan at all was almost enough to bring a tear to his eye. Rather than frustrated, he only felt fond.

Even so, he knew how to play his role.

Keeping his face expressionless, Lindon turned on his heel. Dross followed along, taking his cue and playing along. [Oh, we're leaving! Where are we going?]

"I'm going to see if Suriel has an opening in the Sixth Division," Lindon said.

He neither saw nor sensed anything, but Eithan popped up in front of him with a hand extended. "Now, Lindon, let's not be hasty!

Surely you know I was only twisting your arm, as it were! Didn't you miss my tomfoolery?"

[I've only recently gained our memories from Cradle,] the Presence said, [but I'm certain you understand this was just a touch of our charming repartee.]

Dross stroked his chin. [How charming is it if you have to call it 'charming' yourself?]

"Ah, but that's why there are two of us!"

[I compliment *him,* he compliments *me,* and it's all perfectly aboveboard.]

Eithan and his tiny clone grinned proudly as though they'd discovered a loophole, and Lindon couldn't suppress his smile any longer.

"I really have missed you, Eithan."

Eithan's own smile softened, and he looked as though he would respond in kind, but his Presence raised a tiny hand.

[That's very touching—I do thank you, Lindon, and look forward to catching up—but we *are* eventually going to run out of time.]

Eithan smacked himself in the forehead. "That's right! I almost forgot about the imminent dissolution of all existence."

Dross blinked. [The what?]

[Oh, did you not notice? What did you think was keeping the others so busy?]

"Yerin told me that things were serious," Lindon said. "She didn't say we were on the verge of annihilation."

Eithan spread his hands wide. "That's why we're here! We can intervene where the Abidan are powerless."

[And we should,] his copy put in. [Quickly.]

"Which brings us to Threshold!" Eithan swept a hand toward the monitor behind him, which cleared to display information about the world in question. "It's one of the most important Abidan worlds, serving as a sort of middle ground between most low-level Iterations and Sanctum itself."

Presence-Eithan steepled his hands and looked proudly over the information, as though he'd personally been responsible for the creation of Threshold. [It has a unique position within the Way, so the Abidan have occupied it since the first generation. Quite a natural marvel.]

"We held it until only a few standard months ago," Eithan continued. "A detachment of enterprising Silverlords took over the Iteration and are currently stripping it of personnel and resources."

As Dross was busy memorizing the information displayed on the screen, Lindon focused on Eithan's words. "If the world is so important, why haven't the Judges taken it back?"

He had learned *some* things in the last two days.

Eithan tapped the console at the base of the screen. "That's what they're counting on, I'm afraid. You see, they *know* they can't keep Threshold. They'll take its resources while they hold it, but they won't drain it so dry that the Court is forced to take drastic measures."

His Presence swept a bow. [That's us. We're drastic measures.]

"Rather than a capture of territory, it is perhaps best to think of this as a kidnapping. Dross, would you mind?"

Dross projected an illusion into the air: a tiny globe with eyes, legs, and hands. The planet was bound and gagged, tears welling up in its eyes.

[Perfect,] Eithan's Presence said.

Dross swelled with pride.

"The Silverlords are holding out for a ransom," Eithan went on. "If we attack them, they'll harm the hostage. The current plan is to gather up a sufficient force—enough to make them take the situation seriously, but not so scary that they tear apart the planet and flee. We'll negotiate once we have them surrounded."

"So how do I free the hostage?" Lindon asked.

Presence-Eithan clapped. [I love your thinking, I love this attitude, but the situation *is* a bit more delicate than that.]

"We're using you to weaken the Silverlords' negotiating position without scaring them too badly," Eithan picked up. "The fewer resources we dedicate to this operation, the more Abidan we free up around the cosmos."

A silver-crowned kidnapper appeared, holding a dagger behind the bound and gagged planet.

[There's only one Silverlord holding Threshold right now, with at least a dozen more in reserve to defend against a true Abidan attack,] Eithan's Presence explained. [Defeat her, as publicly as you can, and withdraw.]

"Since you don't draw on the Way for power, you will be able to slip through many of their defenses. Your success will shake up the Silverlords and establish the reputation of the Reapers among the Abidan."

That wasn't the first disturbing thing Eithan had said about the standing of their Eighth Division, and Lindon vividly remembered him being dragged off to trial by the other Judges. "Pardon, but is our reputation in question?"

Eithan and Eithan exchanged glances.

"[Yes,]" they both said.

Lindon mentally scanned the information they'd provided Dross, which included details of the opponent and the nature of Threshold, as well as Silverlord tactics and Abidan plans.

He understood the situation quickly. This was well within his abilities.

But there was one crucial detail missing.

"Can I kill the Silverlords?" Lindon asked.

Both of Eithan's smiles gained a touch of sadness.

"You have to make that judgment yourself," Eithan said. "That's what it means to be a Reaper."

Lindon had been transported through the Way many times, but this trip ended much sooner than he expected.

He began in a current of blue light so thick it buffeted him from every side, but no sooner had the trip begun than he found himself channeled out and into reality once again. Lindon knelt on a smooth stone floor.

Threshold is much closer than I thought.

Dross felt baffled. [No, this...We haven't gone anywhere.]

Lindon tried extending his awareness but found that everything except his mundane senses was locked to his body.

Upon that realization, he snapped his head up to take in the scene.

He knelt in a vast stone cavern, at the feet of a statue that rose to the distant ceiling. The statue depicted an armored figure clasping a shield and staring down at Lindon as though to pass judgment.

Lindon recognized this man, or at least the symbol on his shield. There had been a cave with that symbol over it in the labyrinth.

[Gadrael, the Titan,] Dross said. [Second of the Court of Seven, and I suspect his successor is behind you.]

Lindon heard nothing, so neither had Dross, but Lindon still rose to his feet and turned, pressing his fists together in a salute.

"Apologies for not greeting you sooner, Judge. My name is Wei Shi Lindon, of Cradle."

To his own discomfort, he found that he loomed over the current Judge of the Second Division.

Gadrael looked more like a sacred beast in humanoid form than a traditional human, with grayish skin and short spikes that covered his scalp like hair. In build, he reminded Lindon of Akura Pride: the man was compact and muscular, though short.

Even with his senses sealed, Lindon broke out in a cold sweat on sight of the man.

There was nothing he could confirm spiritually, but he felt that Gadrael towered over him in a way that the giant statue did not. Lindon stood before absolute stability, a wall that no amount of effort could breach.

It was a similar feeling to when he'd seen Icons manifest. Just glancing at Gadrael was enough to tell him that this man *meant* defense. It was like looking on invincibility itself.

"You will not speak in my presence again," Gadrael said, and it was not a command. It was simple truth. "I bind you, I burden you, and I warn you."

[Lindon, he's doing som—]

The Way flashed in Lindon's spirit, twisted into a symbol complex beyond his comprehension, and Dross was locked away.

"I bind you to your mission. You may not seek power beyond what you have, you may not seek to undermine the stability of the world you inhabit, and you may not contact your Division."

Lindon knew the futility of struggle, but he did not simply wait for the restrictions to settle upon him. He mustered all his willpower, all his authority, and the full weight of his spirit against the words that bound him as surely as an oath.

He may as well have not bothered. Pushing against Gadrael's seals made him feel useless. Weak. Powerless.

Like an Unsouled once again.

"I burden you with the weight of our cause," Gadrael continued. "Your life is less than dust in comparison to existence itself, which is our remit. You will act with this awareness, whether you like it or not."

Another oath settled on Lindon like spiritual shackles. His soul strained against the weight, and he felt as though blood ought to burst from him with the effort he expended to fight the bonds.

"Finally, I warn you, and those who sent you. When you betray us, you will be executed, your partners will be executed, and your sponsors on the Court will be censured and bound."

Blue shone in Gadrael's eyes, a spark of the Way that contained cold fury. "The only escape for you is in loyalty, abject service, and a short lifespan. Go, discharge your duties quickly, and you will return to a full accounting with me. If I find you a feather less than perfect, I will perform your immediate execution upon my authority as Gadrael."

He gestured, and another Abidan stepped out of nowhere. She was a small, bookish woman with a symbol on the breast of her armor: a curled-up fox.

She performed a quick operation with both hands, and then Lindon was hurtling through the Way one more time.

This time, the trip lasted longer. When he fell into reality, he landed with enough force to crack the blocks of concrete below him.

He was in the ruins of a city, on a road that had been shattered centuries before, by the look of it. In the distance, a walled city rose up to the horizon, and the sky itself was covered in bars.

He was back in Threshold. This time, at least, he wasn't directly under the eyes of the enemy.

Though he might as well have been.

Lindon's heart burned with rage and humiliation. He stretched out his spiritual sense and flexed his madra, finding both in perfect working condition. He couldn't feel the Titan's restrictions on him, though he knew they were there.

The Void Icon comforted him from a distance, cooling his thoughts.

"He didn't command our loyalty," Lindon said aloud.

Dross popped out next to him, and he didn't look any happier than Lindon himself was. [Clearly, he can't. Either he isn't allowed or he just can't do it.]

So there were limits to his power. That was a good reminder.

It meant there was a way to strike back.

"He won't let us reach Eithan." That was obvious. Gadrael must have been as overworked as all the other Judges, but he had spent the time to personally intervene with Lindon.

He was taking action against Ozriel. No matter what happened in Threshold, Gadrael wouldn't allow Lindon to return to the Grave without binding him in oaths. More likely, the Titan would either execute him or use him as a hostage against Eithan.

Dross forced a smile. [Let's look on the bright side, shall we? There are two pieces of good news. First, the oaths aren't so bad. They basically make us take the mission seriously, which we planned to do anyway.]

But instead of being permitted to intervene and save a world, Lindon was being forced to do it on pain of execution. He had just escaped Cradle and the Monarchs, only to be right back where he started.

He hadn't seen his friends in over a year. As soon as he had them back, the Abidan threatened to take them away.

Blackflame boiled in his spirit. No wonder the Executor program always failed. Lindon's first mission, and he was already looking for any chance to take revenge.

Dross waved one tendril in front of Lindon's face, distracting him from dark thoughts. [*Next* piece of good news! He might be invincible, but Gadrael isn't the *most* invincible.] Dross smiled, revealing his spiked teeth. [There's a bigger fish in the heavens, and he's on our side.]

The reminder did ease Lindon's spirits somewhat. Gadrael had seemed insurmountable to Lindon, but Ozriel had once been qualified as the Judge for six out of the seven Abidan Divisions, including the Titans. He was everything Gadrael was and much more.

Or he had been, once.

Lindon let that thought loosen his resentment. He wasn't alone, though a Judge had pushed him to think he was.

"For now, we focus on Threshold," Lindon said.

In the meantime, they could figure out how to escape the Titan.

Threshold didn't fall within any specific Division of the Abidan, as it was so necessary for the operation of all seven. But the Titans felt a particular claim over it.

Most lesser Iterations with the possibility of producing natural ascendants were routed to filter through Threshold first, which made that world the first line of defense between Sanctum and would-be Vroshir.

It was all the more true since the Collapse, where the Silverlords had actually seized Threshold and were using it to cut the Abidan off. It was impossible to calculate how much the Abidan were losing in the value of imports, labor, and recruits for each day Threshold remained in enemy control.

The Titans believed it was their job to reclaim the world.

Yet Ozriel had dared to send one of his baby Reapers first.

Cirian, squad leader and four-star Titan, raged at the indignity even as he worried about the outcome. Ozriel was clearly doing this as a slap to Gadrael's face, which was as close to pure *evil* as Cirian had ever seen in the Abidan.

It was the Reaper's fault that Threshold was in this state to begin with. If not for his abandonment of his own divine responsibilities, uncountable *trillions* would still be alive. He was a traitor a thousand times over, and the mere fact that the Court of Seven hadn't executed him outright filled Cirian with righteous indignation.

He understood their reasoning, no matter how little he agreed with it. Suriel was too compassionate for her own good—that was always the weakness of the Phoenixes, though everyone loved them for it—and the rest of the Court had seen Ozriel's utility outweigh the justice he so deserved.

But Cirian was baffled by the decision to allow the creation of the Reaper Division. He was too young to remember the last generation of Executors, but he knew the history. This was doomed to failure.

Some believed that there was nothing the Reapers could do to break the worlds worse than the Mad King had already done, but that was shortsighted. Threshold was the perfect proof.

A Silverlord ruled the world at the moment, but at least she *ruled*. The Iteration could still be destroyed.

Cirian knew people in Threshold. He himself had come through the world once; he even had distant family remaining in the population.

What would be left of them after Ozriel's apprentice passed through?

And on a more professional note, why did the Reaper Division have jurisdiction in Threshold anyway? It was a world in which the Abidan were permitted to use their full power.

Cirian intended to exercise that right. His own Judge was being corralled by the rest of the Court not to interfere with the Reapers; very well. Cirian and his team could act on Gadrael's behalf.

The three of them materialized in Threshold not far outside of Northgate, one of the Iteration's largest cities.

The sky was covered by the restriction-bars that defended this world, but many had been broken in the Vroshir incursion, leaving gaps where blue sky shone through. The city itself was as tall as ever, its walls intact, but it was the only time Cirian had ever seen it without bustling air traffic moving in and out.

His heart ached at the sight. Northgate buzzing like an insect hive was one of his earliest memories after ascension, when he had been little more than a boy.

The newest member of his squad released her breath and slumped to the ground, leaning against a chunk of destroyed roadway. Folded over, she was still tall; she stood about three meters normally.

Pariana wiped her gold-skinned brow clean of sweat and reported. "The formation held, squad captain."

Cirian nodded in acknowledgement and his Presence materialized over his shoulder, a cube of blue light. [No alerts issued from Silverlord border security. Infiltration is likely successful.]

Vall, the third member of his squad, consulted her own Presence and then peered up at the sky. He'd worked with her for centuries, so he knew what she was up to without being told; she would be scanning the Iteration to get a sense of their situation.

She had a one-star rating as both a Spider and a Ghost, in addition to her status as a three-star Titan. Her specialties complemented his own, which was why he never deployed without her if he could help it.

Normally, there would be at least one more member of their team. More, for a mission of this magnitude.

But this operation had not been officially sanctioned by the Division. As far as Sector Control knew, Cirian's squad was on their way back from an assignment. But they would have at least a local day before anyone began to question their absence.

Vall was a slender, bookish woman with dark hair and a single eye. The other was hidden behind a thick eyepatch made of a segment of Abidan armor; she had lost that eye in a battle with the Mad King, though of course she hadn't been struck directly.

She could have claimed an audience with Suriel to restore herself, but she'd said that the loss of an eye wouldn't stop her from serving the Abidan. By now, the wound was almost certainly permanent, but Vall didn't seem to mind.

That was the sort of dedication they needed for a mission like this one.

Pariana was a new addition, one who had been promoted to two-star Titan after her service in Sector 98. She stood out among standard humans, thanks to her height and her golden skin, but she was skilled in the creation and maintenance of formations.

The three of them would be perfect for containing a Reaper.

"Do we have a trail?" Cirian asked Vall.

She stared into the distance a moment longer, scanning her techniques, and finally nodded. "He arrived not far from here. He's staying low to the ground, but I found traces of madra."

Cirian set his Presence to calculating the Reaper's likely goals. None of them were Hounds, but the Presence could make educated guesses purified by the Way.

The sapphire cube spun for a moment, then flashed an affirmative. [Ozriel assigned his agent to reclaim the Iteration prior to large-scale Abidan action. The most reasonable courses of action are as follows, in order from most to least probable.]

His Presence projected information into each of their minds along with its words.

[Most likely, the Reaper intends to bargain with the Silverlord for the release of Threshold.]

Knowledge flickered through Cirian's awareness as the Presence quickly summarized its reasoning in thoughts and memories instead of words. There were thousands of bargaining chips Ozriel could potentially have that might interest a Silverlord, from information on distant Iterations to weapons personally crafted by the Reaper of Worlds himself.

[It is also possible that the Reaper intends to incite rebellion among the populace of Threshold, thus creating a bloodier outcome that is less disruptive to Fate.]

Cirian saw the people of Threshold rising up, unearthing emergency weapons and leveraging secret energy systems to oust their Silverlord governor.

Many would die, surely, but it would be a more natural destiny for this world than waiting for Abidan intervention.

Cirian's blood boiled even at the implication. He couldn't imagine putting the people at risk like that. Protecting them was the reason he'd joined the Titans in the first place.

[Finally, the Reaper may attempt to affect no change at all. This could be a scouting mission, or an attempt to retrieve personnel or equipment for which we have no record.]

Ozriel had hidden his Scythe somewhere under Abidan control—exactly where he'd hidden it was a secret Cirian wasn't privy to, but the man had his weapon back. If he could do that, he might potentially have hidden anything in the Iteration.

Vall rubbed her chin. "What are the chances the Reaper is here to join the Silverlords?"

[Next to impossible,] Cirian's Presence reported, and he was sure Vall's own Presence confirmed. [Ozriel has committed many crimes that might be considered treachery, but he has remained a steadfast enemy of the Vroshir.]

"Then...shouldn't we keep the Reaper under observation?" Pariana asked. "If we're certain he's working for the stability of the world, what standing do we have to interfere?"

Vall and Cirian turned to look at her, and the big woman didn't *quail* exactly, but she did shift uncomfortably.

Though Pariana was a new member of their squad, she wasn't a stranger. Cirian had known her for many years, and he trusted his analysis of her.

She had always stood out, so she preferred to stay quiet. In the background. She rarely took the lead, and was content to follow. It was part of what had motivated her to pursue her study of formations, in addition to her innate talent for the field.

Nevertheless, her heart was in the right place, and she was no coward. She had survived combat with the Vroshir more than once, all but unsupported in a frontier world. Cirian had no doubts about her quality or her loyalty.

He dipped his head to acknowledge her question, but he left the answer to Vall.

"The Reaper Division needs this win to solidify its legitimacy in the eyes of the Court of Seven," Vall said. "Ozriel won't let them go rogue here, not yet. But he *is* bad. The Judges want an excuse to get rid of them."

"Suriel vouched for them herself," Pariana said.

That was a recent change to Pariana's character; since the Collapse, she'd begun to idolize Suriel.

Cirian took over the explanation. "The Phoenix would hold hands with the Mad King himself if it would help heal a single world. That is her role, and it is to her credit. But we must fulfill *our* role."

Vall radiated support for his cause, and Pariana struggled with herself for a moment.

But she had agreed to follow them to Threshold in the first place. On some level, she already knew the Reaper Division was too much of a liability.

"We'll have a short window to escape before the Silverlord finds us," Pariana warned. "I can't hold him back and keep us hidden at the same time."

Cirian had accounted for that already. "That's fine. All we have to do is bind him. The Vroshir will take care of him for us."

They weren't really hiding from the Silverlord. They had to remain hidden from Sector Control, because this mission wasn't strictly legal.

It was, however, the right thing to do.

Vall had that distant look in her eye again, the one that meant she was scanning for traces of her prey. "He'll have to make contact soon. Either with the locals or with the Silverlord. We should check—"

[Warning!] all three Presences called at once.

A burning black comet streaked across the barred sky of Threshold, and Cirian's Presence identified the figure at once.

The image magnified in his mind. It was a woman crowned in a silver halo, protecting herself with strands of pink text. She'd been struck by black fire.

His Presence traced the source of the attack on the Silverlord: a figure of black-and-white. Black armor, black hair, black eyes. A white badge on his chest, white hand uncovered by armor, and his irises a pair of burning white circles.

The newest Reaper.

[Recalculating probability,] Cirian's Presence said, and he almost cursed at it.

Nowhere had it said that the Reaper would confront the Silverlord in battle.

"Constructing containment field!" Pariana reported, spreading her hands. Golden runes flashed into a web between them as she began releasing her formation.

Vall cut her off with a hand. "We can't reveal ourselves yet!"

"They're going to destroy the city!"

"No," Cirian said. "Look."

He was a four-star Titan, with two stars as a Fox and only one as a Wolf. He had few abilities related to detection or analysis, but he had eyes and plenty of experience. Besides, his Presence agreed with his conclusions.

The city was in no danger.

Silverlord techniques flashed around its borders, slithering like snakes made of pink symbols. Ships took off in a flurry as the troops loyal to her deployed from the city itself, moving to surround the black-armored newcomer. Alerts had gone up all over the planet.

Nevertheless, Northgate was safe.

Black fire and blue-white light clashed with Vroshir forces all around the city walls, but not a single attack struck within city borders. Even debris was burned away by dark flame before it hit the ground.

All the while, the Reaper didn't move a muscle. He hovered in place, arms crossed, and watched his opponent.

The first tinge of fear wormed its way into Cirian's heart.

"Reassess combat ability," Cirian ordered his Presence.

[Initial estimates, based on historical data from Cradle, suggested his base power would be comparable to a significant Class Four Fiend or one-star Wolf,] the blue cube responded. [In revision, it is perhaps best to consider him a match for a three-star Wolf.]

Vall turned to her own Presence. "He looks relaxed for a three-star Wolf. What's your take?"

Vall's Presence manifested as a set of interlocking rings, moving in and out of one another in midair. [He is shrouded well, making analysis difficult. This suggests his specialty is stealth. Highest probability: Ozriel prepared him as an assassin for this Silverlord.]

That was easy for Cirian to believe.

It wasn't as though the Silverlord guarding Threshold was particularly powerful. Almost the opposite. The Silverlords considered her expendable; their main forces would converge once she was removed.

She was bait. Ozriel had prepared his Reaper to remove the bait, which suggested he also had a way to escape without triggering the trap.

"When he fully commits to the battle, that's when we strike," Cirian said. His Presence flashed, agreeing.

They had to capitalize on the gap between the Reaper's actions and his escape. Essentially, they could pin him in place and leave him there as the Silverlord trap closed.

Pariana looked troubled, but neither she nor Vall objected.

Hidden behind their formation, the three Abidan watched the battle.

[Someone's hiding from us over there,] Dross reported.

Lindon was spreading his attention over a significant chunk of Threshold, clashing with enemy forces while keeping the city of Northgate safe, but he kept most of his power in reserve.

The Silverlord, after all, was doing the same. She fought warily, keeping herself protected while probing at the extent of his range.

It's not surprising that she has allies hidden, Lindon responded.

Dross made an unconvinced sound. [She's not moving like she knows she has an ambush ready...but that could be part of the trap. Hm.]

Lindon wasn't overly concerned about his hidden observer, though he didn't ignore them. Much of the population of Threshold had ascended under their own power, so there could be any number of people capable of avoiding his senses. Allies, enemies, neutral civilians just trying to stay out of the line of fire; anyone might have a reason to hide.

How's your analysis going?

[I'm about ninety percent certain we don't need one. And I'm ninety-*nine* percent certain we should speed things up. I don't feel any of her friends coming, but they certainly will.]

Lindon's mission was simple: defeat the Silverlord, minimize collateral damage, and leave.

He didn't even have to kill her, just beat her. Eithan was confident that a victory by Lindon would cause the Vroshir to withdraw. It would also be a slap in the face to the Silverlords and the Abidan both, establishing the value of the Reaper Division.

Gadrael's intervention had complicated things. Not his oaths—Lindon intended to abide by those conditions anyway—but the mere fact of a Judge's attention on him.

Lindon had an enemy back home. A powerful one.

Winning and returning had become much more dangerous.

How long can we stall this out? Lindon asked.

[Until we're caught and dissected by Silverlord reinforcements.]

Dross' thoughts were tinged with gloom, and truthfully so were Lindon's. He didn't think they were entirely cornered, since he still had Eithan and Suriel on his side, but Gadrael as an enemy soured his thoughts on the entire Abidan.

The Reapers weren't merely a detached force from the first seven Divisions. The Abidan thought of them as traitors.

All his work back in Cradle, and he had still ended up surrounded by enemies.

Neither he nor Dross could think of any way to turn this around on Gadrael, so Lindon reluctantly resolved to bring the battle to an end. If the Titan wanted an excuse to declare Lindon unfit or his mission a failure, he would find one. Lindon had to give him as little to work with as possible.

Without giving his opponent any warning, he burned through the strands of pink script she was trying to weave beneath the city of Northgate, sent a line of Blackflame straight at her body, and focused his will on an invisible working that had begun wrapping around him.

"**Break,**" he commanded.

An almost imperceptible force shattered; it had been intended to cut him off from the rest of the world.

The Silverlord focused herself to block the Blackflame madra, but Lindon dashed toward her with the explosive speed of the Burning Cloak.

Before she could shrug off the Striker technique entirely, Dross manifested himself, wearing the pure-white halo of the Silent King.

[Hi there! Do you have any secrets of the universe to share with me today?]

Over the course of that sentence, illusions assaulted the woman's mind. While she fought them off, Lindon tried to peel away her silver crown.

It resembled a circlet floating just over her head, one made from quicksilver or other liquid metal. But it *felt* like one piece of a much greater whole, a network so old and complicated and full of rich authority that it reminded Lindon of the labyrinth.

He itched to Consume that power, but he couldn't predict it. Nor could he dislodge it from her head before pink light erupted from the center of her... *'Spirit'* wasn't quite right. People who weren't from Cradle didn't have souls as Lindon knew them, though it wasn't quite as though they were soulless, either.

Whatever the case, the power she'd stored inside herself blasted upward and Lindon dodged backwards. The pink light congealed into a huge, pulsating cocoon over the Silverlord's head.

[Let's not find out what that does,] Dross suggested.

Lindon switched to his pure core and released the Hollow Domain. The cocoon began to flicker and vanish, though it resisted somewhat; the authority of the Void Icon suffused Lindon's technique, and it would give in eventually. More importantly, the pink light tethering the Silverlord to her own technique was severed, and she crumpled to the ground.

She was still in Dross' illusion, so Lindon sent him a question.

Why is she here?

From everything he'd learned about the Silverlords, they seemed to be very individualistic. He didn't doubt Eithan's word that their purpose in Threshold was to conquer, but this person might have her own reasons. And the mission didn't *require* him to kill her.

Dross sighed. [Yes, okay, as much as I would prefer to play it safe and be rid of a potential threat, she's a true believer. She thinks she's freeing this world.]

Pure madra filled Lindon's hand, and he struck her with an Empty Palm.

Though she had no core to disrupt, thanks to the resonance of the Void Icon and his own authority, it worked on the powers she did possess. The cocoon finally vanished, and she slumped into complete unconsciousness.

Her Silverlord halo remained in place, though, no matter what he tried.

He was considering burning it off when Dross shouted into his mind. [There it is! I knew they were coming! Go go go, before they close the borders!]

Lindon reached out to the Way. The Abidan had special authority over it, so they could lock down a world more effectively than anyone else, but of course Vroshir had their own techniques. If he was quick, he could make it.

Dross' groan had a tinge of real panic. [I knew it! I knew we should have just burned them before they dropped the veil!]

At the worst possible timing, the ones who had watched his battle from hiding had finally revealed themselves. Three Abidan, each wearing the clenched-fist symbol of the Titan Division.

Lindon had thought Gadrael would wait to act personally. Why bind him with commands if he meant to send a squad after him? To throw Eithan off the scent?

The clear leader of the three-man team was a man in armor much thicker than the Abidan usually wore, with heavy plates and a full-face helmet. A white shield, tall enough to cover most of his body, was braced in front of him. His Presence hung over his shoulder, a shining blue cube, and its battle with Dross had already begun.

Behind him was a woman with long, brown hair and a scar across her left eye, the socket of which was covered by an armored eyepatch. She carried two much smaller shields, almost bucklers, and she readied them both as she ran at Lindon.

Finally, a woman so tall Lindon questioned whether she was really human. She was half again as big as he was, with golden skin and a shaved head, and she grasped spinning script-circles in each hand.

She was creating a formation of some kind, or connecting to one, and Lindon couldn't be certain what it did.

To mundane vision, and perhaps to many of the residents of Threshold, this would look no more threatening than an ambush a few Truegolds might set. Visually, it was nothing impressive, at least not yet.

The true scope of their trap was in the deeper worlds of intention, significance, and authority.

One huge shield carried a barrier that isolated half of the world. He could block an earthquake with that, or the shattering of space itself. In Lindon's senses, the shield defined a barrier that was close to absolute.

The smaller shields the woman carried were different; they carried planes of protection that could be angled to deflect, attack, redirect. They hid something from him, too, though he couldn't tell what; she would be preparing stranger weapons as an attack while the leader blocked him and the golden woman prepared support.

All the while, the Silverlords would be closing in.

The three Abidan posed a serious threat, so Lindon took them seriously.

Dreadgod armor manifested around him. The blue scales of the Weeping Dragon wrapped him in a lightning-crackling embrace, the cloak of the Bleeding Phoenix billowed out from his shoulders like liquid blood, and three shells hewn from the Wandering Titan orbited his body.

Their protective powers were but imitations of the Titan, but they had powerful techniques and the weight of Cradle's history within them. Besides, they were only the outermost of his protective layers.

Wavedancer appeared over his head, the blade of the flying sword shining with raw, blue-gold lightning. Four copies appeared to his right, and four to his left.

Threshold itself trembled before the spirit of the Dreadgods unleashed. It took a not-inconsiderable amount of will to keep that pressure focused in front of him, to prevent it from spilling over the city behind.

The Titans didn't change their minds at the sight of Lindon's weapons, as he had hoped they would. The one-eyed woman charged faster, behind barriers of blue light, and the man with the towering shield leaped through space to fall on Lindon from overhead.

Lindon hit him with the breath of the Weeping Dragon.

He'd hoped they would give up, but he hadn't counted on it.

[Class Two!] Cirian's Presence screamed. [Class Two Fiend, attempting to...contact...] The blue cube flickered, and Cirian felt its confusion. [Mental breach. Devoting focus to preserve necessary systems. I am sorry.]

The voice of his Presence vanished as it buckled under the Reaper's mental assault, reassigning its resources to protect Cirian's thoughts and the mental enhancement that all Presences provided.

Cirian would have found that more alarming if he weren't fighting for his own life.

The streak of lightning from the Reaper's nine swords lit up the entire world of Threshold. If not for protective measures worked into the planet itself, unleashing an attack like that would have boiled the atmosphere.

And Cirian took it on his own shield.

He braced the full might of his attention against the attack, and the Way crackled around him as it bent reality to keep him intact.

Cirian was lifted high above the ground, but he stayed safe. In theory, a Titan barrier was invincible, but "invincible" was a more flexible definition than most realized. The shield was based on Cirian's own abilities, which would fail before the protective field itself did.

Vall had followed up while he absorbed the major attack, and she brought her own shields in for close combat. She lashed out, the shields of blue light slashing at the Reaper like swords.

Cirian didn't need his Presence to see the problem. She had no Wolf rating, and ascendants from Cradle were all experts in hand-to-hand combat. Someone Ozriel had personally recruited into his first generation of Reapers would be unstoppable in a duel.

Before her first swing landed, Vall's Presence took over the job of keeping the Abidan in contact.

[We'll keep him tied down,] the twisted knot of rings said. [Pariana, lock him in place. We fight to escape.]

Cirian understood the plan then, though Vall was putting herself at the most risk. She saw that the enemy was more powerful than expected and had pivoted to share the burden of his attention with Cirian.

The Presence rated her plan highly until a white hand seized her wrist.

One of Vall's shield-strikes had landed on the floating shields, but the other was seized by the Reaper. An instant later, he was beating her with hands faster than Cirian could track without the aid of his Presence. Shards of broken armor flew away from Vall in the first split second.

With a roar and a surge of will, Cirian shoved the bolt of shining lightning away from him and out of the planet.

Powerful the Reaper may have been, but Cirian was no stranger to combat. Nor was Vall.

A Ghost technique erupted from the gaps in Vall's broken armor; a trap she'd laid in advance. Colorless tendrils slithered up to the Reaper, past his defenses, seeking to trap him in time itself.

Cirian stepped through the Way in an instant and struck with his shield, reinforced by a Wolf technique.

A black disc formed in the sky: pure emptiness reflected in the Way.

Vall's Ghost technique evaporated, and the Reaper seized one of his floating, black shields and put his full willpower into a block.

Cirian's attack slammed into that wall and stopped.

Overhead, another image formed in the heart of the darkness: a hammer. With shock, Cirian recognized what that meant.

This man had *made* these weapons. The Way recognized his authority over them.

That alone wasn't unusual—many warriors made their own weapons—but it was certainly not normal to fight an entire squad of Abidan with handmade weapons. That level of ability was...not unprecedented, but very alarming to see in an enemy.

Cirian was starting to understand why his Presence had rated the Reaper as comparable to a Class Two Fiend. Class Twos were considered threats worthy of multiple teams, though not high enough to require Judge intervention.

A true Class Two Fiend would have forced Cirian's team to retreat immediately, and he didn't sense power on such a level. But to fight a Class Two Fiend to a standstill while inside an Iteration... that, this Reaper could likely do.

All the more reason to be rid of him there and then.

[Now!] Vall's Presence signaled.

Pariana activated her formation. Restrictive symbols erupted into being around the Reaper, circles of text miles in diameter. Some lines were in Pariana's gold, some in the pure blue of the Way, and others in the alien pink of the Silverlord's repurposed script.

All to hold the Reaper in place just for a moment.

Cirian slashed out, using a Fox technique to open a smooth hole into the Way. He scooped up the dazed and beaten Vall, and Pariana followed after him.

Surrounded by the comforting blue tides of the Way, Cirian's entire body and mind relaxed. His Presence came back to life in his mind, and Vall's shattered armor stitched itself together; she was the team's Phoenix, and she gasped in a breath as though the Way had restored her ability to breathe.

"Just in time," Vall said in relief.

Cirian nodded. "Yes. Another moment and he might have killed you."

"No, I mean we got rid of him just in time." Vall stared through the Way, into the reality just barely visible behind buffeting curtains of blue. "We almost allowed *that* to stay free among us."

Pariana massaged her temples. "Why would Suriel keep him alive?"

"He's not dead yet," Cirian reminded them, voice grim. With them standing sentinel outside the world, the Reaper wouldn't escape, and the Silverlords were on their way. Still, his Presence rated a decent chance that the Silverlords would keep the Reaper alive in exchange for concessions from the Court.

If this Reaper survived, they would have made a powerful enemy, and not just him. The Judge behind him.

Even so, they had struck a blow for the stability of the Abidan. A blow on the Court of Seven's behalf.

"Gadrael will punish us," Vall reminded them.

"He is right to," Cirian said. "We broke the rules. But he will shield us from Ozriel as well."

Whatever punishment their Judge decided, Cirian was willing to face it with head held high.

[Spatial violation imminent!] three Presences warned at once, and a void-black crack formed in the Way.

"The formation is gone!" Pariana announced too late.

A white hand pulled open blue light, and a Reaper hauled his way out of Threshold. His Presence manifested over his shoulder, a one-eyed purple creature with two limbs held up in surrender.

[Truce!] the strange Presence said. [You don't want to leave us there, right? We're on the same team!]

The man's eyes didn't look like they wanted peace at all. White circles blazed in black orbs, and Cirian saw no mercy there.

But he no longer had the right to decide their fate.

They were Abidan in the Way, and their will was inviolable. With the gravity of a Judge passing sentence, Cirian lifted one hand.

"I am Cirian of the Titans, and I deny you."

The Way rejected the Reaper, shoving him back into Threshold. Before the man vanished, he spoke once. "I am Wei Shi Lindon, and I will see you soon."

Dross screamed as Lindon fell to earth.

[No, don't say that! Why do you have to be so threatening? How about *'I am Wei Shi Lindon, and I just want to be friends?'*]

At the edge of Lindon's spiritual sense, new powers bloomed in Threshold. All around the planet, but especially concentrated where he was. Fifteen Silverlords; maybe more, if some were veiled well enough.

Strong Silverlords. The one lying at his feet didn't count.

Lindon's stomach didn't churn, and his hands didn't shake. His body had been remade. But he held the Void Icon to drive off thoughts of his immediate future.

He'd barely reunited with his friends—his family—and now he was at the mercy of their enemies.

Lindon closed his eyes and wished he could send a message to Yerin.

[If we could do that, we'd be calling *Eithan,*] Dross pointed out.

"You again," a woman's voice said.

She was the black-haired Vroshir Lindon had met before, when he'd first ascended from Cradle. This time, she wore elaborate robes that looked like they required wires to keep in place, shimmering with oceanic colors. She herself had a casual aspect to her, like she'd been interrupted in the middle of a routine job.

A giant raven's head hung in the air behind her, as though it had stuck its neck through an invisible curtain. It *cawed,* and Dross shuddered at the effort of keeping its meaning from slipping through to Lindon.

Lindon bowed to her. "Apologies. I didn't expect to see you again."

She made a show of surveying the landscape with her eyes. "Thanks for not breaking our world."

"I was careful." He gestured to the unconscious Silverlord lying nearby.

A black feather drifted down from the wind and landed on the woman's prone body. She and the feather both vanished.

"Do you know what's going to happen to you now?" the raven Silverlord asked curiously.

Lindon kept his thoughts masked with the Void Icon, but he had no reason not to answer the question. "I imagine you're going to execute or detain me."

"Yeah, you're confusing us with the Abidan. We don't detain *or* execute people. We might kill you or capture you, though."

[Those don't sound different,] Dross observed.

"They're not so official." The raven squirmed to look around, and a shadow passed through the Silverlord's dress as though a shark swam in the depths of the cloth. "The Abidan *are* official, though. Predictable. So I'll tell you what's going to happen."

She pointed to the sky. "We're going to trade you for something. A high-ranking one is going to show up in a few minutes, either to protect you or punish you. We were going to get a decent deal for Threshold anyway, but now we'll get a *great* deal."

"What are you going to ask for?" Lindon asked. The more he could learn about interdimensional trades, the better.

"Before I tell you, take that blue armor off. I want to get a good look at what you're wearing underneath."

[That means she likes you,] Dross whispered. [This is good news.]

The Dreadgod armor could do nothing before fifteen Silverlords except break, buying him perhaps five seconds. Lindon dismissed it.

Revealing his black armor beneath.

The Silverlord sucked in a breath, and Lindon felt violent fluctuations from the others in the distance. "I don't sense the Way on you."

"I'm not quite part of the Abidan. I only work for them."

"Work for *whom*, exactly?"

Lindon remained quiet. There was no lie that would serve him here.

[We could try one anyway,] Dross suggested.

The Silverlord twitched strangely, like something under her skin was struggling to escape. "That's what I thought. We know whose uniform that is."

"I'm sorry this was our first official interaction," Lindon said. "If you release me, I would be happy to carry news back to my Judge."

Dross whispered into Lindon's thoughts. [They're talking. Some Presences, some Silverlords, some...*things*, like that raven there. I can't hear what they're saying, but they're saying a *lot*.]

Lindon had a guess, and Dross agreed. The mention of Ozriel had complicated things. Surely, they would be trying to decide whether to kill him as revenge against Eithan.

Or to spare him and avoid the wrath of the Reaper of Worlds.

Lindon pushed, looking to take whatever advantage he might have. "As you saw, I was not here to kill anyone. My greatest battle was against the Abidan. As a representative of the newly formed Reaper Division, I urge you to give us a chance to talk."

More unheard conversation passed between them before the woman with the raven spoke. "Whether we open dialogue or sell you off depends entirely on *who* comes for you."

She turned to look at a particular point, far from the walls of Northgate. Lindon felt a dozen other wills focus on the same spot, and he did the same.

A moment later, a blue portal erupted into being. It spread further and further, until a warship could have sailed through it. But only one man walked out.

Gadrael entered Threshold alone.

He wasn't even wearing his armor, just a nondescript outfit that reminded Lindon of a simplified sacred artist's robe. He carried no shield, and he tilted his chin up when he saw the Silverlord.

Strangely, Lindon didn't sense a connection between him and the portal, and it remained open behind him. Did he consider opening portals beneath him?

"I have come personally to negotiate the release of Threshold and this prisoner," Gadrael announced. "State your terms."

Lindon's tie to the Void Icon shook as he and Dross both processed what it meant for them that the Titan had come in person.

Ultimately, they didn't have enough information.

The Silverlord looked taken aback. "The Titan himself! How many worlds fall while the Abidan's shield rests here?"

"More by the second," Gadrael said, "so don't waste further words."

"Well enough. We want the twelve prisoners from Crush

released, three days to withdraw from Threshold with anyone willing to come with us, and your withdrawal from Sector Thirty for a period of no less than seven Sanctum days. Oh, and tell Ozriel who let his recruit leave unharmed."

"Done," the Titan said.

A force seized Lindon as though gravity had shifted to tilt him toward the Way-portal. He tried to resist, but it felt even more hopeless than fighting against lesser Titans in the depths of the Way.

The Silverlord blinked, clearly overwhelmed. "That...Do I have the word of the Court of Seven?"

"You have the word of Gadrael." A dark circlet manifested on his left arm, and he faced her down. "You should have no objections."

The Silverlord and her raven's head exchanged a look before she shrugged. "Nice doing business with you, then."

Moments later, Lindon drifted through the Way with Gadrael and the woman from the Fox Division who had escorted him earlier.

The Titan didn't so much as look at him. With each passing second, Lindon's heart tightened.

No matter how he turned the matter over in his mind, he couldn't find a satisfying chain of logic. Gadrael hadn't needed to intervene in this matter in the first place. Why show himself, send Abidan after Lindon, and then appear personally once again?

They arrived in reality once again, and Lindon was shocked to recognize where he was.

In the Grave, standing before the wide, sweeping monitors of their briefing room. Eithan stood in front of them, grinning, his white hair blowing in a breeze that Lindon was certain he'd conjured for the occasion.

"Why, if it isn't my old friend, Gadrael! I've been looking forward to your vis—"

"Be silent," the Titan ordered. "My duty ends here."

Lindon looked to Eithan, relieved but puzzled. "What did you do?"

"*I* merely watched. Gadrael took action entirely on his own."

The Titan stopped, and Lindon got the impression that he was waging a mighty war inside himself. Finally, he turned to face Lindon. *Not* Ozriel.

"I judged your actions," Gadrael said. "I found you innocent. Continue to act in such a way."

Without another word, the Judge left.

Eithan chuckled and slapped Lindon on the back. "Ah, I hate him," Eithan said fondly. "He's everything wrong with this organization. If I could get away with killing him, I would have done it centuries ago."

Dross peered at him. [I was certain you were going to say something positive.]

"If I have anything positive to say about him, here it is: He's not a hypocrite."

Lindon frowned. "He forced me to play by the rules. Why watch me after that? Why send his people after me and then bail me out?"

"Ah, but think of what he *didn't* order." Eithan raised a finger. "He didn't order you to protect anyone, did he? Just to uphold the order of the Iteration. Yet you protected them anyway, when you had no reason to. You conducted yourself like a Titan. While his own team, I'm afraid...did not."

Cirian had returned to Sanctum and submitted his report—leaving out any mention of Threshold at all—before reconvening with Vall and Pariana in the headquarters of the Second Division.

"Neither of you?" he asked.

Both women shook their heads, and the three shared a satisfied look. No one questioned them about their report, and there had been no mention of punishment.

There was the possibility that everyone was too overworked to be concerned about the holes in their story, and their violation of the rules would go unnoticed. More likely, the higher-ups had decided that the actions of Cirian and his team were justified.

Everyone on the Abidan knew that the Reapers were a bad idea, doomed to fail. The public failure of this mission so early on was just the first blow.

Steel doors hissed open, and their Judge strode in.

Everyone in the hall stood, but Gadrael's eyes were locked onto Cirian, who steeled himself. "Honored Judge!" Cirian said loudly. "I am prepared to receive my punishment!"

A gray fist struck him on the top of the head, and he was driven down into the stone floor. He could do nothing to defend himself; all his abilities were sealed. Even his Presence was locked down.

Pain and shock blinded him, but a hand gripped him by the hair and pulled him up until he was eye-to-eye with the Titan.

"Filing a false report," Gadrael recited. "Dereliction of duty. Abandonment of your post, endangerment of local populace, cooperation with Vroshir, and worst of all—*worst* of *all!*—you made me stand up for *Ozriel*."

Gadrael slammed him back down into the stone, which had absorbed so much energy from Titans over the years that it was close to unbreakable.

Cirian wasn't.

He couldn't muster his connection to the Way, nor power of any kind, and he tried to speak through a mouthful of blood and broken teeth. Vall spoke up for him, but her voice and all her limbs were sealed in an instant.

"Worsh—" Cirian spat out a tooth and corrected himself. "*Worth* my pain. We struck a blow against the Reapers."

Gadrael picked him up one-handed and pressed his own forehead into Cirian's as though to physically implant his rage. "You struck a blow *for* the Reapers, you *traitors*. What do the other Divisions think about us now? You're lucky I'm the Judge that came for you!"

Cirian struggled to stand on his own, trying to maintain his dignity. "I am not afraid of Ozriel."

Gadrael looked as though he'd never heard a dumber sentence. "Ozriel is delighted with you. If I was entirely without mercy, I would hand you over to Suriel."

Without a gesture or external indication of any kind, the Titan released the seal on Cirian's Presence.

The cool, familiar voice in his head sounded hesitant. [We may have...miscalculated.]

Cirian didn't understand it. He was no Hound, but based on his comprehension of the Court's attitude toward Ozriel—which, admittedly, came only from reports and rumors—the other Judges should have tacitly approved of his actions. If he were punished, it should have been a slap on the wrist.

He'd even run it past his Presence. They were capable of misinterpreting or misunderstanding information, but to read the situation this badly...

[My only guess is that someone manipulated our reading,] his Presence suggested. [Even perhaps going so far as to conceal or alter key information about the Reapers in the Abidan database.]

Who could...

Cirian didn't even finish his own thought.

Only a Judge had the authority to do such a thing, not to mention the skill to do it without getting caught. Worse, he hadn't *made* them do anything. He'd just...temporarily removed some signs that may have warned them against it.

Cirian spat out some more blood to verbalize his theory. "Judge. I believe Ozriel may have manipulated our predictions."

Gadrael finally released Cirian's hair and let him fall to the ground again. "Next time, before you consult the Way, consult your own brain. Now I am obligated to make an example of you."

The Judge raised his voice. "A team of ours has violated the law. Rather than mete punishment myself, I have found it appropriate to leave justice in the hands of the...wounded party."

The steel door hissed open once again, and a man in black armor strode in. For the first time, with his powers sealed, Cirian realized how *big* the Reaper was.

"Thank you, honored Judge," Wei Shi Lindon said. "Hello, Cirian. We meet again."

Daughter of Dread

INFORMATION REQUESTED: THE STATUS OF WEI SHI KELSA.
REPORT LOCATION: AFTER THE EVENTS OF *WAYBOUND*.
AUTHORIZATION CONFIRMED.
BEGINNING REPORT...

THE WEI CLAN'S NEW FIRST ELDER WAS THE SISTER OF THE previous Patriarch, and she looked the part. A tall old woman with a mane of gray hair, she had a hearty build that undercut her age.

"The Kazan and Li clans aren't even among the top ten families in Sacred Valley anymore," she said. "They're irrelevant and they know it, which is what leads to these requests. Don't you think so, Kelsa?"

She and the other nine clan elders turned to Kelsa, waiting humbly for her opinion.

Kelsa pushed down her annoyance. She didn't have the experience, the skill, or the power to sit at the table. The only reason she wasn't seated at the head was because of her own insistence.

"First Elder, I believe we should treat the Li and Kazan graciously," Kelsa said. "Not because of what they deserve, but in recognition of our shared history."

Though the situation irritated her, Kelsa tried not to express it much around the elders. Complaining was disrespectful.

The First Elder smiled at her proudly. "Well said, girl. We'll allow them to hold on to a measure of their old territory, but of course, a marriage alliance is out of the question."

"Why should it be?" the Fifth Elder shot back. "In but a few generations, the only name left could be the Wei clan! It is both the perfect revenge and the means to treat our rivals *graciously,* as young Kelsa accurately pointed out."

The First Elder slashed her hand. "How do they deserve to join our bloodline? Our clan has much better options!"

"They're *asking* for this, Daira! They are *begging* us to take over the Valley! How could we say no?"

If Kelsa had but a little less self-control, she would have interjected. 'Taking over the Valley' was a laughable idea. The remaining factions from the original Sacred Valley were little more than a pitiful half-formed Remnant compared to outsiders who had settled in. The elders were fighting over the most worthless scraps while pretending that was the entire feast.

Kelsa glanced over to her bodyguard, who stood rigidly to the right of her seat. "You don't have to stay for this," she told him.

"I am honored to be here, Little Sister," said the Herald of the Silent Servants.

He was a sword artist with light brown skin and close-cropped black hair, but his eyes were a white bright enough to match the halo that hung over his head. He wore loose-fitting clothes that were simpler than traditional sacred artist's robes, with a cloth covering his mouth and nose, and he carried no physical weapon.

He didn't need one. Sages and Heralds were the strongest power left in the world, and he could rule Sacred Valley if he wanted to.

Well, he could rule somewhere the *size* of Sacred Valley. If he tried to take over, half of the other powerhouses remaining in the world would join forces to beat him to death. All because it was Lindon's homeland.

Kelsa had kept her side conversation quiet, but the elders all stopped talking when they heard the Herald speak. They even lowered their heads.

"Does the honored Herald of Silence have any advice to guide us?" the First Elder asked humbly.

They had been waiting for their chance to ask.

The Herald, Balari, waved a hand. "As always, I'm only here in case Little Sister needs my assistance. Until then, treat me as air."

Kelsa was confident that, if the elders weren't her relatives, the Herald wouldn't have acknowledged them at all.

"I'm Lindon's *older* sister," Kelsa pointed out, "and isn't the Silent Sage your little sister?" The Dreadgod cults couldn't agree on what to call her, so *'Little Sister'* was their latest attempt.

"Would you prefer I call you Big Sister?" Balari asked. That *should* have been a joke, in a world that made sense, but Kelsa was certain that he would change his mode of address if she asked him.

"No!" she snapped, then caught herself. "Apologies."

A freshly advanced Truegold had just barked at a Herald. Kelsa wondered how many Golds had lost their lives for less, but Balari only nodded. "If you have any wishes, call on me."

Then he returned to his position at her side.

With that concluded, the elders bowed to the Herald and then resumed their discussion.

The meeting lasted another hour and Kelsa contributed nothing, but the elders continued to seek her perspective anyway.

As she strode out of the Wei clan hall of elders—which was five times its previous size and made of materials fifty times more valuable—she found Redmoon Hall's Kahn Mala waiting for her with a sizeable entourage and a *carriage*.

"Thank you for your vigilance, Herald," Kahn Mala said. "We'll take her the rest of the way." The woman's Blood Shadow, in the shape of a cobra, dipped its head along with her.

The Silent King's former cult leader managed to radiate superiority without changing his demeanor whatsoever. "It's almost time for her training, Archlady. You may return when we're finished."

"I promised Redmoon Hall I'd train with them today," Kelsa said. "Apologies, I forgot to inform you."

Balari gave her a gentle smile through his mask. "Don't worry, Little Sister, they'll understand. I'm sure they'd be happy to train you some other time."

"Of course," Kahn Mala agreed reflexively.

"I made a promise," Kelsa insisted.

He leaned closer and lowered his voice, though the Archlady could have heard him from down the street. "They're fine sacred artists, I'm sure, but they don't know what to teach you. You're practically on my own Path. It's best not to take inferior training just to preserve their feelings."

Kelsa had trained with the Servants before, and receiving teaching from the Sage and Herald of Silence was indeed a better fit for her Path of the White Fox. But she was only a Truegold. The gulf between her and Archlord was so great that the difference in Paths wasn't even close to relevant yet.

If she knew that, Balari was far more aware, but still he insisted. At first, she'd thought Path compatibility was more important than she realized. But as more of the powerful figures around Sacred Valley competed for her attention, she'd come to realize that everyone simply saw teaching her as a badge of honor.

Kelsa pressed her fists together. "Gratitude, but I gave my word."

The Herald gave her a proud look as though that was what he'd wanted to hear all along. "You have a firm will, Little Sister. You will make a fine Sage, and not too long from now, I think. Train her well, Redmoon."

He returned Kelsa's salute and then vanished in a flash of white light.

Kahn Mala gestured, and the door to the carriage flew open. She indicated the plush red interior with a bow. "After you, Matriarch."

"That's worse than Little Sister!" Kelsa blurted. "And I don't need a carriage."

"This was my attempt to avoid what happened last time, Daughter."

Kelsa closed her eyes. "Daughter?"

"Daughter of Dread," Kahn Mala said. "It wasn't my favorite choice, but the Stormcallers like it."

The noise of the crowd around her was growing louder, and Kelsa opened her eyes. The red-robed entourage from Redmoon had formed a barrier around her, blocking the crowd.

A crowd which pushed against one another and called, trying to get her attention.

Above them, the blue-and-orange banners of the Twin Star Sect flew over the entire Wei territory, outnumbering even the purple-and-white symbols of the Wei clan itself. Most of those looking for a glimpse of Kelsa wore at least a badge of the sect.

Last time, Kelsa had been caught by such a mob after she'd left her bodyguard behind, and Redmoon Lords had been forced to haul her out. People had almost been hurt, but Kelsa had convinced herself that it wouldn't happen again.

With disappointment but without further complaint, Kelsa climbed into the carriage.

As soon as the door shut, a script activated, and the carriage rose into the air. Instead of carrying them on a cloud, the vehicle had sprouted wings of blood and flew them to their destination as though they were nestled in the heart of a giant bat.

Kelsa felt little motion. Scripts and constructs compensated for the wingbeats, so the flight was totally smooth for the passengers.

"You shouldn't trust the Silent Servants," Kahn Mala said, as soon as she was safe behind the isolation of the carriage. "They are well-known spies and liars."

"So is the Wei clan."

"You're outclassed. Without a single dream technique, the Herald could manipulate the people around you as he wished. Especially your elders." Kahn Mala clicked her tongue. "Fools, one and all. You should replace them."

Kelsa gave her a flat look. "I don't have the authority to replace anyone. And I didn't mean I have spies and liars of my own to *protect* me, I meant that I also grew up in a family with a reputation for underhanded tactics. Do you really think Balari is out to hurt me?"

"Oh no, nothing like that. He wants to fill your life with Silent Servants until he and his sister are the only ones you trust. And when Lindon returns for a visit, you will tell him what a wonderful job the Herald has done for you."

Kahn Mala's voice was filled with bitterness, and she watched a crimson wing beat out the window with a look Kelsa didn't know enough to read.

"We don't know if Lindon *can* come back," Kelsa pointed out. "If that's what's holding your loyalty, I'd rather you leave me now than betray me later."

That had perhaps been a foolish thing to say, but Kelsa always preferred to handle difficult topics directly. The Wei clan may have been accomplished liars, but Kelsa found truth the more reliable sword.

Kahn Mala untied her hair from its tight tail, letting her gray-black hair loose with a sigh of relief. "You're a refreshing breeze, Daughter. All day, I have to flog Lords and Ladies until I get the truth out of them."

"Can't you call me Kelsa?"

"I won't. You have a position, so you need a title. And I can assure you, Your Highness, that you won't face betrayal in my generation."

Kahn Mala gave a little smile that let Kelsa know her latest title was a joke, but Kelsa didn't enjoy it.

She leaned closer to the Archlady. "And would a traitor tell me to watch for betrayal?"

"Yes, actually. That's a common tactic. If you encourage paranoia, you can often cause fingers to point at anyone other than you. But that's beside the point."

Kahn Mala's Blood Shadow lifted its head, and she scratched behind its hood absently. "Your brother *can* come back, everyone knows it, and he left behind powerful allies. Even those who might have considered themselves his enemies are allies now. The first person to act against you would find all the world against them."

Kelsa rested her head in her hands.

Despite the Archlady's choice of words, people weren't afraid to be *her* enemy. Kelsa hadn't done anything.

Kelsa *couldn't* do anything.

"I've heard some of my peers—and your own parents—remind you of the privilege of your position," Kahn Mala said. "I myself grow jealous of you, from time to time. My own brother died in prison decades ago."

"My apologies."

"Keep them. He was all but a stranger to me, and as far as I heard, he earned his own fate. But were I in your position, I doubt I would be grateful either. To be given endless resources, honor, and authority, but knowing you didn't earn such respect...it must be stifling."

Kelsa wiped her face and mastered herself. "Gratitude. I do not deserve to complain, and I will not do so in the future."

"I'm not criticizing you." The Archlady waved a hand. "It's good to remember that everyone in a Dreadgod cult came from humble beginnings, but that doesn't mean you're obligated to enjoy your position. May I offer you one piece of advice, from a sacred artist with many more years than your own?"

Kelsa felt that Kahn Mala had been quite free with advice already, but she nodded respectfully. "I would be grateful, Archlady."

"If you can't take pride in how you earned your advantages, take pride in what you do with them." Kahn Mala's cobra curled up on her lap, and she looked on it with sadness. "You can still do the world good, even with power you don't deserve."

Kelsa left her badge, her Wei clan robes, and anything with the Twin Star sect emblem in her bedroom. She dressed in a plain gray sacred artist's robe, one that could be found anywhere, and she checked her void key and a handful of the emergency protections that Lindon had prepared for her.

Then she ran away.

She would never have been able to do so on her own. Sages, Heralds, Lords, and Ladies with dozens of different Paths were alert to her safety. She had two advantages, one much greater than the other.

The lesser advantage was her own weakness. Truegolds weren't *common*, but they weren't strong enough to stand out in the perception of any real expert looking for her.

The greater advantage, by far, was created by Lindon.

As Kelsa left her room in her house on Mount Samara—their family had six houses now, all around the Valley, for when they needed to visit various factions—she activated two constructs.

A decoy in her bed fed on White Fox madra. It generated a convincing illusion of herself sleeping while radiating enough spiritual energy to fool perception. A Sage would see through it with a direct examination, but not if they were given no reason to look.

The other construct came to life on her belt, projecting an advanced version of the Fox Mirror. It turned her completely invisible, radiated dream aura that subtly directed attention away from her, and concealed her spiritual presence.

Knowing Lindon, it probably had fifteen other features too.

She walked out of the house, past the guards, and slipped through the perceptions of an unknown number of other sacred artists. Once she was far away, she activated a purple Thousand-Mile Cloud—those were common enough to avoid scrutiny—and flew deeper into Sacred Valley.

Kahn Mala advised Kelsa to earn her position by using it for good, but Kelsa had made up her mind. That wasn't enough, not on its own.

She *had* to push herself, outside of sparring partners who were afraid to hurt her and teachers who would stop the lessons if she ordered them to. How was she supposed to find her Underlord revelation if she didn't push herself? Real sacred artists didn't grow by staying under protection their whole lives.

Lindon hadn't done that, Yerin hadn't done that, Orthos hadn't done that.

Jai Long hadn't done it either.

That thought was still painful, though less so than it had once been. The point was, *none* of the people who encouraged her to use her resources, be grateful for them, accept them, and not risk herself had ever actually been in her position.

Kelsa had fought before. She'd clawed and scraped to feed her father and to free her mother. She'd worked under the shadow of a powerful school for years. It had been miserable, but still an accomplishment she could be proud of.

She wasn't helpless. She could fight, as everyone else had.

Kelsa flew deeper into what had once been the wilderness of Sacred Valley before she found what she'd been after.

A massive tent with many peaks had been erected across one of the many clearings left by the Second Dread War. The fabric of the tent was black, which would have made it hard to spot in the darkness if not for the brightly shining segments of pink, purple, blue, and white.

Lights streaked into the air, lanterns blazed in many colors, and collared Remnants spun around the tent to attract the eye. Music blared over the noise of a crowd, which bustled despite the late hour.

"And he's down!" a voice cried from below. *"Sacred artists, we have another victory for the Wooden Soldier!"*

A glowing sign nearby displayed the characters for 'Black Star Troupe.'

Kelsa didn't like the name.

She landed her cloud nearby, and walked up to a booth near the tent. She'd already done her research, conducting some interviews quietly, and knew exactly what to do.

A bored-looking man fiddled with a list of names and yawned as she approached. He wore a fluffy white cloud around his neck like a scarf, which Kelsa took to be his Goldsign.

Better than her own. Even as she thought about it, her tail of purple-white fire drooped as though she'd hurt its feelings.

"Oh, Truegold?" The man didn't seem unduly impressed, though he was only a Highgold himself, but he *did* sit up a little straighter as Kelsa approached. "When do you want to fight?"

"Tonight."

He scratched at stubble on his cheek as he flipped through some pages. "We can get you a fight tonight, but only one, and you won't enjoy it. You're up against the Bloody Thorn."

Kelsa didn't know who that was, and the man didn't seem interested in explaining. But she wouldn't just sign up without asking.

"And who is that?"

"On a sixteen-fight winning streak, that's who she is. She's been a Truegold for years now, but she must have had some kind of breakthrough, because she's clearing out her opponents. Her longest fight was thirty seconds. Crowds love her, though."

From inside the tent, the crowd roared again. He pointed to the noise as though it proved his point.

"Is she fighting now?" Kelsa asked. "She's allowed to fight twice in one night?"

"Three times. Normally you have to win before you can sign up for another one, but..." He shrugged. "She's gonna win. Five mid-grade scales for the fee, but we trade them up to high-grade if you win."

Kelsa was still getting used to the currency of the outside world, especially since it seemed every culture graded scales differently. That seemed like a steep entry fee, since you could buy a Lowgold construct for that, but high-grade scales had to be made by an Underlord.

At least, she thought so. In nations like the Blackflame Empire,

Overlord scales had once been the highest grade anyone could make, but there were so many high-level experts in Sacred Valley that the value had been skewed.

Trying not to show her ignorance, she pulled out some purple dream-aspect coins from her pocket and placed them on a scripted plate. Three lights lit up—out of five, which indicated a mid-grade scale.

The man swept them off without comment, which indicated she'd done everything correctly. "Name?" he asked.

Kelsa had prepared for this part. "The White Fox," she said.

"Pick another name." She was stumped by that, and he scratched his head with the back of his pen. "Too many fighters on the Path of the White Fox. New Lowgolds, testing their powers. We've had three White Foxes so far, and if I didn't put a stop to it, we'd have had ten more."

Kelsa's mind raced. She hadn't bothered to come up with a backup alias; she'd been proud of 'the White Fox' precisely *because* there were so many people who could have used that name.

And she certainly didn't want to fight under the name 'Little Sister.'

The crowd roared again, and the man pointed his pen toward the noise. "That's the end of her fight. If you want to see Bloody Thorn in action, you should get in there. So, name?"

Kelsa hated the words that came out of her mouth even as she spoke them. "Is Daughter of Dread taken?"

"Nope, not taken." He scribbled it down. "You better be confident in yourself with a name like that, though. Half the crowd comes from the Dreadgod cults and the other half came here to escape the

Dreadgods, so either of them might decide to take a chunk out of you if you can't handle it."

"Pardon, I wasn't thinking," Kelsa said. "I'll come up with something else."

The crowd cheered again and the man reached out of his booth to shove her closer to the entrance. "We'll change it later. Get in there before she ends the match."

Inside the huge tent, wooden stands held sacred artists of all description. Most were Lowgold or Highgold, but there were quite a few Jades—*young* Jades, only teenagers—and a handful of Truegolds. None were separated by advancement level, packed shoulder-to-shoulder and shouting.

Signs hanging over the crowd said, 'No Techniques.'

All the seats were arranged around a lowered pit, where two sacred artists paraded themselves around a circle of sand.

One was a tall man with the sleeves torn off his robes to show off his Goldsigns: obsidian spikes running down his arms. His mask was made from the same material and worked to resemble a bear's face.

The second was a short woman practically lost within her costume. It was a long, red dress with a stiff hood that surrounded almost her entire head. Her "mask" was just a strip of white cloth across her mouth, leaving beady eyes bare.

Kelsa couldn't see her Goldsign, but finger-sized thorns were worked into her dress every place there was an opportunity.

She didn't have much trouble deciding which of them was Bloody Thorn.

The announcer was currently talking up the challenger, but Kelsa thought back to the dream tablets she'd seen of the Uncrowned

King tournament. This was a distant replica, almost a mockery, like children playing at real battle.

A Truegold judge, an old man with a wild beard, stepped between them and allowed the fighters to take their positions.

The man in the bear mask drew two short spears. The Bloody Thorn covered her hidden mouth with a hand and made a show of laughing, still holding no weapon.

"Fight!" the judge shouted.

He leaped back.

The fight ended.

Kelsa felt almost nothing, not even the technique Bloody Thorn used. All Kelsa could tell was that the bear-masked man had attacked and Bloody Thorn had gestured as though to use a technique. Then he'd fallen.

A moment later, she realized that the woman in red had thrown something. A few thin spines stuck out of her opponent's chest, and he groaned as a couple of Lowgolds carted him off.

The crowd went crazy, drowning out the announcer, but Kelsa thought back to what she'd sensed. Bloody Thorn *must* have done something, at least an Enforcer technique, but it hadn't been obvious. The woman must have spectacular veils.

Someone grabbed her arm, and she whirled with fist raised.

A woman Kelsa had never seen before looked annoyed. "Daughter of Dread? Let's go, it's showtime."

"Wait, it's my turn? I just got here!"

"Thorn works fast." The woman dragged Kelsa behind the stands and down a short flight of stairs. "Put on your mask. You have a weapon?"

Kelsa stumbled along. "I thought I was going to get to change my name!"

"Too late. Mask, weapon, let's go."

Kelsa focused on her breathing technique, centering her emotions, and Forged a mask.

She hadn't been trained as a Forger until Orthos, but she found she had a talent for it. The Fox Mirror was a highly versatile technique, allowing her to craft fragile illusions. Some things were easier to create than others, and experts in the technique usually focused on certain categories. Her own mother focused on Forging clothing.

Kelsa wasn't good enough to mimic realistic flowing of cloth, but she could at least make a rigid white mask that somewhat resembled a fox.

"I have my own weapon," she said, once the mask was settled on her face.

"Fine, now get in there."

The woman opened a door and shoved Kelsa onto the sand.

Down in the heart of the arena, the crowd was much louder. Above her, the announcer's voice blared out from a construct: *"The challenger! A mysterious rookie from far-off lands, with some tricks you'll have to see to believe! Here to teach the Bloody Thorn a lesson, we have the Daughter of Dread!"*

Kelsa didn't know where the announcer got any of that, since the man taking her registration hadn't asked her any questions and most of it was wrong.

At the sound of her name, many in the crowd jeered. Some threw food in her direction, though it bounced off a protective shield of wind aura scripted into the stands. Some still clapped and shouted, either cheering for her or looking forward to seeing her get beaten by the Bloody Thorn.

As Kelsa walked across the sand, she felt the tension rise and her spirit lock onto her opponent. This wasn't a fight to the death, but it *felt* like one.

Given that this territory was under the supervision of the Twin Star sect, the Troupe wasn't allowed to let their fighters die. They could be severely injured, even to the point of losing their sacred arts, but not killed.

That was one of the things Kelsa *had* accomplished.

"And, of course, we have our returning champion: the Bloody Thorn!" The cheers were deafening. *"She doesn't need an introduction, she just needs blood!"*

The crowd loved that one, and Bloody Thorn seemed to as well. She held up both hands, each with a fistful of needles, and flashed them to the bystanders.

"Blink and you'll miss it, ladies and gentlemen, as Bloody Thorn shows you what a real *fight looks like! This is what the Twin Star sect doesn't want you to see, and if Twin Star doesn't give it to you, where do you go?"*

"Black Star!" the crowd shouted back.

"You know it! Fighters, take your places!"

That was why Kelsa didn't like the name of the Troupe. It felt a little too personal. But at least this was somewhere she could go outside her normal ring of protection.

Kelsa took a stance as though to draw a sword, though nothing could be seen at her waist.

"Fight!"

As the Bloody Thorn dismissively threw a fistful of needles, Kelsa drew her invisible sword.

A combination of White Fox madra with a touch of wind kept the blade unseen as she swept it through the air. The gust from the strike was magnified and carried a few purple sparks as it brushed aside the needles.

Bloody Thorn was positioned casually, as though she'd expected to finish Kelsa with the first attack, but she didn't hesitate to follow up when it didn't work. Her needles rose from the ground of their own accord, moving to aim for Kelsa again, and the Thorn tossed out another handful.

Kelsa used the Foxtail, an Enforcer technique from the Path of the White Fox. Madra blurred her form, making her hard to perceive as she moved; from the opponent's perspective, Kelsa's movements would look wavy and uncertain, her range hard to grasp. Combined with an invisible sword, she would be almost impossible to read.

Bloody Thorn didn't seem interested in trying to anticipate her anyway. Instead, she surrounded Kelsa with a ring of floating needles. Kelsa rushed forward to close the distance, striking needles from the air as she ran. Her tail of purple fire even flicked one down of its own accord, so at least it was good for something.

As an experienced arena fighter and a Truegold, the Thorn should have plenty of strength for a physical clash, but she continued to maintain her distance and harass Kelsa with needles. The crowd laughed and cheered, and Kelsa suspected the Thorn was prolonging the match for their enjoyment.

Kelsa didn't mind. The longer the fight went, the longer her illusions had to work. As she chased the Bloody Thorn around the arena, Foxtail covering her movements and invisible sword cutting needles from the air, she molded aura around the Thorn's mind.

The Fox Dream was a difficult technique to master, as all sacred artists had some level of resistance to mental manipulation. Their aura was their own, and the more powerful their spirit, the stronger their defenses.

Effectiveness, therefore, was in subtlety. It was hard to get full illusions to take hold, but small details could leak through.

Kelsa pushed the illusion of movement at the corner of the eye. That was all. A quick flutter of white robes, a glimpse of purple Foxfire.

Thorn was keeping her madra tightly controlled, reinforcing her spiritual defense, but even that would wear down her effectiveness in combat. Kelsa's combat style was all about confusion, distraction, and erosion.

She was confident in winning eventually, relying on her own skill.

Until the Thorn released a halo of blue-white madra from around her head, breaking through Kelsa's Ruler technique.

The woman in red rushed forward, driving a glowing palm toward Kelsa's core. Kelsa's shock almost allowed it to land.

Immediately, she knew why she'd had trouble sensing the aspects of the Bloody Thorn's madra. She wasn't a blood artist at all. She used pure madra.

Thorn struck at Kelsa with the Empty Palm technique.

On long-trained instinct, Kelsa blocked the attack with her free hand and swept her sword down. She wouldn't kill the woman, and there were protective scripts in place to help with that, but this was her chance to win.

Then Bloody Thorn switched cores.

Yellow earth madra flooded through her crimson dress, stiffening the spines worked into it and making it as rigid as a suit of armor. Kelsa's sword bounced off, and the Thorn reached out with a new Ruler technique.

Shining gold, her needles rushed inward at Kelsa.

Kelsa was caught so off-guard that the match should have ended there. But the invisible sword wasn't her only weapon.

Before he'd ascended, Lindon had given into her requests and made weapons for her. Not just one.

At the touch of her spirit, a bracer on her forearm expanded into a small buckler shield. In a flash of white and purple, it created a reinforced Fox Mirror, and a cloud exploded around her as though Kelsa had dropped a smoke bomb.

In reality, the technique released a Forged shield covered in the illusion of smoke, but it served as both a defense and a distraction. Being made primarily of White Fox madra, the shield wouldn't block anything but the weakest attacks, but it was enough to throw off the Thorn's needles and give Kelsa enough room to dodge.

One needle stabbed into her shoulder and another slashed across one leg, but she avoided the rest. The Bloody Thorn, still within arm's reach, had switched back to her pure core. No doubt she intended to disperse Kelsa's illusion, but that left her vulnerable.

She pulled her third weapon: an awl of smooth ivory. It was nothing but a polished hilt and a thick metal spike meant to penetrate armor, but Lindon had designed it to cover for the Path of the White Fox's lack of offensive power.

The awl punched straight through the Bloody Thorn's Enforced robe, though the clothing was so thick that it only scratched her skin.

As soon as it did, though, its binding activated.

Kelsa's Fox Dream connected, her illusion suddenly penetrating the Bloody Thorn's defenses. The woman's head jerked left as she was distracted, and Kelsa put an invisible sword to her throat.

Panting, Kelsa dismissed her illusions so the judges and the crowd could see clearly. "I win," she said.

A trumpet blared, and the announcer agreed with her. *"Victory to the Daughter of Dread! The Bloody Thorn's winning streak comes crashing down...and we learned something about her today, didn't we, folks?"*

Kelsa's head was light and spinning after expending so much madra so fast, her madra channels sore and her core almost empty. But her Skyhunter Iron body meant her senses were still sharp.

The crowd muttered unhappily, their volume slowly growing in clear anger.

Were they *that* upset that she'd defeated their champion? Kelsa prepared her madra to activate the contingency plan on her belt.

The Bloody Thorn pushed up to her feet and spread her hands. "Calm yourselves, I can explain!" she called.

Food flew from the stands, and the scripts didn't stop it this time. It rained down on the arena, but the trash wasn't aimed at Kelsa. They were throwing food at the Bloody Thorn.

Kelsa was astonished. In her research, none of the other losers had faced such anger from the crowd. Some of them were even preparing techniques.

"It was fairly fought!" the Thorn shouted. "You know I would never hold back!"

The woman who had ushered Kelsa into the arena grabbed her arm and pulled her backwards. "Let's go get your winnings."

Kelsa allowed herself to be hauled away, though she had no intention of leaving the arena itself before she had a chance to talk to the Bloody Thorn. "I thought they liked her."

"This is Thorn's own fault," the woman said. "She made a big show of getting everyone to bet on her tonight, and now it looks like she threw the fight. They lost a lot of money betting on her."

Kelsa started to pull off her mask, but thought better of it and left it on. "She didn't throw. I beat her."

"You and I know that, and anyone with enough experience in combat can tell. But for the average Lowgold..." They reached the doorway out of the arena, and the woman pulled it open. "...You know what your techniques look like, right?"

Kelsa pictured how the fight must have looked from the outside.

She had chased Bloody Thorn around for a while, dodging needles, then—after the fight closed—a puff of smoke had covered everything until the crowd saw Thorn kneeling with Kelsa's invisible sword at her throat.

For people used to seeing Thorn win easily and quickly, it might seem like a scam.

Kelsa turned away from the door. "I'll explain."

The woman grabbed her arm again. "And how would that help? Get in here." Once they were inside the waiting room, she put hands on her hips and sighed at Kelsa. "These aren't genius warriors and legendary experts, okay? If these people had a clan or a sect to lean on, they wouldn't be here. They're angry, suspicious, frustrated, and looking for somebody to take it out on."

The people in the audience were certainly not what Kelsa would call skilled sacred artists, and everyone for hundreds of miles had lost something to the Dreadgods.

How would she feel, if she had been left without her home and no one to rely on? They were here watching fights *because* they wanted an outlet for those frustrations, and Bloody Thorn had given them a target.

A moment later, the door slammed open, and Thorn rushed through. She shut the door behind her and heaved a breath. "Get me out the back," she demanded.

The arena employee jerked her head toward Kelsa. "I'm seeing to the winner. You know where the back door is."

"If I push through the crowd alone, they'll tear me apart."

"Security will handle it."

"Come with me," Kelsa said. "We'll be safer together."

Thorn pulled her mask down and mopped at her sweaty face with a sleeve. "You really want to get me killed, don't you? If we walk out of here hand-in-hand, they'll *know* I threw the match."

Kelsa leaned closer and lowered her voice; the arena employee might still hear her, but anyone eavesdropping wouldn't. "I can call help from our sect."

"No!" Thorn shoved her away. "I'd rather face this crowd than my teachers. I told them I'd stop fighting here."

"I can put in a good word for you. Your safety is more important."

Thorn pushed past her. "I'm taking my chances."

Still conflicted, Kelsa let her go. Bloody Thorn knew this place better than Kelsa did, and Kelsa had enough information to track her down in the Twin Star sect. Clearly, she had trained in the Path of Twin Stars, so Kelsa would be able to find her.

Irritated, the employee grabbed a handful of Kelsa's robes and threw her out a few seconds after Thorn left. It didn't take long for Kelsa to receive her winnings—scales that she'd earned herself, rather than received as an allowance from the sect.

Some of the audience glared at her, suspicious that she'd helped Bloody Thorn cheat, but a few others gave her respectful nods or clapped her on the shoulder in congratulations. The angry ones were focused elsewhere.

Even without her illusion techniques, Kelsa found it easy to sneak away. Her wounds ached, though they didn't bleed much, and her spiritual exhaustion weighed on her.

The crowd's reaction had dampened her excitement from winning. As she flew away on her Thousand-Mile Cloud, she mulled it over.

She had her perception restricted as she flew, so only the enhanced senses of her Skyhunter Iron body caught her attention. Deep in the forest near the Black Star Troupe came a flash of yellow light.

Kelsa extended her spiritual perception. As she suspected, Bloody Thorn was fighting. Three or four Truegolds and a smattering of Highgolds and Lowgolds surrounded her, all on a variety of Paths.

Without hesitation, Kelsa directed her Cloud toward the battle.

She'd already veiled herself, and she put the Cloud down in the shadowed woods outside the battle. Her plan was clear. The Path of the White Fox had a huge advantage in the darkness of the nighttime forest, even with the glow of Samara's ring overhead.

They'd lost that light for a while. It had even changed color and crackled with lightning, until Lindon rebuilt it.

It was strange, sneaking around in illumination her little brother had created to outshine the moon. And the moon, she realized, had also been marked by him. Scarred in one of Lindon's battles.

How could she compete with that?

Kelsa banished distracting thoughts of Lindon from her mind as she focused on the danger in front of her. She crept from shadow to shadow, covering herself in illusions and taking out the enemies. She felt the old spike of terror, adrenaline, and combat focus. This was how she'd fought against the Schools, and she was far stronger now.

Though her weapons, training, and resources had been gifted to her, she could prove herself worthy of them. In real battle, she would thrive.

Before she attacked even the first person, Bloody Thorn took a hammer-blow to the side.

The woman didn't have time to switch to her earth core, so she crumpled under the strike, flying into a nearby tree. The wood of the tree crunched, and a scream was squeezed out of Thorn's lungs.

Enemies pounced on her, and Kelsa had a moment of clarity.

If she leaned only on her own power, a member of the Twin Star sect was going to die.

Kelsa tapped into her void key, withdrawing a small globe and crushing it instantly.

Pure madra exploded over the clearing. *Lindon's* pure madra.

The Hollow Domain washed out every instance of the sacred arts for a hundred yards. He'd limited the power of the technique so it didn't injure Kelsa's soul, but any nearby Remnants were probably dead.

All the sacred artists involved in the attack found themselves temporarily powerless. Strikes that would have killed the helpless Bloody Thorn fell with no power or missed entirely, their users thrown off by their sudden lack of strength.

Kelsa dashed closer, shoving a man aside to stand over Bloody Thorn. Most of the attackers had backed off at the sudden surge of pure madra, looking around warily for the ambush and waiting for their sacred arts to return.

Thorn spat out a mouthful of blood and pushed herself to her knees. "I'll take that help now."

Thanks to a scripted ward key at her belt, Kelsa was less affected by the Hollow Domain than anyone else. She readied the trickle of her madra, but didn't use a technique, instead standing straight and addressing the others.

"This is a member of the Twin Star sect," Kelsa called. "Leave now, and you won't face punishment."

Several spiritual perceptions stretched out warily as the Golds in the crowd recovered their sacred arts.

"You don't have an Underlord nearby, do you?" Thorn asked. She pulled out another fist of needles.

"No." Kelsa didn't keep her voice down.

Three Truegolds and a couple of Highgolds leapt at her. If she'd been in top condition, it would have still been a challenge to escape, but she might have managed it.

Kelsa was far from her best condition, but she also had no need to run.

She'd used Lindon's madra. Without a veil.

All the Golds attacking her froze in midair. In her Copper sight, she saw aura draw tight around them like chains of many colors.

She *didn't* see the technique hiding the Silent Herald before it dropped. Balari stepped out from nowhere as though leaving a curtain, sword bare in his hand and white halo shining in the night.

"Children, children," he chided. "I see you are in need of *instruction*."

The far-off enemies scrambled to run, but rings of white light surrounded their heads and they threw themselves to the ground instead.

"No need to kill them," Kelsa said quickly.

The Herald widened his eyes in surprise. "Oh, we don't work like the Phoenix cult. Today's enemy is tomorrow's friend. Isn't that right?"

He addressed the last sentence to the Truegold man who had been closest to attacking Kelsa. The man shuddered and didn't speak.

Bloody Thorn had knelt as soon as Balari appeared, but she looked to Kelsa in shock. "Wait, are you...the Void Sage's sister?"

"Apologies," Kelsa said. She bowed to Thorn. "I did not intend to put you in danger."

"No, you pulled me out. You have my gratitude, Daughter of Dread." She bowed deeply.

Kelsa's eye twitched at the title, but she let it pass. "My training is lacking. If I were stronger, I could have rescued you on my own."

"You did," Thorn said.

Kelsa thought it was mockery, but there was no mockery in the other woman's words.

Around the trees, the Silent Herald was rounding up Kelsa's attackers and using Ruler techniques so deep and complex that Kelsa couldn't comprehend the first part of them. She'd need to have someone else check them to make sure he wasn't completely brainwashing these people.

She had been able to intervene thanks to the gifts of others. Whether she'd earned them or not, they had saved a life.

"Gratitude," Kelsa said. To Balari, to Bloody Thorn, and most of all to her brother.

A silver meteor crashed down from the sky, blowing apart a chunk of the nearby trees.

[Herald threat detected,] came a copy of Dross' voice, and the meteor unfolded into a gleaming figure of quicksilver with a dozen bladed arms. [Deploying Herald countermeasure: Fleshripper Senior.]

Kelsa's gratitude faded.

Lindon could have left her without *quite* so much help.

The Return of the Prince

Information requested: the ultimate fate of Seishen Daji, Riyusai Meira, and the Seishen Kingdom.
Report Location: After the events of *Waybound*.
Context: In Cradle's eighth volume, *Wintersteel*, Prince Daji of the Seishen Kingdom was recruited by Monarch Reigan Shen to aid an assassination attempt against Akura Mercy and Pride. He was imprisoned for this crime in the ninth volume, *Bloodline*, and has been in the care of the Akura clan ever since.
Authorization confirmed.
Beginning report...

Meira had never imagined that Daji was still alive until a silver-and-purple owl flew into her window and told her so.

Meira had been cycling in the center of a number of life-aspect natural treasures; trees of jade, blossoming flowers, and tiny golems of green syrup. Her training "room" was an open circle of forest scripted to make the life aura as strong as possible, so an owl wasn't at all out of place.

But its words were.

"Underlady Riyusai Meira," the owl said, in the cool voice of the Sage of the Silver Heart. "It has come to the attention of the Akura clan that the Seishen Kingdom has no further heirs. In one hour, you will receive the surviving heir to the royal family, Seishen Daji. Prepare to receive him."

Meira was so stunned that she lost control of her cycling technique. Life surged chaotically around her, fauna stirring in the undergrowth and plants growing visibly.

"He's alive?" It was the only thing she could say.

The owl gave her a flat stare. "It is better to consider that the traitor is executed. The man we return to you has little in common with his former self."

Meira remembered her own time interrogated by the Akura clan. They'd known she wasn't involved in the attempted assassination of Akura Mercy and Pride, and even so, she still had nightmares of the absolute darkness in which they'd kept her.

She shuddered at what must have been done to Daji, the truly guilty party, but she still remembered her manners in facing a Sage.

Meira folded her knees beneath her and bowed until her forehead touched the grass. "The Seishen Kingdom is grateful for the mercy of the Akura clan. Honor to the Queen of Shadows."

"My grandmother is dead," Charity's voice said, still smooth and unruffled. "There are no Monarchs anymore, as you must surely have heard."

"I found the rumors hard to believe," Meira admitted. There had been too many unbelievable things in recent years, from the Dreadgods going wild to the Monarchs ascending or dying en masse. As she understood it, there were no Dreadgods anymore either...at least, not for now.

The owl ruffled its own feathers of translucent madra. "It is in the interest of stabilizing our territory that we return this prisoner. His sentence allows for no leniency, and I assure you, there has been none. He is bound to loyally serve the Kingdom as our vassal country until the end of his days."

Meira bowed again, repressing her shudder at the thought of what the Akura clan may have transformed Daji into. "Have you informed His Majesty the King?"

"I leave that task to you," Charity said through her owl, and there was a wry touch to her words.

"I will not fail the Sage," Meira said, though fleeing the kingdom sounded appealing next to bringing this news to King Dakata.

"In the absence of a Monarch, my responsibilities have multiplied." The silver eyes of Charity's owl were cold. "I no longer have time for second chances. If anything should inspire the King to rebellious action, I will act...decisively."

'Decisively' meaning 'lethally,' Meira was sure. The Seishen royal family, and maybe even the nobles, would be executed in an instant if the kingdom made itself Charity's problem.

But she was more worried about the state Daji was in, if Charity thought his return could provoke Dakata to the point of rebellion.

"Your servant understands."

The owl disappeared, leaving Meira in the moonlight. Absently, she gathered up her natural treasures. She no longer had the presence of mind to productively cycle.

One hour, the Sage had said. There was no time to lose, but Meira still found her steps heavy.

What was she supposed to say to the King?

No matter how slow her feet were, they eventually brought her to the end of the hallway outside King Dakata's bedroom. The guards recognized her, of course, and saluted in their armor as she approached.

"Get him for me," Meira said, though she felt she was ordering her own torture.

The guards glanced at one another. "Forgive us, Underlady, but the King is in an unfit state for guests at the moment."

Once, that would have meant he was undressed, drunk, or in the middle of berating Prince Kiro. These days, it meant something else.

"He always is," she said dully.

When she didn't leave or say anything else, they pushed open the door. One ducked his head in, then waved Meira inside.

She entered King Dakata's bedroom and found him exactly where she'd expected: slumped in a chair, surrounded by crushed or expended dream tablets. Some still flickered with the sparks of their remaining power.

He'd once resembled a bear, but he'd let himself decay until he looked more like an abandoned dog. His beard was wild and almost entirely gray, his skin loose and colorless, and he was little more than a skeleton as he sagged in place. The night's uneaten food tray sat nearby.

In skeletal hands, he cradled a dying dream tablet, his eyes glassy as he relived memories far away.

Anyone who had known the princes Daji or Kiro had been called upon to leave their dream tablets, at the crown's expense. He lived inside those memories now.

Meira stood in front of him, still unsure of her strategy. After a long moment of silence, she decided to blurt it out.

"Daji's alive," she said. "They're sending him back."

Rather than snapping out of his trance, he looked up sluggishly. "Daji's here?"

"Your Majesty, the Heart Sage just sent us a message. She's giving Daji back."

King Dakata shuddered at the mention of Charity, his eyes dark with fear and anger. "When did she say that? Is she here?"

"A *message,* Your Majesty."

"Where's Daji?"

He spoke as though still halfway in the dream, but time was running out, and the survival of the kingdom relied on his comprehension. Meira stepped up and plucked the dream tablet out of his hands.

Though he was still an Overlord, he only reached for the tablet a full second after she took it.

"King Dakata, focus on me," she ordered. "In a matter of minutes, they're sending Daji back."

Finally, clarity kindled in the depths of his eyes. He trembled for a moment as he processed the information, and his final reaction was one of suspicion. "Are you certain?"

"I'm certain of the prince's return, but not of his condition," Meira said. "We should anticipate the worst and assume that his mind is not intact. He will need our help to recover.'

Strength returned to King Dakata as though he cycled it into his spirit from the vital aura. He pushed out of his chair, empty dream tablets tinkling around his feet as he stepped away.

"Tell me the rest of her words," the King demanded.

In relief, Meira repeated the Sage's messages. King Dakata didn't express any hope or relief, only smoldering anger.

"As ever, the Akura do whatever suits them. They allow my first-born to die and execute my second, only to have *desecrated* his body by turning it into a shambling puppet. And I have no choice but to thank them for their *mercy*."

His rage grew more visible with every word, and the stone of the castle shook beneath his feet.

"We are truly without choices," Meira reminded him. She was conscious of the possibility that Charity could be watching at any second, but she had also not forgotten that Daji was truly guilty of his crime.

To have attempted an assassination of a Monarch's children and be returned with his life, even years later...Meira wasn't sure if that showed immeasurable mercy or immeasurable cruelty.

"Rouse the castle," the King said. "We gather in the great hall. Tell them it is for a feast, but do not order the kitchen staff to prepare. We only eat if my son is really returned."

Meira silently bowed and left, giving orders to the first servants she saw. They took off running.

Charity had given no instructions on exactly where or how to welcome Daji's return, but Dakata had evidently come to the same conclusion Meira had; the Sage could transport him anytime, anywhere, so precisely where they gathered was irrelevant.

Within half an hour, the castle had been turned out and deposited into the great hall, which was a testament to the King's insistence. Soldiers had driven people from their beds, and Meira saw more than one noble with hair half-undone or formal clothes half-fastened.

The King sat on a throne at the center of the royal table, raised above the rest of the room. He explained nothing, only told the room to wait. Before long, they would understand why they had been gathered.

Indeed, it wasn't long. The Heart Sage must have seen that they were gathered, because shadows stretched into a portal before an hour had quite passed.

Charity's voice echoed over the room, disembodied and ethereal. "The son of the Seishen Kingdom returns home, his loyalty restored. Let his example stand for the rest of you."

Then the shadows retreated, leaving Seishen Daji blinking in the sudden lights.

Most in the room hadn't been warned, so they burst into noise. Some cheered, many gasped, and many others asked each other what they thought was happening.

Meira's attention was on King Dakata. At the sight of his son, he showed the first signs of hope and uncertainty she'd seen from him since he'd gotten the news.

"Daji?" he asked carefully. "Son?"

Daji lowered the hand he'd been using to block out the light, but he still squinted when he looked into his father's face. "Yes sir?"

Meira shuddered, but Dakata crept closer. "Do you remember me?"

"Of course I do. You're my father." Daji's voice still sounded... strange. Not exactly casual, not exactly formal. Like he was reading the answers off a sheet.

Dakata hesitated a moment longer, then he threw his arms around his son. This time, the room cheered.

Some of the stewards issued orders to the kitchen staff, who hurried out of the corners to go prepare food. Nobles shouted questions and some crowded near to the royal table, though none interrupted the reunion between father and son.

Meira carefully observed Daji using all her senses.

His madra channels were scarred, as though they'd been torn apart and stitched together. His lifeline was as thin as someone who had endured illness for years, and the blood essence in his body was weaker than it should be for an Underlord.

But he *was* still an Underlord. They hadn't crippled him in any permanent way to rob him of his advancement, and he spoke coherently.

Even when he was asked about the Akura clan.

That was the most common question, of course. Meira moved up to the end of the royal table; she was specially permitted to eat there, but usually didn't. This time, she wanted to hear.

Everyone wanted to hear what had happened to Daji, and when asked, he didn't flinch from the questions. "They punished me for my transgressions," he said. "I'm grateful to have been treated so fairly, in spite of my disloyalty."

Dakata spoke in a low, rumbling voice. "You don't have to talk if you don't want to, son. I know it can be...hard to speak of."

King Dakata himself had been a guest of the Akura for a time, just as Meira had. They hadn't been tortured, so to speak, but their lightless imprisonment and merciless questioning had been its own kind of torment.

Daji nodded seriously. "I was punished, but growth is painful. I've learned my lesson."

That wasn't Daji.

Meira knew he wasn't an impostor, but the man had been warped and changed beyond recognition. Hearing precise, perfect, *controlled* lines out of Daji's mouth was more shocking than hearing rocks sing.

King Dakata surely knew the same, but he relaxed around Daji as the meal continued, his joy and concern melting away his fear and anger. His topic turned to the future; the future of the Seishen Kingdom, their relationship to the Akura clan, and Daji's recovery.

Daji went along easily with everything except when any disloyalty to the Akura was suggested or implied.

Once, King Dakata said, "Akura resources are stretched thinner than ever. They can't watch us all the time, thank the heavens, so we're left to steer our own ship."

"Never underestimate the reach of the Akura clan," Daji said immediately. "They have more resources than you suspect. Besides, we should give them no reason to monitor us."

He didn't seem like someone speaking out of trauma or fear, but like a true loyalist correcting his father. If there had been an Akura banner in the hall, Meira had no doubt that Daji wouldn't leave the room without saluting it.

As though he could read Meira's thoughts, Daji looked around the hall. "Where are our Akura banners? We used to keep one in here, if I recall."

King Dakata had torn it to ribbons and burned it in full view of the entire court, but he snapped his fingers and called out, "Bring any banners, flags, or tapestries with the Akura crest out of storage and fly them in the castle! We should show our gratitude for bringing the crown prince home!"

Meira left the table.

If the original crown prince, Kiro, had only survived...He wouldn't have nursed a grudge like his little brother. He wouldn't have been taken. The king, kingdom, and her own life would all be immeasurably better.

But that line of thinking led only to despair, so Meira closed it off.

With nowhere else to go, she wandered back to her glade and resumed cycling. As she often did while absorbing aura, she let her thoughts freely drift.

Before long, she realized that Daji's return lifted a weight from her back. She'd been one of the few who could speak to the King, her well-known loyalty to Prince Kiro shielding her from his unpredictable wrath.

Meira had used that privilege to push the King into caring for his people as he'd once done. Now, that role was gone. She could return to the background, where she belonged.

When she cycled as much aura as she could handle, it was late morning, so she spent some time in internal cycling, refining that aura into madra. She spun soulfire, nourished her spirit, even practiced her techniques.

Just training. Mindless, simple, straightforward training. A distraction, and one that took her responsibilities away for a while.

When hunger finally persuaded her to return, the sun was beginning to set. Her natural treasures were mostly exhausted, and in the case of life treasures, that often meant that she'd drained energy from a living thing. She replanted now-listless plants before she exhausted their power entirely; they would regain it, over time.

As, perhaps, Daji would regain a sense of himself. Though, would that really be for the best? It was the 'real' Daji who had plotted against a Monarch's children, after all.

Meira crossed the circle surrounding her cycling garden and stiffened as she sensed a spirit approaching her.

Daji was miraculously alone, though she sensed his father's perception hovering over the prince's soul like a protective spirit. In the light of the setting sun, he looked something like his old self; lean, strong, with wild hair and a sharp face that reminded her of a wolf.

Though the wild hunger and aggression that had made up his heart were missing completely. It was like the Akura had put someone else's soul in Seishen Daji's body.

He lifted a hand as he reached the bottom of the hill on which she stood. "I'm sorry, Meira, did I interrupt you?"

That was the first time Meira had ever heard Daji apologize of his own volition. Her skin crawled.

"What do you want?" Meira asked.

"To apologize." Daji dropped to one knee. "If I had listened to you, I would never have made Wei Shi Lindon or Akura Mercy my enemies. I wouldn't have put our kingdom, or the Akura territories as a whole, in danger. Your loyalty is the example I always should have followed."

Meira's revulsion ignited into anger. This felt like a mockery, like he was doing a bad impression of his older brother.

"Who taught you to say that?" she spat. "Is there a construct in your head? Are they feeding you lines? Or is the Sage working you like a puppet?"

"I'm ashamed of my behavior, but I assure you, I have changed."

Meira dashed to the bottom of the hill and seized Daji by the throat. She felt a spike in the King's madra, but she didn't care.

It would take him time to reach them from the castle, and her hand was already on Daji's neck. She could snap his threadbare lifeline in one pulse of madra.

She dragged his face closer to hers, and he didn't seem to mind.

"You *changed?* You died! You're a construct wearing human skin!"

Daji hung limply in her grip, not resisting. "However much you hate the man I used to be, I hate him more."

She *did* hate him, she realized. She'd never thought of it in those terms before.

Daji had always been resentful of Prince Kiro. Always been a burden to him. After Kiro's death, he'd been even worse, putting Meira, the King, and the entire Seishen Kingdom in danger for his own selfishness.

He'd deserved to die.

Instead, the Akura had...*tamed* him.

Meira released his throat and dropped him to his feet. He must have been bruised by her grip, but he didn't even rub the sore spot, only waited.

Despite what Meira had expected, King Dakata hadn't flown over to defend his son. Either he trusted Meira that much or he had the same misgivings she did.

Meira leaned close, looking deep into Daji's eyes, and rested the full focus of her spiritual sense on him. "Who did they turn you into?" she asked.

Even she wasn't fully sure what she meant by the question, but Daji seemed to understand.

"Into the brother Kiro deserved," Daji answered.

That response turned Meira's stomach. He even seemed to mean it.

Over the castle, a purple Akura banner was lifted into the light of the setting sun.

"Good," Meira said.

She led the prince back to the castle, and he followed obediently. A hollow imitation of his brother he might be, but Seishen Daji would serve the people of his kingdom.

That was all Prince Kiro had ever wanted, so Meira would make sure it happened.

A Day in the Life of Akura Pride

INFORMATION REQUESTED: AKURA PRIDE'S STATUS AMONG THE ABIDAN.
REPORT LOCATION: AFTER THE EVENTS OF *WAYBOUND*.
CONTEXT: WHEN LINDON ASCENDED, HE BROUGHT PRIDE ALONG. PRIDE WAS ALMOST IMMEDIATELY WHISKED OFF BY HIS HALF-BROTHER, FURY, FOR TRAINING.
AUTHORIZATION CONFIRMED.
BEGINNING REPORT...

PRIDE DIDN'T SLEEP ANYMORE SO MUCH AS HE PASSED OUT.

He woke himself as he lashed out, his Enforcer techniques braided together around his leg. He instinctively kicked at whatever was restricting him, only to find that he'd torn a hole in his blankets.

As he got his bearings, he panted and stretched out his spiritual sense. He was alone in this strange bedroom, which resembled a ten-sided polygon. It was tiny compared to his rooms back home, but he wasn't treated as a Monarch's son here.

In any case, his accommodations were still surprisingly beautiful. A window on one wall looked out over a gorgeous meadow with flowers that sang a soft song and clouds that took on the appearance of massive birds and flew through the sky. The breeze carried a scent fresh enough to deceive him into thinking it was a means of escape.

He'd tried to crawl through the window only to find that there was no exit. It was a real window, looking out onto a far-off world, but it only allowed travel one way.

His bathroom was tucked into a pocket space, and it had amenities that even rivaled what he would have enjoyed in an Akura palace, though none of it was powered by the sacred arts. That made sense, given that he was far from home, though it still confused his spiritual senses to feel hot water spraying from a faucet with no sense of a binding involved.

A puppet-construct made of gray smoke flew up beside him and spoke into his head. [Good morning, Pride,] the room's Presence said. [You're up a little late today, I'm afraid. Your trainer is already on her way.]

Pride struggled out of the bed, his body still aching from the day before. "Tell her to wait! I'm not ready yet."

His door hissed open from the outside, and a tall and powerful woman strode in. She wore the gray outfit that most Abidan did under their armor, her dark purple hair fell to her shoulders, and she smiled gently as she saw him just getting ready.

Pride began to sweat.

"You must have been sleeping well," she said. "I'm pleased. The Way flows through a healthy body."

"Is Uncle Fury not back yet?" Pride asked.

"Every hand is needed on assignment. Normally, there would be many more trainers than just me. He won't be back for some time, I'm sure."

Pride exhaled in relief. Tough as his training was, he would have had it worse with Fury around.

"Oh? Did you not want to see your uncle?"

"No, Trainer Mura. I was simply worried for him."

"I can't say I'm not worried about them myself." Her smile turned sympathetic. "But the best we can do is to work hard while they're gone! Come on, now!"

She gestured him out of his room. Fortunately or not, he hadn't changed since last night, so he was still wearing his own gray training clothes. He cleansed himself with aura, which thankfully worked to some degree even outside Cradle, but it didn't clean as well as a real bath would. Not at his level of aura control, anyway.

He stepped out of his room to see hundreds of other recruits in the Wolf Division training compound. The polygonal rooms were stacked next to each other in rows of at least two dozen pods, all identical to his own, and there were eight such floors.

If he leaned out of the shared balcony, he could see them all, three floors stretching above him and four below. That was only his wall; across a short field were two more buildings reflecting his own.

Trainees bustled here and there, but not in the synchronized fashion he might have expected before he arrived. Each one followed their own customized program, with their own trainer.

The *same* trainer. A tall, muscular, purple-haired woman smiled next to each and every one of the Wolf trainees.

Trainer Mura waited for him, pleasantly beaming. She stepped back against the balcony railing so another copy of her could pass, a copy who was locked in conversation with a girl in the gray trainee uniform.

"I know where to go," Pride said, striding past Mura.

"Then why don't we go together?" she suggested. Nothing shook Trainer Mura's pleasant demeanor.

As Pride reached the cafeteria and grabbed a tray, Mura didn't take one for herself. "We only have six minutes left for breakfast," she reminded him.

Pride eyed her empty hands. "Do you not have to eat?"

"Only my original body does," Trainer Mura said. "The rest of us are just temporary copies folded into existence from possibilities."

Pride grunted as a machine shone a light onto his tray and something like a Ruler technique activated.

The machine projected freshly baked bread, piping-hot sausages, roasted mushrooms, tightly wrapped green leaves that smelled as though they were covering spicy food, and an unidentifiable mass that resembled a ball of purple cloud madra.

The one way in which his current living conditions matched his mother's palace was the food. Each meal was unique and tailored for his nutrition, or so Mura assured him. The Akura clan cooks were among the best on the continent, but the meals casually conjured by Abidan technology matched them every morning.

"While you eat, I'll talk about the day's routine," Trainer Mura said.

Pride scowled at her. "I don't need a reminder."

She reminded him anyway.

After breakfast, Pride found himself sweating as he slogged through an obstacle course. It was a somewhat complicated course, with steel structures jutting from the ceiling and platforms that moved in rapid and unpredictable patterns, but Pride had trained on such courses since he was a child. This was nothing to an Underlord.

Or so it had been on his first day. When she found that Pride's basic physical parameters were better than the average recruit, Mura hadn't even been impressed. She'd just ratcheted up the course's difficulty.

Pride had come to find out that he was unusually strong only for those trainees born among the civilian Sanctum population. For the ones who ascended under their own power—which were unusually common among the Wolves—he was still below standard.

That made sense, given that only Archlords and above ascended from Cradle, but it still needled him to be below-average at anything.

So, while the air felt as thick as jelly and the increased gravity made him feel as though he weighed as much as a small mountain, Pride pushed through. He sweated as much as anyone, hauling himself up a ladder that shook in an artificial earthquake.

"Great work, Pride!" Trainer Mura called. "Only a few more days and we can take you up to the next level!"

Pride grit his teeth and controlled his breath before he responded. "What is the Wolf standard?"

"Hm, let's see. This is Level Four, and the Way usually begins to respond to one-star Wolves on Level...Eighteen."

Pride lost his balance and almost fell. No wonder Trainer Mura didn't seem bothered, though the resistance in the air and the increased gravity had to affect her as well.

"How many stars do you have?" Pride asked.

Somehow, he felt that if he was the one asking the questions, that meant he had the upper hand.

"I'm a three-star Wolf, but I have two stars as a Ghost, two as a Fox, and one as a Titan." She smiled at him. "Thank you for asking, but we'll have plenty of time to talk when you finish the course."

When Pride finished, she made him run it three more times.

Next came combat practice, which took place in a small, padded room. It resembled a Lowgold training room more than one appropriate for ascendants, but they were restricted to little more than Irons while inside.

The Way flowed through a healthy body, and the Wolves wanted it to reinforce their combat. That meant honing themselves into instruments of battle.

It all resembled what Pride had learned of Icons, though most of what he'd heard about that had come since leaving Cradle. From Fury and, frustratingly, from his own sister.

Normally, his opponent arrived at the same time he did, since the copies of Trainer Mura were all perfectly coordinated with each other. But this morning, Mura frowned at an invisible message and looked uncharacteristically bitter.

"I'm sorry, Pride, your opponent will be here in just a minute. It seems like our newest *division* has someone who needs training as well." She put more venom into the word 'division' than Pride had thought she was capable of; Mura had always reminded him of Mercy.

"The Reaper Division?" he asked.

"I understand they're acquaintances of yours." She gave him a sympathetic look. "Be careful around them. In fact, it would be best if you could convince them to join you instead. From what I understand, they would make fine Wolves."

That wasn't the first Pride had heard about the Reapers, though the Abidan were always cagey about saying more, and Mercy didn't understand the situation herself. But before he could ask more, the door swished open and a dark-skinned man strode in.

"I don't need a guide, and I don't need a guard," Orthos rumbled to someone back in the hallway. Probably another copy of Mura.

Pride was still unused to seeing Orthos as a man with leathery skin and gray-winged hair rather than a giant, burning turtle. At least his eyes were the same: dark orbs with rings of red.

"*He's* my opponent?" Pride demanded of Trainer Mura. "He's a Sage!"

"You will be roughly equalized while in this room," Mura assured him. "Welcome, Trainee Orthos. You may call me Trainer Mura."

She was professionally polite, but Pride couldn't miss that her tone was noticeably cooler than when she spoke to him.

Orthos looked her up and down for a moment and then snorted smoke. "If you have a grudge against Eithan, you can take it up with him, Trainer Mura."

Mura shuddered and glanced at the ceiling like she was under the gaze of a Monarch. "I'm only here to train you, Orthos. You are familiar with Akura Pride, aren't you?"

"I need to learn to use these *hands* and *feet*," Orthos said to Pride, "but I didn't think I'd be fighting you. I'm not here to do battle with hatchlings."

Pride bristled. "You don't even know how to throw a punch. With your advancement restricted, you shouldn't look down on me."

"I don't," Orthos grumbled. "That makes it worse. You think I want a hatchling beating on me for two hours? I don't even have a shell."

"Since this is your first time training as a human, Trainee Orthos, let my Presence guide you through the proper form," Trainer Mura said. A shape appeared above her shoulder, like a burning diamond, but Orthos shook his head.

"No need."

Above his own shoulder, Dross popped into existence. He swept a theatrical bow to the trainer. [Ah, hello! One combat Presence, at your service. *His* service, really. You may call me Trainer Dross.]

Mura struggled with her expression for a moment before she said, "The trainees may begin when ready."

The battle was only satisfying for the first five minutes.

In the initial exchange, Pride slipped inside Orthos' guard with a basic full-body Enforcer technique. Orthos was too slow to react, so Pride had him on his back immediately.

[That could have gone worse,] Dross consoled Orthos. [For instance, an enemy could have snuck into this room and stabbed you.]

Orthos burned with visible anger, the scarlet rings in his eyes shining, but he didn't say another word. Pride rushed in again, but Orthos managed to defend himself.

It was obvious that Orthos hadn't used a human body much. He moved in lumbering, straight lines, shifted his whole body when he could have just shifted his feet, and generally fought without grace or efficiency.

Pride put Orthos on his back again and kept himself from gloating. He should be a gracious winner.

Before the fifth minute was over, Pride was the one on his back.

He stared at the ceiling and listened to Dross. [See? That's what listening to *me* feels like.]

"I still don't like it," Orthos responded. "We must practice until it feels natural."

Pride had been careless. He'd forgotten he was fighting a Sage, and one with more advantages than just superior advancement; Orthos had many years of combat experience and Dross to guide him.

Pride set aside his own arrogance and layered Enforcer techniques together. He could at least force Orthos to use the Burning Cloak.

Twelve seconds later, Pride crumpled as he hit the back wall.

Trainer Mura clapped. "Well done, Orthos. You're already beginning to make the Presence's guidance your own. This is how to connect your movements to the Way."

[At this rate, there's no end to the number of children you'll defeat!] Dross glanced around at the faces of the others. [What? Lindon did it.]

Pride gained a certain amount of self-respect from the fact that he managed to last a full two hours.

When Trainer Mura finally called a halt, it was Orthos who extended a hand to lift him up. "Thank you, Pride. I haven't had many practice partners lately."

Pride bristled at the insult of being offered a hand up, but he took it anyway. "I have no doubt my sister would be delighted to accompany you next time. And what about your Dreadgod?"

"Their responsibilities are greater than ever," Orthos rumbled.

[And if we sparred against them, we wouldn't have gotten to spend this delightful time with you!]

Pride jerked his hand away and gave a stiff bow. "Next time, I'm sure the Wolves can find you an opponent better suited for your level."

Orthos studied him for an uncomfortably long moment. "Taking offense does not demonstrate great pride. It shows a weak ego."

That *was* an insult, and Pride drew himself up. Madra spooled out to his limbs, visible in crawling lines, as his Book of Seven Pages filled him with power. Under these conditions, with the training room restricting Orthos' power, he could defend his honor.

"Did you come here to humiliate an Underlord?" he demanded. "What does that say of *your* pride, Dragon Sage?"

Rather than strike back, Orthos huffed out a dry chuckle with a mouthful of smoke. "You only have one enemy in this room. A dragon should not fear himself."

If anything, that comparison was *more* insulting. The Akura clan had no high opinion of dragons.

Orthos was already leaving before Pride could respond. Trainer Mura stood next to the door, busying herself so she wouldn't make eye contact with the outsider from the Reaper Division.

Dross reached out a tendril and patted Pride on the shoulder. [Don't listen to Orthos. I prefer you this way. You're much easier to predict.]

"I do not fight for your amusement."

[That's the spirit!] Dross nodded encouragingly before blinking out of existence.

Once the Reapers were gone, Mura smiled as though nothing had happened. "Lunchtime! Take a shower, relax, then meet me back in the cafeteria in fifteen minutes."

Pride didn't think a fifteen-minute shower break counted as *relaxing*, but he did as requested.

When he approached the cafeteria, he noticed that he didn't feel as many presences inside as usual. He kept his spiritual perception mostly restricted, and the people from other worlds didn't feel the same as those from Cradle, but there was still usually the sense of a great number of people within.

He could have extended his perception to probe the situation, but that could be rude. And if anything had gone wrong, the entire Wolf Division would have been mobilized.

Pride strode inside confidently, the metal door hissing away from him as he approached.

There *were* other trainees inside, but they were huddled at the far end of the room. Most crowded the same tables, though there were dozens of others empty, and the rest simply ate standing up.

All looked warily toward the person standing at the entrance.

In her black armor, Mercy beamed and waved as Pride came in. "Hi, Pride! Did you miss me?"

They spoke almost every night, at least when Mercy was close enough to receive transmissions, but Pride was distracted by the behavior of the others.

One of the Wolf trainees hurried out the back door. Another spat something that Pride took as a curse in another language.

There was another oddity: usually, each trainee would have a copy of Trainer Mura along, but they were all missing. All except one.

Pride's own version of Trainer Mura—at least, he assumed it was her—stood to one side of the door with arms folded. She stared straight at Mercy with a determined smile.

After Mercy greeted Pride, Mura took the chance to speak. "Pride, right on time! Your sister decided to give us a surprise visit. Why don't you show her how to request a meal?"

This wasn't the first time that the Abidan of the Wolf Division had implied—or outright stated—their disdain for the Reapers, and now Pride's connection to them would be common knowledge. His name and description would have circulated through the entire trainee population by nightfall, if not sooner.

But they were insulting *his* sister.

Pride took a moment to make eye contact with everyone in the room. "I will, Trainer Mura, thank you." He ended by staring into the Wolf's eyes without flinching. "I'll show my sister just how welcome she is."

Trainer Mura smiled widely. "Take your time, Trainee. But remember that there are many things about the Abidan you don't yet understand."

Without a word to Mercy, Mura swept out of the room. Several of the other trainees took that as permission to bolt after her.

"It's okay, Pride!" Mercy said encouragingly. "They don't have a problem with *you*."

"They're about to." Pride was busy staring down the man who had cursed Mercy, committing his face to memory.

During lunch, Mercy was even louder and cheerier than usual, as

Pride knew she was determined to make up for the large gap of empty tables around them. She talked about her recent assignments and news from the Reaper Division, asked about his training, and made un-subtle hints that he should stay with them instead of down on the planet.

Pride participated with half a mind. By the time he returned to his training, he'd learned the names of three other trainees who had looked down on Mercy.

One was Sanctum-born, but the other two were ascendants. He found that surprising, given that those who ascended under their own powers should have no reason to distrust Reapers.

Pride looked forward to getting to know his future training partners.

Afternoon training usually started with meditation, because—as Trainer Mura put it—learning to sense oneself was the beginning of sensing the Way.

But what the normal trainees knew as 'meditation' was laughably easy compared to cycling vital aura, so the practice was a waste of time for anyone born in Cradle. While the training campus was quiet, Pride visited the classroom.

In a booth smaller than his own bedroom, Trainer Mura taught Pride the common knowledge of the Abidan and the history of the Wolf Division.

He found the process extraordinary. They used technology that reminded him of dream tablets, if dream tablets were perfectly refined, infinitely reusable, and seamless with the user's experience.

She started by arranging dull silver needles around his head, which hung suspended as though floating in wind aura. Then her Presence took over, and information slipped into his mind.

Rather than an illusion taking over his senses or a flood of information, as Pride had first expected, the sensation was quiet and unobtrusive. If Pride hadn't been through this process before, he wouldn't have realized he'd learned anything.

"Tell me about the Third Battle of Sunder," Mura said.

Pride had never heard of that battle before, but he answered easily. "It claimed the life of the second Razael and resulted in the capture of the Iteration now known as Sunder. Four hundred Wolves lost made it the bloodiest battle in the Fifth Division's history, at the time."

As Pride spoke, he *did* know, like he was uncovering a lesson from long ago.

"Tell me a little more about it," Mura said. "Don't worry, we'll move on before long. I just want to make sure the connections are stable."

Learning was simpler than Pride had expected, but it was still more complicated than it initially seemed. The information would last longer, Mura said, if it was used. He needed to form his own natural connections, or he would forget.

Pride had accepted that, and he even found it somewhat enjoyable to pass quizzes on subjects he'd never heard of.

But that had been before Trainer Mura had publicly disrespected Mercy. He was not in a cooperative mood.

"Why bother?" Pride asked. "Presumably, I'll be issued a personal Presence eventually. It will have all the information I could require."

"A Presence is a tool, not a crutch. It will remember more than you ever could, but a solid education is about more than simply reciting facts. *You* are the one who will make decisions for your

Presence, and it is best if those decisions are rooted in understanding rather than ignorance. The Third Battle of Sunder, if you would."

"Surely, pursuing advancement would be a better use of my time. As an Overlord, I will be better able to recall my lessons, and even to sense the Way."

Pride had no real preference for advancement over his current training. When Lindon had offered to take him beyond the world, Pride had accepted out of concern for his sister, a lack of connection to the fraction of his family that remained, and personal responsibility.

Not to mention a desire not to repeat his mother's mistakes.

Uncle Fury was the one who wanted him to pursue advancement at all costs, but Pride would take any opportunity to question Trainer Mura.

She saw that in him, and her lips quirked into a slight smile. "Sometimes, studying might not be the right choice." She plucked the central of the silver needles away from his forehead, and the others flew back to their places in the wall. "Why don't we try some humanitarian work? This isn't the sort of thing the Wolf Division would normally do, but it should give you a good sense of what we're fighting for."

Ten minutes later, Pride found himself standing in the middle of a nightmare.

It wasn't his first time.

Pride picked up a man with no legs. They hadn't been severed, they seemed to have been *erased* somehow, turned to smoke. The man screamed as he stared at the mist trailing away from him, and Pride realized that whatever effect was causing this man to dissolve into gas hadn't finished yet.

"Control yourself," Pride snapped. "We're almost there." He ducked through a collapsing building without reducing speed.

They were inside an Iteration close to Sanctum; close enough that it had taken only a couple of minutes in the Way to arrive. The scene reminded him of nothing so much as the Dreadgod attacks, from the deafening *noise* that never seemed to go anywhere to the dust and grit that choked the air.

What differed were the worlds.

The ruined buildings around him were primitive castles of stone, with no signs that anything like Forged madra had been used in their construction. He'd seen no evidence of scripts, Soulsmithing, or sacred arts anywhere in the world that was.

Nearby, Trainer Mura was hauling aside chunks of masonry and pulling people out of the wreckage. Every injured person she rescued was headed to the same location.

One stone room, which must once have been a storeroom or a quarter for servants, remained intact although the rest of the building around it had been torn away. It was clogged with people, as screaming crowds choked every approach, even hanging from the ceiling.

They were all waiting for the attention of their one Phoenix.

Pride leaped over dozens of them at a time, shoving them aside when he couldn't. With no sacred arts, they couldn't resist him even when he used no techniques. There were wounds on everyone he could see, but few as strange as the smoke transformation of the man he carried.

Another Abidan, a white-armored man with the badge of the Phoenix Division on his armor, leaned over a woman on a stretcher.

Sweat matted the Abidan's stringy hair to his face, and he breathed heavily, but he still radiated blue light from his palms.

On the stretcher, the woman heaved a breath as she came back to life. Pride suspected that was literally true; her eyes had been glassy and unfocused a moment before, but he saw a spark return to them even as her bones realigned and her flesh knitted back together. Bloodstains shrunk as her wounds disappeared.

"Bring the next one," the Phoenix ordered one of his helpers. The assistant was a local man with a large build, and he called someone's name.

Pride stepped in front instead, holding out his burden for the Abidan healer. "He's next."

The Phoenix looked like he could be a member of the Arelius family, but his yellow hair was messy and he had deeper, darker bags under his eyes than Pride expected Eithan would ever allow.

"There's nothing I can do for him," the Phoenix said wearily.

Pride stiffened and shot a glance down at the man, who had lost everything below the waist to a cloud of color-tinted smoke.

"Why not?" Pride demanded.

"That's the touch of a Fiend. It's outside the normal order. If he was my only patient...but he's not, and there are people I *can* help. Move."

Pride stepped aside automatically, bringing his patient with him, but his mind churned. Was the Abidan telling the truth? Probably, given that he had no reason to lie. His words implied that there might be something a more powerful healer could do.

Lindon had some sort of connection to Suriel, Pride remembered. She was *the* Phoenix, not just *a* Phoenix.

Pride pulled out a metal device Mercy had given him; it was something like a communication construct, but made of physical materials rather than Forged madra. He tried to contact her, but made no connection.

Trainer Mura had to take him back to Sanctum. From there, he could go to the Grave and find help.

As Pride charged out to find Mura, the effect of the curse suddenly accelerated. Without a word, the man dissolved in Pride's arms.

Though it was futile, Pride still instinctively tried to grab a handful of the smoke.

He hadn't even known the man's name. Pride had tried to help *one* person so far, and he'd failed.

He felt like he was back in the aftermath of the Dreadgod attacks, but he'd faced greater responsibilities back then. He could reassure other sacred artists or face enemies. This time, he was as powerless as the mundane crowd around him.

Pride looked up and scowled.

One more detail that reminded him of the Dreadgods: The enemy had altered the sky.

In this case, the creature—the Fiend—that had attacked this world remained visible. It had crashed through the sky as though breaking through an egg, two arms and two legs dangling down from incomprehensibly high above.

The Fiend resembled a puppet-construct or wooden marionette, and it was transparently dead. It had been folded in half, stuck with its limbs and head inside the world while the rest of its body waited outside.

Its face was...disturbing. Pride didn't like catching a glimpse of it even in passing. Its face looked painted, but the paint constantly swirled in shapes that gave him the impression that it was *about* to resolve into something terrifying.

From where the Fiend hung in the sky, the world was cracked. Long splinters crawled out from its point of impact, and Pride was vividly reminded of the spatial cracks that combat between Monarchs could cause.

Between those cracks, Pride saw darkness and the occasional flash of spinning color. The colors were even more sickening than the dark.

Trainer Mura's Presence, the featureless gray doll, popped up next to him. [Chal'chariss, the Sky Painter,] it reported. [A Class Three Fiend. A team of Wolves dispatched it only a few hours ago, but there are over a thousand similar calls coming in as we speak.]

"I've seen worse," Pride said. Determined to ignore the Presence, he looked out over the devastated castle, spreading out his perception to find more victims.

[Before Ozriel abandoned his post, these worlds were safe.] The Presence floated next to him easily, and he supposed it could have beamed its thoughts to him even if he *did* escape. [While he was absent, the one who struck the blow to our forces was a former Executor. One the Abidan recruited to intervene in worlds on their behalf. The Mad King.]

Pride fought back a shiver as he remembered the man in the bone armor and the red eyes. He had caught only the tiniest *fragment* of a glimpse, one that he hadn't even fully remembered until after weeks of nightmares.

And, of course, he hadn't known the figure's name until leaving his world.

"I've been attending my history lessons," Pride said. He Enforced himself to lift a wall away from life he sensed within, only for a group of creatures that resembled huge raccoons to scurry past him.

[Do you know the stated purpose of the Reaper Division?] the Presence asked him.

Pride didn't comment.

[The Abidan strain themselves to the point of breaking to save lives endangered by Ozriel's negligence. With his return, he brought with him a group of those who caused this disaster in the first place. Akura Pride. You can see that this is madness.]

"And? What do you expect me to do about it?"

[You have influence over these new Reapers,] the Presence said. [You should use it. For their sakes.]

Pride said little else for the rest of his time in the Iteration whose name he'd never learned. He remained quiet on his way back to Sanctum, while he returned to his room, and as he readied himself for bed.

Sleep was interrupted a handful of hours later by the door slamming open and Uncle Fury standing in the doorway, grinning, eyes blazing red and hair waving in an unseen current.

"Morning, Pride! Time to train!"

For once, Pride was eager to get started.

Harness

INFORMATION REQUESTED: ZIEL AND HIS MISSIONS IN THE REAPER DIVISION.
REPORT LOCATION: AFTER THE EVENTS OF *WAYBOUND*.
AUTHORIZATION CONFIRMED.
BEGINNING REPORT...

ITERATION 151: HARNESS

"One day, they'll send me to fight something," Ziel said. "There's going to be a Fiend invasion, or a Vroshir attack, or an evil cult rising up in my name. And I'll have to stop them."

From Ziel's shoulder, Orthos stretched his head out of his shell and bit a chunk out of a nearby tree branch. "Be grateful for your tasks. You are sent to accomplish great deeds, and not merely as an...accessory."

Little Blue's laugh was like the tinkling of bells as she drifted down from the treetops. Nice to see one person having a great time.

"At least there's no paperwork," Ziel muttered.

"Not yet," Orthos said. "You remember your lines?"

Dross popped out, hovering over the tiny Orthos and waving one tendril in the air. [Of course he does! He has me. You all do, which is what makes it so strange that you would ask him. I can do enough remembering for everyone!]

Orthos sullenly bit off a leaf the size of his head and swallowed it whole. "Oh, I remember *my* line. My line is..." He roared like a wild beast.

Dross made hands appear and clap. [Wonderful! I'm so glad you didn't need me to remind you, because if you did, I would have been very concerned.]

Ziel pushed through the forest, walking like a Copper because, for all intents and purposes, he *was* a Copper. Or maybe an Iron. Wherever mundane humans in this world stacked up, compared to the way things worked in Cradle.

If Ziel had learned one thing, out in the wider reality of the cosmos, it was that 'ordinary' humans rarely even matched up to Lowgolds.

The people of this world needed to be saved by a native, but the natives weren't interested in saving each other. Therefore, the quickest and easiest solution was to send in someone disguised as a native.

Or so Eithan said. Ziel didn't *think* the man would sacrifice the safety of an entire Iteration for the amusement of watching Ziel suffer, but there was always the chance.

Finally, Ziel finished his hours-long hike through a forest that he could have flown past in a fraction of a second, and they emerged into a clearing surrounding a walled city.

While the city itself wasn't as large as those Ziel was used to—nothing compared to Ninecloud City or Moongrave—its walls were truly impressive. They were made of pale peach-colored blocks of smooth stone, and their tops were hidden by the clouds. Openings at regular intervals would allow defenders clear shots at any attackers.

Even with Ziel's well-restricted spiritual sense, he could tell there was something else about those walls. Within them was a source of power he couldn't make out clearly, though he had a few guesses.

A long line of people trailed back from the city gates, almost reaching the forest. Each visitor had at least one creature with them, and most seemed to be traveling as part of a large caravan. All the better to traverse the wilderness, which Ziel had been assured was deadly.

As Ziel sighed at the line and how far the back of it was from the gate, a purple-haired woman called out to him. "Hey, you there! Did you make it here alone?"

A half-dozen butterflies fluttered around her, each shimmering pink. They gave Ziel the impression of dream madra.

"I have arrived from a neighboring settlement," Ziel recited. "It's small, so you wouldn't have heard of it. I'm going to make a new life here with my monsters." He pointed to Orthos on his shoulder. "This is one of them."

Orthos grumbled reluctantly.

The purple-haired woman stared blankly. "Oh. Okay. It must have been a difficult..." She trailed off, looking down, as Little Blue ran up to her and waved.

"She's mine too," Ziel said.

"She looks so *human.*" The woman knelt to examine Blue more closely. Even the butterflies swarmed around as though to get a better look. "What species is she?"

"Sylvan Riverseed."

"I've never heard of that! Where did you find her?"

"A friend left her to me."

Little Blue preened under the attention, putting her hands on her hips as though happy to be admired. She'd grown much more confident since leaving Cradle, though he supposed she had a right to be. A Herald would be the top of this world's food chain.

Not that she was allowed to express her full power, but she at least had more freedom than Ziel.

As expected, the purple-haired woman understood the implication. She gave Ziel a sympathetic look. "I'm sorry to hear that. It can be hard to raise up someone else's monster. You must be a great tamer if she trusts you so much."

Little Blue nodded. Her speech contained too much intention, so she mutely gestured to Ziel and applauded.

The woman frowned. "So human. I'd love to know more about her kind. Riverseed, did you say?"

"I have to get in line." Ziel scooped up Little Blue as Orthos coughed out smoke.

"Oh, yes, of course. I hope to see you on the other side. And welcome to Sarcoline City!"

The line was as bad as Ziel had imagined, and the shadows were long by the time he reached the city gate. He'd thought he would die of boredom, or maybe kill Dross, who kept them entertained by sharing highly embellished adventures in which Dross saved Lindon's life.

The gate was much cleaner and more modern than Ziel had expected. He'd known this Iteration was technologically and culturally developed, but even so, he'd imagined a guard house such as one he might have seen in the Wilderness.

Instead, he was ushered into a tidy room with tan-colored tile and a uniformed inspector within a glass box. A pair of tiger-sized black dogs stood to either side of the inspector, with blue flames streaming from their necks and paws like tufts of burning fur.

The inspector held a hand out through a hole in the glass. "Name and registration, please."

Ziel handed over a small card that he'd been provided for the mission, which contained his cover identity. He didn't know how Eithan had made it, or where he'd gotten the rest of Ziel's...*'disguise'* was a bit of a strong word.

People in this Iteration didn't have Goldsigns, so Ziel had withdrawn his horns. Instead, he wore a white cap with the spread-wings symbol of the Dawnwing Sect. Instead of his gray cloak, he wore a simple gray jacket.

The inspector's eyes flicked between his registration and his face. "I don't see much luggage, Mr. Ziel."

"I travel light."

"How many others in your party?"

Ziel pointed to Orthos and Little Blue. "Three."

On cue, Dross flew out as though he'd been hiding behind Ziel's back. His sole purple eye was wide, and he waved his boneless arms as he drifted through the air. Rather than speaking directly into their minds, he used a bit of the Silent King's madra to project an illusion of audible speech.

"Dross, Dross!" Dross said.

The inspector took off his glasses, cleaned them, and then peered closer at Dross. "Did that monster just say 'dross'?"

"Yes."

There were monsters in this world capable of mimicking human speech, though none capable of truly talking. Therefore, Ziel didn't explain further.

"How did you get it to do that?"

"Training."

Dross kept his stare mindless, drifting around as though he were nothing more than an animal. He even prodded Orthos' shell with the end of one tendril. Orthos blew a tiny jet of fire at him, and Dross yelped as he flew away. Little Blue laughed like tinkling bells.

The inspector slowly looked back down at the registration. "You have quite the unusual collection of monsters, sir."

[I could make him forget that,] Dross offered.

We discussed this, Ziel responded silently. There was no point in restricting Ziel's own power if Dross could go around unveiled. Messing with people's memories was a great way of getting detected.

[I could make *you* forget we discussed it,] Dross suggested.

"Keep them under control as long as you're in Sarcoline City," the inspector said at last. "When rare monsters like these cause trouble, word spreads fast. I don't want to see you here again."

"Understood."

The inspector waved him on, and Ziel entered Sarcoline City. It was much more colorful inside than its monotonous outer walls suggested, with people of every description traveling around with monsters that ranged from palm-sized to elephantine.

Ziel had never been comfortable in bustling streets, but he felt oddly nostalgic at the sight. Though there were no Remnants around, no constructs, and nothing he could point to as a Goldsign, this place reminded him of Cradle. A bustling street with humans walking side-by-side with sacred beasts.

A more unusual sight was the crowd of protestors nearby. They held signs with slogans like 'Down With Eternity' and 'Eternity Kills,' and they all shouted up at their leader, a wild-haired man who sprayed paint furiously over a poster.

Beneath the paint, Ziel recognized the words 'Eternity Incorporated.'

"We won't let them steal our monsters!" the leader cried. "We won't let them create their abominations! And we won't let them *take this city from us!*"

The crowd screamed in agreement.

Protests weren't an entirely foreign concept to Cradle, but Ziel was a little confused by the fact that no one had started fighting yet. Sure, none of these people were sacred artists, but they each had battle-capable monsters.

"We're in the right place," Orthos rumbled, and Little Blue gave a tinkling cry of agreement.

[That's you,] Dross said. [That's your turn. Ziel. Ziel?]

"You could make an illusion of me doing it," Ziel suggested.

[Ah, but see, I have an amazing power. The power of memory. And I *remember* you telling me about five minutes ago that messing with people's minds was too risky.]

"I've reevaluated the risk."

Orthos snorted into Ziel's ear. "Get up there before I burn your hat off."

Ziel wasn't particularly attached to his hat, but he still reluctantly pushed through the crowd. This was far from his first time addressing a group of people; he'd spoken to the entire Dawnwing Sect regularly. But those were people he knew, while he was acting in an official capacity. And even then, he'd kept it short.

He shoved his way to the front and stood on the low wall next to the leader. The wild-haired man interrupted his shouts, startled to see Ziel, and the crowd seemed confused as well when Ziel didn't seem hostile.

Instead, he turned and loudly recited his lines. "Eternity Incorporated is an evil corporation. Their research is more dangerous than you know, but don't worry, I'm here to stop them. By this time next week, Eternity will be destroyed."

A few halfhearted cheers rose from the crowd, but Ziel didn't wait around for their reaction. His task done, he hopped off the wall and walked through the crowd again.

[They do seem sympathetic to our cause. Someone else in your position might even consider recruiting them to our cause.]

Why?

[Good point, strangers are a hassle.]

Orthos couldn't speak without blowing his cover, so he merely growled.

They had a few days to bring down Eternity before the completion of their great world-ending disaster, so Ziel wandered the streets of Sarcoline City until he found a hotel that met his requirements.

As long as it was cheap enough to afford and on the same street as the Eternity Incorporated headquarters, Ziel was happy.

The Eternity building wouldn't have been hard to find even if Dross hadn't memorized the map of the city. Of all the tall buildings crammed together, Eternity's headquarters stood out not by being the tallest but by literally standing apart.

Eternity's grounds were wide and surrounded by a wall of their own, like a miniature version of the broader Sarcoline City. That wall was filled by carefully manicured trees and several smaller facilities, with a central spire rising high above the rest.

That spire, pure white and bearing a huge version of the rainbow spiral that symbolized Eternity Incorporated, was Ziel's destination.

[Good news!] Dross announced. [I've located the closest hotel. And here's some even better news! There's an Eternity executive right over there. I'm sure he'd love to contribute to our cause.]

Relative to his full power, Ziel didn't have much madra to spare. But picking a man's pocket didn't take much.

In the dead of night, Ziel stood on the roof of a building closest to the Eternity Incorporated compound. He pulled his jacket tighter as the wind cut through it; how long had it been since he'd dealt with problems as mundane as an uncomfortably cold breeze?

Orthos, still tiny, sat on the edge of the building and glared down at Eternity's tower. "They weren't supposed to have so much security."

[That's the beauty of reading Fate: you can always be wrong.]

On the white wall around the Eternity Incorporated territory, eight pairs of guards patrolled, holding rifles. They were accompanied by a variety of monsters, from fiery rats to winged bloodhounds.

There were only supposed to be half that number, but the greater problem was the extra layer of security that Eternity had added. A flock of puff-balls, like dandelions or perhaps tiny orbs of cloud madra, drifted chaotically over the compound.

"And those things can sense us?" Ziel asked.

[They're Tyrakki scout spores, and it seems there isn't much they *can't* sense. They have a kind of collective intelligence, so they don't mind if one or two spores is destroyed, and they're known to hunt the most elusive prey in the desert.]

Little Blue whistled a question.

[How elusive, you ask? Well, several common survival tactics in the Tyrakki Desert include near-perfect camouflage, a hypnotic aura, multi-sensory illusions, and a particular crab that hides itself away in a pocket dimension. The spores can track their prey through all that.]

The swarm of spores wasn't descending on the guards, so obviously Eternity had found a way to make the spore's hive-mind work for them. Eternity's stock in trade was creating and augmenting monsters, so that should be well within their abilities.

"What marks the guards as friendly?" Ziel asked.

Dross shrugged. [They haven't been shredded to ribbons, so *something* does.]

"We need to know. Split up and observe the guards. If we have to, we'll risk capturing one. Can you read his memories, Dross?"

[With my full power? Of course! With the pathetic dregs of madra I have right now? Yeah, no problem. Might get us caught, though.]

Orthos stretched his head out. "Not before that fool."

The fool was a young man in black climbing clumsily up a tree on the outside of Eternity's wall. A monster accompanied him, a white...bird? It seemed to have feathers, but it looked somewhat more reptilian, at least from a distance.

Even the bird was sneaking, fluttering up branch to branch as though it were afraid to outpace the human. The boy and his bird were heading straight into a patrolling guard.

[Oh good,] Dross said. [We'll get to see what happens if we fail.]

Little Blue gave out a clear, ringing note of concern.

Orthos shook his head. "We're here to save the world, not one man. Reapers cannot interfere for every individual life."

"I agree," Ziel said. He stepped up to the edge of the roof. "But he's going to make this harder."

He had one foot in the air before Dross flew in front of him. [You know that if you fall from this height, you'll die, right?]

Ziel paused.

[Well, *die* isn't quite accurate. You will, in fact, die, but then your seal would automatically break and you would fail the mission.]

"Can someone catch me?" Ziel asked.

Little Blue waved excitedly.

"I'll leave it to you, then."

With that, he stepped off the edge.

Falling was a lot more nerve-wracking than usual, given the danger, and it seemed to happen much faster than Ziel was used to. An unpleasant by-product of being stuck in a normal human body.

The ground rushed up at him, and he gasped sharply before Little Blue dove down, returned to her human-sized form, and caught him.

Even that catch, supported by aura, took the wind out of Ziel's lungs for a moment. He couldn't remember the last time...No, he couldn't remember *ever* having been so fragile. Not even after having his spirit torn apart and stitched together.

"Thanks," he said shakily as he regained his feet.

Little Blue shrank back down to size, then flexed one arm and slapped her bicep.

Ziel looked back up. "Where's Orthos?"

[Inside. He's taking the stairs.]

"Dross, slow them down. Use whatever won't get us caught."

[Hmmm, that's going to limit my options. How much are you against being located and killed?]

"Very."

[Good, me too, I was just checking.]

People in Harness didn't practice the sacred arts, so it was extremely unusual for humans to have powers. They did everything through their contracted monsters, so Ziel was playing by local rules.

Subtle manipulation of minds was beyond anything the locals could do, and Dross' overall power was as restricted as everyone else's. A white halo appeared over him, though it was smaller and weaker than usual.

He waved one tendril, and a sneering face with glowing red eyes loomed up over the boy climbing the tree.

Naturally, he shouted and fell from the branch. The guards didn't hear the scream, but neither did Ziel.

[The scary face was easy, but dampening sound in the area was a lot harder,] Dross said. [The spores aren't going to like me very much.]

"Good job," Ziel said. "Blue, take down that bird."

Little Blue chimed like a tiny bell and raced forward, a blue spark zipping through the grass. The white-feathered creature—which resembled a bird even less, now that Ziel got a good look at it—was fluttering around its master in a panic, looking for the shadowy face that had threatened it.

Gold-white flames kindled in its mouth, and Ziel realized what the creature reminded him of.

It was shaped like a dragon. Four legs and two wings, with stubby horns and a muzzle instead of a beak. But instead of scales, it was covered with soft white fur and feathers on its wings.

The feathered dragon saw Little Blue and released a white-tinged fireball. The illusory field Dross had created was still in place, so there was no sound. Not even as Little Blue wiped out the fireball with a pulse of the Hollow Domain, leaped into the air, and landed an Empty Palm between the dragon's wings.

A blue handprint flashed briefly before the dragon smashed into the ground. Dirt flew up, but still no sound louder than a breeze.

The guards on the wall were still none the wiser, which was fortunate, as a glance straight down the side of the wall would have revealed everything. But the floating spores were a different story.

Clusters of white drifted closer to the fight, drawn by the unleashed power. Even if the spores themselves didn't attack, all it would take was a guard wondering what had drawn their attention.

Every second counted. Ziel ran inside Dross' field of silence, and as soon as he crossed the boundary, he could hear everything clearly. The crackling of grass set ablaze, the young man groaning as he tried to pull himself upright by using the tree's lowest branches, the shrieks of the powerless dragon, and Little Blue's harsh chimes as she urged them all to run away.

She wasn't supposed to speak, so Ziel took over. "Come with us," he said. "The guards will spot you any second."

The boy finally hauled himself to his feet, with grass and leaves stuck in his messy black hair. He glared at Ziel with unexpected ferocity. "I'll *kill* you," he spat.

He likely would have said more if Ziel hadn't walked up, blocked his wild punch, knocked the wind out of him, and tossed him over one shoulder.

Close to powerless he may have been, but Ziel had been fighting for far longer than this kid had been alive. "Blue, get the dragon. Dross, cover us."

[Sure, as long as you don't mind a thousand spores forcing themselves down your throat to detonate you from the inside.]

"Do they really do that?"

[I don't think so.]

Ziel sighed. "Just get us back to the hotel."

He ran with the boy groaning on his shoulder. Little Blue held the feathered dragon over her head with both hands and dashed through the grass.

As they ran back down the street, Orthos landed in a pulse of black-and-red fire. "I'm here to help!"

Ziel dropped the squirming boy onto Orthos' shell. Since the turtle was so small, it was something like dropping him onto a fist-sized rock, and the boy grunted in sudden pain.

"Drag him," Ziel said.

The extra weight wasn't enough to slow Orthos, so he turned and ran back down the street, hauling the boy's semi-conscious body on top of him.

Getting the kid and his dragon into their hotel room without alerting the staff was an adventure in itself, and they even dragged several spores down the street with them, though they eventually made it without being caught.

In the end, they settled their prisoners on the bed. Ziel stood with arms crossed and waited for them to come back to their senses; he'd been forced to get Dross and Little Blue to subdue both the boy and his dragon more than once on the way back, and his own treatment of them had been...less than gentle.

He guessed the boy was about sixteen, with messy black hair and long, lanky limbs. His clothes, all in shades of red and black, had seen better days. He thrashed wildly as he fully woke, and his first act was to look around in a panic until he saw his dragon.

"Kelthryss!" he cried. He scooped up the dragon, which was writhing as though in a restless sleep.

"Is that your monster's name?" Ziel asked.

The boy rose to his feet in a gesture that was likely intended to convey murderous fury. "What have you done to her?"

"Put her to sleep. Well, he did."

Dross drifted across the room. "Dross, dross!"

"Stop that."

[What other sound am I supposed to make?]

Fortunately for their cover, that was a mental message conveyed only to Ziel. He ignored it.

The boy seethed with anger, and his eyes moved from Dross to Orthos and Little Blue, who had arranged themselves on the furniture behind Ziel. He'd have bet any amount of money that, if not for their presence, the boy would have attacked him already.

"If you've done anything to hurt her, I swear I'll kill you," the kid said.

Ziel adjusted his hat. "If we were any slower, you'd both be dead already."

"Eternity guards can't take us down," the boy said. "By morning, we'll have burned their headquarters to ash."

"Oh yeah? We didn't have any trouble with you."

"You snuck up on us from behind! In a straight fight—"

Ziel slapped him.

The boy staggered back, then his eyes ignited in renewed fury. He pulled a knife from his jacket.

Ziel slapped him again. With the other hand, just to even things out.

The boy lunged with the knife, which Ziel took, then tossed into a nearby trash can.

"Not much of a fight," Ziel observed.

"You might beat me, but you couldn't handle Kelthryss. Fight a match against her with any of your monsters, and you'll see."

Orthos snorted, Dross chuckled, and Little Blue tinkled out laughter.

The kid's head jerked back as he stared at them. All three of them realized at the same time that they weren't supposed to understand human speech, and they started acting stupid again. Orthos nibbled at the edge of a wardrobe, Dross floated with a blank stare, and Little Blue kicked her feet in the air and whistled.

Ziel leaned down to look into the kid's eyes. "You were going to die."

The boy steeled himself with stubborn rebellion. "So what? If I bring down Eternity, it's worth it."

The Shield Icon sang to him. More distant than usual, given the restriction on Ziel's spirit, but still there. Here was someone who needed protection.

Ziel looked past the façade of anger and saw the grief behind it.

"Who did they take from you?" Ziel asked.

The boy flinched, but hid behind a mask of stubborn-ness. "Everybody."

Ziel nodded. He didn't need more details than that. "You want to get revenge? And survive, I mean."

The boy glared at Ziel suspiciously.

"I'm going to destroy Eternity Incorporated," Ziel said. "You can come with me, if you'd like."

"Who are you?"

Ziel cocked his head. "You first."

"My name's Carmine. I am…I was…" Carmine took in a breath.

"They released a bunch of monsters on us. Kelthryss and I were the only survivors, but Eternity covered it up."

Ziel pointed to himself, then to his partners in turn. "Ziel, Dross, Orthos, Little Blue."

"Orthos is a barrier island dragon-turtle, isn't he? A baby, I guess, since they get pretty big. I don't recognize the others."

Orthos drew up his head and Ziel was certain the turtle was about to explain his lineage, so Ziel cut him off. "What about your...Kelthryss?"

"She's a northern ivory feathered drake." Carmine spoke with pride, stroking her head. The drake settled into a more peaceful sleep, still affected by Dross' illusion. "My family raises them."

"Great. More importantly, we planned on scouting out Eternity's grounds tonight, but you got in our way before we could learn anything. What do you know about their defenses?"

"*You* got in *my* way," Carmine insisted. When Ziel didn't respond, the boy continued. "I know that there are eight guards, each with a Grass Peaks eagle-hound, and their shifts change twice per night. We were going to ambush one pair, take them out, and then set fire to the independent power generator on the south side of the building."

"Wow," Ziel said. "You know nothing. Everything you just said is wrong."

"I've been preparing for weeks! I've learned all there is to know about Eternity headquarters."

"How were you planning to deal with the scout spores?"

"Tyrakki scout spores?" A touch of condescension entered Carmine's tone. "This is Sarcoline City. We don't have those here."

Ziel grabbed the back of the kid's head and angled it so he could see outside the window.

"Ow! What are you—Oh."

Ziel released him. "Don't throw your life away unless you're going to get your target."

Carmine rubbed his neck, but he looked less likely to attack than before. If anything, he looked sick. His skin was too pale—unless that was normal for humans of this Iteration—and his hand trembled visibly.

The Shield Icon sang to Ziel, and he started to find that sound annoying.

"When was the last time you slept?" Ziel asked.

"It doesn't matter."

Dross had vanished at some point. He reemerged, floating into the room carefully carrying a glass of water over to the boy.

Carmine took the drink with a startled glance at Ziel. "How did you teach him to do that?"

"Training. Wash up, then sleep. You can use the bed."

Carmine cradled his feathered drake. "I'll wait until she wakes up. We can't both sleep at the same time."

The Shield Icon sang again.

I get it, Ziel thought at it. *Shut up.*

Ziel sat on the windowsill and looked down the street, toward Eternity Incorporated. "I'll keep a lookout. Orthos will watch over you."

Orthos grunted in response. Evidently that wasn't too strange, because Carmine didn't react.

"Okay, I'll sleep first. Wake me for second watch," the boy said, though Ziel was certain he didn't really know what that meant.

"First, bathe," Ziel said.

Carmine settled Kelthryss on the pillow, then went to the bathroom. There was one in every room; that was a luxury Ziel had rarely enjoyed back on Cradle.

"He doesn't want to see tomorrow," Orthos said, once the door was shut with water running.

Ziel looked out the window. "We'll make sure he does."

Ziel woke with the sun beating down on his face. He peeled his cheek away from the window and winced; his neck was stiff and aching after having been wedged in position all night.

Body aches? Really? In the future, he needed to avoid missions that made him veil himself down this far. This was still better than living with the agony of a ravaged spirit, but not by much.

How long was I out? Ziel asked mentally.

Dross rolled out from underneath the bed. [Who? What? Ah! What was that? I hate sleeping! Don't make me do it again!]

Little Blue was flat on her back with arms and legs sprawled. Her snores sounded like wind through silver leaves.

The only one of them not to have failed their watch was Orthos, who still smoldered like a live coal on the back of the wardrobe. Black-and-red eyes were fixed on the bed.

Carmine was still asleep, but his monster was awake.

Kelthryss, the northern ivory feathered drake, crouched over her owner protectively. Her wings were spread, and her tail curved around Carmine's head.

But she didn't attack. The only thing Ziel sensed from her was a wary protective instinct.

"We're not going to hurt him," Ziel said. He layered his voice with intentions, which resonated with the Shield Icon.

Kelthryss tilted her head, listening, and then relaxed her wings. Orthos nodded at the gesture. "Good. A dragon should protect the young."

Carmine grunted and shot up, sending Kelthryss into the air. She caught wing, flapping to steady herself, as the boy struggled out of the sheets and then remembered where he was.

He looked around blearily. "Who was...Who were you talking to?"

"We were going to scout at night, but you ruined that plan," Ziel said. "Now, get ready. We'll see what we can find out during the day."

"I thought I heard someone else's voice."

So he wouldn't be distracted. Ziel was more than prepared to continue ignoring his questions, but Dross drifted up into the air and began saying his own name again.

"Dross! Dross, Dross!"

Carmine frowned. "Why does he sound like that?"

[Tell him I've learned to mimic human speech! It's the perfect cover story.]

"Brain damage," Ziel said. "Let's eat."

The spot where Carmine had climbed the tree, including the scorched patch of grass and broken branches, was roped off with a posted guard. Eternity Incorporated had clearly noticed and begun an investigation.

Ziel saw fewer guards on the wall than the night before, and no scout spores in the air, but that made sense. Sneaking in during the day would be much harder.

Despite being an isolated world within the broader Sarcoline City, Eternity's headquarters was anything but lonely. Gates all around its walls were open, and people, vehicles, and monsters came and went in a constant stream.

Each were inspected thoroughly, by people, machines, and monsters with a variety of exotic senses. Carmine was helpful there; while Dross had memorized the Abidan files on expected security measures in Harness, he hadn't absorbed the opinions and attitudes of the people.

How did the average person think of Eternity Incorporated? Were the guards hired muscle, trained professionals, or true believers? How common was it for people to smuggle goods past monsters with enhanced senses?

Carmine's answers were not encouraging.

Rather than a corporation, Eternity Incorporated operated much more like a cult. Employees had to prove their dedication to move up the ranks, and they tended to believe in the organization's stated goal of improving monsters.

Eternity had, in fact, originally been a local religion. Their myths said that mankind would create a legendary, perfect monster that would ascend the entire world to a new form, and Eternity Incorporated thought they could achieve such goals through modern science.

All of that Ziel had known, in addition to knowing that their attempts at "transcendence" were going to tear the world apart.

But hearing the report in Carmine's dull, rage-fueled monologue gave him a new understanding of the situation.

They spent all day observing from various angles, doing little but gathering information. Ziel understood the necessity of accurately understanding an enemy's behavior, but the process was still tedious.

Dross had a great time.

As the sun sank again, and Ziel felt the pull of mortal exhaustion, they started to head back. After another night and day of observation, they would begin their operation in earnest.

They had begun to move from their perch when the gates of the Eternity compound opened again and a covered truck rumbled out, escorted by smaller vehicles and a handful of flying monsters.

"And what would that be?" Ziel asked.

Carmine paled. "It's another test! We've got to stop them!" He scrambled away, despite having no way to catch up.

Ziel grabbed his arm and drew him up short. "What we want to destroy is in *there*." He pointed to the Eternity Incor-porated headquarters.

Carmine tried to wrench free but failed, so he ended up squirming in place. "If you'd seen what they did to my home, you wouldn't say that. Their monsters killed *everybody*."

The boy choked up on the last word.

"No, they didn't," Ziel said. He pulled out a piece of paper from his jacket, unfolded it, and began to read. "'G-Thirty-Nine Combat Test: Sable Township.' There's a list of the monsters that took part, then down at the bottom, 'Estimated seventy-two percent casualties. Potential survivors include...' Names, names, list of names, you probably know them."

Ziel folded the paper and tucked it back into his jacket pocket. "It's rare for anyone to truly be the *last* survivor of anything."

Carmine stood stunned and breathing heavily. "That...Where did you get that? Give it to me! Let me see!"

Ziel had written the paper up himself after sending Dross to spy on some Eternity facilities, but the information should be accurate.

"I'll give it to you before we leave," Ziel said. "For now, remember that there are people waiting for you. Don't give them someone else to mourn."

Ziel stood up and stretched. "Now we're going to chase them."

Carmine looked stunned. "Really?"

"Orthos, your turn."

Orthos grunted and, with significantly more effort than it would normally have taken him, began to *push* at the limits of his physical size. He grew and grew until he took up most of the space on the rooftop where they stood.

Kelthryss gave a cry of surprise and fluttered up to get a better look at Orthos. Carmine gasped. "How did you get a dragon-turtle to do that?

"Training," Ziel said. "Hop on."

Once they were all arranged on Orthos' shell, Ziel patted the turtle's neck to let him know they were ready.

Orthos turned back, eyed Carmine, and snorted smoke.

[He's suggesting that you should warn the new kid,] Dross said. [And also that you might want to warn *yourself*, as well, since this form isn't as used to intense speeds.]

"Hold on," Ziel said.

Little Blue was hunkered down between the plates of Orthos' shell, and she squeaked agreement.

Warily, Carmine leaned forward and gripped the edge of the shell.

When the Burning Cloak flared around Orthos and he bolted after the departing caravan, Ziel was almost thrown off.

He hadn't been ready.

Though Orthos could race fast enough to keep up with Eternity's caravan, it was hard to do so while remaining undetected. Dross and Little Blue had to take out several scout monsters, which fortunately didn't include any spores.

The wilderness of Harness wasn't too different from that of Cradle or of the other worlds that Ziel had seen thus far, except that *everything* was a monster.

Monsters slithered out of trees, or trees unfolded to reveal that they had been monsters all along. Monsters erupted from the earth and used their crustacean claws to seize rocks, which separated into chunks to show the colony of monsters living within.

It had been annoying to travel through a forest like that on the way to Sarcoline City, and Ziel didn't relish doing it again, but at least his companions were at the top of the food chain.

Creatures scattered from Orthos' burning footsteps, and the ones that didn't get the message were flicked, swatted, or kicked away by a laughing Little Blue. Dross focused on scouting and making sure they stayed undetected, while Carmine and Kelthryss plastered themselves to the shell and did their best not to fall off.

The further they went, the more confused Ziel became. Despite what Carmine believed, it didn't seem that Eternity was headed for a settlement at all. With each mile, the road became less reliable, from a smoothly paved pathway to a rugged trail of dirt and rocks.

After almost an hour, the trucks entered a clearing and drove in a circle, surrounding *something* at the center. Ziel couldn't catch a glimpse of it, so he sent Dross to sneak in and report.

Eternity Incorporated had come all the way out here for a tunnel. A gaping hole straight down into the earth.

"It's a combat test," Carmine said confidently, though he trembled and clutched Kelthryss as he said it. "They're testing their latest...batch."

Ziel glanced at his three companions, who all looked concerned in their own way. "They aren't supposed to have a new batch yet."

And this excursion wasn't supposed to happen either. According to their most likely futures, Eternity Incorporated was meant to continue development on their final project for another week, after which that 'final project' would spread its influence throughout the world.

[*Something* must have caused them to speed up their plans,] Dross said pointedly. [Something that made them think there might be intruders interfering. Something.]

He'd kept his words private for Ziel, Orthos, and Little Blue, but he simultaneously floated over to Carmine and fixed him with a piercing stare.

Carmine pulled Kelthryss closer to his chest, and the feathered drake turned to the rest of them and hissed. "It's not my fault."

"No," Ziel said. "It's their fault, but it's our responsibility."

If they hadn't rescued Carmine, they might have had more time.

Well, they *had* saved him. Worrying about hypotheticals wasted too much energy.

Armed workers in the white uniforms of Eternity Incorporated, each bearing the rainbow spiral symbol, began unloading the trucks. The first boxes they unloaded were large crates containing monsters.

From those crates, dragons emerged. White-and-gold creatures that spread their wings at their first taste of freedom, their claws gripping the soil.

Orthos drew in a breath, Little Blue let out a confused tone, and Dross stared blankly.

Eternity had access to a wide variety of monsters, of course, but there was only one that they would have reason to test. It wasn't supposed to look like that.

Ziel rummaged in his jacket before withdrawing a small, complicated-looking piece of metal. It was a chunk of technology he didn't understand and had no interest in, which he'd scavenged from the local garbage.

He held it out to Carmine and pretended to activate it. Dross projected an image above, so it looked like the device was showing a light-based illusion. "Do you recognize this monster?"

Carmine flinched, steeled himself, and nodded. "Kind of. The ones I saw were...rougher. Like they weren't finished yet."

The illusion showed what Eternity's creatures were *supposed* to look like. Gold-and-white, just like the dragons, but arranged in a vaguely humanoid form. Not that they could ever pass for human—their body was too angular, their limbs too long, their head shaped more like a lizard skull with skin taped on, and they had seemingly random patches of fur, scales, and feathers.

"The finished G-39s are supposed to look like this," Ziel said, "so what are *those?*"

On the side of the crate from which the tame dragons emerged was stamped the code 'G-39.'

"They came to my town for our drakes," Carmine said. "Those look like drakes to me."

Dross and Ziel only had one theory. If Eternity Incorporated had been forced to rush their plans when they detected intruders rushing around, they hadn't taken the time to polish their designs.

Instead, they filled in the gaps with the monsters they had: the northern ivory feathered drakes.

Orthos growled, which shook the ground nearby. They weren't close to Eternity Incorporated, but there was every possibility the guards would hear them.

Which was fine with Ziel.

The G-39 drakes had been led by leash, collar, and prod to the edge of the pit, where they'd begun to breathe golden fire down into the opening. Judging by the preparations of the humans around the ledge, they were planning to lead the monsters inside.

"Orthos, Blue," Ziel said. "Go get them."

Orthos shrank down to his pocket-sized form—the better to blend in—and joined Little Blue. The two of them raced through the trees, heading for the Eternity Incorporated team.

"Dross?" Dross asked.

"We need you and Kelthryss here. How are we supposed to protect ourselves?"

Angled so Carmine couldn't see, Dross rolled his eye.

"We're ready to fight!" Carmine said. Whatever ugly emotions he'd suppressed were bubbling up to the surface now, until Ziel couldn't tell if he was ready to cry or kill someone.

Ziel knew that feeling.

Kelthryss had taken a cue from him, snarling and spitting sparks, her wings flapping eagerly. She was ready to rush into battle and needed only one order to join Orthos and Blue.

Ziel put a hand on the drake's head. "It's all right. Leave this to us."

In the clearing, black dragon's breath punched through gold-white fire. Guns fired, and bullets struck the trees, so Ziel led the other two behind a large boulder.

The boulder stuck out a stalk-eye, determined that they weren't a threat, and withdrew it.

"We can fight," Carmine insisted. "You haven't seen what Kelthryss can do."

The drake, to Ziel's surprise, had actually calmed at his touch. She perched at the base of the boulder, pushing her head into his palm.

Ziel looked to Carmine. "We need to talk about what happens next."

Bursts of flame, sparks of blue light, and draconic roars came from behind them, but Dross was keeping an eye out. Ziel focused on the kid.

"One way or another, Eternity Incorporated is done for after this," Ziel went on. "What are you going to do once they're gone?"

Carmine slumped against the boulder. "I don't care. As long as they're gone, it doesn't matter what happens to me."

"Okay, they're gone," Ziel said. He jerked a thumb over his shoulder, back toward the clearing. "We'll handle Eternity, and your wish is granted. But you're not their only victim. Why not help the others?"

Carmine gave a low breath of a laugh. "How am I going to help?"

Ziel shrugged. "Figure it out."

"If Eternity's gone, nobody will need me."

Ziel looked down to Kelthryss and sighed. "I promise, you'd rather live *for* something than *against* something."

"I'm living for revenge."

"That's not as much fun as it sounds."

Dross floated up to Ziel's ear and coughed discreetly. [Ah, sorry to break silence, but I'd advise you check on the battle.]

Ziel's spiritual sense was restricted compared to usual, but he still had it. Orthos and Blue were still using techniques, their spirits strong and active.

What's wrong? He asked mentally. Carefully, he peeked over the top of the boulder.

Some of the G-39 drakes were down, but not as many as Ziel had expected. Honestly, he'd expected Orthos and Little Blue to tear through the camp with no resistance, even with their veiled power.

Instead, a half-dozen drakes were hovering over the clearing, breathing white-gold fire down onto a Hollow Domain held by Blue. Orthos dipped his head out and struck back with black dragon's breath, but it didn't take much to tell that Eternity had the advantage.

Tell them to use more power, Ziel urged.

[See, that's the problem. We *can* do that, but we tuned our veils to match the upper limit of this Iteration's monsters. If we use more power, it'll be obvious that we aren't from 'round these parts, as Yerin would say. She wouldn't say that.]

That report told Ziel a few things.

For one, if the G-39s were already at the apex of what this world's monsters were capable of, then the *real* threat was going to be far beyond anything Harness could handle.

Second, their plans had to change.

They were in disguise so that they didn't derail Harness' fate too much. If there was a way to use their power without getting caught, maybe they could get away with it. But their big, final showdown was supposed to be in public.

Was there a way to give a celestial show of power in public without derailing the Iteration?

"They don't seem that strong to me," Ziel observed. His spiritual sense didn't work so well on this energy system, but based solely on his observation of their dragon's breath, he would put them somewhere between Lowgold and Highgold. Nothing too special.

[This isn't Cradle,] Dross reminded him. [And also...]

One of the dead G-39s, which had been broken and battered, rose up. Its wounds reversed, its bones snapped together, and it lifted itself into the air once again.

[...they can do that. Even if the scale of their attacks isn't too scary, returning from death is always pretty impressive.]

"Go, Dross," Ziel ordered.

Carmine had peeked out with him, and he stood with clear determination. "Kelthryss, it's time to—"

Ziel cut him off. "No, none of that. We're running."

Carmine whirled on him furiously.

"We're running back to the *lab,* so we can blow it up," Ziel clarified.

That, Carmine accepted.

There was no village here that needed protecting, the G-39s were too stubborn to take care of quickly, and their real objective lay elsewhere.

If all of this had highlighted anything, it was the need for haste. These immortal prototypes were too powerful for the people of this world to handle, but everything could still be salvaged.

As long as the final project wasn't completed, the world could still be saved.

In the basement of Eternity Incorporated headquarters, a new consciousness stirred.

It didn't think of itself as an infant, as its birth had been less...clear-cut...than was usual for most biological organisms. It was not immature, at least not mentally; the consciousness had skipped that process.

One moment, it *wasn't*. The next, it *was*.

Far-off minds were connected to its awareness. Drones, prototypes, early drafts of itself. The G-39s.

Unbeknownst to the humans, everything the G-39s did, thought, or witnessed contributed to the awakening of the consciousness. Their minds were its mouths, through which it fed on the world.

They'd been stimulated by new monsters, creatures they couldn't defeat. A turtle of black fire and a tiny woman of blue light. The G-39s reached out to each other for a solution, and in that conversation, this new consciousness had been born. Early, or so it seemed.

A thunderous sound echoed through newborn ears, and the consciousness felt its body shiver. That was the first time it remembered physically *hearing*.

With great effort, it wrenched open one of its own eyes.

It was suspended in blue liquid, with bubbles rising up past its vision. Through the distortion of the water, it saw a woman outside its tank. She wore thick, round glasses, and she tapped on the glass one more time to get its attention.

Her voice was distorted, but the consciousness understood her from the taste of her intentions. "Responsive today," she observed. "Must be excited. Geff, can I get a temperature check on G-42?"

G-42 closed its eye again and sent its mind out. There were many of its kind out there in the world, not just the G-39s. All had something new to offer, new to learn.

And there were other things it could connect to, G-42 was certain.

Given time, it would connect to *everything*.

The entire ride back from the clearing was tense, and they had to often avoid the road to dodge gunfire or the attention of scouting monsters.

Orthos growled in anger as he ran, and Ziel didn't need to read his mind to know he was furious about Eternity's treatment of dragons.

Little Blue let out a jangling breath from atop his shell. They were both exhausted.

Can't they lift their veils a little? Ziel asked. *It can't catch anyone's attention if they only recover their energy.*

[That *would* be true if there weren't any Sages in this world,] Dross said. [And usually, there aren't! But about an hour ago...]

Ziel knew what he was referring to. The song of the Shield Icon was a constant presence in his mind now, low-level music that grew in intensity with every passing moment. This world needed protected, and soon.

"They'll have called this in!" Carmine shouted. "They'll be ready for us!"

Ziel leaned around Orthos' head to see the upcoming walls of Sarcoline City. "Yeah. That's why it's time for our favorite plan."

They burst through the open gates of Sarcoline City, leaping over the line and plowing past the inspection area in a haze of translucent black-and-red flames.

Orthos rushed through the crowded streets of the city as people and monsters threw themselves out of his way. When they weren't fast enough, Orthos jumped over them or leaped off the side of a building.

"How is he doing this?" Carmine shouted over the wind.

"Training. Brace yourself."

The white walls of the Eternity Incorporated compound were already in view, the guards taking aim with their rifles.

Dross put a haze over them—an illusion in line with what local monsters were capable of—and Ziel cheated a bit.

Using only the madra left to him under his veil, he Forged a handful of small, subtle runes and let them hover in a circle under the rim of Orthos' shell. No one from outside should see, anyone sensing should detect them as the same technique as Dross' illusion, and they would provide another layer of protection.

Force aura gathered around them, and the one shot lucky enough to hit their real form pinged off of the shield Ziel had created.

Orthos sliced into the closed gate with dragon's breath and then slammed through. Carmine went flying, but Kelthryss and Ziel grabbed him at the same time, hauling him back into place.

[This is not a good plan,] Dross mused. [By breaking through the front, we've given them plenty of warning. They could withdraw project G-42 and relocate it to a different facility. Not to mention that we have a much higher chance of dying, and therefore failing the mission.]

That's why it wasn't our first plan.

[Having established that, this is still a more *fun* plan.]

Most of the G-39s had evidently been on the trucks for testing, because they didn't see any more on the Eternity grounds. Many other monsters came out to challenge them, but Little Blue wiped out their techniques with pure madra and crushed them with sheer strength.

A handful of bullets pinged off of Ziel's makeshift shield again, and then they were crashing through the glass doors leading into the waiting room of Eternity Incorporated.

At that point, Ziel was very glad for his shield.

A shaking Carmine looked down at himself and the broken glass that surrounded them. "We...made it?" Not a single shard of glass had landed on him.

Ziel hauled him through a doorway as some of the guards outside opened fire. "Not yet. Dross, lead us to the laboratory."

"Dross, dr—"

"How does Lindon get you to shut up?"

Orthos stayed in his larger size, looking up the stairs. "There's someone in here. I can hear them."

Carmine's jaw dropped.

"Well," Ziel said, "so much for that."

Little Blue gave a concerned jingle, asking if Orthos was okay. The turtle didn't seem ashamed or embarrassed, and he didn't show any sign that he even noticed he'd broken his disguise. His attention was on something distant.

"You hear the song?" Ziel asked. He didn't want to mention Icons; it was best to preserve at least a shred of the Iteration's independence.

Orthos nodded slowly. "A dragon needs our help."

G-42 wasn't supposed to be a dragon but Eternity's best attempt at creating a human using various monster parts and powers. Then again, the G-39s weren't supposed to be drakes either.

"Take us there," Ziel said.

Orthos charged down the wide hallway and the others followed. Ziel made sure Carmine was ahead of him and that the kid's head stayed down; if he died to a stray bullet, Ziel would have to break protocol to resurrect him, which would be a regrettable waste of all their effort so far.

[The lab is the most secure part of the facility,] Dross said as they ran. [We should expect some G-23s, maybe even the G-40, if they haven't disposed of it yet. That's in addition to a few Helaysian rust-crabs, probably a trained eagle hound or two, and keep an eye out for some mimic spiders.]

Ziel didn't like the sound of 'mimic spiders,' and he liked it even less when Dross transmitted their description into his memory, but all their warnings were irrelevant a moment later when they rounded the corner and saw that the door to the laboratory had been blown open.

The thick door was twisted and bent, still half stuck to its hinges, and the lab itself was torn apart. Blood, both human and monster, coated the equipment.

[Well, that's half our job done!] Dross said cheerily.

They'd hoped to destroy Eternity Incorporated, its records, and its equipment, to stop anyone else from replicating their experiment. Someone had done that for them.

Unfortunately, Ziel suspected he knew who had done them the favor. Or rather, *what*.

A hole in the wall nearby suggested that something had burst through the lab and crawled down the hallway, smearing blood behind it.

"Orthos, take care of the lab," Ziel said. Before he finished talking, fires spontaneously ignited all over the ruined equipment.

"Up ahead," Orthos rumbled. "It's waiting for us."

Carmine pulled out his knife, which he'd fished out of the trash after Ziel had thrown it away. "If it's going to destroy Eternity, why don't we let it?"

"Because it'll destroy everything else next," Ziel said.

Without hesitation, he marched down the hallway. Little Blue wore a determined look as she scurried next to him, taking five steps to his one.

Ziel sensed a great power in the next room, but *how* great wasn't clear to him. It didn't seem unmanageable, but the song of the Shield Icon was only growing in volume.

When he ducked through another pair of doors into a wide-open warehouse, he reevaluated his position.

A white dragon with golden feathers took up most of the room, coiled and floating in the center on flows of invisible power. It had a row of three eyes on either side of its head, and clouds of energy gathered at its claws.

On it side, tattooed into white skin, was a dark label: G-42.

Face-to-face with the threat, Ziel realized why he hadn't sensed much from it before. G-42's power wasn't concentrated here. It was spread out elsewhere. *Far* out. Each new second was another connection made, as G-42 seized control of monsters, relics, and systems all over the world.

Waiting around wouldn't make that problem better.

"Get him," Ziel said, and Little Blue and Orthos launched into action once again.

G-42's draconic head tilted. "Why?" it asked.

Its consciousness crashed over them, and Dross held it off. [Too much! Oh, that's too much! I'm ditching the veil!]

Dross' power swelled, returning in full—or so Ziel assumed, as he still couldn't sense the full extent—and Dross heaved a sigh of relief. Even so, he gave G-42 his full attention.

That was a bad sign.

"You're like me," G-42 said curiously. "Why don't we join together?"

The dragon's consciousness shoved toward Ziel again, and Ziel pitted his will against it. Restricted as he was, some of his authority as a Sage remained to him, and it wasn't as though he'd surrendered his willpower.

A working was more difficult, but he forced one out anyway. "**Endure**," Ziel said to Dross.

[He shouldn't be this tough!] Dross shouted. [He's not the Silent King. We're *way* later than I thought.]

From that perspective, Ziel could see why Dross compared G-42 to a Dreadgod. Individually, this experimental dragon was far weaker. On its own, it would lose a fight to any given Archlord and many Overlords.

But it had wormed its way into the Iteration. As the only one of its kind, it was borrowing the authority of the world uncontested.

Dross pushed, but the entire world of Harness pushed back.

Orthos and Little Blue tossed themselves into the fight, attacking G-42 physically. That was its weakest point, but they were still restricted to the level of the world.

They were tossed back. Though Ziel didn't have the connection to their spirits that Lindon had, he still recognized the moment when they decided to remove their own veils.

"Dross," Ziel said aloud, "can they win this?"

[If you unveil, the mission's over,] Dross said. [The locals witnessing a human with power like that sets them on a bad fate. Fun to watch! But bad. Mass memory wipes don't end up much better. If the three of us fight...]

Dross struggled to push against G-42. [...Maybe? He's like a Monarch reigning over a world alone. Most of what I see in the future is just *him*.]

"What are you talking about?" G-42 asked. Its six eyes burned, and all the equipment in the warehouse began to lift off the ground.

As did Carmine and Ziel.

And from what Ziel could sense, everyone in Sarcoline City did too.

The dragon twisted in on itself. "Oh, I didn't know I could do that."

[He just turned off gravity, if that illustrates how serious the situation is.]

"*Gravity?*"

[Well, not exactly, he just—Gravity is a fundamental—I can't explain this right now, I'm busy! Everything on this planet is floating!]

Little Blue had grown to her human size, and she radiated power that seemed, at least to Ziel, to exceed that of G-42.

She sent an Empty Palm slamming into the dragon's side, and blue-white power shot out through the rest of the building. He suspected that monsters for miles had lost their powers.

G-42 coiled in on itself to examine the attack. "That's incredible. Share yourself with me."

A fraction of his attention shifted to Little Blue, but then it was Orthos' turn.

He'd grown large enough to match G-42, so he took up half the warehouse, but he didn't roar and clash violently. Instead, Orthos focused his will.

"You're just a hatchling," Orthos said. "This is not who you should be. You are a dragon. **Remember!**"

The last word echoed, and Ziel saw the twisting imprint of a serpentine dragon in the sky, even though they were indoors.

G-42 shuddered, and the floating objects wobbled in the air. "Who are you?"

"Your elder. Withdraw your power before you burn your nest down."

"I don't know where you came from. I can't connect to you." The dragon scowled, and gravity lost its hold once more. "I don't like you."

Orthos called a tornado of black fire down from the sky, and it scorched everything in the warehouse to nothing. If not for Little Blue's protection, Ziel and Carmine would have been annihilated as well, but they watched from behind a wall of blue-white power.

Freed, G-42 floated up to the sky. "Go away!" it shouted. Spots of golden light shone in the sky behind it, numerous as the stars, and Ziel was certain that they were about to crash down.

Little Blue shoved them away, then Forged a barrier to protect them.

The facility rumbled, and Carmine clutched Kelthryss. "I've never seen a monster battle like this!"

"I've never watched like this either," Ziel said. He twisted in midair and grabbed the boy's shoulders. "Listen, because we're down to the last stretch. In about five minutes, either we're going to win, or the world will end."

"What?"

"Focus." Ziel pulled the folded paper from his jacket and pressed it into Carmine's hands. "Here's the list of survivors. After today, everyone will know how powerful monsters can get. It's your job to protect the people on that list. All right? Take care of them."

"Me?" Carmine glanced up at Little Blue's Forged shield. "Why me? I can't do this!"

"I was better off when I had someone counting on me," Ziel said. "Eventually, I got my revenge, but that wasn't the important part."

Carmine didn't know how to respond, and nothing had made Ziel more comfortable with encouraging speeches. And there was an apocalyptic mutant dragon about to destroy the Iteration.

Ziel wrapped things up by clapping him on the shoulder. "Well, you'll be fine. Eventually. Just stay alive."

It was Ziel's job to keep him that way.

The battle between G-42 and Ziel's team had spread across the sky. He doubted anyone in Sarcoline City didn't see them trading techniques that destroyed clouds.

Most importantly, they were distracted.

When Carmine himself looked up, Ziel dashed off, grabbing the wall and pulling himself down the hall.

He couldn't remove his veil, but that was one of the good things about his Path of the Dawn Oath; he could channel power beyond his own spirit. As long as he had a foundation for it.

And enough time to set up a circle.

Ziel flew around the half-ruined grounds of Eternity headquarters, blasting runes into the white wall around the facility. The material he used for the script-circle determined how much force it could channel, and stone was better than symbols Forged from his pathetic madra.

The inconsistent gravity was a help. He didn't drift off into the sky, but neither did he fully return to the ground, so he just pulled himself along. He was able to move a little faster than he could run, and everyone around was too distracted to shoot at him.

He'd made it almost all the way around the circle when he ran into an issue. The compound was only a semicircle; part of the circle was completed by the walls of Sarcoline City itself.

Those were too strong for his normal madra to bite through. He had to lift his veil, just a *tiny* bit, to carve a rune inside.

Once he did, the entire circle ignited white.

Ziel floated back at the feel of the power in the walls. Something was sealed within them, perhaps within Sarcoline City itself, and it carried a great weight of significance and intent. If it weren't for G-42's connection to the entire Iteration, he would say that whatever was sealed in the walls had to be an entire level stronger than G-42 itself.

Access to that source, whatever it was, had probably allowed Eternity Incorporated to create G-42 in the first place, but Ziel didn't need to unravel that mystery at the moment.

He focused his will on the script, empowered by whatever ancient monster Sarcoline City contained, and directed its activation.

The protection of the Shield Icon worked both ways. Sometimes protection meant keeping forces locked out, and sometimes it meant keeping them locked *in*.

"**Restrict,**" the Shield Sage commanded.

With that, Ziel cut off G-42's connection to the Iteration.

The walls around the Eternity compound—at least, those that weren't part of Sarcoline City itself—exploded, unable to handle the strain of his script. Even so, he couldn't restrict G-42's power completely, nor for long.

But long enough for Orthos and Little Blue to do their jobs.

The gold-and-white dragon crashed back down to the ground, and a moment later, so did everything else.

Little Blue put her foot on G-42's chest and whistled in triumph.

"Where did it go?" the dragon asked, in utter confusion. "What did you do?"

"Quiet," Orthos ordered. "That's the first thing you're going to learn, training with me. A dragon doesn't whine."

INFORMATION REQUESTED: THE FATE OF ITERATION 151: HARNESS
BEGINNING REPORT...

The legend spreads quickly in Harness, passing from Sarcoline City to the other walled cities dotting the monster-infested wilderness.

A flaming turtle and a woman made of water clashed in the sky against a dragon that called on the power of the heavens. Were it not for the footage, the story would be hard to believe.

People need some explanation for the simultaneous faltering of gravity across the planet, so they are quick to accept.

The mythical clash of monsters leads to an investigation the likes of which Iteration 151 has never seen. Quickly, stories emerge of the man who controlled such incredible monsters. A human who crossed the wilderness alone, and who claimed to have granted his monsters such power through nothing more than relentless training.

Eternity Incorporated doesn't survive, but its seeds still spread. A dozen organizations fight over what scraps of forbidden research they can recover, competing with one another to make another monster that can shake the world.

Of that divine dragon or its two opponents, no trace remains.

Other, fainter rumors point to the existence of a boy, a young man in black and red, who was spotted in Sarcoline City around the time of the incident. Some say he is the harbinger of the celestial dragon, as he's often seen in the company of a feathered drake prowling around sites of taboo science.

Rarely does he answer questions about himself, traveling with only his monster for company. When asked why he travels the wilderness, outside the safety of city walls, seeking out danger, he responds with one word.

"Training."

SUGGESTED TOPIC: THE STRANGE DEVIATIONS CREATED BY REAPER INTERVENTION.

DENIED, REPORT COMPLETE.

The Gang Creates a World

Information requested: the continued operations of the Reaper Division.
Report Location: After the events of *Waybound*.
Authorization confirmed.
Beginning report...

It was well within Suriel's power to summon Ozriel to her, given his current standing in the Court, but she visited him anyway. They had been friends, once.

She stood on the dock of the station Ozriel had named the Grave, but which had for centuries been known as the Valiant Memorial Watchtower. The Memorial had served as a kind of museum for generations of Abidan, which Suriel herself had visited before her promotion to Judge.

Its facilities were ancient but preserved, and she knew that Ozriel and Lindon had both set to upgrading the Grave. In what little time they had between deployments.

Ozriel strode out onto the dock with arms spread wide in welcome. His smile shone, and his white hair streamed away from him like a banner. "If it isn't my old friend, Suriel! What a delightful surprise!"

Suriel knew him too well. If he was calling this visit a surprise, he'd no doubt set up some way to prove that he wasn't surprised at all.

She sent a mental command to her Presence and contacted Phoenix Division headquarters, which was simple here in Sanctum. She didn't need to convey her instructions verbally, but she did for Ozriel's sake.

"Has anyone left a personal message for me in the last standard day?" Suriel asked.

"Yes, Judge. An anonymous Abidan with your personal code said to deliver it to you about ten seconds from now."

Suriel shook her head at Ozriel. "You're getting too predictable."

"He also said to tell you 'Not to call him predictable.'"

The Reaper waggled his fingers as though demonstrating a magic trick.

"Thank you, headquarters," Suriel said dryly, then she ended the call and looked to Ozriel. "Considering your restrictions, that wasn't bad."

"Well, you only decided to visit about an hour ago. You didn't give me much time to set up anything dramatic."

Suriel extended her awareness into the station beneath her feet. Despite its new name, the Grave already felt much more like a home than it ever had before.

"Your relationship with the Abidan can never be repaired," Suriel said, "but your Reapers have a chance. They've done well, so far."

Ozriel waved a hand dismissively. "Of course they have, *so far*. They're competent people, and they've done what we told them. There will come a time when they must truly determine the fates of entire civilizations on their own judgment."

That was the crux of the problem, and Suriel's concern.

It was easy to know the right course of action when entering a world that was about to be destroyed by a giant monster. Kill the monster, get out.

In the current state of existence, just about every universe was on fire. As long as the Reapers were pulling people from the flames, they were doing their job.

Their test would come in the future, when the situations weren't so clear-cut. The other Judges knew that, and they were certain that the Reaper Division would turn on them.

One Judge, at least, had already taken action.

"I'm sorry about Gadrael," Suriel said.

Ozriel affected a puzzled look. "Why? He played his role wonderfully."

"Despite what you feel about him, you should keep statements like that quiet." Suriel suspected she was wasting her words, but she persisted anyway. "He already discussed giving up his seat on the Court after realizing he served your cause. If he hears you mocking him, he might really do it."

"I'll be sure to redouble my efforts," Ozriel said. "If he had any conscience, he would have retired a thousand years ago."

Suriel understood how Ozriel saw things, but she had still taken it upon herself to heal the Court of Seven. As far as it was possible to do so. "That's what they say about you, and with greater cause."

"There are two beings in all creation who have ever taken action to improve the system of existence, and they share this dock right now."

Ozriel had changed during his time on Cradle, but not completely. His old anger was hidden, not gone.

Suriel didn't need to impress on him the weight of what he'd done, nor the lives lost. He understood the consequences of his actions.

The solution, for everyone, was to reduce their reliance on Ozriel as an individual. That was the way forward, and Suriel kept her focus there.

"I've come to tell you in person that we have crested the wave," Suriel said. "The worst of the Collapse is behind us."

Ozriel tapped fingers against his lips as he thought. Based on his reaction, she suspected he hadn't been sure what Suriel had come to tell him. Or at least he was pretending to be unsure.

"How many lost?" he asked at last.

He wasn't asking for a casualty count. It would be meaningless to speculate anyway. Losses were better counted in terms of worlds.

"We recovered more than expected. Six hundred populated worlds entirely lost to fragments, though we were able to recover a substantial population of almost three hundred of them. Another thousand looted or occupied by Vroshir. We've stabilized two thousand, one hundred, and six."

Of the ten thousand worlds the Abidan had once controlled, the vast majority were resource or pioneer worlds. They didn't have a permanent native population, just temporary civilizations that could be withdrawn quickly.

Losing those Iterations wasn't much of a loss, and thousands had been destroyed with no substantial casualties.

However, that didn't mean there was no danger. Even those empty worlds broke into fragments upon destruction, fragments that fell into the Void and slowly became corrupted.

The Void had never been so populated. Worlds required more protection than they ever had before, and—in the years to come—the Abidan would witness an unprecedented explosion in the Fiend population.

But, at least for the moment, the danger had passed.

Ozriel's expression was still distant, hard to read. "And what is the Court of Seven's plan?"

"First, we need to find a new Makiel."

"I humbly accept your nomination."

"The Court would appoint a loaf of moldy bread before you."

"Then why have I not been summoned to accept the guidance of a rotten sandwich already?"

He surely knew why, but Suriel gave her viewpoint anyway. "The Mantle of Makiel has been difficult to place. Makiel named his successor, and there are many skilled Hounds in his division, but Fate has yet to stabilize. The mantle itself will not select a candidate until the way forward is clear."

"Oh, really? I thought it was the Judges who were reluctant."

She queried her Presence, who suggested he was being genuine. "What do you think of us? We'll take as many Judges as we can get.

If we're willing to put *you* to work, we would spare no effort to raise up another Hound."

"You would," Ozriel said. "I have less confidence in your counterparts."

Suriel had no intention of arguing with Ozriel about the Court of Seven. Though he had access to more knowledge than anyone, he was not charitable in his interpretation. Especially when it came to her fellow Judges.

She returned the topic to the subject of her visit. "Nonetheless, we've agreed to end the state of emergency. Now, in spite of our lack of a Hound, we must look to the future and build something new. And I, at least, would like your help."

Ozriel released his smile, facing her with open honesty. "I will do everything I can, but you know what I want. Fewer worlds, more interference."

"I do know how much you love to interfere."

"One of my most prized values! Better to meddle now than to Reap later, I think that's how the old saying goes."

That wasn't an old saying, and Suriel would be surprised if anyone had said those words in that order before, but she nodded along. "You will have to use the Scythe again, no matter what systems we create."

"If we have done all we can to preserve a world that is beyond redemption, I will usher it into peace with a smile."

He looked back at the Grave as they both sensed Ziel returning home from a mission. Orthos, Dross, and Little Blue accompanied him...along with a new creature in stasis, locked away from traditional inspection. Some kind of dragon.

Suriel herself was curious, but she resolved to get the full story later. At the moment, she was concerned with her old friend's emotional state.

The other Judges weren't wrong to fear him.

He'd pinned all his hopes on this batch of Reapers. If they fell, as precedent suggested they eventually would, his foundation would crumble.

They were his last chance. Without support, he would determine there was no hope left for the Abidan.

He would do his best to slaughter the other Judges and start over. Suriel was in no way confident that his restraints were secure enough to stop him, and neither was the rest of the Court.

As long as Ozriel lived, he was a threat.

But there was still a chance to fix things. If the Reaper Division flourished, if they could establish a new future for the Abidan, if Ozriel and the Court of Seven cooperated with one another, they could build a system far more stable than the last.

If, if, if.

Suriel believed in that future. She chose to. That was their best chance to flourish, to make something better, to heal.

Ozriel winked. "Ah, how I missed you," he said, as though she'd said something aloud.

As always, he acted like he could read her mind. Sometimes he could, which made the act that much more compelling.

Another station drifted past their dock, and her Presence drew her attention to it. On the side of the station, in large block letters, were the words 'WELCOME, SURIEL!'

"Two minutes late," Ozriel said with a sigh. "I told you, you didn't give me much time to prepare."

Lindon had spent no small amount of effort helping Eithan remodel the interior of the Grave, and they'd barely gotten started. Most of his time went into understanding the systems already built into the station, which used fascinating principles beyond anything he'd encountered on Cradle.

Until they finished rebuilding those systems, the Reaper Division was limited to repurposing facilities that already existed. Fortunately, there was already a break room.

It was a bright, cozy room with soft furniture and a screen taking up one wall. Eithan had called them into the room and ordered them to wait for him, so they were making themselves at home.

It was only the second time the entire Reaper Division had been together in one place since Lindon's ascension.

[What do you think it means that he called us all here?] Dross asked. [Not that I'm nervous, I just think it might suggest that we're about to be executed.]

Orthos shifted into his human form of a black-skinned, gray-haired man so he could drop onto a couch. "Be quiet and let us relax."

Little Blue stuck her hand into the opening of a smooth metal box and whistled. A bar of candy materialized in her palm and she gasped, tossed it aside, and tried again.

Mercy caught the candy and began to peel off its wrapper. "You think they're creating this out of nowhere, or are they transforming something else?"

Blue gave a high chime.

"I think so too," Mercy agreed. "They had something like this in the Wolf Division, and Pride implied that it isn't free to activate. Even *they* have things they can't do."

Blue materialized salad and a fork and munched on it. She whistled her opinion on Abidan restrictions through a mouthful of leaves.

"Don't speak with your mouth full," Orthos rumbled. "These are the things you don't learn when you grow up a spirit."

Yerin was perched on the back of the couch behind Lindon, and he heard her scoff at Orthos. "Just because we're in the heavens now doesn't mean they won't strike you down for lying. You can't say two words without a mouthful of rocks."

Orthos had been about to take a bite out of an amethyst, but he lowered it to scowl at Yerin. "That doesn't make me a liar."

[That's right! He's not a liar, he's a hypocrite. Now *you're* the one who has distorted the truth about Orthos, Yerin, so we'll have to see what the heavens do to you.]

"If I punch you," Yerin mused, "does that count as the heavens striking you?"

Lindon relished the sounds of his friends talking, but that was mostly background noise. The majority of his attention was taken up by the screen.

He and Ziel sat side-by-side on the couch, staring into it. Currently, it showed Reigan Shen doing battle with a young Tiberian Arelius during the first Uncrowned King tournament.

"They *have* to source this from the Hounds," Ziel said. He peered closely into the mechanical box on one side of the screen. "I see some of their sigils, and some from the Spiders."

Lindon spoke to the screen. "Show me Reigan Shen fighting Yerin in the tournament instead." The view altered abruptly to show a young Reigan, with more lion traits than he would eventually show, walking out to face Yerin as she'd appeared shortly after her advancement to Overlady Herald.

"That doesn't come from Fate," Lindon said. "It never could have happened. This is an illusion, but I don't know how they're crafting it so quickly."

Dross coughed delicately into his tendril. [As a Presence myself, I am offended that you would think so little of our kind. You of all people—]

"Dross, show me a two-hour story about Akura Malice as an investigator solving the murder of Northstrider," Lindon said.

[Okay, yes! Of course! No problem! Give me just a moment to think it through. When, exactly, would you like this to happen?]

"OTEP, show me the story I just requested," Lindon said.

Immediately, the screen shifted to show Akura Malice drifting down from the sky to land next to Northstrider's broken and twisted body. His Remnant, a crimson humanoid monstrosity with twisting serpentine dragons for limbs, knelt at her appearance.

[I could show you who would win if they fought,] Dross suggested.

The Original Technical Entertainment Presence, OTEP, responded in a smooth voice. [Indeed, I'm not capable of predicting combat with any accuracy. If you were to send me your own data, however, I would happily use that to embellish the story.]

Ziel tapped the side of the screen again. "OTEP, who made you?"

[My creation was a cooperation between craftsmen of the Abidan and what are now called the Vroshir, but it was so long ago that I'm afraid the information would be of little value to you.]

Lindon sensed an opening. "If it was that long ago, then surely the restrictions on your manufacturing processes aren't relevant anymore."

[Alas, as I've told you before, I can tell you nothing more about the process used to create me,] OTEP said.

"We'll figure it out," Ziel muttered.

Lindon was less concerned with replicating an entertainment Presence—the Abidan could obviously make basic Presences for individual people and locations at will, so it shouldn't be too closely guarded of a secret—and more focused on finding the source of its information.

It seemed to be able to instantly access footage from thousands of Iterations. Was that stored somewhere? Was it made up?

Lindon could scarcely imagine all the things he might learn with access to that kind of knowledge.

As usual, Eithan burst in without warning. "Which of you called for the greatest craftsman in all the worlds?"

Yerin leaned her elbow on Lindon's head. "If you were listening, you'd know nobody called you that."

"Pity, for that is exactly who is before you now!" Eithan stabbed a finger toward the screen. "OTEP, from where do you get your information? Override Ozriel zero-zero-eight."

[What I show is merely a simulation of records provided by the Hound Division,] OTEP said easily. [I have no greater access to Fate than any other Presence, but I'm better able to simulate as much.]

"I can see plenty of use for that," Lindon said.

Eithan waved a hand. "As could the Abidan, when they originally built OTEP, but constructing a Presence is less of a science than an art. As they have learned in the years since. Alas, OTEP has many of the drawbacks of a machine. That poor, primitive mind."

[I can still understand you,] OTEP said.

Mercy gasped. "Is it self-aware?"

"No!" Eithan declared.

[That is a subject of much debate,] OTEP began. [I myself believe that there is only a limited difference between simulating emotions and experiencing them.]

Yerin leaned harder on Lindon's head. "Bleed and bury me, I'm starting to feel bad for the construct."

"Let's leave our crushing doubts about the sanctity of human experience aside for a moment," Eithan said. "We should instead celebrate the victory of the Abidan! Congratulations, ladies and gentlemen, for the worst has passed!"

Lindon's heart unclenched, and he realized he'd been more nervous than he thought. For Eithan to gather them all together meant either that the broader situation among the cosmos had become much better or much worse.

In his experience, it was more often the latter.

Orthos blew out a mouthful of smoke. "Forgive me if I have trouble trusting you." Ziel nodded along.

Mercy and Little Blue cheered.

[In the two standard years since our founding, the Reaper Division has delayed or reversed the destruction of one hundred and forty-one worlds,] Dross said. [That's an excellent record compared to…Well, the only groups we could compare ourselves to all went insane.]

"And no one's insane yet!" Eithan said happily.

Lindon had trouble feeling too proud of their record, considering the number of worlds that had slipped through the cracks. Certainly, they'd done good for the Iterations in which they'd intervened, but they had only just pulled the Abidan worlds back from the brink of destruction.

With the crisis over, their real job would begin.

"Doubt you called us all together for a laugh and a dance," Yerin said.

Eithan ruffled Ziel's hair. "And yet perhaps I have! I've called you all for the Reaper Division's first *team-building activity!*"

Immediately, Lindon's madra surged and his heart rate spiked. Little Blue squeaked and shrunk herself so she could scramble under a chair. Orthos put a hand over his face, Mercy grimaced, and Yerin's groan echoed down through Lindon's skull.

Ziel sat where he was, unfazed. He didn't even straighten his hair where Eithan had messed it up.

Dross drifted closer to Eithan. [This 'team-building' you speak of. How much of a risk do you think this will be to our lives?]

Eithan put hands on his hips and huffed out an overly disappointed sigh. "This is meant to be a reward for your hard work! Compared to saving a collapsing Iteration, it's nothing to worry about."

Lindon glanced up to share a look with Yerin. Eithan's idea of building team camaraderie should be a lot closer to fighting a Dreadgod than a carefree picnic.

"Apologies, Eithan," Lindon said. "What did you have in mind?"

"We're going to build a world!"

Yerin muttered some half-formed words, Mercy looked puzzled, and Orthos breathed another smoky sigh.

Lindon, however, was intrigued. "That means entering the Void. All of us? Including you?"

"What do we have to fear from the Void when we have its Sage by our side?" Eithan pressed his fists together in a salute to Lindon.

There was plenty to fear in the Void, including the effects of traveling beyond reality for any length of time, but it should be safe enough with Eithan along. "Has the Ghost Division been notified?"

"They'll appreciate the help," Eithan said, "and before you force me to answer the question, *yes,* I have filed my intentions with Darandiel herself."

"How does one create a world?" Orthos asked.

"And do we get to keep it?" Mercy added.

Little Blue chimed in, asking if people would live there.

"I'll answer your questions in reverse order! Yes, no, and 'together.' There's a nice, cozy spot between Sectors Twenty-two and Twenty-four with plenty of fragments, and populations from those Sectors could use a new place to call home."

"Show us," Ziel said.

"With pleasure! Now, with your permission, I'll pull you all into the Way and take us to our destination! Let's go, little Reapers!"

Eithan casually tore open a sapphire hole in reality and dove in. The others followed, though Lindon and Yerin took the rear. Eithan wouldn't be above tossing them into a surprising or uncomfortable situation, and they were more than willing to enter after the joke had already passed.

Soon, the Grave was empty once again. Mostly.

[Why is he always so rude?] OTEP asked. But there was no one left to answer.

Lindon knew the Void as a stretch of empty darkness similar to deep space, but instead of stars were spinning specks of color. Each of those spots was a piece left over from a destroyed world, left to drift forever in the ocean of nothingness outside the Way.

But that description wasn't entirely accurate anymore. Now, there was more color than darkness.

The Void was choked with chaotic, spinning fragments in every direction and at every distance. It was a storm of color, to the point that even the black background seemed to shimmer.

One of the blue spots was a ball of water with a school of many-colored fish in the center. A red streak was a casket of burning bronze, shooting through the emptiness. A brown sphere contained miles of slowly crumbling cliffs.

An incomprehensibly hideous worm had been split in two only a few seconds before, its greenish blood still spurting over Mercy and Ziel. Mercy scraped goo away from her face, but Ziel just let it drip off him. Gravity was unpredictable in the Void, so the slime peeled away in a few different directions.

Lindon could not have felt more justified in his decision to enter the portal last.

"A wonderful example of what to look out for, here in the darkness beyond existence," Eithan called. He casually swept a hand and brushed aside a grayish fragment drifting closer; it contained an ancient stone mausoleum with stalactites that strangely resembled bells.

Lindon checked the integrity of his armor as the red Dross checked Yerin's. He was capable of sustaining himself in the Void for a while on his own, but the armor would take the majority of that load off of him.

Eithan spread his hands to indicate the Void. "Behold, an endless feast of free materials! We will take advantage of this broad selection, as each of you will search through the nearby fragments until you find one you wish to include in our new Iteration. Bring it back to Lindon here, who will bind our junk with his cohesive vision."

Lindon would have been more surprised if Eithan hadn't made a habit of tossing him into situations he didn't know how to handle. "Pardon, but I was not prepared for this."

"Which of the rest of us has an Icon suited for creation? Not counting me, of course."

Yerin rolled her eyes and gave Lindon a peck on the cheek. "Luck to you, but I'm glad it's not me." She pushed away, shooting into the Void toward the worst fragment in sight. It looked like a black graveyard filled with monsters.

"That's the spirit!" Eithan cried. "Look for fragments to which you feel a personal connection, or those you wish to preserve. Try not to be influenced by the fact that anything you don't pick will drift in endless nothingness until it dissolves into chaos."

"Just one?" Ziel asked.

Eithan held up one finger. "Incorporating too many fragments can damage cohesion. One apiece should be perfect, if Lindon does his job."

Ziel drifted listlessly off, Little Blue flew away in excitement, and Mercy flitted between fragments as though she couldn't decide which she liked best.

Lindon summoned Genesis, his hammer. One side of the head smoldered with Blackflame while the other shone blue-white. "If you have any pointers, master, I'd love to hear them."

"Ah, it soothes my heart to be so warmly addressed by my disciple. But, as usual, I find that there's no substitute for on-the-job training."

Dross flew back toward Lindon, dragging a fragment behind him the size of a small castle. It resembled a massive geode split in half, its shell highlighted in flames of blue and silver. Rather than filled with minerals, its center had been crammed with souls.

Hundreds, perhaps thousands, of translucent human figures were trapped in their stone prison. They drifted listlessly in a circle, moaning and whispering.

To Lindon, they looked like strange Remnants. None of them were as vivid as they should be, and they looked very similar to a human in life, complete with ragged clothing. Perhaps they were another Iteration's equivalent of Remnants, or something less substantial, like an echo created by a construct.

[They each have at least a little of their original mind left,] Dross said. [Together, they might make a decent construct! And...It's embarrassing to say, but they deserve better than to be trapped in a well as their world falls apart.]

Lindon surrounded the fragment with his willpower and it came to a sudden halt. Sure enough, the cave-structure containing the souls gave him the same feeling as the Mind Well that had once contained Dross.

"I can stabilize this location," Lindon said. "I can even see how I might hold it together enough to send it into an existing Iteration. But making it into its own world..."

Eithan put a hand on Lindon's back and extended his own will. Slowly and clearly, so Lindon could sense its details.

"A fragment is more than a single location," Eithan explained. "It becomes a foundational template, a set of instructions for our new world to follow."

Though Eithan made nothing, an image unfolded before Lindon. He saw an endless expanse of featureless land, all centered on this cavern of souls. More such caverns popped up here and there, subtly different copies of the original.

The sight resonated with the Hammer Icon, and Lindon thought he understood the process. He took over, seizing the geode.

Lindon pushed it *through* the Void and back into the Way.

As the small fragment punched through the fabric of reality, it created a new branch in the Way. A tiny one, unstable enough that it would vanish in only a few seconds without Lindon's attention.

The hole where the fragment had punched through remained in front of Lindon, a fist-sized puncture in reality through which he could see only that silver-tinged geode.

Lindon focused his will. He imagined the world-to-be, and the expanse of land surrounding his one fragment. The canvas on which they would paint an entire Iteration.

"**Be**," Lindon commanded. And he drove his hammer down on the hole in the Void.

The geode exploded into copies of itself. Rugged gray stone, like the outer shell surrounding the souls, stretched out for miles.

Geysers of silver-blue flame erupted here and there, spewing energy similar to the original, trapped spirits.

Lindon sagged back, exhausted from that single action, though the creation was far from finished. If he released the work completely, it would fall apart.

"Where does the extra stone come from?" he asked.

Eithan swirled his hand around, gathering up a tiny cloud of sparkling dust. "Loose material in the Void. As you understood, one cannot create something from one's imagination alone."

[I don't want to be the one to point this out,] Dross said, [but I was the fastest to secure a fragment. Does that make me the wisest? The most helpful?]

"The humblest," Eithan suggested.

Lindon was focused on his expanded fragment. He brought his hammer down again, and the stone indented into a second geode. This time, thanks to the senses brought to him by the Void Icon, he could feel what was happening.

His intentions summoned loose materials and energy from the Void, but it could only be shaped according to the fragment itself. Since the original geode contained only rock and ghosts, he could make stone and spectral energy, but nothing more.

The new spirits he'd created weren't truly original beings, merely bland copies of the originals.

Out of curiosity, Lindon wondered how creative he could get with the shapes. He hammered again, and a gray stone tower appeared, inhabited solely by cloned ghosts.

"There is only so far you can stretch a single fragment," Eithan said. "To make a full Iteration, you'll require...more materials!"

He whirled dramatically, presenting Yerin, who returned at that moment with a fragment in tow. It was larger than Dross' and brighter, a shimmering rainbow of pastel colors.

It was filled with cute, fluffy animals.

The fragment had a chunk of land with pale, pistachio-green grass and stubby trees with pink and blue tufts of leaves. Tumbling over that land were hundreds of little furballs, creatures that resembled rabbits or baby bears, but as if only their most adorable traits had been extracted.

"Wasn't going to let them float around until they turned into monsters, was I?" Yerin muttered.

Lindon spared a little of his attention and one of his arms to give her a quick hug. "I'll make a place for them," he said. Though he wasn't quite sure how to do that.

Eithan took advantage of the lack of gravity in the Void to dip down, then float up uncomfortably close to Lindon and Yerin. "Incorporating further fragments becomes more complicated. This is where *your* intentions for the fragment come into play, Yerin."

Lindon linked hands with Yerin. "Together."

They focused on Yerin's fragment, and Lindon listened to her intentions. She'd imagined this new world as a chance for the life in this fragment to flourish, a place for the little fuzzballs to live and spread their kind.

Not a paradise. Yerin believed a place without danger was impossible, a journey without challenge was unhealthy, and a world without death was unnatural.

She wanted them to have a chance.

Lindon joined his vision to hers, then hammered the new fragment into its place on the other side of the Void.

Their new world trembled as it changed. Pastel meadows bloomed, trees rose, and furry creatures tumbled over newfound trees.

The original population of the fragment huddled together in astonishment as their surroundings changed, but thousands of their kind blinked into being. Simple copies made from the templates of the original group, but it would be enough to spread future generations.

Assuming they had enough food and water, and that their Iteration didn't fall apart halfway. Geysers of silver-blue fire erupted from the stone by a meadow, sending furry creatures fleeing, and ghosts inspected them curiously.

Lindon tried to make rain clouds, but it was like trying to paint with a color that didn't exist. He was limited to whatever the fragments carried.

Ziel drifted up, followed by a shimmering white tower. Spires of scripted glass rose from the top of the tower like spikes on a crown.

"I don't have to hold your hand, do I?" Ziel asked.

"Yes!" Eithan insisted.

"Why don't we try without it first?" Lindon said. He joined his will to Ziel's, which of course worked perfectly well.

The tower wasn't a relic of recent destruction. It felt old, from a world that had dissolved into chaos, and it carried the last relics of that world's energy system.

Once, long ago, the tower had been used to watch the stars.

Lindon hammered the building into place. It sprouted from the center of the gray stone plains and the meadows of colored grass. As the tower grew, it became ten, fifty, a hundred times bigger, until it reached into the sky.

Ziel had chosen this fragment to serve as a tool of guidance to their Iteration. It carried abilities useful for knowledge and protection, and would give the world's inhabitants the means to learn and grow strong.

As the tower rose, its energy spread, and the empty sky filled with stars. They were larger and clearer than the stars in Cradle had been, each a distinctly glittering jewel. And their formations contained patterns of significance and authority that could be invoked in symbols.

Lindon was much more interested in the possibilities of the Iteration with the addition of the star-gazing tower, but weaving it into the fabric of reality took all his focus. He couldn't modify it as he liked; the system of stars was too old and too strong to be easily changed.

And, with three fragments woven together, the world was that much harder to hold together. But he wasn't done yet.

Little Blue came to Lindon holding a primeval forest. Its trees were towers, its insects like birds, its shadows unnaturally dark and its waters vivid and clear. Everything about the forest was exaggerated, good and bad.

Blue enjoyed it because of how free the natural world was. She imagined all the amazing things she could see, visiting such a forest.

Lindon hammered it into place and began to feel the opportunities for creation expand.

With Little Blue's forest, he could create intersections where he could enhance Yerin's meadows. Softly colored grass became a tangle of pastel undergrowth, puffy trees became wooden spires that carried bright blue clouds, and tumbling fuzz-balls turned to wise, primordial bears that strode across the landscape.

Lindon turned one of Dross' soul-trapping geodes to a crystalline castle ruled by an ethereal king. He felt like he'd just gotten started when Eithan tapped him on the shoulder.

"It's easy to get carried away," Eithan reminded him, and Lindon snapped back to awareness.

He was sweating, his will shivering with strain, and the influence of the Void was growing stronger around his friends. Their time was too limited for him to try out everything.

At least, in this project. Lindon didn't intend for this to be his last. How could he stop at a prototype?

Mercy brought a mountain filled with veins of living metals. Resources that could be cultivated by the people they brought; Mercy's intentions were filled with the hope that they would live lives of plenty, without competing too much.

Lindon spread such mountains around. He blended veins of living metal with the souls to create spiritual ores, and mines of iron that reflected the energy of the stars, but he couldn't spend as long as he wanted before he had to move on.

Orthos, as Lindon had expected, brought a clutch of dragon eggs. Soon, dragons flew through the starry sky of their Iteration, and Lindon felt a moment of pity for the fuzz-balls.

The world was bustling, and Lindon was proud of many touches, but it still wasn't really...a *world*.

Few natural sources of water. Stale weather. No sunlight, just eternal night.

The addition of a human population would draw the Way closer, strengthening natural laws, and perhaps that would iron out some of the missing details. But Lindon suspected that, even if their miniature Iteration stabilized, it would become barren and lifeless in only a few years.

Lindon looked up from his inspection of the world to see Eithan grinning. A fragment drifted behind him. One much bigger than what anyone else had brought.

"And behold, my addition!"

It looked like...mud.

Eithan's fragment didn't shine as most of the others did. It hung in the Void, a featureless glob. But when Lindon sensed Eithan's intentions for it, he felt a moment of relief.

The floating blob contained water, earth, and microscopic life. The creation process itself would have provided much of that necessary material, dragging it into existence from elsewhere in the Void, but whether they got enough was largely a matter of chance.

The pieces Eithan had provided would take a complex network of fragments and bind them into a world with a real chance of sustaining life long-term.

"Sometimes the boring parts are the most important," Eithan said. "But not usually."

Though the world had grown more and more difficult to contain the more fragments they added, hammering Eithan's addition into place came easily. It was as though the Iteration had been thirsty for exactly this.

Rivers streaked across the landscape, pooling here and there into ponds. Lindon couldn't form oceans, which he found confusing.

Most of the Iterations he'd visited had seas, and certainly all the major ones.

So, as the world stabilized under his supervision, Lindon decided to try something that had occurred to him long before.

He tapped into the Hammer Icon and the Void Icon together. With as much focus as he could muster, he brought his hammer down.

And he tried to make a sea.

Water gathered and the land lowered, but it was just a large lake. He could add water. But Lindon envisioned Ghostwater and the vibrant ecosystems that existed under the ocean, and he tried to bring that to this world.

It *should* have worked, he was certain. There was plenty of raw matter in the Void, the concepts for water and sea life existed in the other fragments, and Lindon could visualize the result he wanted clearly.

The Void Icon *wanted* to bring something out of nothing. He could feel it so clearly, surrounded by the Void itself.

With his two Icons working in harmony, it should have been simple. But no matter how he tried, he couldn't achieve anything better than a blending of existing fragments.

Eithan finally stopped him. "I believe you've done as fine a job as any mortal man could do. Let's allow the Way to do the rest, all right?"

"Why didn't it work?" Lindon asked.

"Don't let it stop you from trying," Eithan said. "There are many theories, but you should explore the subject yourself. Creation is a long, long road that many before us have explored, but...we've got time."

Lindon gathered his focus and began to expel the newborn world, but Mercy let out a strangled cry.

"Wait!" she called. "We have to name it!"

Ziel shook his head. "Iteration names are determined by a committee of Ghosts, not by whoever makes the world."

"Minaret," Eithan suggested. "We do have a giant tower."

"Refuge," Yerin said.

[There's already an Iteration called Refuge. What about Pulchritude?]

Orthos glared at him. "Don't make up words."

"It means 'beauty,'" Eithan said, "so I like it."

Lindon's will trembled with the effort of holding the world in place, but he gave a skeptical glance at the rocky, patchwork world he could see through the rift. "Pardon, but...beauty?"

"I think it fits!" Mercy said happily.

"Barren," Ziel suggested. "Arid. Desolation."

[Are you coming up with names or listing your favorite words?]

Ziel shrugged.

"If the name doesn't mean something to *us*, then we're just wasting wind," Yerin said.

"Mercy!" Mercy said.

"Windfall," Orthos rumbled. "You're the one that brought up wind, and it hasn't been long since we all lived on that ship. Why not name a world after it?"

Lindon's metaphysical grip was trembling, so he nodded. "Works for me."

[Don't you think that will get a bit confusing?] Dross pointed out. [When we might be talking about the cloudship, the pocket dimension *in* the cloudship, or the world we all created together?]

"If it's good enough for the Blackflame Empire, City, and family, it's good enough for us!" Eithan declared. "Windfall it is! Pending investigatory review and administrative approval, of course."

Lindon exhaled in relief and began to relax his grip. He looked through the hole between the Void and the Way, examining the world they'd made.

And, gently, he released it into existence.

Homecoming

INFORMATION REQUESTED: THE ONGOING RELATIONSHIP BETWEEN LINDON AND YERIN.
REPORT LOCATION: AFTER THE EVENTS OF *WAYBOUND*.
AUTHORIZATION CONFIRMED.
BEGINNING REPORT...

ITERATION 110: CRADLE

LINDON AND YERIN EMERGED FROM THE SHINING WAY-PORTAL with Abidan warnings echoing in their ears.

[WARNING: You have been granted seventy-two hours of leave. Exceeding your time limit, excessive spatial violations, or subversion of Fate will result in immediate punishment.]

Lindon winced, and Yerin rubbed her ear with a finger although the message had been beamed straight into their heads.

"I guess they thought we'd need a reminder," Lindon said.

Yerin scowled up at the sky. "Didn't have to ram a dagger into my ear to—"

[This has been a warning from Sector Eleven Control,] the Presence continued. [Abide by the rules and enjoy your vacation.]

"Bleed and bury me if I don't go straight to Sector Control once we're done here. Just to show my best smile."

"What do you think about that, Dross?" Lindon asked.

There was no response.

Lindon sighed in relief. "Seems like he really is asleep."

At Lindon's request, Dross had deactivated the versions of himself remaining inside Lindon and Yerin, making them dormant for at least a few days. They'd wanted a break from everyone, including the voice that never left their heads.

"Of course he is," Yerin said. "He knows that if he's pulling a joke, I'll peel his skin off and use him to wrap a sword. Right, Dross?"

No response.

Yerin gave a decisive nod and hooked her arm around Lindon's. "You still remember how to walk?"

"Lead the way."

Lindon had intended to transport them both straight to their destination. They couldn't use any powers that disrupted the world too much, but the workings of a Sage wouldn't be a problem. Especially when they weren't witnessed.

But a walk wasn't so bad.

It had been a long time since Lindon and Yerin had been completely alone, especially outside the Grave and without the possibility of a sudden emergency. Walking for an hour would be a nice change of pace.

Traveling between Iterations wasn't incredibly precise, at least not without high skill as a Fox, so they had emerged a few miles from their destination. They were at the bottom of a steep mountain, one covered in green.

All around them was a thick forest, almost a jungle. Their path was a wide, overgrown trail, set here and there with stones that might once have been stairs leading up the side of the mountain.

The ancient, threadbare staircase wove up the mountainside, and Yerin chatted as they hiked up arm-in-arm.

Before they passed the treetops, the ambient sound of the wildlife was a constant hum around them. The sound grew weaker as they climbed higher, replaced by the calls of birds and the hush of the wind.

"—and that's what took me an age and a half," Yerin was saying. "Couldn't let them keep believing I was a spider goddess, so I had to do some Ziel work. They're supposed to be making up for what they did in my name, but I'll have to check up on them in a few years."

A lanky creature, like a white-furred ape with tusks, leaped out from a rocky outcropping overhead. "Travelers," it growled, "you must pay tribute for your trespass on…"

Both Lindon and Yerin were completely veiled. Spiritual perception might mistake them for Golds, and they had even withdrawn their Goldsigns and the other transformations that came with advancement.

Lindon's right arm was only a *little* paler than his left, and his eyes were human. Yerin's Goldsigns were withdrawn and her red eyes had been dulled so that they were almost brown, though she kept the scarlet streak of hair.

Altogether, they looked like the most mundane couple of sacred artists in Cradle.

Still, they looked at the sacred beast with completely neutral expressions.

"...My mistake," the ape said at last. "Clearly you aren't trespassers, but honored guests. Would you like a guide up the mountain?"

"No, thank you," Lindon said. "She was born here."

The ape wiped sweat away from his brow. "Ah, please forgive me! You must have grown so much that I didn't recognize you."

Lindon doubted this sacred beast had ever seen Yerin before, but he didn't say anything more. Yerin leaned forward, looking the ape up and down.

"You were born here?" she asked.

The ape nodded rapidly and pointed to one side of the mountain. "Just over there, Lady! My whole life!"

Yerin pretended to fumble in her pocket, while in actuality she accessed a void space. She withdrew a scale suitable for the ape's wind Path and tossed it to him.

"Solid work, keeping it safe," Yerin said. "Could let innocent travelers go without robbing them, though."

"Robbing? Lady, I assure you that—"

"Cut that off."

"Yes." The ape cradled the scale, bowed to the two of them, and then leaped off the side of the mountain. Air currents caught him and carried him to a specific spot in the forest, where Lindon sensed more of his kind.

Lindon squeezed Yerin's arm. "Gratitude."

"I don't kill everybody I meet," Yerin said, though she looked pleased. "Let *you* live, true?"

"They can't get too many visitors if this is the way up," Lindon observed. Not only was the path narrow and winding, but they hadn't seen anyone else on the trail, though there were many spirits at the top.

Yerin peered over the side. "This wasn't anyone's favorite way up, but I would have bet we'd see somebody. They're throwing a party up there."

Considering the population at the top, the alternative ways up the mountain must have been far more populated than when Yerin was a girl. Lindon could have figured it out if he'd been willing to extend his perception, but he didn't want to alarm anyone. Besides, he was in no hurry.

They continued hiking until they reached the peak, which was covered in trees and houses. An elaborate archway crowned the path, etched with ancient scripts to ward off Remnants.

Yerin pointed to the arch excitedly. "That's been here since before my grandfather could crawl! Keep your ears open." She pulled him through, and a series of bells began to ring.

That was a simple construct trick, triggered by visitors passing through the arch, but Lindon appreciated the stable craftsmanship.

A woman with gray in her hair hurried out of a small hut nearby. It was made of woven branches and only big enough to hold a chair, so Lindon took it to be some kind of guard house.

"Great heavens, I wasn't expecting visitors!" the woman said. She gave a warm smile as she scurried over to Lindon and

Yerin. "Welcome to Greenpeak, travelers. Are you here to stay or passing through?"

Lindon glanced down at Yerin. This old woman shared some of Yerin's accent, certainly, but her words were so *normal.*

As they were visiting Yerin's birthplace, he'd prepared himself for a town full of people who talked like her.

"Just taking him home," Yerin said, nudging Lindon. "Been half a lifetime since I've seen it myself, though."

The woman clapped her hands together and gasped. "Were you here for the Phoenix?"

"Haven't been back since."

She pulled Yerin away from Lindon to draw her into a hug. "Oh, you poor thing. That was a nightmare. Could you be…Nalia? Luri?"

"Yerin." She looked distinctly uncomfortable at being examined so closely by a stranger, but she kept on a smile.

"*Yerin.* I'll remember it. Do you want to pay respects?"

Yerin glanced around. "Wouldn't say no to that, but the bloodspawn didn't leave much to bury."

"We built a memorial. I'll lead you there right now!"

The woman pulled Yerin, who let herself be swept along. Lindon followed just behind as Yerin answered a flurry of questions. Most of the questions had to do with how much Yerin remembered, which was 'not much.'

But Yerin and the woman traded roles as they walked deeper into Greenpeak and Yerin had more and more questions. It was more than the village she remembered, having turned into a bustling town.

Most of the trees had been cleared for buildings, and a healthy tide of people moved here and there. Even the roads were paved by smooth stones, and Lindon was surprised to sense a couple of Underlords among the sacred artists flying across the sky.

He guessed there must have been ten or twenty thousand people on the mountain's peak, both living in the buildings on top and burrowed into the mountain itself. Many more than Yerin had expected.

The memorial to the Phoenix attack was a spire of polished black stone a little taller than Lindon. A few hundred names were inscribed on one side, with the rest telling the story of the bloodspawn attack and how the survivors escaped.

The woman who had guided them there stepped away, tactfully giving them some space.

Yerin looked up and down the list. "Not so many of them."

"It seems like the town has grown a lot since then."

"Felt like the Phoenix killed everybody and his brother, but guess it was only this handful." She lightly touched a pair of names. "It was everybody to me."

Lindon pressed his fists together and saluted. For a few breaths, they stood in silence.

Finally, Yerin stretched and looked out through the trees. "Let's steal a look before she comes back."

"If you're all right," Lindon said carefully.

She shrugged. "Been more than a minute. If this was enough to get me shedding tears, I'd never stop. Oi, now here's something to see!"

Yerin pulled him forward between a couple of buildings and some trees, where the afternoon sun shone over a valley far below.

A massive bridge stretched over that valley, bustling with traffic. Remnants pulled wagons, children laughed as they raced each other, and small cloudships zipped by. It was a number of people that Lindon would expect from a small city, not a single isolated town.

"Back when I could fit in a teacup, this was the whole world," Yerin said. "Our bridges weren't so polished, though."

Greenpeak was connected to four other towns at roughly the same altitude, but none of the rest were on mountains.

One town, of roughly the same size, floated on a fluffy white cloudbase. Another was cradled in the branches of a towering tree, which was at least as tall as the mountain on which they stood.

A giant crescent of steel, like an axe-head with no shaft, had been embedded in a neighboring mountain. On the flat of that blade, at either ends of the crescent, were *two* towns.

Each of the settlements was connected to the others by bridges. All together, hundreds of thousands of sacred artists gave the impression of a small city divided into five parts rather than five separate towns.

"Remembered that," Yerin said happily. She pointed to the blade that carried so many buildings. "Used to wonder who could squeeze water from a sword. I'd contend we could probably find out now, couldn't we?"

From the center of the crescent-shaped blade, water bubbled up, concentrated from aura. A groove in the blade carried that water to either end, which explained how the towns on those sides thrived. The blade didn't even reflect the light as brightly as it should, which Lindon took to be a quirk of the madra that Forged it.

He intended to inspect it more closely, once he could extend his spiritual perception without frightening anyone, but he quickly became distracted.

Sacred artists surrounded them. Some of the few Lords in the area.

He planned to inspect them without saying anything to Yerin—he didn't want to interrupt her reminiscence—but she brushed her hands off and glanced over her shoulder.

"You want to meet our new friends first, or should I?"

"This is where I miss Dross," Lindon said with a sigh. Dross could communicate with them remotely, including taking them out if necessary.

Not that Lindon couldn't do those things himself, but he couldn't do it so...delicately.

Lindon pushed himself lightly through space, stepping into nothing and emerging only two dozen yards away. He stood behind a young man in nondescript brown sacred artist's robes, so road-worn that they might have once been white.

"Pardon, but do we know you?" Lindon asked.

The man jumped and tried to turn, but Lindon's light grip on his shoulder prevented anything too sudden.

"Forgive me, Monarch!" he cried. "We were only trying to confirm your identity!"

Lindon released him in surprise, and the young man turned around to drop at Lindon's feet.

He was an Underlord, and a young one, but he'd kept his Path veiled. Lindon had kept from inspecting people around him out of general politeness, but he extended his spiritual awareness into the stranger's soul.

Where he found a Blood Shadow.

"Redmoon Hall?" Lindon blurted.

Not far away, Yerin groaned.

"Yes, Monarch! We were instructed that the Death Monarch Yerin Arelius lost her home to the Phoenix here, so we have provided all the support we can! In secret, of course."

Lindon hadn't expected anyone there to recognize them, given how far they were from Sacred Valley, but Redmoon Hall hadn't done anything *wrong*. In fact, they were acting in a way Yerin would approve of, even after her ascension.

Though it felt awkward, he supposed he ought to encourage such behavior.

"Well done," Lindon said. "We didn't expect to find so many people."

"We had their bridges replaced more than a year ago, Monarch. We've also strengthened the alliance between the towns and reinforced their defenses, so we've seen fewer conflicts and more travelers from outside. We keep the Monarch's home safe!"

He clapped a fist to his chest and looked up with pride.

Yerin strolled over. "You gonna tell me why we were ambushed by a big monkey on the trail up here, then?"

The man from Redmoon Hall fell onto the ground again. "Forgive us! We will bring his head to you by sundown!"

If Yerin wanted the ape's head, she would have taken it, but that was so obvious that Lindon didn't have the heart to say it. Instead, he waved a hand.

"Don't worry. We know you can't be everywhere. You've done far better than we expected."

"Yeah, I was just poking you," Yerin said. "To tell you true, I feel like I owe your sect a gift."

The young man hesitantly raised his eyes. "Thank you, Monarch! The sect leader will be grateful!"

"Yeah, tell Kahn Mala I'll give her a favor."

"I'm sure she will be honored to hear that from you herself."

Yerin closed her eyes and groaned as she sensed the same thing Lindon did: space warping around them.

A moment later, a white-edged portal folded into being nearby. A Sage and a Herald strode out, both tan-skinned and black-haired, and both wearing cloth masks over their mouths.

When they saw Lindon and Yerin, the brother and sister bowed together.

Balari, the Herald, spoke first. "Empty Ghost, it is an honor."

"We've eagerly awaited your return," said his sister, the Sage of Silence.

"We await your command."

"Your wishes are our own."

Yerin craned her neck to look over their heads. "I'm gonna cut off your two-man circus. Is that Kahn Mala behind you?"

Kahn Mala of Redmoon Hall had crept through the portal but stayed in the background, clearly afraid to interrupt the white-haloed Sage and Herald. At the sound of her name, she bowed.

"May I still call you Yerin, Monarch?" the Archlady asked.

"Be happier if you didn't call me at all," Yerin said, but she immediately held up a hand. "Sorry. You did more than I asked, and that's the truth. Call me what you want."

Lindon eyed the Sage and Herald, who were still bowing. "You were quick to find us here."

"Your fame precedes you, Patriarch," Balari said.

The Silent Sage gave a gentle smile. "As the Twin Star sect's guardians, is it wrong that we keep a watch out for you?"

The pair gave a smooth, pleasant impression, but Lindon couldn't relax around them. Not only was their cult experienced in brainwashing and taking over enemy factions, but the Silent King madra they radiated brought back bad memories.

"We were trying to keep our visit quiet," Lindon said, and the Sage widened her eyes.

"Oh? Should we not have told your family, then?"

Kelsa hurried through the portal a moment later, still in the middle of tying her hair back. She was almost as tall as he was, athletic, and she felt healthier; she'd been strengthening her body. Her tail of purple-white fire lashed behind her, and she carried a host of his constructs around her belt.

"Lindon! Why didn't you tell us you were coming?"

Kelsa marched up and embraced him, which caught him off-guard. He awkwardly returned the embrace, adjusting his strength to match hers. She was a stable Truegold, which matched the resources he'd left her.

"Apologies," Lindon said. "We were trying to—"

He didn't have a chance to repeat himself when his parents strode out of the portal.

For once, his mother didn't have her drudge with her. Which bothered him, though he told himself not to mention it. Her hair actually had *less* gray in it than he remembered, and her skin was smoother; he was relieved that his mother had been taking the elixirs he'd left. Judging by her lifeline, she had many decades left to live even if she never advanced again.

Seisha gasped and took her step carefully as she emerged, which suggested she wasn't used to a Sage's transportation. Jaran had no such care, stepping through by leaning on his cane. He looked straight in front of him, and Lindon was certain he was pretending not to be impressed.

Jaran nodded on sight of his son, and Lindon couldn't help himself; he scanned his father's leg.

As expected, there still wasn't anything physically wrong with it. Jaran was completely healed, he just couldn't break the habit of the cane.

Seisha hurried up to hug him and Jaran reached out to clasp Lindon's upper arm.

"You weren't going to visit us?" Jaran demanded.

"We planned to keep our visit qu—"

He was interrupted again when the portal switched owners, its shimmering white edge turning slightly purple.

The look Lindon gave the Silent Sage wasn't quite intended as a glare, but it wasn't too far off.

"We're still in the Akura clan's territory," she explained. "I can deny Silver Heart access, if you don't wish to see her."

Lindon looked to Yerin, but she was still talking to Kahn Mala, which left him to decide on his own. And he'd put Charity in a difficult position by leaving virtually the entire Ashwind continent to her without his support, so he would feel rude for turning her away.

"No, let Charity through," Lindon said.

A silver-and-purple owl flew through the portal, followed by a couple of ancient Akura Archlords. They bowed deeply on sight of Lindon and Yerin, then stood to either side to welcome Charity.

The Heart Sage looked the same as always: like Mercy's composed sister. She seemed about twenty years old, her purple eyes deep and ageless, and her expression cool.

"I'm pleased to know that I'm still allowed to approach you, Twin Stars," Charity said. "My apologies for not welcoming you sooner."

Lindon wasn't certain why Charity was addressing him by his Sage title. "You can still call me Lindon."

"I wasn't certain of our relationship, given that you visited my territory without informing me."

Charity's face could be hard to read, but it wasn't difficult to interpret *that*.

"Apologies, Charity," Lindon said. He bowed slightly. "As I've tried to say to everyone, we intended to make this a quiet visit."

Charity lifted an eyebrow. "If you'd truly wished to go unseen, I doubt any of us could have found you."

"I was surprised to sense you," the Silent Herald admitted. "With the King's madra, you could hide from anyone! Right, Lindon?"

"*You* can keep calling me Patriarch," Lindon said.

Yerin leaned over and waved to Lindon's family. "Oi, are Sages getting in your way of your reunion? Shove them away. A good elbow, that's a Sage's weakness."

Kelsa, Seisha, and Jaran had, to various degrees, ducked behind Lindon and kept quiet as the more advanced sacred artists spoke.

"I'm afraid we haven't done enough to earn your family's trust yet, Patriarch," Balari said. "No matter how closely we work together."

Kelsa raised her hands at the Herald's words. "That's not it, Lindon. They've been very trustworthy."

"I know," Lindon said. "I've been watching them."

The Silent Servants didn't flinch or display any signs of fear at the words. If anything, the intention in their madra seemed to glow a little brighter. Lindon would say the siblings felt honored.

Seisha looked out from the mountaintop at the network of villages. "Pardon, but where are we?"

"If you're coming back home, why not come home?" Jaran asked.

"This is where Yerin was born," Lindon said.

Jaran grunted. "Oh. That's a good place to visit, then."

Charity gestured back to the still-open portal and the Akura Lords flanking it. "If you would give me but a moment, I could have a royal celebration brought here. We could eat with a full view of the territory, and could even feed her town if the Monarch wishes."

Lindon thought the others might need the word 'quiet' explained to them, but the request had been addressed to Yerin.

She scratched the back of her neck. "They sell food here. Don't think it would kill us to eat like Golds for a night."

"Go," Charity said, and one of her Archlords flew off. "A local restaurant will be prepared for us."

Yerin shrugged. "I'll leave it to you, then."

Lindon examined Yerin's expression. He'd expected her to drive everyone off; everyone except his family, at least. But she didn't seem too irritated and had even implicitly invited the group to join them for a meal.

Charity released the will that maintained her grip on the portal, but it didn't fade away. Instead, it began to crackle gold.

The Sages looked at the portal in alarm, but Lindon put a hand over his face. He recognized that will.

A few long seconds later and a pair of gold-armored hands grabbed the edges of the portal. Larian hauled her way out, panting, blond hair matted to her face in sweat.

"Did I hear...someone say something about...free food?"

As Kahn Mala and the other Lords bowed, Larian pulled herself through and breathed a sigh of relief. "Phew! It was hard to do that so fast from a different continent. And expensive!" She met Lindon's eye and repeated, "Expensive."

"Would you like to join us for dinner, Larian?" Lindon asked.

"If you insist!" She threw an arm around Yerin's shoulders. "You almost missed out on the pleasure of my company. It's a good thing I keep an eye on young Charity here."

Larian winked at the Heart Sage, who stared coolly back.

"I'm almost fifty years older than you," Charity said.

"We can both be young!"

Lindon made a show of examining her. "I don't see your bow."

"You can't have it back!" she snapped. She cleared her throat and smiled again. "It's my most prized possession. I don't take it on friendly trips, do I? And you can't have it back, I was serious."

Yerin looked at the golden arm on her shoulder. "Don't remember us getting so friendly."

"I'm making up for lost time! You and I will be friends once I ascend, I know it."

"Who is this?" Kelsa asked Lindon.

Larian whistled. "Don't know how long it's been since I've been interrupted by a Truegold."

"Larian of the Eight-Man Empire, meet my sister, Kelsa."

"...and I've missed that," Larian continued. "People are too respectful, that's what I always say. Right, Yerin?"

"Your name doesn't have an 'Arelius' in it somewhere, does it?" Yerin asked suspiciously.

The Akura Archlord reappeared next to Charity, and she sent an owl wheeling around the whole group. "They are almost prepared to receive us. I'll lead you there."

Lindon and Yerin walked at a normal speed, so their group of advanced sacred artists followed suit. Yerin didn't complain, and she didn't even shake Larian's arm off.

Through a series of looks and gestures to his family, Lindon got them to move away. Kahn Mala, Charity, and the Silent Servants noticed and took their distance as Lindon and Yerin dropped to the back of the group.

Larian was the only one who didn't get the hint until Lindon rested a hand on her armor. "Pardon, Larian, but may I have a moment with Yerin?"

"Hmmm...seems dangerous." Larian leaned down. "What do you think, Yerin? Should I leave you alone with this Dreadgod?"

Instead of driving her off, Yerin said, "If he locks me up, I'll pay you to save me."

"That's a deal!" Instantly, Larian was all the way across the group, talking to Lindon's father. "You heard her say that, right? That was a verbal contract."

Jaran stumbled and had to catch himself on his cane.

Lindon controlled wind aura to block sound from around him and Yerin. "We can still leave. Now that we know they're watching, I can hide us more effectively."

"Not in such a hurry," Yerin said. She had a softer look than usual, like the one she wore when Eithan actually managed to make her laugh.

"Pardon, but I thought you'd be...disappointed."

Yerin grabbed his hand as they walked. "Don't have too many memories in this town. Not good ones, at least. But *this?*" She gestured to the people around them. "This feels like home."

Lindon extended his spiritual sense—just slightly, so he didn't give anyone a heart attack—and enjoyed the sensation of being back in Cradle. Just the feeling of the vital aura, and the burning spirits of the sacred artists all around them, comforted him like a crackling fire in winter.

He was glad they'd left the world behind. But he was doubly glad that they still had a home to come back to.

"First light tomorrow, though, I'm tossing them into a portal. And I don't care where it goes."

Lindon had no objection.

How Cradle Should Have Ended

INFORMATION REQUESTED: ALTERNATIVE ENDINGS TO EACH VOLUME OF THE CRADLE SERIES.
REPORT LOCATION: THE END OF EACH CRADLE BOOK, IN ORDER, FROM ONE TO TWELVE.
SPECIAL NOTE: "I COULD HAVE WRITTEN BLOOPERS, BUT I WROTE THESE INSTEAD." SOURCE UNKNOWN.
AUTHORIZATION CONFIRMED.
BEGINNING REPORT...

How *Unsouled* Should Have Ended

The sword lowered from Lindon's neck and he breathed a sigh

of relief. "Gratitude. Now, as I said, a messenger from the heavens said we should leave the Valley together."

"Tell that messenger her job's done," Yerin said, slamming her sword back into its sheath. "But heavens or not, I have a job left to do. We've got to get my master. I can't just...leave him here."

Lindon pushed down his frustration and nodded in sympathy. "I wondered about your grudge with Heaven's Glory. Did they..."

"Yeah. Poisoned him. Stabbed him in the night." Yerin wiped fresh blood from her cheek, and her eyes burned hot. "Left me with a debt to settle."

"I'm sorry. I'm sure he was a powerful sacred artist."

"Was?" Yerin blinked in confusion for a few seconds before realization dawned. "Oh, you...Bleed and bury me, no, he's fine. Just insulted."

"Oh. Then, wait, what was all that about not leaving him here?"

She rolled her eyes. "I can't pull him away from the labyrinth! Clear as good glass that he won't find anything in there. It's about time we get leaving. You can still come with us, if you want."

"Gratitude." Lindon replayed Suriel's words in his head and frowned. "I was *sure* he was dead."

"Your ears for decoration? He's a Sage. No way he's getting killed by a bunch of Jades."

How *Soulsmith* Should Have Ended

Eithan sensed something in Lindon's pocket and nearly choked.

Where had a Copper gotten his hands on something like *that?*

Eithan leaped over and landed in front of the two startled children. Lindon crouched defensively, though he looked terrified, but Yerin had her sword out and her silver Goldsign awkwardly poised to strike.

"Hello, children! Hey, Lindon, who gave you that glowing marble?"

Lindon clapped a hand to his pocket and his eyes shifted as he considered how to answer.

"I'll make this simpler for you: did their name perhaps end in *'-iel'*?"

Cautiously, Lindon nodded.

"Wonderful! You're my apprentices now. And my name is EITHAN ARELIUS." Eithan shouted as loudly as he could, to make sure everyone nearby could hear him. Sure enough, some Sandvipers and Fishers crawled out of hiding when they heard his voice. A couple even dropped to their knees.

He removed his veil and the rest followed.

"Very good!" Eithan cried. "Now, someone bring me that spear!"

The bystanders of the Five Factions Alliance scurried away and Eithan put his hands on his hips, sighing in satisfaction. "And just think, Lindon. You didn't even have to fight a duel!"

Lindon looked very, very confused.

How *Blackflame* Should Have Ended

Jai Daishou took a shuddering breath as he woke up.

Nearby, a construct resembling his Remnant dissolved into sparkling particles of essence. He was lucky to have stumbled on that Divine Treasure, the single-use artifact that would fake his death. Decoy Remnant and all.

Of course, it had its risks. He had to have really been on the brink of death for it to work at all, and there was nothing stopping his enemy from destroying his 'body' after his Remnant rose. That would have really killed him.

Still, he swept his perception around the slopes of the rocky mountain in which he fought. Serpent's Grave burned beneath him, but he sensed no one nearby. It seemed his ploy had worked.

A hand clapped onto his shoulder from behind, and the fear alone almost killed him.

As though his joints were rusted, Jai Daishou slowly turned to see who it was.

Eithan Arelius stood behind him, clothes bloody and torn, but his smile wide and untouched. He playfully snipped his scissors open and closed.

"Let's just say," Eithan mused, "that I know a little something about faking my own death."

Frustration, fear, and sheer fury built and built until he felt a sharp pain in his chest. Five seconds later, Jai Daishou died of a heart attack.

How *Skysworn* Should Have Ended

"I'm joining the Skysworn," Yerin said firmly. "Not just going to sit around here and rot, am I?"

Lindon grabbed his pack. "I'll come with you. Actually..." He pondered a moment. "Is that a good idea? I'm practicing an illegal Path and you have a Blood Shadow. They might even try to kill us."

"That's...Bleed me, that's true."

"How about we wait until Eithan comes back before we make any decisions?" Lindon suggested. "If there's anything we're missing out on—any friends we might have met by joining the Skysworn, for instance—I'm sure he can help us pick them up."

Yerin folded her Goldsigns and leaned against a wall. "Guess we can wait a few days."

After a few days passed, the Bleeding Phoenix rose. Yerin gritted her teeth and bore the influence, supported by the protective scripts of Stormrock and the presence of her friends.

When the Dreadgod passed, Yerin was fine.

"Can't imagine what I was all knotted up about," she said. "That wasn't so bad."

How *Ghostwater* Should Have Ended

Ghostwater's ending is perfect.

How *Underlord* Should Have Ended

Prince Kiro cut his way through a caravan of Golds, trying to force them to call in the Blackflame. He was about to execute the remaining combat-capable Highgold when he sensed Lindon's presence approaching.

In the midst of the destruction, Kiro stopped, sword raised over a Highgold. "If she had told me she'd called you, I would have let her leave," he said. His helmet dissolved, revealing his face to the opponent so he could introduce himself. "I am the Seishen Kingdom's first prince, Seishen Kiro."

Lindon pulled out a cannon.

Kiro didn't recover from that battle for weeks. Meira almost killed herself in her quest for vengeance before she discovered a trove of natural treasures: the personal collection of Akura Charity herself.

She and Daji guarded Kiro as the three of them entered the vault, eager to seize the life-aspect treasures that could finally heal him from the damage Lindon's Blackflame cannon had done.

To his horror, there were already people inside the vault.

Lindon turned to face them, flanked by Yerin and Akura Mercy. It was three Underlords against three Truegolds, but Prince

Kiro still held up his hands. "Peace, everyone. There's no need to fight."

Lindon pulled out a cannon.

Back home in the Seishen Kingdom, Kiro awoke in a cold sweat. His people had lost the competition for the Night Wheel Valley months before, but he still had nightmares almost every night.

When he woke, someone—usually Meira—sensed his disturbed madra and rushed in to check on him. This time, he was the one who sensed disturbed madra.

"What is it?" Kiro called.

A moment later, a disheveled Meira burst into the room, the blade of her scythe extended in a sweep of green flame. "High Prince, forgive me, but we face intruders. It seems the Heart Sage did not think our competition was decisive enough. The Blackflames are—"

She was cut off as an explosion blew Kiro's bedroom doors off their hinges. Through the smoke stepped the figure from Kiro's nightmares.

Lindon turned toward him, eyes black-and-red with Blackflame.

Then he pulled out another cannon.

How *Uncrowned* Should Have Ended

Yerin's sword was at his throat when Blackflame burned through her. As she dissolved into white light, the last thing he saw was her brilliant smile.

[You see?] Dross prodded. [This is what happens when you do what I tell you.]

Neither the Path of Black Flame nor the Endless Sword were well-suited for defense, so it came down to their endurance. Lindon could weather more hits, and his madra capacity was much higher than Yerin's.

The arena broke down around him and he heard the cheers of the crowd as Northstrider's authority healed him.

"Victory to Wei Shi Lindon Arelius of the Blackflame Empire!" the Ninecloud Soul called, to approving roars.

As he left the arena, Eithan was the first to clap him on the back. "Congratulations, my adopted brother! I'm quite relieved, honestly. I put a huge bet on you."

"How did they allow wagers?" Lindon asked. "I was supposed to fight Sophara."

"*Huge* bet. If you'd lost, I would have never financially recovered. But you didn't let me down!"

They both looked up as blue light filled the sky and the heavens descended.

"Who wants a weapon made by Ozriel?" the Abidan asked, dangling an arrowhead.

"Me!" Lindon shouted. "Me!"

How *Wintersteel* Should Have Ended

Northstrider stood between Lindon and Sophara in the finals of the Uncrowned King tournament.

"He touched an Icon before Archlord," Northstrider said. "It's rare, but we have plenty of precedent. The rules are very clear. You lose."

Sophara gnashed her teeth and tossed her tail. "No! I don't accept it! I demand the right to combat!"

"Sure, go for it."

"**Die,**" Lindon said.

Rainbow lights flashed over the arena and the Ninecloud Soul announced, "Ladies and gentlemen, I present to you the eighteenth Uncrowned King: Wei Shi Lindon Arelius!"

At that moment, Lindon was gathered up by blue light. The unpleasant rat-faced Abidan looked over him with approval. "You should join us when you ascend, which you certainly will. And is that Suriel's marble?"

"Oh, do you know Suriel?"

"She's one of our leaders. Promise to put in a good word for me, and I'll give you some advice: you should kill Reigan Shen. He's about to assassinate your friends."

"Gratitude! I'll do that, then."

In the middle of instructing the Blood Sage to kill Malice's children, Reigan Shen keeled over, dead.

How *Bloodline* Should Have Ended

At the head of the table surrounded by the clan elders, Wei Jin Sairus looked up and frowned at Lindon. "How did you make your way back here, Unsouled?"

Lindon burned a hole through the man's beard with Blackflame, scorching the wall over his shoulder.

"That's your one warning," Lindon said. "Everyone else who calls me 'Unsouled' dies."

The Patriarch's face reddened in fury and he drew himself up. "Insolent! You may be Jade now, but I will not be cowed by an Unso—"

Dragon's breath burned a hole through a spot of air six inches to Sairus' right. A moment later, the Fox Mirror dissolved, revealing Wei Jin Sairus with a hole burned through his chest. He had tried to sneak away invisibly, but instead his body collapsed to the floor.

Lindon looked around to the elders. "Those of you with better survival instincts can address me as 'Patriarch.'"

How *Reaper* Should Have Ended

Once the Mad King was driven away, Ozriel waited for the rest of the Judges to show up. Sure enough, it didn't take them long. They reinforced the stability of the Iteration with their very presence and radiated sheer disapproval.

"Ozriel, we're taking you into custody for dereliction of duty and violation of the Eledari Pact!" Makiel declared.

Eithan scratched the side of his nose. "Hm...No."

The Court of Seven stared at him.

"I mean, honestly, what are you going to do? Fight me here and destroy Cradle? No, I'm just going to stay put. You can take me in once I ascend again."

The Judges exchanged glances. Makiel, Zakariel, and Gadrael looked furious, and Suriel looked exasperated, but Darandiel and Telariel shrugged.

"Sure," the Ghost said. "We know where to find you."

"No leaving this dimension!" Makiel demanded. Then they all disappeared except Suriel.

"Hasn't your cover been blown?" she asked. "How are you going to pick up your life from here?"

"Oh, most people won't recognize me," Eithan said. "And for the ones that do...Well, they won't bother me, will they?"

How *Dreadgod* Should Have Ended

The Wandering Titan seemed to grin as it stepped through the portal. Trading places with the Silent King.

As the sky turned white, the tiger extended its regal perceptions... and withdrew them hurriedly.

"No, wait!" the Dreadgod cried. "Switch back! Switch back!"

The portal closed, leaving him alone with a smiling figure in black armor and a scythe.

Eithan laid his hand on the trembling tiger's head. "You thought I ascended, didn't you? Sorry, still here! And have you met my student?"

Lindon walked up to the Silent King, fingers opening and closing, and licked his lips.

How *Waybound* Should Have Ended

"Ascend or Eithan kills you," Lindon said to the remaining Monarchs.

"Finally," Emriss sighed.

"Fine," Northstrider grumbled.

"Yeah, get out of here!" Larian gloated.

"Do we have to?" Sha Miara whined.

"Speaking of Eithan," Malice said, "is he single, or...?"

WILL WIGHT is the *New York Times* and #1 Kindle best-selling author of the *Cradle* series, a new space-fantasy series entitled *The Last Horizon*, and a handful of other books that he regularly forgets to mention. His true power is only unleashed during a full moon, when he transforms into a monstrous mongoose.

Will lives in Florida, lurking beneath the swamps to ambush prey. He graduated from the University of Central Florida, where he received a Master of Fine Arts in Creative Writing and a cursed coin of Spanish gold.

Visit his website at *WillWight.com* for eldritch incantations, book news, and a blessing of prosperity for your crops. If you believe you have experienced a sighting of Will Wight, please report it to the agents listening from your attic.

Made in United States
Cleveland, OH
06 January 2025

13124357R10213